The Extra-Ordinary Heroes of USPRE

Series

Dorene McLaughlin

This is a work of fiction. Names, characters, places, and incidents either are the product of the author's imagination or are used fictitiously. Any resemblance to actual persons, living or dead, events, or locales is entirely coincidental.

Book cover design by Caleb Covak

www.dorenemclaughlin.com

Fiction2Reality

To the greatest author of all,
the One who deserves all the praise.

Prologue

The tires protested against the pavement as the pickup truck rolled into the turning lane, the blinker pulsing in the dark. The July heat made the asphalt a rude companion for both machine and man, and no one knew that better than the boy and his father making their way in the pre-dawn temperatures toward the corner gas station. Even at 4:12 a.m., the temperature reached 87 degrees in Mesa, Arizona, a dismal fact of life for construction workers. They began their day before the sun, trading intense heat for darkness. The driver, Bruce Radison, had managed his own crew with quiet pride for over a year now and the magnitude of that accomplishment spilled over to his son in the still morning heat.

Wayne simply didn't have enough moxie to acknowledge his father's hard work. Success and pride meant little to the fourteen-year-old; what mattered to him was that at 4 a.m., two days a week, all summer long, his dad would wake him to journey to the current work site for several hours of labor. Separating piles of debris into different dumpsters was tedious, but good pay for a teen. Still, more than an income, the job provided the chance for father to bond with son, a return on the hours stolen by hard labor throughout Wayne's childhood.

The trouble was the boy was now discovering just how much he didn't know about this man that had raised him. From his slouched position in the passenger seat, he shot a furtive glance at his father who remained silent and stoic. There was a time when that dark hair and those small eyes held a kinder countenance, something time and experience had taken away. The eyes were mostly blank now, seldom breaking into sympathy or humor. When Bruce did find something funny, the laugh lines that appeared around his narrow eyes made everyone around feel slightly more at ease. But those moments were few.

Wayne dared not look at his father long for fear of being caught and questioned about his scrutiny. He turned his attention back out the windshield, the silence within the cab impenetrable. No matter. There was something comforting, something right about this time together even if conversation was hard to come by. The teen all but forgot about his own oversized glasses, spreading acne, and his skinny frame that held together his insecurities; he found himself oddly content with this pre-dawn opportunity.

The truck and trailer rattled into a longer parking slot in the rear of the building and sighed to a stop. The door gave a familiar soft jingle as the two Radison's made their way inside, the clerk giving them a nod of welcome into the empty store. The teen moved through the few short aisles looking at the overpriced treats, part of the ritual. Although he would inevitability settle for the donut, he prolonged the moments with his father in every way possible. He studied a pack of gum, lingered over the mints, eyed the chips. His father slowly mixed his coffee and creamer as if he understood the game, watching his son with neither smile nor frown.

"Only one left," the father said with a jerk of his head to the case.

The boy glanced over to see one lone glazed donut amid the crawlers and eclairs. Leftover from last night, no doubt. He shrugged away disappointment. "You take it."

The man squinted his uncertainty.

"No, really. I'll get something else." The teen moved on to the next aisle to find nuts and granola bars. He grimaced when his father couldn't see and headed back toward the chips until a red package caught his eye on the bottom row. He knelt before a row of trail mix, one package labeled *Adobe Fire*. He examined the fiery spices attached to the nuts and crackers within, debating. The next package was called *Spicy Mix*, a little less intimidating, and he put the *Adobe Fire* back and adjusted his glasses.

"Need an iron stomach for that breakfast," his dad said, kneeling beside him.

The boy hid a grin and reached for a third package labeled *Habanero Heat*. "What would Pedro say if I showed up with this?"

"He'd tell you that you were finally earning some hair on your chest." The kid chuckled, and they looked over the other spicy choices neither of them intended to purchase. The soft bells jingled again unnoticed. Several seconds passed in silent consideration when a rough voice turned the father's head. Bruce stood for a moment and instantly took a knee again. A vice grip dug into the boy's shoulder and Wayne winced. He turned toward his father to find his dad's finger pressed into his lips. The boy had never seen his father's eyes carry such intensity, and an instant chill ran down his spine. His ears finally tuned in the angry voice issuing commands at the counter. A quick glance at the corner mirror revealed the distorted, curved image of a figure in a dark hoodie. The figure carried a gun.

The armed man had the same distorted view of two figures crouched down in the second aisle and in an instant, the gun swung in their direction.

"Hey, you—you!" The man beneath the hood cursed at them and began to dance nervously in front of the counter. "You two! *Get up here*!"

The boy had no legs of his own as his father pulled him to his feet and shoved him behind his taller frame. With feet of lead, Wayne followed his father toward the front. He felt stupid, almost as tall as his dad, but trailing behind. His father's eyes that held such distant pride and resolve, had shown a glimmer of something Wayne had never seen before. A fear that had nothing to do with the gun, a fear the boy couldn't understand; it was a fear mixed with knowledge that promoted both strength and wariness. The father stopped at the end of the aisle and put his hand behind his back which the boy eagerly grasped. He couldn't see much of the potential robber except the black hood and swaying frame.

"Stay there," the armed man barked. His gun whipped back at the clerk and his voice rose to a scream. "*Get that money now, you moron*!"

The boy jumped and tried to suppress what he presumed was pure, raw fear. The intensity of this new emotion sucked the breath from him and something inside quietly screamed for his dad's strength to transfer to him. If he could just get another look at his father's eyes....

The Indian clerk, calmly and carefully, opened the drawer and dug within, when the soft bells chimed again.

From the outer darkness appeared a man with rich brown skin, cloaked in a black t-shirt and jeans. His stature dominated the room, his size and build conspicuous in the crowding space before the counter. But his presence was more than just his mass of muscles and shapely form; his eyes took in the scene in a second without a single blink.

The gunman cursed again and began screaming orders. "Get over there! Get! I SAID MOVE!"

The man's hands remained relaxed at his side, his narrow lips and piercing eyes emotionless. The air stopped moving around them as all eyes turned to the newcomer in fear, in hope, in uncertainty.

But the figure didn't move. Tension created a thick blanket around the hostages.

"*You think I'm playing, fool? You see this gun*?" In the heavy, heated air filled with the shouts of a desperate man, the clerk's movements caught the boy's eye. He had clumsily reached under the counter to retrieve a hidden rifle. The hooded gunman swung his sights back to the counter, weapon facing weapon.

What happened next would be the moment that baked itself into hot summer nightmares for years to come for a terrified boy of fourteen. As if all in the same second, he heard the shots, and his father moved forward toward the robber—or had the robber moved first?

His father lay on the floor before the shots stopped ringing in Wayne's ears.

But none of that would register or make any difference in the burning memory of the figure in the doorway who seemed to be everywhere at once. As if a burst of lightning had blazed in the room, he was in front of the clerk then on the gunman, beside his father. There would be no way then or in the long evenings to follow to slow the images down in the boy's mind to understand the movements of that speed and precision.

Wayne stood helplessly by as the air sucked from his lungs and no breath would come to him.

His father lay at his feet, the thief beside him, both slowly becoming engulfed in a spreading pool of red between them. The stranger had been there a second ago but now reappeared from behind the checkout where the cashier had fallen. He leaped over the counter as if on springs and bent down by the blood spill, the hood of the robber no longer protecting his identity. Lifeless eyes, half closed and unblinking, made Wayne reel backward. Large, thick eyebrows, a broad nose and lips—all unable to ever move again. His father's eyes were closed, denying him an explanation of the fear and knowledge his stare had held.

The boy felt hot tears on his cheek and found the piercing eyes of the stranger in the black shirt upon him.

"He's dead," he said with the lack of emotion his expression held.

The boy gasped. But as the man moved on, kneeling over his father and putting his fingers to the motionless neck, the boy realized he had been speaking of the gunman. Wayne's breath came back sharply, in tight uncontrollable gasps, his stiff body planted powerlessly looking over them all, staring down at the stranger's neat military haircut. In the folds of the thick neck, he could see a tattoo, something written in script, unreadable within the folds of skin.

"He's alive, and he'll be ok," the black eyes rising close, bringing the full strength of their intensity with them. The teen's own eyes clouded and burned with uncontrolled tears. "The blood isn't his." A groan arose from behind the counter and died out again. The stranger kept his gaze on the boy's as if deciding something.

"What's your name, son?"

"Wayne… sir. Wayne Radison."

"This your dad?"

"Yes, sir."

The man attempted a smile but seemed unfamiliar with the mechanics of it. "Wayne, I want you to listen very carefully to me. This is what happened. Your father tried to stop the shooter and was knocked out. If it weren't for your dad, this guy would have killed that poor stiff behind the counter. He's just winged. He'll be alright." The sound of distant sirens pierced the silent morning. "You listening? The clerk fired on the shooter and hit his mark. You saw it all, and that's what you're going to tell them. That's how it happened. Wayne? You hear me?"

Wayne's gaze traveled to his father's motionless body, and the tears wouldn't stop. "Y-y-yes, sir."

"And Wayne, this is the most important part. I was never here. You never saw me."

Wayne swallowed and his eyes involuntarily moved to the camera in the ceiling's corner. A distorted smile followed Wayne's gaze. A nod of approval.

"Good thinking, kid."

The stranger got up and moved to the camera, pushing a pallet of soda with the toe of his foot as if it were no more than an empty box. Like an animal—an insect or small cat—he scurried between the window and up the pallet, seemingly touching nothing, as if moving on air—and toyed with the camera, only for a few seconds. In what could have been a blink, he had moved the pallet back and stood once more by the bodies. His black eyes made Wayne shiver from the depths of his gut. Something unnatural, unreal existed before him, and he fought against the terror of facing it. The figure turned to kneel beside his father once more as the sirens grew closer.

"Wayne, I'm going to save your father now, but I need you to say it first. What are you going to tell them?"

The teen—caught in the horrible grasp of half child, half man, in need of his father that he had so recently found connection with, and so much left to discover—cowered under the veiled threat and felt his lips move as if beyond his control. "You were never here."

"You know they'd never believe you anyway." The man placed his hands on Bruce Radison's unmoving chest. "Now watch me." He straightened his posture as he began compressions. The tattoo on his neck straightened and Wayne read:

Señor Epus

"Have you ever learned CPR?"

"No, sir."

"Now's your chance." The sirens sounded as if they had just rounded the corner, seconds away. "Come here." Wayne obeyed. "Put your hands here... like this. Good.... Remember what I told you. Your dad's a hero. And so are you."

Wayne said nothing as his heart pounded in rhythm with his arms. His dad's lifeless face terrified him. As the mysterious stranger disappeared, Wayne tried to will his father awake.

If only Bruce could have seen what he saw. If only there was someone to share his disconcerting secret with... an untold tale that would haunt his nights for many long, lonely years to come.

Part I

Chapter 1

Aisles of overpriced produce and gluten-laden food turned out to be the perfect background for the mentally struggling population on a Friday night.

Not that a tired, overdressed school teacher shopping there would say there was anything peculiar about this night of the week. It had been Laney Whyte's experience that her neighborhood market contained at least one weirdo on any given day—the guy who squeezed the melons a bit too enthusiastically; the woman who nonchalantly wore her pajama bottoms or a see-through shirt (or both); the bargain-hungry mom clutching a handful of coupons, bent on purchasing a year's worth of cereal and bragging rights for less than a dollar.

On this random, average Friday night, a surplus of odd characters filled up the rows.

Laney just never suspected she would be one of them.

But there she was, bent down by her cart, grapefruit in hand, staring at her shoe in a physical and mental lockdown, unable to move. The dull yellow citrus that rolled from across the grocery store aisle had landed unapologetically beside her feet. For some reason, mid-bend, her gaze shifted from the fruit and locked onto her normal, everyday foot—wearing the perfectly wrong pair of shoes.

"Oops," Urie said sheepishly from across the wide aisle. She had tried to palm the softball-sized fruit with one hand while the other attempted to grip the slippery cellophane bag.

The runaway fruit wasn't responsible for this catatonic state. Heaven only knew the number of spills this family of three caused in their lifetime. Laney wasn't even annoyed at her young daughter for bruising the produce she'd sent on a wild roll. It was the darn shoes. Brown, strappy cork wedges, perfect in color and height, purchased with excitement over price and fit, given a place of honor in the closet until the day they would match a complementary outfit and be strutted with a juvenile type of pride. Friday shoes for sure.

Did other people even have Friday clothes? she wondered, as she struggled to break free from the hypnosis she was under. It had been a high school thing, dressing for the weekend, that she had never quite abandoned. Not because she would be going out, doing anything special—just because it was Friday, the end of a workweek. No matter what the weekend held, *Friday* gave a good enough excuse to dress in her favorite things. The clothes that made her happiest, that she felt good and confident in, whether comfortable or stylish—these she saved for Fridays.

Now here she was, on a weekend night, in the flawless textured brown leather strappy wedges, a designer brand she had gotten for a steal. And no one would ever notice but her. The grocery store? So pathetic. Even if she was divorced and living the hard-knock-life of a single mom, her Friday shoes deserved better than this.

"Mommy?" Urie called in bewilderment.

Feet shuffled by her and Laney tried to care, but some unseen glue held her fast in her near-fetal pose. Fatigue? Stress? Probably both. Since D-day close to two years ago, Laney thought she had successfully put the pieces together again. But at odd moments like this, the ocean of grief Laney kept at bay seemed to inexplicably charge the shore and threaten to engulf her.

Her eyes clouded over as they locked in on the soft fabric lining under her foot as if she were watching the uninvited tidal wave of self-pity well up around her, sucking her into its vortex. Laney Whyte let herself be swept further and further in the ocean of nothingness. Done. No longer available for—

A tug on her sloppy blonde curls tethered her to shore.

"Mommy!"

Those words. So sweet. So wrenching. The only reason to come back to reality.

"Mommy! Get it!" insisted Ella. Sitting in the cart in front of Laney, the younger daughter swung her feet excitedly, almost knocking Laney's glasses off one ear. Slowly, painfully, she pulled at the sucking tide that wanted to trap her, willing herself to become a mother, if nothing else.

"Got it," Laney shakily reassured the miniature version of herself; she stood and handed over the naughty fruit. Wiser than her older sister, Ella used two hands to capture and secure it against her chest, then grinned at Laney. A lady in a head-to-toe leopard print jumpsuit was staring at her. Good grief, how long had she been huddled on the floor like that?

"Yessss!" Ella hissed with glee, acting like they'd just roped a wild bronco.

"Sorry, Mom," Urie sing-songed in her practiced six-year-old way.

"Hey, keep an eye on those rascals," Laney said, voice odd and dull. She couldn't meet her daughter's eye as she internally scrambled to pull herself together.

Urie brought her bulging bag over to the cart. She tried to haul it over the side, almost falling backward to counter the weight. Laney reached to help and bumped heads with Ella on the way. Ella whimpered and Laney's grip slipped; grapefruit ripped out of the bag and rolled every which way. A large woman with a cart full of dog food strolled by, eyeing the scene with vague sympathy.

Divorce sucks: the mantra popped into Laney's head for the thousandth time, but she needed to get them out of this grocery store. It was time to corral grapefruits and kiss smarting foreheads, be bright, cheery "Mommy." These little blondies—not the children she had ever intended to mother—were all she had, all that mattered in life. They needed her, and she would never *not* be there for them.

Urie's voice slowly brought her back, and Laney realized her daughter was talking to someone else.

"You're welcome," a male voice replied.

Laney turned to meet a set of oddly familiar eyes, a mixture of smoke and darkness, framed by a thick set of lashes that no woman could view without jealousy. The owner of the knockout eyes was handing her daughter a grapefruit. She locked gazes with the man for a silent moment until a generous grin broke out on both of their faces.

"Michael?"

"Hi, Laney," the grinning man replied in a rich tone. "Long time no see."

The words rolled off his perfect lips while Laney fumbled with a reply. Michael?—the finest specimen of young, unobtainable bachelorhood Laney had ever met—at the grocery store? So she wasn't the only one without a weekend life apparently.

Words failed her, and as Michael held out a grapefruit to her, Laney thought to ask about his work partner when a second set of helpful hands appeared, each filled with grapefruit.

"Donavan," she smiled even wider at this second familiar face, but a lump formed in her throat immediately making the grin wobble before she could set it. The instant glow of old friendship was tainted by the cold remembrance of the end of all things Charlie & Laney. It never got any easier being around one of Charlie's old friends, even someone as friendly as Donavan.

"Laney, how are you?"

Equal in height to the breath-taking dark-haired Michael, Donavan's smile spoke of warmth and kindness amidst sandy brown hair and a five o'clock shadow. He gave her a half hug and she surprised herself by returning it without balking.

"I didn't recognize you at first with the tie and all," was all she could come up with. Her ex-husband's best friend made a great companion to jeans and t-shirts which is all she knew of him. Backyard barbeques and casual gatherings at the Peterson's house had been common place…back when. "I'm fine... good," she finally answered him. "You know, shopping."

As if on cue, sweat formed on the lower quadrant of her back and she nervously pushed her hipster glasses back into place up on her nose. She lost many things in the divorce—her house, her car, full custody of the girls... but the second greatest thing stolen from her was the group of friends that had been made through Charlie. Ramdon encounters like this instantly made her awkward and uneasy, not exactly knowing where she stood.

"Girls doing okay?" he pressed and Laney had a vague remembrance of this easy-going voice. He had a great casual confidence about him, something that commanded authority yet didn't scream *police officer*. She tried to look at him directly, but his eyes held that kind of knowing that made her uneasy. Many months later and she still was unable to simply have a normal conversation with anyone about the split.

"Yeah, they're great. You know kids. So... resilient." Resilient? Right. They weren't fine or great or resilient. They were hurt, confused and... well, maybe they were okay, but they shouldn't have to be shuffled between two households at such a young age. It was rough enough that she knew a day would come when she would have to tell them of their past without having to add the injury of split parenthood.

"Well, you guys look good," Donavan reassured her, one hand casually tucked in his pocket in a familiar gesture. She hoped her unruly curls were in place and wished that she had removed her glasses, but there you go. The first and greatest thing lost in the divorce—dignity. She couldn't even stand in the grocery store and carry on a simple conversation with a man she had known for almost nine years without feeling inadequate and ashamed, no matter what shoes she was wearing.

Ella looked from Laney to Donavan and stuck a finger in her mouth with uncertainty. A deep, low rumble came from the sky, and for a moment the gathering clouds drew their attention away from Laney's awkwardness.

"I think it's been about a year since I've seen Charlie." Donavan graciously provided a way to ease the tension. He glanced at Michael and got a slight nod of confirmation.

"Oh?"

"I think the last time I saw him was... uh, before the playoffs, I think," Donavan continued. "We went to see a game together."

"Right, the game," she echoed. That would have been less than a year ago, maybe ten months ago when the Cardinals were on their way to the playoffs. Charlie had scored tickets and taken... her. Charlie and his new bride had gone with Donavan and Kelly, she now bitterly remembered.

The sky shook with thunder and the store along with it.

Donavan remarked on the unusual weather which led to a two-minute catch-up of their kids' school and activities, a couple of harmless shared memories. The casualness of it should have relaxed her, but the river down her back continued as rain pitted against the wide windows at the front of the store.

"So how's Kelly?" she asked in a last attempt to appear sane and normal, but there was a quake in her voice that made her turn away. It was a pitiful jealousy she had toward happily married people, something she couldn't seem to smile her way through. Michael kindly busied himself checking his phone. Laney kept her hands from shaking by rearranging Ella's curls while her daughter swatted her hand away. Urie had finally reappeared from around the cart and was tugging on her shirt.

"Mom," she whispered, and Laney bent down to hear her ask, "Is that Parker's daddy?"

She smiled. "That's right. This is Parker's dad," she said loud enough for Donavan to hear.

Urie grinned.

"Ah, you remember Parker, don't you?" Donavan's smile matched the little blonde's, warm and playful. "You remember playing in his bouncy house?"

"Yeah," she answered shyly and bit her bottom lip which didn't quite keep her from beaming.

"Wow, good memory," Laney said. The party, a year back, seemed so long ago and misty.

"That reminds me," Donavan said. "Parker's seventh birthday party is this Sunday at Peter Piper Pizza. You all should definitely come." He switched his pocketed hand, letting the thumb serve as a hook to keep it from completely disappearing. Laney analyzed his look for any insincerity. But there was none. His hair, overdue for a cut, swept across his forehead indifferently, his eyes warm and comfortable. Of course he meant it. Donavan was one of those guys. He wouldn't have invited them if he didn't want to.

"That's so nice of you," she said, surprised that her voice still didn't sound controlled, "but we don't want— "

"Mommy, pleassssssssse," Urie interrupted. "Peter Piper!"

Ella caught on and joined in, rocking the whole cart with all the enthusiasm of a four-year-old. "Peeper Piper, Peeper Piper!" she chanted, and Donavan and Michael let out a laugh.

"Well, I suppose you have your answer," Laney agreed weakly.

But Donavan had real sympathy in his look. Not as if she were pathetic or unavoidable or in need of someone to force themselves upon her to rescue her. Not like other people. It was more like... he understood how hard it all had been. But she had no idea how he could with his picture perfect house, remarkable wife, and adorable son.

"Great," he smiled, his voice reflecting his understanding. "It will be great. You know, balloons, video games, screaming kids on a sugar high—your normal Sunday afternoon stuff."

"Yay, can't wait," Michael mumbled with a slight flick of his eyebrows. He was a good sport, always showing up to Kelly

Peterson's parties, which were plentiful. Michael would come, usually solo, and manage to look like he had a good time. As Donavan's partner for at least five years on the Gilbert police force, he was rather obligated. Regardless of how well he interacted with the kids, his eye roll told Laney he was looking forward to a noisy kids' party as much as she was. The girls squealed with delight making up for any lack of enthusiasm on her part as Donavan gave her the time and location.

Outside, the brewing storm let loose.

Laney Whyte managed to check out and load the car in brown strappy shoes while two restless girls whined for dinner. The car got as far as the US 60 interstate before the patient-mom façade began to fade away.

The rain had been kind, quick, and erratic. About a mile into the drive, drops faded from the windshield, but taillights began to glow in rapid succession. Laney groaned. She crawled to the first exit ramp, congested with cars that had the same avoidance strategy. The traffic report on the radio caught her attention when she inched her way off the freeway. She turned up the volume.

"—temporarily closed due to a major accident on the East bound section. Witnesses report seeing what appeared to be large remote-controlled recreation vehicles racing across both lanes causing the pileup...authorities are questioning whether the sightings have any connection to reports earlier this week of similar machines responsible for the accident Tuesday on—"

"Mommy!" Urie pouted. "Why are we going this way? It will take forever!"

"There's an accident, sweetie." Looking down off the exit ramp, she startled at the number of mangled-up cars involved. Vague images from Tuesday's wreck played back in her mind from the newsfeed she had seen. If some prankster were operating a big mechanical toy onto the freeway for fun, the joke was lost on her. There were certain to be injuries in both incidents. "We'll be home soon, I promise."

But the hungry complaining continued the whole way off the ramp. The Friday night feeling Laney had hoped her clothes would produce disappeared like the fading light of the dying day.

She drove in silence amid her children's whines and the weekend rush hour traffic trying to escape the freeway.

Stupid shoes.

By the time Laney got to her apartment, a truly rotten mood threatened to engulf her. To make matters worse, there wasn't an open parking space close to her door. Her designated space sat down the lot a way and she relied on the closer "guest only" spots to make her trek to the second floor quicker while keeping an eye on the girls.

Laney sighed. She'd just have to have the girls run back and forth with her to get the job done. No use grumbling about it, she told herself. Just get it done—another familiar mantra.

On their first trip up the sidewalk to her stairs, she spotted two dark heads chatting by the mailboxes.

"Hola," called out Maria, the neighbor who lived with her family below Laney.

"Got more of those?" the man beside her asked.

"Plenty."

"I'll get 'em." Rodney, unemployed but solidly likeable, recently moved in with Maria's sister, Angela, on the second floor near Laney.

"Oh, no way." Her relief was unbridled. "You're a lifesaver."

He gave a grin that took up a large portion of his face and headed down the sidewalk in the direction of her car.

Up the long stairs, to the second floor, to the first door on the landing, next to grumpy old Mrs. Preese. Urie ran ahead to unlock the door. Laney barely got the girls in the door and the bags in the kitchen before Rodney appeared with the remainder.

"Luuuucey! I'm hooooome!"

She laughed. He might be able to pass as a Latin singer, but she could never be a Lucille Ball with her tight blonde curls, oblong-framed glasses and petite stature. "Just put them anywhere, 'Ricky.' I'll get them, thanks."

"I locked up the car for ya."

Urie charged out of her bedroom after dutifully putting her shoes away in the closet. Ella's were strewn across the entryway.

"Hola, mi chica!" Rodney called out.

"Buenas noches, Rodney!" Urie sang out and tripped into the dining room, doubling back to hand her mom the keys. "Here, mom. Didn't need them. Gracias!"

"She's six and she knows more Spanish than I do," Laney complained. She frowned then at Urie. "What do you mean, sweetie? You didn't need the keys to get in?"

"Our door wasn't locked," Urie called, flitting away to join her sister in front of the Little Animals Play Zoo. Laney was about to grill her, but Rodney interrupted her thought.

"Ah, give me another month," he grinned. "You won't sound like a gringa no more." He made himself comfortable, leaning on the counter semi-blocking Laney's view of the girls. She let Urie's comment go and began to stash away her goods while her company watched. Broad and muscular and a little thicker around the middle, Rodney stood only slightly taller than her when upright. The shorts and light windbreaker and sneakers were his normal wear, his dark hair cropped close, his skin a warm tan.

Laney didn't miss the look that passed over his face as he surveyed her little apartment. His face grew still like that when he was around her and the girls. He came from a large family, but she always got the impression that her domestic life somehow made him pity her...more than that, it actually made him seem uncomfortable. Her own discomfort made her prattle on.

"Give me a week, and you won't be saying 'no more' anymore." She stashed several boxes of mac and cheese in the tiny pantry and slammed the door before they could fall out.

"Oh, I forgot. I've made friends with an English teacher. My worst nightmare!"

"Your worst? Surely, you can think of something more frightening than proper grammar?"

"Hmmm... your cooking?"

She threw a dishtowel at him.

"Maria just made a fresh pan of tamales. Want me to score you some?"

A scene of domestic contentment flashed through Laney's mind as she pictured Rodney's family all around the table, eating and laughing. The jealousy stung.

"No, thanks. It's Friday—pizza night." She waved the frozen cardboard box in the air.

Rodney grimaced. "You would pick that over Maria's tamales? I have a lot of work to do with you, gringa."

"Tell Maria I'm open for trade agreements."

With a wave and grin, Rodney sauntered out.

Once the groceries had been housed for the week, Laney stood in the kitchen watching the girls at play. Her apartment was small but fit her more than any other model she had looked at, so she had compromised space for appeal. The unnecessarily large entryway opened like a fan into the three general living areas: the kitchen before it, the living room to the right with a window that faced a large grass patch before the parking lot, and the dining area to the left with a one small window that looked onto the landing. The kitchen had a rounded island that pushed out toward the door. The dining area was out of the line of vision as you walked in, so Laney had chosen to set up plastic drawers with toys for the girls there instead of in the living room which everyone could see. It helped immensely on the weeks she didn't have the girls to not be overcome with longing to see them and hold them every time she spotted a Barbie.

Since it was just the three of them, she had pushed the small dining table into the corner so the girls could eat on one side and she could eat on the end, but the other seats were blocked by the wall. This made the area more accessible to play for the girls and let her eat with her back to the kitchen she routinely disasterized before each meal.

It wasn't as nice as their house had been, of course....

Laney shook her head and grabbed the pizza box. She had no energy left for a proper pity-party tonight.

Chapter 2

The Friday traffic through Gilbert rushed from light to light, giving commuters no better speed than the congested freeway ramps. Summer wasn't giving way easily to fall, and the muddled mass of vehicles at each stoplight had windows up, air blasting, and drivers squinting into the blazing horizon sun that had popped out below the rain clouds.

Donavan happily took the right on red, escaping both the jam and the glare as he turned into his subdivision. He pulled up to the mailboxes first—heated metal receptacles piled together—and yanked out his mail as quickly as he could without touching the hot surface, steamy with the evaporating raindrops. He parked in his drive, his attention on the small stack of letters when he walked in the door. A coolness greeted him as he threw his keys in the dish on the side table and dropped his small bag of grocery items to the floor. The echo of its jingling clang went unnoticed while Donavan intently examined envelopes, looking for something in particular.

Something caught his eye, a swift motion, perhaps a glare from a windshield that blazed a streak of light across the room as it rolled by? He jerked his head up, trying to find the source of movement, but all around him, the house sat quiet.

"Hello!" he called out and listened to the un-answering silence. *Right.*

A further scan revealed a tidy house, no dirty socks or dishes about, a tell-tale sign his mother had been there. What's more, the carpet had been vacuumed, the side table free of dust, jobs undone since Kelly had left.

Slowly Donavan inhaled and let the breath escape his drawn lips. *Riiight.*

Without giving himself a moment more to think, he went back out into the menacing temperatures and walked three houses down to a similar door.

An older woman opened the door and eyed him warily. "You walked over?" Her gray hair sat neatly in place in short waves, and her kind eyes matched Donavan's in color and shape.

"Yeah." He really hoped he didn't have to explain that he'd forgotten Parker was here, that he'd driven home first before picking up his son... again. His mother didn't press him any further as she widened the door to let Donavan in.

Parker came running from the other room into his father's arms.

"How was soccer practice?"

"Good." Parker wore his standard *daddy's-home* smile that would have been there even if he had said, "Bad."

"Hot," Donavan's mother answered, never known for mincing words. "Not sure they should be playing the kids in this heat." Parker looked at his grandmother. "But the kids don't seem to mind, and he's such a good little player," she added for his benefit.

"The dishes. You didn't have to—"

Nellie Peterson waved her son's words away. "Made some Chicken Cacciatore for dinner. It's packed up and ready for you to take with you so you can get home and relax a little. Parker's had a shower, but he's hungry and a bit tuckered out."

"Okay, let's see what's in the backpack." Donavan set his son down.

"Homework's done," Nellie intervened and handed him a paper bag with handles, dinner boxed within.

"Oh. Thanks, Mom."

"Now get out of here and eat while it's still hot," she said, chasing them both out the door.

At sixty-three, Donavan had to admit that his mother had her life even more together now than when his dad had been alive. More precisely, she had *his* life more together than ever. As a widow of nearly thirteen years, she had moved close enough to see her grandson as often as she liked and had become an invaluable part of their lives. He couldn't have made it through a week without her, and Parker wouldn't have let him try.

Dinner, predictably delicious, was consumed quickly by father and son. Donavan tried to care about the little odd jobs that needed attention but too easily caved into Parker's request to watch *Transformers* together. He made sure teeth were brushed and jammies on before letting his only child snuggle on top of his chest on the couch.

Donavan absently stroked the small head while several cases from work ran through his mind. He wished giant robots and elaborate car chases on the screen could keep his mind from wandering. Occupational side effect; you never really punched out.

Without drawing attention to his free hand along the back of the couch, Donavan got out his phone, swiped to his news app, and tried to read headlines. Nothing of national interest concerned him enough to read on. He was about to close the app when a story out of Phoenix caught his eye. He struggled to sit up and get a good look at the article, but Parker protested in response.

"Sorry, kiddo." Donavan readjusted his couch mate to a more comfortable position. He opened the full article: "Man Captures Highway Menace on Video" with Parker still reclined against him. He had been following the story from last week, when some crazy, custom-built vehicle had driven others off the freeway. Only eye witness accounts existed, presumably, each with incredibly different descriptions, and, thus, mostly unreliable.

Donavan read on to discover that another incident had happened just hours ago, not far from the store he had stopped at with Michael. More cars than last time. More eye witnesses. And this time, a *video.*

After turning the phone volume down to keep from competing with the chaos on the television, Donavan pressed play and waited with climbing curiosity as the video loaded. The stretch of freeway he recognized, though not in the direction that would take him home if he had ventured into traffic. Something dark moved between cars, almost as if from nowhere, and then, there—a millisecond glimpse before it disappeared to the other side. *What the...?*

Donavan shifted into a better angle, then backed the video up and paused to capture that one tiny glimpse. Frustrated, he began surfing for other articles and found exactly what he was looking for. A still frame image of the video highlighting a solid, black mass moving between the cars, the top an odd triangular slope. A vehicle? No, thinner and taller. Maybe like an animated amusement park oddity. A mobile device with an elongated pyramid top. The angle made it difficult to see if it moved on wheels, but its motion was smooth and easy like that of a road-ready machine. Then it vanished.

How could no one see it or find it after it left the freeway?

"Daddy! You're missing the best part!"

"Oh, no!" Donavan feigned his regret. "Com' on, let's get comfy again." He lay back and let Parker bury himself into the hollow of his armpit, the boy's favorite place to rest. Parker gave a contented sigh, and Donavan put his phone away, his remorse real now. These moments were few and precious, he reminded himself. The kid grew so fast, and soon snuggling on the same sofa like this wouldn't be possible.

He knew the movie by heart now, and almost as soon as he'd resolved to stay engaged, his brain turned back to work; one case, in particular, continued to plague him. Maybe because he had so little to go on, and that bugged the snot out of him. No details to help him, no clue where to begin. Just an odd string of vandalized construction sites that began in the valley, spread out toward New Mexico, and found its way back again. The latest had been close to home, but their only suspect remained annoyingly elusive. A grainy surveillance tape, a few dead-end leads, and countless hours of door knocking had gotten them nowhere.

A soft snore came from the small body by his chest. He smiled despite himself and let his eyes drift unwittingly over to the vacant chair at the end of the couch. If he squinted, he could see her, legs tucked under, chin in hand, enduring a "guy" movie, as Parker called it, just to spend time with them. This room used to have so much life, savory memories that had faded into the corners like unswept crumbs left over from a grand party....

When he woke sometime later, the TV screen had gone blue, and Donavan had developed a stiff neck. Parker would likely suffer the same fate, twisted oddly in his sleep, half-on, half-off his paternal mattress. Night had fallen around them, and shadows occupied the outer rim of the room, still empty and lifeless. Donavan clicked the remote off and resituated Parker beside him but made no attempt to leave. His eyes adjusted to the pale street lights sneaking through the cracks in the blinds, and he waited miserably for sleep to return.

Sleep avoided him too often these days. He wanted to blame it on a nagging feeling that something lurked out of his line of vision. Every little movement stirred him, but empty space always glared back. Work had him in knots more often than he ever let on to anyone; it could be the easy answer to his recent restlessness.

Tonight he soundly subdued it with closed eyes, willing a peaceful night's slumber to come to him while the shadows remained ominously close by.

§ § § § §

The courtyard streetlamp in Laney's complex cast a huge shadow across her walls in the evening, mimicking a giant hand with wispy fingers as the light cut through the trees. Laney blocked out the incoming shadows with the pull of the curtains and settled in her beloved chair, staring at her favorite feature in the room—her fireplace. With her apartment slightly smaller than the others on the upper floor, the builders must have wanted to compensate. Hers was the only apartment that contained the luxury.

Though the fireplace peeked reluctantly out from the wall, plain and impractical in the desert climate, it suited her. She preferred to read most evenings, and nothing added more ambiance than the glow of a fire. October still proved too warm to turn on the gas, though the evenings now brought a hopeful chill with them. Instead, she placed pillar candles along the narrow hearth and lit them. Together with the small lamp beside her chair, they provided the room's only light on a quiet evening.

Tonight a worn copy of *The Count of Monte Cristo* served as her companion; she was reading it for the umpteenth time after one of her seniors had chosen it for their literature analysis. It had been quite a few years for Laney and time for a refresher. The pages did their best to work their magic, searching for harmony with the candlelight, soft music, and wine...until Laney's glass ran dry.

She sighed and went back to her book until Maria's trilling laugh made its way through the floor that separated them, and she found it hard to concentrate. Rodney loudly teased someone; his voice boomed above the murmur of the rest of the family. Laney pushed herself further into the chair, but when another of Maria's laughs followed by the loud roar of the others made her repeat the page a second and third time, she gave up. She eyed the empty wine glass and caved.

Laney had learned quickly after Charlie left that one glass led too easily to another, one night worked as well as another. So she gave herself the one-glass-Friday-night rule and vigilantly stuck to it. Nothing out of the ordinary should have brought on this rebellion tonight. It just seemed like too much work to analyze *why now*? as she reached for the bottle.

The refill cradled against her in the chair, she ditched her glasses on top of the book and slipped unwillingly into the last part of her Friday night routine. Unlike cardboard pizza and engrossing books that were habits of choice, this custom had developed purely in an attempt to deal with the blow that hit harder than her loss of dignity.

Rejection.

No matter how she tried to reshape it, avoid it, excuse it, there it waited: the defeating idea that Charlie had rejected her. She wasn't good enough. She wasn't woman enough to hold on to the man she was raising two children with. It was somehow *her* fault that he had run off with Victoria. The pain, all the heartache she had learned to brilliantly disguise, attached like gravity to her very core and pulled her into a spiral of despair. A week's worth of careful control gone in a blink.

Her knees had found their way to her chin, and she rocked as she clung to them. Somehow her cheeks were wet, and to her surprise, her glass lay empty again. Dang it.

She sucked in a ragged breath. *I wouldn't want him back*, she reminded herself. She grasped at the anger to regain her composure. *He's a two-timing, soul-sucking dirt bag, and I don't need that in my life!*

Tonight that just wasn't strong enough. He was gone and she was alone, and the pain of that was too heavy for her fabricated courage.

Rodney's loud laughter rose outside just as a sob ripped from her chest. She quickly buried her face into the collar of her long-sleeved shirt to muffle the sound.

Okay, just one more good cry, she told herself. And then she would find a way to bury the pain far out of reach, perhaps in the back of her closet with those ridiculous, strappy, Friday-night shoes.

Laney stumbled out of the car two days later when the heel of her ridiculous, strappy shoe caught on her too-long jeans.

"Mommy, *huwwy*!" Ella implored.

"It's okay! We're on time, Ella." Laney tugged at the gift bag wedged in the back of her SUV.

"But the pawty," she whined.

"Hold my hand, Ella," Urie whispered. Her older daughter's glance both ways made it clear that she meant to cross the parking lot without Laney if she didn't "huwwy" herself.

"I'm coming! Don't move." Laney shut the car door, swung her purse onto one shoulder, and pushed the door lock button on her key fob with the hand clutching the gift. Her heel caught again, and she righted herself.

Okay, so her Sunday shoes proved even worse than her Friday night pick. But at the last minute, she just couldn't wear Keds to Parker's birthday party. It had been ages since she had seen most of these people, and she wanted them to think she was doing okay. Nothing said defeated, I-got-no-one, soccer mom better than sneakers.

"Alright, let's cross." The girls scurried alongside her, one on each arm. A long strand of naturally curly hair escaped from its clip and trapped itself between her eyes and sunglasses. She hoped Urie was leading them straight.

She needed to get out more, to have more adult contact outside of work. Well, here you go. The social equivalent of a Cinderella's ball for a lonely mom. Glass slippers might have worked better than these shoes set on sabotage.

A blast of noise hit them as they entered Peter Piper and sent her two girls into a hyper frenzy. She discarded her sunglasses to see children running among the tables as adults simply tried to not get knocked over. Video games blared, tokens jingled, and children, every single one of them, all spoke with high-pitched intensity simultaneously. Climbing tubes took up a corner of the room, and purple and red balloons punctuated the tables hosting birthday parties.

The prayer for survival threaded itself through every parent's face.

"Mommy, where's the tokens?" Urie asked.

"Mommy, heewa's my shoes! I wanna go up darw!"

"Can I go get the tokens myself?"

"Mommy! Mommy! HEWA!"

Within minutes, Laney had added two pairs of shoes to her load but was ten dollars and two daughters lighter as they disappeared into the throng. Apparently, they had none of her misgivings about seeing these "friends" they had not seen in a year.

She stood awkwardly for a minute and looked between the parties until she could make out the "Happy Birthday, Parker!" sign across the room. Weaving between the tables while trying not to drop anything, Laney soon saw familiar faces. There was Kimberly and what's-his-name. That one was Augusta, she was pretty sure. Lots of familiar faces, but the names had faded for some. Where were Donavan and Kelly? Laney arrived at the gift table just as someone she *should* have recognized squeezed by. Jack, Jerry, Jim? Dang it, he was going to say hi.

But all she got was a nod, and she smiled back in relief. The gift bag deposited, she found the shoe cubbies, passing two more moms she knew for sure: Peyton and Gail. She couldn't remember if she had ever liked them, but knowing their names gave her confidence to say hello.

"Hey, how you been?" they asked in that surprised-to-see-you voice all women used. "What have you been up to?"

Laney played at the small talk as long as she could but soon sensed they would rather be chatting without her. She glanced around for another safe spot but saw none.

"I haven't seen Donavan or—"

Two very rowdy kids pushed against her, producing a patient sigh.

"Say 'excuse me,'" she said to her daughters.

They were talking a-mile-a-minute, and she could barely hear them above the din. She finally understood Ella's need to find the restroom, and Urie had run out of tokens. *Already?* Well, she had shared some so that other kids could play with her. Laney turned to excuse herself from Peyton and Gail, but there was no need; they had already moved away.

Laney sighed again. She might find it harder to dance at the ball than she'd anticipated.

She whisked Ella off to the restroom; Urie found Parker on the way. They both giggled with recognition and ran off together as if no more than a day had passed since they'd last played. The resiliency of kids.

By the time Laney and Ella made it out of the bathroom, Urie and Parker were up in the tubes playing hide and seek, a game Ella readily joined in. Laney headed back to the grownups, then hesitated. It seemed polite to seek out Kelly and say hello, but the hostess' friends weren't making it easy. At the moment, Laney found the potential fake smiles and uncomfortable conversations too draining. She found the perfect little niche under the curve of a big tube. A globed window above her made it possible for the kids to peek out to see her.

Michael? He had to be here somewhere. After twenty minutes of crowd scanning, she finally gave up. She had seen the back of Donavan's head twice, but no sign of the others she cared to see—no Michael and no Kelly.

When trays of steamy pizzas arrived, the kids begrudgingly made their way to the seats. Food offered a weak substitute for the lights and noise of the arcade. The party table held fourteen, just enough for Parker and his thirteen friends. That meant standing room only for the adults. Laney found a safe spot where she could see the girls and keep an eye on their manners, but she wasn't brave enough to lean in for her own piece of pizza. Kimberly brushed by without so much as a glance, her long, blonde hair in perfect, beautiful curls, as only Barbie could wear.

Laney twirled her own thin, tight curl with a finger and tried to tuck it back into the clip but soon gave up. She had dealt with the streaky, naturally-curly hair all her life, but couldn't complain. Since she had moved to Arizona nine years ago, she found the one place her hair would actually behave. With the desert air virtually void of humidity, her tight curls (with the aid of a few styling products) agreed to a sort of organized compromise. She couldn't lie and say that manageable hair wasn't one of the reasons she stayed put in Arizona instead of moving back to her folks in Colorado.

Her stomach rumbled. She looked longingly to a pepperoni pie not yet touched and tried to summon the courage to take a slice.

"Hey, where's your plate?"

Finally. A friendly face.

"There you are. I thought maybe you'd decided to skip out on your own son's party."

"Not a bad idea," Donavan mumbled. He walked over the table, grabbed a plate, and filled it with two slices of pepperoni. He handed it to Laney along with a napkin.

"Oh. Thank you." *No use acting too ladylike to accept when drool is practically running down your chin.* "The kids seem thrilled to see each other again." She ripped off a piece with her teeth, trying not to burn her lips.

"I know. Parker got so excited your girls were coming. He remembers them from his last party. Apparently, they made quite the impression."

"Anything to do with Ella lifting her skirt for all the boys to see her new undies?" She ripped off more pizza.

Donavan grinned. "I have no idea how you guys do it. Little girls make me nervous. Keyed up one minute, emotional the next. Parker plays with the neighbor girl all the time, and at least once a week he comes home shaking his head, utterly baffled by something that went wrong. One day football is her favorite thing in the world, and the next day she runs screaming when Parker tries to throw her a pass. Poor kid was crushed.

"Two days later she rang our bell to say she had gotten a snow cone maker and wanted Parker to come over because he was her best friend. Kid was so confused."

"Phhh, it's not as complicated as all that. She likes him, that's all," Laney said between bites.

"Likes him? Half the time she won't even look at him. She ignores him on the playground and then when they get to class, she throws a fit if he tries to sit anywhere but next to her. It's driving him nuts."

Laney paused her feast long enough to stare him down. "Seriously? You're *that* clueless about women? Poor Kelly." She shook her head and took a couple more nibbles, ignoring his wince at her words. "That little girl's got it bad for Parker, that's all I got to say. Tell Parker to ignore her on the playground too, and see what she does. If that doesn't bring her around, it means she doesn't want him but doesn't want anyone else to have him either. Classic jealousy. And if she sits by him in class *and* plays with him at recess, then she actually thinks they're a couple."

She tore off a huge hunk of crust just as Urie caught her eye. They waved at each other, index finger style with wrinkled-up noses. Urie pointed at the uncut cake, but Parker was just reaching for another piece of pizza, so Urie slumped down to wait.

Laney turned to find Donavan staring at her. "How could you possibly know all that?" he asked incredulously.

"Whaa?" Laney mumbled through a mouthful.

"That's just freaky. Give me a boy any day!"

"Oh, all those mud pies and LEGOs in the washer can't be much of a tradeoff." Who was she kidding? With a tomboy like Urie, Laney had that too.

"Maybe we'll switch kids for a week, and you can let me know," he said, leaning closer in conspiracy.

She realized how safe his presence made her feel among all these pretenders.

"Two for one? I don't care what the gender, you got yourself a deal."

He laughed. "Want another piece?" He reached for her plate. It was empty. Dang.

It doesn't matter what kinda shoes you wear – if you can wolf down two pieces of pepperoni pizza in under two minutes, you should probably forget about impressing anyone, Laney.

"No, thanks. I'm good." *But please cut that cake soon!*

She saw Kimberly lean over and whisper to a dark-haired lady Laney didn't know, and they both glanced her way. Her earlier discomfort returned in a rush. Any minute Parker would finish his last piece of pizza, and then Donavan would have to be birthday- dad host again.

"So," she began, leaning closer to Donavan and her feeling of security returned, "What are you doing at Gilbert PD these days?" They had skipped any specifics at their grocery store meeting.

"Still detective."

"That's great."

He nodded. "How about you? What grades you teaching?"

"Juniors and Seniors English. I have one mixed lit class."

"Yikes."

"Okay, you catch bad guys for a living and you say 'yikes' to high school English?"

"Some of the worst years of my life," he said with a shudder.

"Get out of here," she laughed and saw a third lady join Kimberly. The whispers intensified. "Don't tell me Shakespeare is as horrifying as some drug addict waving a gun at you?"

"No. Chaucer."

She opened her mouth to protest, then hesitated. "Okay, I'll give you that one."

"And grading all those papers...."

"You only have to grade them if you assign them," she jested. "That's not as bad as all the rehearsals right now."

"You still directing drama?"

He seemed genuinely interested, so she told him all about her latest high school production while Kimberly's stare turned to ice. Was Kelly seeing all this?

"It's coming along rather well, though. This one might be right up your alley."

Donavan tried not to grimace, and she laughed. "Is it about sports?"

"No. It's Sherlock Holmes."

"Interesting. Maybe if my root canal gets canceled, and I don't have to rip up my tile—"

"Okay, okay, I get it. Just remember, there are no spontaneous outbursts of singing—"

"Ahh, a play not a musical. That's a plus."

"—and someone gets murdered." Laney wiggled her eyebrows conspiratorially.

"Speaking of *criminals* did you see the accident on the freeway Friday night? Would have been about the time you left the grocery store."

"Actually, yes! We must have just missed that thing, whatever it was."

"See anything?" he asked. Laney tried to hide her smile as she thought of him forever "on duty."

The cake was presented and a huge cheer rose up. Laney recognized Donavan's mother for the first time, Parker's Grandma Nellie, setting the cake in front of him. Laney adored the no-nonsense older woman, the coolest grandma she had ever met, hands down. Whoever got to meet a real life ex-FBI agent? Nellie, now retired, always took an active role in family functions, but Laney found it very curious she would be taking the lead role today.

"Where's Kelly? And Michael?" she asked, but Donavan was headed toward the candles with a lighter in his hand. Soon the cake blazed and everyone sang the familiar chorus. Kimberly and friends turned their backs on Laney as she came to accept her piece of cake. Kelly was nowhere in sight, despite everyone celebrating the birth of her son.

"Has anyone seen Kelly?" she finally got the courage to ask Gail once she was close enough.

"She couldn't make it," Gail answered casually.

"Oh?"

Gail looked at her like she was an idiot. "She's sick," she said while adding lip gloss to her patronizing smile that walked away with her.

Wow. No warm fuzzies from that one.

After Nellie wiped Parker's sticky fingers, it was present-opening time. Squeals of delight from the youngsters, nods and exclamations from adults. Twenty minutes later, and it was time for cleanup.

Nellie gave the girls each a balloon and a goodie bag, and Parker politely gave his thanks with his shy, cute smile under the Donavan-ish hair sweeping his forehead. Laney led her bouncing, giggly girls toward their SUV when they crossed Donavan's path on his way back from depositing the gifts in his car. Perfect timing. Not a single glowering woman in sight.

"Thanks again for inviting us. The girls had a blast."

"Not you?" he teased.

"It was very… fun," she hedged. She decided not to ask about Kelly's illness in front of the girls. "We'll have to get the kids together to play again soon."

"You bet." He started away but then turned back. "Do you have our number?"

"No, actually, I don't." *Charlie has it, but please don't make me ask him for it.*

Donavan took out his cell phone. She tried to swing her purse around, but he held up his hand. "Just give me yours, and I'll call you so you have mine."

"I'll tell him!" Urie piped up. "I know Mommy's number!"

"Perfect," Donavan said, and he listened patiently while she told him the number missing a different digit each time until he pieced it together. Donavan rubbed both girls' heads and promised a play date soon. Urie smiled. Ella batted his hand away with a devious laugh.

"We're considering a Summer's End party again this year," he said, speaking of one of Kelly's many legendary parties of the year. "I'll have to let you know."

"Please do," she grinned, and fervently hoped he wasn't inviting Charlie.

With a wave, he disappeared into the noisy parent trap again while she led her girls toward the car with a mixture of chagrin and relief.

Chapter 3

The goodie bags from Parker's party contained mesmerizing items, aka, cheap toys dressed up to become coveted party favors. The girls eagerly unwrapped Tootsie Rolls and shoved them in their mouths while zinging bouncy balls throughout the SUV and stretching Slinky's to maximum capacity. The whole scene would have been aggravating chaos if not for the laughter that lifted the car like wings.

The girls' giddy mood redirected Laney from her normal weekend cleaning routine. She only had a couple of precious hours left with the girls before she had to hand them over to Charlie (and *her*), and she didn't want to spend the time doing chores.

Laney and Ella camped out on the dining room floor with Ella's best-loved puzzle spread out in front of them. Ella's favorite goodie bag item turned out to be a "sticky hand," a gelatinous but tacky palm on a bungee tether. To Ella's delight, she realized she could use it to grab out-of-reach puzzle pieces. Collapsing in fits of wild giggles, Ella again and again flung the sticky hand at the pieces Laney sent her to retrieve.

"Not that one!" Laney would say in mock frustration and fling the puzzle piece back to the pile. "*That* one!" And Ella would collapse in wild laughter all over again.

Urie watched with amusement, but a Chinese finger trap from her goodie bag intrigued her more. Eventually, she stopped pulling and removed one finger at a time, the woven tube only then allowing its victim to escape. Magical enchantment in a handheld toy—right up the tomboy's alley.

"That's it!" Laney cheered Ella on as she made an accurate fling. "That's the piece! Okay, let's put it... right... Wait.... *Noooooo*! Ella! It doesn't fit!" Laney dropped back on the carpet with a dramatic faint of disappointed exhaustion. Ella toppled onto her, laughing harder than Laney had heard in a long time. Both girls rushed to "revive" their fallen mother, holding her cheeks and petting her hair, and when that failed, they attempted to shove a Tootsie Roll in her mouth. Laney laughed now, trying to keep her mouth closed to avoid their cure.

With a roar, she returned to life, sending the girls running and screaming with mirth to their bedroom. The game started as chase but ended with Laney's famous somersaults. She rolled end over end down the hall, a trick left over from years of gymnastics—a surefire way to produce giggles from her little ones.

When she was good and dizzy, Laney collected the girls onto the sofa to read with them. Disney stories always captured their immature imaginations, so she let them talk her into reading *The Little Mermaid* although it was personally her least favorite. They couldn't yet know that the story made Laney want to puke a little in her mouth. She'd have to tell them someday that this was their real mom's favorite, how they got their names and had come to live with her instead, but today wasn't that day, and she couldn't deny them their story. After all, having those curly heads tucked under her chin provided a swell of love her heart desperately needed.

All too soon, it was time for Laney to over pack bundles of accessories the girls would probably not even use for their week away. She didn't care. She'd never give Charlie a reason to call her an unfit mother. The fear of losing the girls strongly outweighed the fear of being unwanted and single forever.

Her stomach knotted as she loaded the SUV, and she fought waves of nausea driving toward the meeting point, a solid half-hour from her apartment. Despite all she had lost in the divorce—the car, the house, furniture—meeting on neutral ground was one point she'd held firm on and won. Laney refused to let Charlie pick up the girls at her place. It was her new world, her created space away from the happy newlyweds, and she never wanted the embarrassment of seeing them stand in the doorway, pitying her inadequate belongings or mocking her meager grasp on happiness. They had agreed on a shopping plaza parking lot instead.

Experience had taught her that no matter how civil Charlie could be, she would be physically ill by the time she reached the store's lot. Hence the stash of antacids in her glove box.

Today, she took two.

Such stupidity, she ranted in her head for the thousandth time. How could the courts allow for this arrangement, this sharing of kids? Her girls were way too young to shuffle between parents. Her husband had left her for another woman—his *secretary,* if that didn't beat all—but still the authorities saw him as a fit role model, worthy of being in the girls' lives.

Okay, so maybe he wasn't an unfit father—Laney wouldn't pretend that—but a fifty percent role in their lives seemed more than he deserved. Still, Charlie had married Victoria, then Victoria had quit her job to be always available for the girls. They could then provide a stable home environment. Next to the stepmom, Laney paled by comparison, single and working full time.

Right on time, a car pulled up several spaces from Laney with two well-dressed, smiling figures inside.

"Hey, there are my girls!" a voice rang. The sound of it made Laney's stomach grind as if it had teeth.

The backdoors swung out and Urie and Ella squealed, "Daddy!" in unison as they bolted from the car. Laney's heart tugged and twisted. Maybe it was good for them to get used to this two-family thing so early in life. Maybe it would make it easier, more natural, as they got older. They had adjusted well so far... right?

"Tori!" the girls called, and acid crept up Laney's esophagus.

Victoria stepped out of the vehicle, her short, dark hair neatly framing her face and oversized sunglasses. A masterful side part and shiny, smooth swoop gave her hair a classy modern look. She grinned and bent to hug her stepdaughters, her perfume enveloping them all with a perfectly balanced bright, sweet scent. She whispered into their ears, and they excitedly climbed into Charlie's car, looking for Tori's inevitable gift of the week. Role as superior maternal figure thus secured, she joined Charlie in greeting Laney.

"Looks like you got everything," Charlie teased as he glanced into the back of the SUV.

"Always," Laney answered lightly.

Charlie appeared nervous as Victoria wound her arm through his. Victoria stood slightly shorter than her new husband when not wearing monster heels, which was almost never. Charlie, compared to her undeniable head-turning appearance, had a boy-next-door smile from thin lips, and his small squinted eyes now hid behind lenses, too.

"Hello, Victoria." Victoria's smile faltered for a second, giving Laney the jab of satisfaction she was looking for. Saying *her* full name was the only dig Laney could find to give the woman who'd stolen her man. Everyone else called her Tori. But the smile bounced back all too quickly.

"Hi," Tori answered, turning her eyes toward Charlie. He seemed to hold his breath. Something was up.

"Laney," Charlie began.

Uh-oh.

"Laney, we have good news."

No. Please, God, no. Laney remained frozen, her smile untouched by the sudden panic racing through every vein in her body. *Please, don't say it. Please....*

"Tori?" Charlie prompted.

She squeezed his arm as if she'd float away without him.

"I'm pregnant!" Tori squealed. She bobbed up and down like a preteen at her first concert, stripping her of all maturity she may have achieved from her careful wardrobe selections.

"Well, congratulations," Laney didn't hesitate in saying. Her tone, her smile—static. Arms still crossed. Oozing *no big deal* from her own pores. *You can do this, you can do this. Hold it together.*

"Oh, thank you! See, Charlie, I *told* you she'd be happy for us!"

Laney laughed, impressed with how natural it sounded. "Of course I am. How fantastic for you guys." She oughta win an Oscar.

Charlie seemed reluctant to buy it, and an uncomfortable silence lay on the horizon. Laney's mind raced for something more to say. "And you know...I'm pretty sure I still have some of the girls' things in storage if you need them. I have their crib, their stroller—"

"Oh," Tori laughed. "Um, thanks, that's sweet. But I think we'll be getting all *new* stuff for the baby." She wrinkled her cute little nose as if that made her comment sound less demeaning.

"Good idea," Laney countered. "I'm sure you'll love to pick it out. That's part of the fun."

Tori pulled up her shoulders in an excited shrug at the word "fun" and gave Charlie a glance that gushed with meaning. It was Urie's call that pulled her away then toward the car.

Charlie had the decency to look at Laney apologetically. "I was going to call you," he whispered. "But she was so excited. She insisted on telling you together."

"Right, no, I get that," she said, still light, still in control. "It's her big news. She wants to be the one...." A slight crack in her voice betrayed her and she stopped, hoping he hadn't heard. Her practiced smile still held.

"I know how hard this is for you," he said, reaching out to touch her arm.

That did it. The building wave crashed into the lining of her stomach so hard it made her almost retch.

She shrugged off Charlie's hand with all the casualness she could muster and maintained her Emmy-winning smile. "Don't pity me, Charlie," she managed evenly. "I have all the love I could possibly ask for. I don't need to go looking for more." She gazed past him to the two curly-headed girls who had tricked Victoria into putting her fingers into the Chinese finger trap. She was soundly stuck.

Laney began unloading the bags from the back of her car.

"Laney, I want to talk to you about Hawaii."

Laney burst into a sudden hysterical laugh as she wielded the bags onto the ground.

"*Really?* You want to bring up Hawaii *now*? You can't be serious?"

"Laney, please," Charlie continued. He closed the SUV's door and took his sunglasses off to eye her. How many nights had she lain alone in bed, wishing that those familiar eyes were beside her, staring at her? She made herself stone still and kept her sunglasses in place. "We don't have much time now. Tori can only travel for a few more months, and then we won't be able to go again for years."

"So go! I'm not stopping you from your silly little honeymoon!"

"Laney. *With* the girls." He was leaning closer now, begging with every ounce of his body language. "Please, Laney. You know what a fabulous time they'll have."

"Who wants them to come, you or Victoria?"

He gritted his teeth. "Both of us do, Laney. You know that Tori loves those girls like a—" He stopped himself.

"A mother?" Laney tersely finished for him.

"You know what I mean." He refused to look at her.

"It's ridiculous. Why wouldn't you want to go alone? Have a romantic getaway? With the girls along you'll never have a moment's peace! It makes no sense."

"Tori's sister, Michele, *lives* there. She's great with kids and very excited to meet her new nieces. She's agreed to watch the girls for a couple of evenings so we can go out. And I'll get some time alone with the girls while Tori hangs out with Michele. This is really important to me, Alex. Please."

"Don't. Do *not* call me that." Laney, the childhood nickname she had taken for Alexandria, was the only name anyone ever used except for Charlie. She had outlawed his use of *Alex* after the divorce and demanded he go back to *Laney*.

Regardless of what he called her, the courts had made it clear that neither of them could break the one-week-on, one-week-off pattern without the other's consent. She knew Hawaii meant a lot to Charlie; he wasn't trying to be greedy, and she wasn't trying to be vindictive. But the thought of the girls flying so far away for so long made her acid reflux climb to new heights.

"Why not Vegas? Texas? Disneyland, for crying out loud. Why does it have to be Hawaii?"

"It's where we want to go. It's where her family is. It's a beautiful time of year...." With an irate motion of his hand, he donned his sunglasses once more. "Will you at least consider it again? Please?"

"Daddy!" Ella ran over, and without another word, Charlie brushed past Laney to scoop up his girl. "Look at my sticky hand! Mamma made me waff when we did da puzzle."

Laney's little one gave her a fully loaded, ear-to-ear smile that was just for her, and Laney's heart twisted in new and softer ways.

"Have fun, my babies," she called to her daughters without approaching Charlie's car. Urie waved from the back seat. Then she gave her daughters her usual line, "Remember I love you *very* much!"

And without pausing for an answer, she jumped in her car and sped out of the parking lot, not caring about the responsible, single-mother act. She kept her focus until she knew she was out of sight and could pull over unnoticed. With her hands shaking and stomach rolling, she was pretty sure she could vomit. Taking deep breaths until the urge waned, she reached for the antacids in the glove box and popped a couple more.

Chapter 4

"Mrs. Whyte! Mrs. Whyte?"

The urgent voice of an approaching teen cut through the noisy hallway between second and third period. Laney turned to see the head of a dark-haired girl swimming through the pond of unconcerned classmates.

Laney had long ago learned to tune out the din of the corridors—the slamming lockers, squeaking shoes on lack-luster floors, sudden shout outs—that had the potential to produce a migraine in micro-seconds. But ever the teacher, Laney couldn't block out the occasional curse word that floated too close by. An evil eye over the rim of her reading glasses produced the necessary apology, and she shuffled on. She kept her own stack of books tucked tightly in her arm to ward against wiggling loose as today she waddled through in a pencil skirt and low heels.

The tenacious voice continued to follow her. "Mrs. Whyte?"

Laney couldn't ignore the girl at her elbow now, weaving through the masses with a matched gait. The teacher tried not to grimace at the use of "Mrs," but no matter how often she corrected students to say "Ms," they would revert to the familiar form out of habit rather than disrespect. Jordan, astute as she was, was no different.

"Jordan," Laney acknowledged. "What can I help you with today?"

"The Radster is messing up the production schedule." She gave a weighted scowl, then continued in a slightly louder tone. "Amber asked the Rad—er, *Wayne*, if everyone needed to be on the set Wednesday for rehearsal and he said *no*."

Jordan's eyes searched her teacher's with emphasis.

"So then the answer's no," Laney replied.

"Mrs. Whyte. Seriously."

Laney paused along the lockered wall, letting the surge of adolescence pass by. Jordan, an excellent student gifted in the theatrical arts, stressed over being the *assistant* to the assistant director for *Sherlock Holmes*.

"Yes, seriously, Jordan." The heels boosted Laney's height; paired with nerdy librarian glasses on a long, beaded cord around her neck and a thin, drapey gray cardigan, she felt authoritative despite her smallish stature. Pulling back her semi-tamed curls and letting the strays fly where they may added a hint of mad scientist, which complemented the *don't-mess-with-me* vibe she shot over the rim of her spectacles. She punctuated every word as she said, "What Wayne says goes."

Jordan's mouth gaped open while the hallway progressively quieted.

"But Mrs. Whyte. We've *always*—"

"No, Jordan, *you* have always," she interrupted firmly but not unkindly. "It's not you this time. You have to give Wayne an opportunity to run things. He can do this."

"The set crew always goes to rehearsals. We only have three more."

"And we also have a group of seniors with very busy schedules. If they don't need to be there Wednesday, let them get caught up on their work. They'll be all the more productive at the dress rehearsal."

Jordan's lips became a hard, determined line of dissension.

"Listen, Jordan. Give him a chance, would ya? They don't call him The Radster for nothing."

"They call him the Radster cuz his last name is Radison."

"Yeah, but *The* Radster," she teased. "It's '*The*' that commands respect."

As if on cue, Wayne burst from a door across the hall and darted in the opposite direction.

"Wayne!" Laney called out.

Wayne turned so suddenly that he almost tripped himself. He pushed his dark, thick-framed glasses up his nose and dumbly took in the two familiar figures. His opened-mouth stare wasn't helping Laney's case.

"Jordan was just complaining—" Jordan shot her teacher a venomous look

"—about the number of books she has to carry. Can you help her out with that?" Laney smiled sweetly at the narrowed slits that had once been Jordan's eyes.

"Um, yeah, sure." Wayne hustled over and grabbed Jordan's top two textbooks and threw them on top of his huge three-ring binder covered with stickers from different software companies. Squeezed in between the stickers, written in Sharpie, were single foreign words in block letters sculpted with creative twists at the ends. Laney had noted them before but could never make out the language. Today their puzzling presence caught Laney's eye again.

"Where you headed?" he asked Jordan.

"Spanish."

"Right," Wayne said and headed down the hall without waiting for her. His thick, black hair flopped along with him as he hurried.

Jordan rolled her eyes at Laney. "Thanks a lot."

"Oh, come on. The guy's had a crush on you for a year now. Can't throw him a bone once in a while?"

"Is putting him in charge part of your twisted plan to provoke some kind of romantic scenario?"

Laney laughed a little. "As if I'm that clever. Give him a break, Jordan. He's not that bad. With a little encouragement, he could be good at theater production."

"Not that bad? He's like a brainiac—and not the good kind that gets rich cuz they invent something sick. The weird kind that, you know, drools over equations and doodles insane stuff. Have you seen his binder? His notebooks? He scribbles stuff all day and hangs encryptions on his locker door. It's so... *weird*!" She wrinkled her nose and glanced at the boy in baggy jeans making good time with his jostling, off-kilter steps.

The deserted hallway warned that the bell would ring any second. Shifting her books again, Laney whipped out a pad of paper from her cardigan pocket and wrote a hall pass for Jordan and one for Wayne to ensure they wouldn't be marked tardy.

"What's that about, anyway?" Laney asked. "What's he writing in, Italian?"

Jordan snorted and took the passes. "English."

"I don't get it. He invents words?"

"No, it's like inverted letters. You know, with the same letters but in a new order?"

"You mean an anagram?"

"Yeah, that's it. He writes anagrams. His Tumblr name is Neway or something. Y'know, Wayne mixed around."

"MEAN SPUR. What's that mean? Those are the letters across the back of his binder."

Jordan shrugged, bored with the conversation and eyeing the disappearing Radster. "Sorry, gotta get to class. See you after school."

Laney watched them go. She liked Wayne. She really did. Under all that geeky, insecure nonsense grew a kid who had experienced a lot and come out of it remarkably well. His passive acceptance with peers, perhaps just tolerance at times, came from reverence for his remarkable back story. Gilbert may be a decent-sized city, but there wasn't a student in the high school of thousands that didn't know the famous moment that had slammed Wayne into high school as a hero instead of a zero.

Over two years ago, the papers told the story of a robber that had entered the Quick Mart and pulled a gun on the clerk in the predawn hours. Wayne and his father had been unfortunate enough to be the only customers that morning. The written account told of shots fired, a wounded cashier, a dead thief, and a stunned teen. His father, hailed as a hero for intervening, had been shot in the process. The bullet would have proven fatal if Wayne hadn't tackled his father and made it miss its mark. The boy performed CPR until the medics arrived and afterward became the only person in the Mart to walk away unscratched.

Heroes, both of them.

That's how the story went.

The story Wayne and his father would never speak of.

An odd mixture of awe and sympathy from his fellow students had let Wayne escape the usual harassments of someone with his social inclinations—smart, acne-ridden, shy, non-athletic, drawn to theater. Laney had to admit, she treated him with added respect, too, considering the harrowing ordeal.

Resuming her own trip down the hall, Laney mauled over MEAN SPUR as if it were a clue revealing what was going on inside Wayne's head.

Laney poked her head into the teacher's lounge before entering, not always comfortable with the company she found there. Today Dawn sat over a bag of chips and a stack of math tests. Laney saddled up next to her.

"How's the diet?" she teased.

Dawn's eyebrows shot up and eyes widened like a guilty child. She paused mid-crunch. "Wan'sum?"

Laney laughed. "I'm afraid I'll get bitten if I reach in there!"

Dawn sighed and crushed the bag. "How's the play coming?" she said, licking salt from her fingers.

"Three more rehearsals, then the real deal. I think they're ready."

"Wow, you seem pretty calm."

Laney shrugged, digging for the change at the bottom of her purse.

"Well, Doug and I were gonna have you over for lunch next weekend, but I have a feeling you'll be preoccupied."

The play ran two nights, Friday and Saturday of the following week. By that Sunday, Laney'd be dead. The thought of a long, uninterrupted sleep, even six feet under, sounded more tempting than Dawn's house. Still, Laney appreciated Dawn's attempts to keep her from imploding socially from post-divorce withdrawals.

Laney's exhausted expression must have peeked through because her friend's eyes shot open. "You don't have the girls this week, do you?"

"Oh, no. There's no way I could manage this week with them around. It's kind of a good thing they have Charlie while mama turns into Hyde."

"True. But next week—"

Laney waved her off, not wanting sympathy. "I have it covered; don't worry."

"Alright," Dawn shrugged and stood. "Gotta use the ladies' room before the bell."

Laney moved to the vending machine, but a quarter slipped from her fingers before entering the slot. It rolled across the floor till a foot stopped it at the lounge door. She tried to control her *oh great* grimace as the owner of the foot bent to pick it up.

"Drop something?" Mark Radison asked needlessly, offering his best crooked smile.

"Thanks," she said, reaching to take it from him.

He reached for her other coins instead. "I got it. What do you want?"

Laney steeled herself against her co-worker's weak attempt at chivalry. She handed him the change, bound into conversation with him now. "A granola bar is fine."

Mark happily purchased her snack and plunked himself to her table, straddling his chair the wrong way around. His leg twitched like a running motor. "How's the play coming along?"

Seriously, did no one have anything else to talk to her about? She really had to get a life. "Fine. Good."

"No troubles, huh?" He started fiddling with Laney's discarded granola wrapper the second she set it down, darting glances at everyone else who came and went.

She chewed quickly as she eyed the exit. Mark wasn't a bad guy. Good looking. Fun. Single. But he was wired like a squirrel on crack. He seemed to get endless delight in flirting with her, probably because she would do anything to avoid him.

"No. Looks like it'll go off without a snag."

"Awesome." His nervous energy made Laney want to scratch something.

She checked her phone for messages. "You coming?"

"You inviting me?" he asked, elbowing her.

It took serious effort not to roll her eyes. "Everyone's invited, Mark. Tickets are free for faculty." She set the phone down with a thunk.

"Expecting a call?"

"The guy bringing the fog machine should have called by now."

"Holy cow, what year did you get this thing?" Mark laughed, picking up her ancient cell.

Dawn came back in time to hear. "You don't want to know."

Mark snorted, flipped open the phone, and messed with the buttons. "No wonder you haven't heard anything. No one has a Fred Flintstone pterodactyl to call you with."

Dawn burst into laughter with him.

"Ha, ha," Laney said, used to the teasing. "Give it back or I'll ban you from the play."

Mark gave a mocked look of horror. "Oh, no! What will I do with myself on a Saturday night if I can't go to a melodramatic high school play?"

Laney gathered her things and held out her hand. Mark snapped the phone shut and smiled. "My number's in there now in case you change your mind."

"About what? Banning you?"

"I might just swing by to give my nephew a hello."

"Wayne will be thrilled, I'm sure." But she hoped for the kid's sake Mark never showed. Wayne had a weird notion that it would be great if his uncle and Ms. Whyte hooked up. It gave her shivers.

"Hey, Dawn says you were on the freeway during one of those RC pileups."

"Sort of. Got there right after it."

"See anything?"

Her eyebrows arched at the wildly drastic change of subject. "Nope. Not a thing." With all that was happening with work and the girls, she had forgotten all about it. Obviously, the rest of the world hadn't. "Gotta go. Later." She left with her phone in hand, still grossly warm from Mark's grip.

§ § § § §

Mondays, hated by most, always provided a recharge for Donavan. He had the weekend to unwind from his nine-to-five schedule. When the weekdays returned, his mind refilled with a flood of ideas to follow up on. Donavan and Michael had been working with the property crimes division for more than a year now, and the rock yard case was by far the most intriguing in their stack of files. And most baffling.

So when the call came that the case had been reassigned to the violent crimes division, Monday felt ruined. He had to hand over his hottest case? He'd spent hours on his leads. *Violent crimes?*

"What's got you so worked up?" Michael asked as he dropped heavily into the passenger's seat next to Donavan.

Donavan arched an eyebrow. "Worked up?"

"Come on, man. You carry that casual chill around to throw everyone off, but I can tell you're gritting your teeth behind every 'Good Morning' you throw out there."

Donavan gave a half grin and shrugged. "So you're not the least bit *mad*?"

"To let go of a case that's going nowhere? Seriously? Couldn't be happier."

Donavan started the vehicle. "Yeah, well, we have to meet the detectives at the scene to brief them. Make any sense to you?"

"Relax. They found blood, man. They have to check it out. It's out of our hands."

Donavan shrugged again as if the matter was dropped, but underneath he felt betrayed by Michael's nonchalance.

By the time they pulled up to *Dickerson's*, Donavan had let the warm air relax his tensed shoulders. When Michael pointed out that the sign had its last six letters weathered off, Donavan could even joke about the sun's inappropriate graffiti with him. They closed their car doors in unison and made their way across the dusty lot to a trailer that served as *Dick's* hub.

Detective Stanley Greer greeted him at the door of the supply yard office. It was a small, shed-like space that took up the corner of the lot out of the range of lumber, metal, and rock. Construction vehicles blocked the road beyond the open gates. Any would-be thieves would have to drive around the stacks of materials and would have difficulty maneuvering out with any kind of load. Only with the heavy equipment off site and out of the way would someone have the room to bring a vehicle into the yard to do any pilfering. They obviously couldn't walk out of there under the cover of night *without* some way to transport large materials. But somehow that's exactly what their elusive suspect had done, so it seemed.

"Thanks for coming," Stan said, creasing his face with a partial smile. Donavan had always liked Stan, and he tried to keep that in mind now. Wizened and leathery, Stan had the look of Jack Palace mixed with Marlboro man. Squinty eyes set in a wrinkled mask gave him a *don't-mess-with-me* countenance even before he spoke.

The office, a portable trailer anchored in for a more-than-temporary stay, wouldn't let four officers and the manager in all at once. The manager got a call and excused himself while the others tried to squeeze in. A desk against one wall faced the large, dirty window; its surface held a computer, files, and grunge. A tall filing cabinet sat in the corner while a couple of folding chairs took up the available standing room. Stan's partner, Jaclyn, grabbed them and folded them into the free corner, inspecting her hands afterward.

"Whatta we got?" Michael spoke up. Donavan kept silent and stuck his hands in his pockets to lean on the doorframe.

"Wondered if you could lay it out for us—how you found the place the morning after it got hit," Stan asked.

"It's like we said in our report," Donavan said with a shrug. Michael eyed him, and Donavan instantly got the message: *get over yourself and let's help these guys.*

"We'd like to ask you about some stuff we found, but it would help if you could talk us through this," Stan tried again.

"When we got here, the guard gave us his statement," Michael began. He squeezed himself into the room and looked for a clean spot on the desk to lean. Finding none, he leaned anyway. "He said there was nothing unusual about the night. He kept watch till ten and all the trucks were in and accounted for. The gates were closed, and there was no movement in the yard. When he left, he said it was quieter than church on a Monday."

Jaclyn laughed a little. "Those are the exact words according to your report. Good memory." Jaclyn Caudill, a short brunette woman, had joined the force after Donavan and Michael. Donavan didn't know much about her except that she put up with Stan's sass well enough.

"Emilio was his name," Michael continued. "Anyway, he locked up and went home for the night. They don't have a guard on duty from ten to five, just surveillance cameras."

"We checked the tapes," Donavan decided to get to the heart of the matter a little quicker; he'd rather not be here all day if he wasn't going to get to work the case. "Caught a glimpse of this guy—our perp—moving between the stacks of lumber and rock. At one point, he's in a forklift. Several pieces in the yard get moved around, but we don't always see him actually moving them."

"How'd he get in?" Stan asked.

"No one knows," Donavan said. "We don't see him come or go."

"What kind of damage did he do? How did he cart supplies out of here?"

"That's just it," Michael picked up. The place was a mess the next day. They filed a report of random items missing—some piping, cement, hardware, random items. The weirdest part is that they are pretty sure a few ton of rock and stone had been either moved or taken. But it's just not possible without the proper machinery."

Stan produced an almost inaudible grunt. Donavan knew what he was thinking.

"This isn't an isolated incident," said Donavan. "Two other sites hit in the last six, eight months. Same thing every time. This location had the most items taken, most damage done, and the most visibility, and still we have no real motive."

"Inside help?" Jaclyn asked.

"You tell me."

Stan and Jaclyn exchanged glances.

"That's why you're here, right?" Donavan persisted. "No money was reported stolen, no computer fraud. When we worked this, we found no sign of entry into the office and no evidence that any of the accounts had been tampered with. So has that changed?"

"No, that's accurate." Stan rubbed the back of his neck and waited a moment to speak. Donavan rested back into the door frame; he knew Stan wasn't someone he could rush. "The problem's been compounded—we really can't call it a theft anymore."

"All the materials are back," Jaclyn spoke up while Stan focused on a spot on the floor.

"They were recovered?" Michael asked incredulously, shooting a look to Donavan, then back to Stan. "When? Where?"

"Here."

A heavy pause pushed its weight around the room.

"I don't get it," Michael said what Donavan was thinking.

"It's as if they never left. They are all accounted for."

"That makes no sense," Donavan said in a low, controlled voice. "What's going on?"

Stan weighed his words like a man who knew what he was saying was too implausible to be counted as fact. "We've double, triple checked. There's nothing missing."

"We've been pouring over this office," Jaclyn interjected to help out Stan, "to find out if perhaps he was acting as a distraction for someone else." Michael glanced at Donavan. This had been one of the dead-end theories they had considered. "There's no sign that anything happened in any of the site offices during the break-ins. No indication of book tampering or bribes. Clean as a whistle. If we hadn't looked so long and hard here, we would have never noticed."

"Noticed what?" Donavan asked.

"Some items have exact counts," Jaclyn explained. "Like the piping, wire rolls, concrete. Other things like rock and sand are measured by the ton. Not so easy to detect theft. Still, the bins—or whatever they're called—the large area with boards they stake out for different supplies? They have depth markers on them. Lines drawn on the boards to help indicate the quantity. All the rock levels are back to where they started." She paused, giving her senior partner the chance to jump in.

"Went back to the other two sites and found the same thing," Stan struggled to confess.

"How did *that* happen?"

"Same way he got in and out of here," Stan smirked. "Magic."

"So this has nothing to do with blood?"

"Some of the so-called 'returned materials', pipes in particular, have blood smears on them. Emilio reported them. One day the pipes are gone, the next they're back with bloody streaks. No other evidence of a victim. For all we know this guy cut himself...."

"Did you—"

"Collect a sample? Of course."

Michael insisted on seeing the inventory himself, a worthless attempt at grasping for explanations in Donavan's opinion. Equally futile was Donavan's attempt to eyeball the room, peer out the window to the yard, survey the parked vehicles, hoping to find the thing they missed. The crowded room stifled his thought processes so he excused himself outside into the shade of trees that grew by the cinder block wall next to the busy road. The rustling palms overhead could either be oblivious to the crime that had unfolded beneath them or conspirators to its secret. He stood a while and listened as he thought.

Had he not been so still, Donavan might have missed movement in the parking lot when an employee got out of his vehicle. The man's eyes darted to the plain detective's car, and he hesitated.

Recognition led Donavan over to the car. The man glanced around nervously with nowhere to go now that he'd been sighted.

"Hey, there," Donavan greeted in his best easy-going tone. "Officer Peterson, remember? We spoke on the day of the break-in?"

The short man with warm dark skin nodded, his sunken eyes wide and his hands shoved deep into an oversized windbreaker.

"Weird turn of events, huh?"

Emilio looked confused.

"Have you heard? The supplies have been returned. The ones stolen."

Wide little eyes and silence.

"Any idea how that could happen?"

Something close to fear flickered for a second, a fraction of one. He mumbled something is Spanish that Donavan missed. The wind rustled his jacket and masked the words.

Donavan analyzed quickly, like second nature, flipping through files on the man's personality, reactions, and knowledge to come up with the right probe. Two chains with different charms hung about the employee's neck, the image quickly filed along with the rest.

"So odd," Donavan continued, rapidly deciding on a course of interrogation. "They disappear… and reappear," he spread his fingers out wide now as if an illusionist, his onlooker frozen, "like... magic."

"I only know what I told you before," the man croaked.

"There's something strange going on here," Donavan mused, looking about. "If I were you, I'd get a priest or something in here. This stuff doesn't just happen. You watch your back, okay? At the other lots that got hit... well, I shouldn't say. Just... be careful."

Donavan turned to go when the man spoke up in a more desperate pitch. "I don't believe in magic."

Donavan turned back. "No? Well, you might want to. Seems like—"

"Sometimes there are signs, though," the man interrupted him as if he suddenly had to get the words out. "Things that happen, that you see, and you just know it means something. Like...."

"Omens?" Donavan provided. "Like good luck and bad luck?"

"Yeah, yeah," the man continued, his voice relaxing a little though his body remained stiff. "It's not magic, it's just, some stuff happens, and you knew it was gonna because you had a sign. Anything like that happen at the other yards?"

"Did you have a sign that this was going to happen?"

"Not like that, no. But I found this." The man looked left then right before pulling his hand out of his pocket. It revealed nothing more than rubble.

"A rock?"

"Look at it."

Donavan took it and examined it more closely. He barely knew the difference between granite and flagstone, but the sheen of the rock in the light told him this was neither of those. A myriad of greens, in flecks and stripes, wove their way from the core and around. Donavan squeezed it, weighed it in his hand.

"What do you make of it?" he asked Emilio.

Emilio shrugged. "I don't know. Never saw rock like that before. I found two of them in one of our loads. Kept them in the office, and they seemed to make my luck change, you know? Like a good luck charm. Got a raise, got back with my girlfriend." He shrugged again as if adding nonchalance supported his superstitions. "I took one home with me; kept the other one in the office."

Donavan turned to glance at the office where Michael and the others now exited toward him. He flipped through mental pictures of the room.

"The rock's gone from the office?"

The man nodded slowly with a weighted pause. "I don't know what's going on, but yesterday I noticed it was missing. Nobody else knows what happened to it. But I'm thinking it's not good luck anymore. Me and my girlfriend are fighting again, someone broke into my house... I don't know. And all this weird stuff—the supplies coming back? I don't know, man. Just weird."

"Bad luck, huh?" Donavan frowned as if seriously contemplating. "So why are you carrying this around?" Michael was saying bye to Stan and Jaclyn, buying him a few more seconds.

Emilio flicked his head toward the yard. "I'm putting it back. Get things back in order." He laughed a little, hiding a flicker of fear that most would have missed.

"Sounds like a good idea," Donavan nodded, turning the rock over in his hand. "Mind if I do it?"

Emilio looked doubtful, but Donavan gave him no chance to answer. Instead, he slapped the man's arm in solidarity just as his partner joined him. "Thanks, Emilio. Everything will go back to normal."

Emilio walked warily away when Michael approached. Donavan pocketed the rock, unsure why he didn't want to share with Michael just yet.

"Well, that was a waste of a morning," Michael said, heading toward the car. "Let's go grab some coffee."

Donavan quickly agreed; coffee was never a bad idea. Michael drove this time, giving him the chance to push aside the impossible case and make a few phone calls. He had been putting off being social ever since Kelly had left—those words were still hard to even think, let alone say out loud—but Parker's party had really helped motivate him.

Nellie had been pushing him to "get back out there." Maybe this was the perfect time to rinse his hands of this case and do just that. He decided to put this next get-together in motion.

Back at the station, there was no sign that others had had the unproductive morning Michael and Donavan had shared.

Commotion in processing deterred Donavan from heading to his desk. Instead, he ventured a peek around the corner. Sounded like a lot more attention than the usual unruly offender required.

"Got yourself a live one," Michael quipped to Browser, their resident IT expert who watched with mild interest from behind his desk.

Browser gave them an eyebrow. "You guys might want in on this one." He clicked a few buttons on his laptop and exposed the processing form with a picture and name. "Looks like they caught the guy connected with that rock yard funny business."

Donavan straightened and glued his eyes to the slight man in handcuffs, mid-thirties with a jet black hair in a greasy ponytail cursing out three officers that surrounded him.

"Well, wadda ya know," Michael mumbled.

"Hold this," Donavan said, passing his coffee off to his partner. "Time to get us some answers, don't you think?"

Chapter 5

Laney took a breather before lunch, much needed after forty-five minutes of grading lukewarm essays. She dug out her phone from her cardigan to check the time, pushing her glasses up her nose. Three missed calls. That hadn't happened since Gary Walkowski left his inhaler at home on the day he could break his own record at the track meet; his Mom had called every soul in the school.

Curious, Laney went to her voicemail.

First call: Charlie. Had she had time to think more about Hawaii?

Ugh.

Delete.

Call two: Mom. Wanted to know how the play was coming and really missed her. *Awww.*

Save.

Call three: not a number Laney recognized. More surprise to find it was Donavan.

She switched the phone to her other ear and knocked over a stack of papers. She grimaced at the mess and wrestled them back onto the desk as the message began.

"Hello, Laney? Donavan. How's the play going? Or did I miss it? Sorry, you'll have to remind me of the dates again." (Little laugh). "We're going through with the end-of-summer party this weekend. So just wanted to call and invite you… and the girls… and whoever. We'll start at five for the kids but come whenever. That's Saturday night." He breathed in as if he had not a care in the world. Just the sound of his breath made Laney smile. "You know, same casual stuff. No need to call back. Just show up if you can."

Laney played her mom's and Donavan's messages twice each. It was nice to have messages from two friendly voices. They chased away the blues Charlie's nagging tone gave her. Donavan wouldn't invite him, right? Bring the girls… *and whoever*? Who would she take?

She put the phone away and sighed. Another social event stag. Not so bad unless married couples made up the rest of the party. She'd need another shot of confidence to tackle this one. Looked like the strappy shoes might have to come out of retirement early.

§ § § § §

So far, October had cruelly mislead its adorers with deceptively cool evenings and milder days. It taunted Valley dwellers like Donavan with a reminder of why they called this once barren land home. But just when it convinced people to put away their tank tops and pool towels—*wham*. Another sprint of intensely hot days, as if the sun wouldn't give up its prime time without a finale.

With the depressing resurgence of summer sending a stream of moisture down his back, Donavan yanked his car door open and threw his tie across the seat. There it melted into a lifeless pile, as relieved to be rid of its owner as its owner was of it.

In the stifling heat of his car, the detective breathed the torturous temperature deep into his lungs. He pushed back the agitation that heat might ruin his weekend barbecue. Instead, he simmered like the heat waves rising off the hood, a different anger building.

With gritted teeth and jerking motions, he started the car and turned on the air conditioner, letting it blast its initial scorching wind to further provoke him.

The steely silence that trademarked Donavan's calm, collected demeanor started to collapse. With a sudden burst, he slammed his hands into the steering wheel, put the car in motion, and took off out of the lot.

Vincent Valentine. The sole thought that consumed him now. The menace, the shadow, the elusive... Now that Donavan had him in his grasp, *he* had become the one caught.

The hero now the victim.

Just like that.

The scene from moments before replayed in his mind like a broken newsreel.

He tried to redirect his thinking like he always did when he found his emotions taking hold. It made him good at what he did—the ability to keep his cool, to keep a composed, reassuring smile or an intense stare without giving away more than he needed.

His sergeant knew that. So for anyone to believe he would let some greasy-haired criminal get the better of him was laughable. Brutalizing a perp? Openly and intentionally? Who would believe it?

The burning sensation coming from the steering wheel helped him relax his hold, and he slouched back in his seat, brooding as he drove.

What did it matter that he got time off without pay? If it came to that, he needed the rest anyway. Every day seemed longer than the next, and he tired of the constant feeling of being dragged behind the car at the end of each shift. Periodic insomnia didn't help. Rest would be… good.

At the thought, all the long hours on the go caught up with him in a rush within the vehicle's oven-like conditions. The clock read 4:45 pm. So now what? Parker would still be at practice. The house would be empty and lonely. He couldn't fall asleep now even if he tried to nap, so… more caffeine?

Impatiently tapping the steering wheel, he waited for a red light to change until he felt his hands clenching once more. He turned into a corner gas station instead and sped out the other side. He had to move, had to leave the day behind somewhere.

I don't need coffee, he decided. *I need to find something stronger.*

But where?

He headed down Arizona Avenue, not sure it led anywhere he wanted to go. The City of Chandler's older sections inter-fused with newer subdivisions, the need for modernization leading to rebuilding downtown. New businesses lined the heart of the city. Donavan passed them with wary interest, seeking. The mental image of a cold glass enticed him, but something more than that pushed him on.

A new wine cellar tucked between two restaurants peeked its pretty painted sign out at him. He could hear Kelly now, tugging at his elbow like a child: "Pleeeeeease? Oh, doesn't it look so cute?" She would love a small, swank place like that.

The vacant seat next to him mocked him. She wouldn't be joining him for excursions to new places. The thought urged him on until he found a bar—no, an old restaurant masquerading as a friendly hang-out with its new paint job—but no available street parking. He continued to a small lot in the back, more a widened alley, really, where barely five cars could fit.

But even more unusual than the parking was the door he found tucked into the side of the adjacent building. An ancient sign hung in the window carved out of faux wood, metal wire around lights punched through holes, looking like a Pinterest project gone wrong. *Jake's* it read, in small dimly lit bulbs. The weathered door and windows, both sprayed with several shades of dirt, told of an establishment long vacated... except for the dim lights glowing within and the distant sound of a TV.

Donavan got out of his car and thought of a dozen reasons he should get back in. The dust on the other vehicles indicated they hadn't moved in days. Weeks? Not a great sign. He didn't need a beer that badly. Just walk around the corner and go into the far less seedy door of the bar and grill. Better yet, drive until a more suitable parking spot opened up rather than park by a dumpster in an alley-sized lot.

Donavan did neither. After locking his doors, his feet carried him to the dismal bar, and he walked inside before he could stop himself.

Guess he *did* need a beer that badly.

The building, more a shed than a bar, stretched before him, long and narrow, as he pushed the door. With his first tentative step in, Donavan reeled with disorientation until he took off his sunglasses and let his eyes adjust. Motionless for a moment in the doorway, he stabilized until he could find the outline of the bar itself.

His head swam with a scent—no, a feeling. The light, dim and obscure coming from the hanging bulbs, paled in comparison to the sun that streaked in from high, small windows. It tinted the dust motes suspended in its beams. An ill-fitted collection of tables—some wooden and round, some metal and square—wound their way around the L-shaped bar. The backroom attached itself like a drunken afterthought, needing the larger room, a sturdy, sober friend, to cling to.

Donavan found his way to a stool, as if he'd staggered through a fog, the feel and draw of the place a mysterious pull on his being.

"Draft," he told the barkeep, a solid balding man, a bit nondescript, almost like the old creepy Wooly Willy toy, where you add magnetic shavings to a blank face to give it character.

The man nodded in return and removed a glass, a little suspect in its cleanliness, from the back shelf.

A dark mountain of a man, sitting at the bar in front of an empty, wet mug, took in the newcomer with a critical gaze then turned back to watching an old clock without giving Donavan so much as a nod.

The clock hung monstrously behind the bar, an ancient, round metal beast, a rusty relic from another lifetime, its lackluster hands pointing to Roman numerals at six-ten, almost an hour ahead.

"You're late."

Donavan's throat tightened at the black man's voice, hard with authority. He must be mistaking him for someone else. When the man nodded toward the clock, Donovan got the joke and slumped in relief.

"Depends on who's keeping the time," he replied.

The man gave a fraction of a smile and went back to timekeeping. One of the pool players emerged from the back shadows and peered at Donavan from the far end of the counter. His neighbor shot a glance that way, sending the pool player ducking back again.

A TV in the corner murmured and Donavan pulled his attention to it until he felt his shoulders relax, the odd sensations diminishing. *Just one,* Donavan told himself. But the beer was more than good, it was therapeutic. The clock kept up its insane ticking but never moved an inch, as if capturing its occupants within a cocoon that subdued thought. *It's a time warp,* Donavan mused to himself. *If only it could back me up to a couple of hours before I met Valentine.*

His shoulders tensed again, and he swallowed more therapy.

A second-rate comedy rerun took up the five o'clock slot before the news at six. By the end of the second drink, a second pool player managed to steal several more glances from the dark shadows. A slow lazy afternoon group.

Donavan should stop after this second mug, the questionable cleanliness a nagging thought, but as he neared the bottom and the six o'clock weather began, he knew he'd be staying.

"Same thing as last week," the bartender mumbled. "Hot. What we need a report for?"

The Goliath next to him laughed and shook his head. "Some folk are just hopeful, Rufus. Fall's just around the corner."

"It is fall, and it's still hot. This is desert. Gonne be hot. Don't everybody know that?"

"Hard to accept," the patron continued. He finally gave Donavan his attention as if he'd been waiting for the right moment. "Been in Arizona long?"

"Long enough to know Rufus is right."

Rufus snorted his justification.

After the promise of cooler temperatures in the near horizon, the program turned to local news.

Elusive vandal Vincent Valentine: arrested and taken into custody early this morning.

Donavan gripped his now empty mug. Rufus brought another that he ignored. *Valentine has been linked to several industrial crimes in the Phoenix, Albuquerque, and San Antonio areas.*

Then Donavan appeared on the screen, leading Vincent in cuffs. The backside of his head anyway. Thank God the camera had been on the opposite side of the mongrel, and only Donavan's hair made the shot. Then they climbed the stairs inside the station.

Clips changed to sketches. *Valentine, whose identity had eluded police until very recently, has been linked to vandalism at several construction sites; he is accused of damaging property and stealing equipment....*

"That's not all," the big guy snorted and muttered something more Donavan couldn't hear.

Donavan controlled his impulse to whip the man a quick look almost too late. He saw the man give him a sidelong glance. Donavan calmly took a sip, trying to ignore his heart pounding in rhythm with the clock.

"...has a prior record of petty theft and larceny. Police hope to learn a motive for his actions in the industrial crimes. No trial date has been set."

Donavan steeled himself, but the story changed to a major accident on the freeway. His own actions weren't revealed, what had led to his suspension, to this moment here on a bar stool instead of on the job. But there was no doubt his part in this horrible day would soon reach the public.

Vincent's greasy sneer appeared in the suds of the mug that Donavan stared down. He'd put his share of guys behind bars and had always let their insults fly past deaf ears. It was the job, and no matter whose blood stained perps' hands, what vile offense they were accused of, Donovan treated them the same. The guys who hurt the innocent set his teeth on edge, but even then he could compartmentalize it. Vincent had done his best to shake his controlled façade.

"How's your wife?" Valentine had hissed from between damaged teeth. "Man, she good." That was a new one for Donavan. He said nothing, though Michael shot back a "Yo mama" comment to Vince. Donavan kept his head in the game, helping with the booking. He hadn't brought Vince in. He shouldn't even been the one, but pride had gotten the better of him, and he wanted to be the one to navigate the suspect toward the cells. That's when he felt Vincent's mood change.

"She doesn't know, does she?" Vincent's voice grated into a cackle, thick from smoking, with an edge that exposed a world of experiences. His dark Hispanic hair lay slicked back and pulled into a tight ponytail at the nape of his neck; he kept his five-five frame hunched over as if trying to hide something under his loose T-shirt. "You haven't told her, eh?" He laughed. "She'll find out. She'll probably know it before you do. That's what's driving her *loca*, ese."

Donavan refused to acknowledge him, but as he shuffled Vincent along in cuffs, Donovan grew warier. An image of Kelly popped into his head and wouldn't leave. *Loca.* It only took that moment of distraction for Vincent to make his move. It happened so fast Donavan couldn't place it all in proper sequence. Vincent stumbled the same instance Donavan reached up to signal for the cell door. The stumble caught Donavan off balance and, as he quickly tried to catch himself against the bars with Vincent in between, his prisoner went down hard, head rapping the cell bars so solidly that a *thunk* had echoed across the small space, resounding with Vincent's cries. By the time they untangled and got on their feet, Vincent was screeching "Police brutality!" from his bloody and bruised head.

The images surfaced on the screen and all but brought Donavan to his feet. But his bar buddy didn't seem to notice, his comment still floating like a lure between them. Donavan kept his seat long enough to fish some more: "That Valentine guy's a load of trouble."

Big guy bit. "You can say that again."

"Wonder how come police couldn't snag him sooner."

The man turned toward him with a slow smile as if he shared the inside joke. "Yeah, I wonder."

Another sip, another pause. In a moment this guy would finish his beer and might walk out without having satisfied Donavan's curiosity. "How come you know about him? Valentine."

The answering eyes had gone dark, but they didn't turn all the way toward Donavan. "They just said he had priors. That kinda guy's trouble."

"You seemed to know about his priors even before the TV mentioned it. How so?"

A slow smile. "You ask a lot of questions."

"Can't help it; it's my job. I do it all day."

The man stayed quiet for so long, Donavan thought it was a lost cause.

"He's bad news. The kind that hurts people. Shows up where he don't belong. Makes the world a worse place." For a moment, their eyes locked. That brief moment was enough to make Donavan question the randomness of their meeting.

"Name's Harley."

Donavan took his hand and shook it. "Donavan."

Again, Donavan glimpsed a smile that seemed to have a private meaning. "Well, Donavan, I reckon it's time to hit the road."

"I reckon it is."

The thought didn't dawn on Donavan until he was halfway to his car that Harley wasn't the one leaving; *he* was. A chill spread through him, despite the heat, and he turned back to scowl at the small lights on the rusty *Jake's* sign.

What *was* this place?

Chapter 6

"Having fun?" Laney asked.

Rodney stood beside her, racket in hand, sweat on his brow, intensely studying the people across the net. He snapped out of his competitive mode for a minute to give Laney a crooked grin.

"Yeah, you?" She nodded back and swatted the birdie with satisfaction right over the net.

"Plus one" wasn't a phrase Laney usually allowed into her vocabulary. When Donavan had called with his invitation to the end of summer party, his comment to bring "whoever" had thrown her off. Who wanted to go to the party with a "whoever" hanging over them? So Rodney it was. She considered either him or Mark Radison, and the shudder at seeing Mark's name in her phone contacts made Rodney the less painful choice. She would have eradicated Mark's number from her list... if she could figure out how.

Little girl giggles tempted her to peek across the yard at her girls engaged in unbridled fun with kids they barely knew. It was perfect timing that this was the one week out of the month she got the girls on Saturday instead of Sunday so Charlie and Tori could compete at their tennis club. It was worth having the kids as a buffer with all these other families and to see Urie play chase in her sparkly jean shorts, neat French braids flapping in her wake. Ella, meanwhile, sat in the sandbox in her pink tutu, constructing mounds of nondescript figures that only a four-year-old's imagination could bring to life.

Had she known about the backyard sports, Laney wouldn't have worn her white gauze skirt and a coral short-sleeved shirt. But she surprised herself by jumping right into the action after Donavan had greeted them both warmly, dressed in blue jeans and t-shirt—the Donavan she remembered well from years gone by. She and Rodney had joined the call to play badminton while Donavan moved off to play host. They were on game three, and already Laney had downed two bottles of water. Rodney, in contrast, was working on beer three.

As the opponents rotated and alcohol flowed, Rodney's good spirit grew more intense. She could be competitive herself, so his aggression had only sparked her best effort. To her amazement, they were winning, and she was having fun. How'd that happen?

She remembered all the moments of stress over the play that had given her reason to not attend this party. Next weekend: opening night. But she had *wanted* to come in a strange, inexplicable way, despite having to bring a date, despite having to face happy easy-going couples, despite all her stupid baggage.

And she was here and having a good time. Would wonders never cease?

In the middle of one more set, Rodney was *not* having fun. Laney thought she heard him curse under his breath at lucky shots from the other team and missed birdies of his own. When he missed a birdie just beyond his reach, he became genuinely irritated and shouted, "Out of bounds!"

Dissension arose from spectators, but the other team just wanted the game to go on. Laney remained nervously silent.

"Just let them have it," a tall guy named Mike said casually. "Forget the points. Let's just play."

At that, Rodney threw his racket down harder than necessary and sulked off.

Laney stood stupidly frozen when another woman rushed in to take his place. Uncertain what else to do, Laney played a few more rounds, trying to pretend nothing happened.

By the time she made it to the other side of the yard, Rodney was talking to two men she didn't recognize. *Perhaps he's feeling better again*, she thought. This dating thing was tough. She hadn't planned on worrying about someone other than the girls tonight.

She stood awkwardly alone when Donavan appeared from the side of the house with a huge tray of ribs still smoking in his mitted hands. He was the master griller, and Laney's spirits picked up again. She might be a poor date chooser, but she could put down ribs like a champ. The thought made her mentally drool.

Laney scanned the yard to find Kelly; she still hadn't reconnected with her old friend. Her gaze fell on the back patio where a group she recognized stood gossiping. She hesitated. It was hard to just jump in, but given the choices of standing alone and being with Rodney, she decided it was worth the risk.

She took a big breath and headed over.

"—the most amazing chicken salad," someone was saying. Pam? She looked like a Pam with soft brown curls and friendly, round face. She was married to Gary; Laney knew that for sure. Gary was a mechanic and had helped them get discount parts for her car years ago. He was a good guy, eager to please and easy to like; she'd met "Pam" only once.

"Hey, there!" Peyton, of course. And Gail. Kelly had met them at a playgroup when Parker was little, and Laney had tagged along a couple of times. This was one of the women who had smiled and waved at her at Parker's party.

"Laney, do you know everybody?" Peyton asked graciously. "You know Gail and this is Megan and Eve." She pointed to Gary's wife.

The semi-circle of faces contained none that belonged to Kelly. "Hi, everyone. Long time, no see." So Pam was an Eve. That'd take some getting used to. She looked nothing like an Eve.

"We were just talking about *food,*" Peyton said, and all the women giggled at some inside joke. "It seems like Gail is determined to torture us with the topic."

Gail playfully hit Peyton with her free hand while the other one held a soda. "I am not that bad! I was just telling them how horrible my eating habits have been. I just found out I'm pregnant."

Good grief, not another one. But out loud, Laney cooed, "Oh, congratulations!"

"We've been giving her a hard time because whenever we mention a place, she starts talking about the food there." Open laughs of agreement.

"Like the convenient store on Baseline is the only one she can find that sells Flaming Lime Torittos," Megan added. "I don't even know what those are!"

"They are awesome, you guys! Seriously, it was worth the drive."

"I couldn't eat anything spicy when I was pregnant with Brandon. I swear, he would have kicked me out of my own body if I'd even *read* a label that said 'flamin'."

Okay. I can handle this. Fun conversation about pregnancy eating habits. Laney looked longingly at the rib table and glanced about for Rodney. *Just don't let the conversation come my way. Best to head it off.*

"How's the baby feel about ribs?" Laney asked in what she hoped was a playful tone.

"Don't they smell incredible? I wish Gary could grill like that."

"Baby would love some!"

"Do you think they're ready yet?"

"I heard Kimberly and Dyana say they're bringing out the side dishes first."

Dang.

"So have you guys been picking out names?" Peyton asked. And they moved right back to babies.

"I'm only four months along. We've got lots of time to think about it."

Agreement and opposition arose. Some had waited, this one had picked the name this way, others had a list, each silly reply revealing meaningless choices to others in the group while being personally imperative to each parent. On and on.

Laney shifted her weight and angled for a way out. Maybe they needed help in the kitchen. But she could see through the long dining-room windows that too many bodies already crowded the kitchen.

"Laney, how about you? How'd you come up with Urie and Ella?" And so the name game had come around to her.

Laney smiled and hid the sigh she felt inside. "Easy. Just used the names they came with." She let everyone squinch their faces in confusion for a minute. "I adopted the girls." In this company, Laney would never share the explanation behind Arie's odd baby names.

There were a couple of nods and glances at the girls until Gail laughed, "She's kidding," and she swatted at the air to wave away any awkwardness. "They aren't adopted. Look at them! They look more like you than *you* do, Laney." Eve/Pam laughed with her, half convinced.

Laney kept smiling. "Yeah, actually, they *are* adopted. They're my sister's kids."

The group stared dumbfounded. Awkward *Oh's* and *Ah's* replaced laughter.

"That's right," Peyton drawled. "Now I remember us talking about it once at playgroup. When you'd only had Urie a little while. But Ella. I would have never guessed in a million years. Urie looks like you, but Ella could be your clone!"

The others agreed.

"My sister is my twin, so…"

A chorus of "wow" and "unbelievable/so cool" followed.

And eventually—inevitably—someone braved the question everyone wanted to know. "So what happened to your sister?"

Car crash. Sky diving accident. Drugs. Shark attack. Peace Corps. Anything sounded better than the truth. How do you explain to a group of mothers whose world revolved around their kids that some moms just don't want that? Laney couldn't comprehend her sister's decision any more than an outsider. Regardless, she somehow felt disloyal saying anything derogatory.

"She had issues," was Laney's best excuse. "Let's just say she wouldn't have been… the best mother."

The moms nodded and *umm*ed just as a train of guests exited the house carrying big bowls of green salad, baked beans, potato salad, corn on the cob, and what looked like plenty of kid-friendly mac and cheese.

"Well, the girls are just the sweetest," Peyton said as she led the group toward the tables.

"Hey, where's Kelly?" Laney asked and got a blank stare back.

"You don't know?"

"Know what? She's sick?" Ravished party-goers hurried toward the tables.

"Donavan and Kelly divorced."

Laney stopped in her tracks. "Wait—what?" Good thing the others had gone on ahead.

Peyton grimaced sympathetically, but suddenly hungry children bombarded them, holding empty plates like little Oliver Twist's. The noise and activity rattled Laney further as she tried to wrap her mind around this new information. "How long?"

"Since January, I think," Peyton managed before an impatient offspring pulled her away.

Urie and Ella tugged Laney from either side. Laney hurriedly did the math in her head. Nine months? They divorced nine months ago, and she had no idea? Charlie never told her, but then Donavan said they hadn't spoken since before Christmas.

An odd sense of disappointment tangled with... betrayal. No one had told her.

Donavan hadn't told her.

Laney distractedly filled the girls' plates when she remembered she was with someone. Rodney. *Oops.* She caught a glimpse of him heading back into the house. Bathroom? She hoped she wouldn't offend him if she got in line without him. The girls made a great excuse. She only filled *their* plates on the first run.

She waited outside the back door while the girls ate. Her eyes moved to Donavan, across the yard, talking with Michael, Parker up on his shoulders. Donavan's normal poise, solid and casual, seemed so natural as he wiped his hands on a kitchen towel and laughed at something Michael said. The light in his eyes confirmed for Laney that the split had to have been several months ago. No one who went through a breakup could laugh like that so soon.

But what could have kept Kelly from an event like Parker's birthday? Her mind wandered as she watched the soft cotton of Donavan's denim blue t-shirt stretch with his movements, his muscles obvious under its pull. She tore her gaze away, mind racing.

The girls finished and moved on to play. The seating overflowed with families and couples, leaving Laney on the edge of the yard. It was a beautiful space, with a rock garden surrounding the interior grass plot, bougainvillea in bright, showy pink blossoms and unusual peach hibiscus sprung up in various places in the stone border, giving the grassy center the perfect, complemented edge. Kelly always did have a green thumb and had spent years on this yard. How had she left all this? Or had she? Had Donavan asked her to leave? How had Donavan gotten the house?

Mulling over the questions, she looked for Rodney again when she noticed more ribs remained, but there was no line.

Okay, just one helping, then she'd find Rodney.

The other grownups had finished and were cleaning up their sauce-covered kids. The sun dipped and Kimberly rounded up the strays with a promise of a special surprise. Donavan appeared in cahoots with her about the secret something for the kids. Laney noticed how the other woman's eyes shown and how her face lit up as she talked to the host. Hmmm. Laney glanced over at Kimberly's husband and wondered what he thought about that relationship.

Okay, now she was just inventing stuff to explain Donavan's divorce.

Rodney finally emerged from the house and hunted her down with rapid glances. She waved sauce-covered fingers at him, his expression much different from the fun guy swinging a racket an hour ago.

"These ribs are incredible. Grab some before they're all gone."

"Nah," he answered. "Hey, my buddy Hernandez just called. A bunch of guys are meeting at Maria's and she's got a big spread. What'd you say we blow this party and head back to the apartment?"

Laney searched for her napkin, but it had slipped from her hand and lay lost somewhere in the twilighted grass. "Umm. Well, I thought we'd stay a little longer. The girls are having fun, and they have some kind of treat later for the kids."

"Angela's kids will be there. The girls would have fun with them." He texted someone while he waited for her answer.

An uncomfortable chill settled over her. "I... I think we should stay." She loosely gripped her plate in front of her, trying to keep her sauced-up fingers from touching anything. Was she wearing it all over her face?

"Well, I want to go," he said, barely able to stand still. "Finish your food and let's get out of here." His voice had escalated, and Laney could feel her heart rate joining the climb.

"The girls—"

"So, what, they get to decide how you're gonna spend your Saturday night?" The comment came with an awkward laugh, but his features held an unfamiliar distortion of her once friendly neighbor. His hand ran through his hair with increased impatience, his feet in a restless shift.

With sudden clarity, Laney paused before she spoke again. "No, Rodney. We're going to stay. How about you have some coffee—"

He scowled as if suddenly disgusted with her. "Forget it." He swung his arm in agitation and barely grazed Laney's plate. But it was enough to send it spinning from her loose grip. In a second, her white gauze skirt streaked dark red with trails of BBQ sauce.

She sucked air in horror and held her breath. As people along the fringes of the yard turned her way, her cheeks began to burn.

"But you're our ride," was all she could manage.

"So get cleaned up and come with me or stay." An ultimatum. From Rodney. The *let-me-give-you-a-hand* guy next door, now the world's worst "plus one."

And then there were more than just two of them standing there.

She hadn't even seen Donavan cross the yard or known he saw any of this. But there he stood beside them, one hand in his pocket, the other around a soda can, as poised and relaxed as if he meant to chat about the weather.

"Hey, how's it going?" For a fraction of a second, she thought he was completely oblivious. She examined his passive face quickly, but it was enough. It was there, behind Donavan's calm brown eyes, the nonchalant smile, the casual stance. He knew exactly what was going on and had come to her rescue.

A little of her courage resurfaced. "Rodney was just leaving."

Rodney's eyes pierced them both. She held her ground as he said, "How you getting home? I'm not coming back."

"I think we can find her a ride," Donavan interjected. He took a sip of his soda and stared Rodney down. No one moved. "Thanks for coming, Rodney. Let me show you out."

Rodney said something in Spanish that Laney didn't understand as he walked away. Donavan followed him through the back door, shoulders relaxed and hand in his pocket.

Laney fought the urge to collapse into a puddle. She bent to pick up the fallen plate and realized she was shaking. *Please don't let anyone be staring at me, please.* But she knew the wish was futile.

"Piñata time!" someone yelled.

Perfect timing. Kids scrambled to assemble, and their disorganized delight took precedence over Laney's disaster. The party collected en masse beside the badminton net, where a colorful flower-shaped piñata dangled from the neighbor's jacaranda branch. With her retrieved napkin, she timidly poked at the red smear on her skirt, relieved to be alone in the grass as the darkness closed in.

Relief was short-lived.

Floodlights kicked on by a dusk timer, and the brightness made everyone turn to notice her, as if for the first time, standing by herself in the middle of the yard, the white canvas of her skirt displaying the masterpiece her plate had painted on its way to the ground. She prayed for a hole to fall into when Donavan returned through the back door. A blush—a hot, red, stupid blush—spread until her entire head felt on fire. Just when she was sure only death could be worse, fate played its cruel hand. With everyone else off the grass and headed toward the piñata, the sprinklers suddenly came to life and began to drench everything in the center of the yard.

And the only thing in the grass *to* drench was her, Laney Whyte—messy dateless divorcee—showcased in the brilliance of the floodlights with a crimson stained skirt that just about matched her cheeks.

She stood in defeat and let the water drown any hope of recovering the evening.

Chapter 7

Donavan stood in the doorway to the backyard, relieved that the piñata had distracted the guests when Laney needed it most. Kimberly organized the kids with a blindfold and single-file line while Laney had slinked into the house. Donavan maintained a "nothing to see here" smile, watching Michael enjoy himself amid the dads who egged boys on to improve their aim and coaxed little girls out of timidity.

Laney silently emerged from the hallway into the kitchen as he turned. Her forehead creased between the eyes under his gaze, her hand smoothing the material of the only thing he could rustle up for her: a simple swimsuit cover, nothing more than a large square of fabric that wrapped around her body then crisscrossed to tie behind the neck. Kelly was taller and leaner than Laney, so finding something left in the house wasn't easy. The turquoise sarong covered Laney, and her damp hair had disappeared into a severe knot in the back of her head as if being punished for playing in the sprinklers. Only one stubborn, short curl had escaped and swept across her forehead.

"I put my wet stuff in the dryer," she spoke softly. "Hope that's okay."

Donavan wished somehow he could take away her embarrassment. But trying would only make it worse. "Yeah, sure. Come watch the girls swing at this thing. Ella is cracking me up."

Laney hesitated before taking the spot opposite to Donavan in the door frame where they watched her four-year-old princess clobber like a Viking. Her smile held, though hollow and forced; he sensed her gathering courage to speak. Waiting without expecting worked best with women. Especially one who had something on her mind.

"Thank you for earlier." Laney cast her eyes down when she spoke.

The next kid finally smacked the piñata hard enough to make a dent.

"No problem," he said lightly, not in the least sorry he'd ushered Rodney out. To be honest, Laney's episode had been just the distraction he needed. He had been imploding for days, waiting for the captain to call him, to find out what the Valentine case would mean for his career. Rescuing Laney from her terrible date had given him something much more comical to focus on.

"I was thinking... I thought I'd just Uber when the piñata is finished." She grew noticeably paler with these words.

"Really? Michael lives over your way. I'm sure he'd give you guys a ride."

"I don't—I just don't want to make anyone…." She stopped, and he could imagine the entire spectacle of the evening playing all over again in her head. He hid an amused grin.

"Look," he said, and she finally peeked at him from the corner of her eye. "Don't worry about Uber. Sit back and relax a little while, and we'll get you home, I promise. Don't let some *guy* ruin your evening."

She glanced down at her clothes and grimaced.

"And by some *guy*, I meant Rodney," he added. "And, yeah, sorry about the, um, sprinklers."

She matched his chagrined smile, and together they laughed.

"Seriously, of all the moments for them to come on—" she said.

"I swear, I thought I turned them off before the party."

"—and there was no one out there but me!"

"I don't know what happened. *Really* sorry."

"And the flood lights just *had* to come on?"

"Complete bad luck, I know."

She sighed and the natural color returned to her cheeks.

"My clothes were ruined already. Just gave me a reason to change. Thanks... I think."

A loud crack and excited squeals told them the piñata neared destruction.

"Come here." Donavan led her inside and pointed to a seat in the kitchen where the sink faced one side, a long counter and stools stood opposite. "Have a seat." He uncorked a bottle of wine and set out two glasses.

"Oh, no thanks," she declined from her perch. "I still have to get the girls home, and I'm already wiped.

Donavan placed half a glass in front of her and poured the second for himself. Heavens knows *he* needed it. Her eyes held uncertainty.

"Laney, in about two minutes, a herd of people will come through those doors while they let their kids get high off of penny candy in the backyard. They will stare at you, see you in that sorry excuse for a dress without your date, and be full of questions that they may or may not ask aloud. Most likely they'll just whisper behind your back." He watched her face grow pale again. "Now, you can pretend you got this thing under control or you can find a little courage from that glass. The choice is yours."

An explosion of cheerful glee erupted in the backyard; without a doubt, the piñata had broken open.

Laney raised her glass. "Bottoms up."

As predicted, grownups filed into the kitchen, relieving themselves as piñata guardians. Kimberly floated in and controlled the disruption of desserts like the ringleader of a circus. Laney arched back to scan outside, but Donavan, aware of the many eyes turned her direction, drew her attention to her glass again.

"I can see them," he reassured her. "I think Urie is helping Parker get more candy, and Ella's taking it back out of his bag."

She smiled. "That's my girls."

Kimberly offered them pastries, her smile on Donavan for a second too long as he declined. It didn't escape Laney's notice like he'd hoped.

"So what's the story with her?" Laney asked.

Donavan grimaced internally but kept his practiced outer mask in place. "We used to date right after high school. She's like an overprotective big sister." *And a giant pain in my backside,* he wanted to add. But Ron, her husband, had been a good friend for years. So inviting them to functions was often a package deal.

"Right." Laney sipped her glass as the room filled with more people. Donavan studied Laney then, leaning into his detective mode over that of friend. The eyes hiding behind the rim of her glass revealed a woman not easily fooled. Perhaps more perceptive than he would have given her credit for. Truth was, he really didn't know Laney as well as he should. Things are different when you hang out as a foursome. You learn about some people only as an extension of the group, without individuality. He had never thought of her as being any more than Charlie's wife until now.

"You're doing well. No one would know you just kicked your date out."

"That's me—theatrical master. Or 'drama queen' as Charlie used to say." But his diversion didn't stop the next question from coming, her eyes fixed tightly on him. "So you and Kelly are divorced?"

He shrugged, and as much as he wanted to, he didn't look away.

"Why didn't you tell me?"

He opened his mouth, but the words took a second to form. "It…never came up?"

She cocked her head and eye-balled him harder. "You knew I thought you were still together. You could have mentioned it."

"I wasn't sure what you knew; it's…difficult to talk about."

"Better I hear it from Peyton or—"

She stopped mid-reply, mouth agape, eyes seeking an unknown source. "Wait... what song is this?" Music piped through speakers in the corners of the room. "Is this Cher?"

He froze. "Maaayyybeee."

"What are you listening to?"

Donavan looked toward his living room but knew it was too late to reach his stereo and change the tune. "Um, it's from Parker's iPod."

"You have Cher on an iPod?" She stifled laughter with a hand over her mouth, her head dipping down into her shoulders.

He grinned despite himself at her sudden distraction. *Thank you, wine.*

"It's Parker's favorite. He likes all the oldies. I never deleted it," Donavan said, defending himself.

"Liar!"

"Okay, I let Parker load my player and—"

"Still lying!"

"All right! So I haven't updated my music in ten years—"

"Or fifteen."

"I just loaded all my CDs onto my iPod years ago when I got it. It's so old; I just passed it on to Parker. He hooked it up to the speaker for tonight. Honest." He threw his hands up in innocence. "I had nothing to do with tonight's playlist."

"Does Michael know his partner listens to *Cher*?"

His humor overshadowed any embarrassment she was pressing for. Laney's real laughter, pure and infectious, felt welcome in his house. "He's still not letting me live down the pink cupcakes my mom baked for tonight. Please don't tell him. He'll make me replace my gun with a rolling pin."

Her laughter gave him a chance to fill her glass again. "Your music collection seriously needs an overhaul," she scolded.

"Louie! Kari! Great to see you again." Donavan waved at the people moving toward the door.

"Thanks for inviting us. Take care."

Donavan was glad Laney couldn't see the look of pity Kari shot her way. Still, somehow, Laney instinctively knew.

"At least they'll have something to talk about on the drive home," she mumbled before another sip.

Parker rushed in to show off his half-eaten loot followed by the girls and their stash. Ella was a sticky mess from ear to ear, so Donavan produced a washcloth for Laney to use. Once cleaned up and candy-free, Parker begged to show the girls his Transformer's room. Donavan had warned him that all play would be outside during the party to keep his room from getting trashed. But looking around, he found most of the other children being hauled out the door.

"Okay, bud. But just Urie and Ella."

They disappeared down the hall with a whoop, a squeal, and a flounce of pink tulle bringing up the rear.

Donavan said goodbye to two more departing families, walking them to the door this time. When he returned to the counter, Laney alone occupied the kitchen, intently twirling her wineglass. Her sarong gaped to reveal more of her shapely leg than she probably knew. He decided not to draw attention to it as he sat on a stool and reached across her to retrieve his drink.

"I never should have invited him," she said, surprising him with her willingness to talk about it. "What was I thinking?"

Donavan sipped and glanced up at the painting above the stove where the vaulted ceiling jutted inward. The painting's large canvas perfectly filled the gap between the cabinets. He slumped down onto the bar closer to Laney and dropped his voice. "See that painting?"

His closeness captured her attention like he'd hoped, and she turned to the painting. "Yes."

"I've sat here every morning for years eating my breakfast, looking at that painting. What do you think of it?"

"It's... nice."

"Okay. Look some more."

Her head leaned to one side while he studied her face. Her cheeks glowed with the warmth of the wine and the house. Small sprigs of hair had escaped their trap as they dried and now coiled along her face and neck. Her shoulders lay exposed in her makeshift dress, golden and smooth. "It's a perfect balance of reds and oranges and yellows," she said. "I mean, all the colors are perfect for this room. It's like it was made for this space."

She didn't have to say that Kelly had exquisite taste and had impeccably decorated the house. Most likely the painting *was* made for the space. He had no idea.

"But just random curves, right?" He examined the black outlines that surrounded the color trails, remembering the morning it had become so much more. "Do you see the rooster?"

"The rooster?"

He put his arm around her and drew her beside him so their eyes aligned to the same spot. "There. Behind the big red curve. A rooster."

The hidden outline of a proud chicken became clear to her, and she nodded, "Well, I'll be."

He moved back but only a little. "Years and years and I never saw it. Then one day she's gone. And I'm sitting here alone, and I see it. I see a stupid rooster. And it's been in front of me all this time." He could hear her soft breath with her face so close, hunched together over their wine, shielding out all else. A flicker of understanding glowed through from beneath her pain, and for once, neither of them turned away from it.

"Why did she leave?"

The moment became too raw to avoid answering. "She's ill, Laney. No, not just 'ill.' That sounds like she has a cold, and if she just blows her nose she'll be all right. She's very... mentally unstable. She left because she had to."

"That's... awful. I'm sorry." It surprised him how much her genuine concern meant to him. "It's only been a little while, Donavan. It takes time. Soon it won't hurt so bad."

He tried to smile. "Time heals all wounds, right? *Time*... that just seems so... indefinite. Can you give me a time frame? Because every day feels the same."

She took time with her answer. "A year. After one year, take stock and see what's changed in you, around you. Every day until then, just put one foot in front of the other, and do the best you can for Parker."

"Is that how long it took you?"

"Umm, roughly. Totally different situation for me." She took a sip, and he stayed quiet. She smiled cynically as she swallowed. "Charlie doesn't have crazy to blame for his actions... oh, sorry, I shouldn't have said—"

"Not offended. I'm sorry, too."

"No, it's okay. My divorce is much older than yours, so I'd better be able to talk about it if I'm going to preach time-healing to you."

"All better?"

"Not by a long shot, but I don't cry myself to sleep every night, so I've made massive progress."

His heart pained for her, and it must have slipped into his expression because she shook her head. "No, really. I don't... miss him. It's like your rooster. I ate breakfast across from him every day for nine years, and I had no idea who he was, that he was capable of lying and cheating." She winced and scrunched up her nose. "Forgot—he's your friend—"

"The Charlie I knew wouldn't cheat on his wife. The Charlie that would is not my friend."

"I never want anyone to take sides."

"I stopped seeing him a year ago, Laney. That wasn't me taking sides. One year ago." He sighed despite himself. "And a year is all it takes to get over this? That's it?"

She smiled a little. "There's no secret formula, Donavan. People process pain differently. You're a tough guy." She lifted her shoulders in a hopeful gesture. "One year." Her eyes held a promise of healing, so encouraging and friendly, he wanted to drink in every syllable of her. She patted his hand, finished her glass, and stood up. "I'm going to check on the girls."

Chapter 8

More guests left, and if he were honest, Donavan had intentionally hurried them out the door. Back at the kitchen bar top, he refilled Laney's glass in selfish hopes she'd stay a little longer. The conversations he consistently avoided with others, even Michael and Nellie, seemed to fall out of him in a natural flow with Laney. There was still tension in her shoulders as she reappeared from her second trip now down the hallway to check the kids, but she smiled despite her stress and motioned him to follow her. "Come see."

In Parker's room, Ella lay sleeping in a cocoon of pink princess frill on the bottom bunk. Beside her, on a huge bean bag chair surrounded by action figures, lay Urie and Parker, viewing the movie playing on the dresser TV with half-closed eyes.

"Pllleeease let me finish the movie, Mommy!" Urie begged and then bit her lip in a surprised smile when her mother nodded yes.

Back in the kitchen, Laney eyed her glass that held the last remnants of the wine bottle.

"I have some bad news," Donavan spoke before she could. "First of all, the bottle is empty. Secondly, Michael already left. But don't worry, I can take you and the girls home in a bit."

"Oh." Uncertainty again clouded her composure. "I'd hate for you to bother. Please just let me Uber."

"You don't really want to, do you?"

"Well, no." She hesitated before voicing her concern. "If Rodney is outside with his family when I get there, I'd rather not have to walk past him alone. I'm sure it would be fine, just... awkward."

"No, I get that. I'll definitely drive you home as soon as those folks make it out of here." He nodded at the last two families graciously cleaning up the backyard for him, lost in happy conversation while they did. Tonight had turned out to be more than just an attempt to turn post-Kelly life into normalcy. Everyone had had a good time. To his amazement, that included himself. "Don't worry about it."

He now just had to make sure Laney felt the same.

"Thanks," she said. "And I'm sorry."

He directed her back to her stool. "Sit."

"I haven't been the best company tonight." Her face registered remorse. "You've been babysitting me forever and hardly got to see your friends at all."

"Not true. I talked to them plenty while Rodney was here. Great guy, by the way. Where d'you meet?"

"Very funny. Neighbors. And don't do that."

"What?"

"Keep trying to focus the topic on me." She patted the stool next to her. "You sit."

"I have to say I'm extremely curious about how he came to be your first choice for a date."

"Stop. It's not funny." But he could tell she was laughing along with him. "I won't say another word about Rotten Rodney until you tell me everything about Kelly."

"Everything takes a really long time. And we've got maybe twenty minutes. Thirty, max." He leaned over the bar to the sink and got a glass of water to sip on. "But I'll bet the Rodney story takes all of five."

"Uh-uh. Spill it."

He wasn't sure why he hesitated so much. Everyone knew some version of his and Kelly's split, everyone but Laney, and if he didn't tell her, she would hear a distorted account from somewhere. Shared pain made Laney easier to talk to, but he tried to avoid realism these days. Escapism equaled survival.

"She checked herself into Barro's Mental Health Institute in January."

Laney's eyes registerd shock. "Donavan. I had no idea. What happened?"

He almost shrugged, but even that gesture got weighed down by the darkness of the truth. "Well, you want the five-minute version or the twenty?" She didn't seem to find any humor in his remark, so he sighed and stumbled to the beginning while peering down through the clear liquid in front of him.

"Kelly had always had 'episodes,' let's call them. When we met, she told me about them, but it was just some vague talk about depression and anxiety, stuff she'd already seen doctors about. Sometimes when she was sick or exhausted and stressed, she would not be herself, but nothing 'concerning.'

"When her mom died over a year ago—that was the first time it was bad. Just... bad. She wasn't herself, couldn't get a grip, ended up going to the doctor and getting all kinds of medications and going to counseling. I thought it was just grief, and it would take time. I didn't pay attention to which doctors she was going to or her medications. Looking back, maybe if I had asked more questions I would have understood better." He shook his head subconsciously at the thought. "After about three weeks, she acted almost like herself again. But…"

He took a drink then because he didn't know how to finish the sentence. Everything he said was true. Conveying the look in Kelly's eyes, the nervous way she withdrew from him, the *thing* she would never say…communicating that part of the story wasn't so easy. He didn't know *what* made her unravel. All he knew was that Kelly at some point had become un-Kelly.

"But what?"

His throat suddenly felt dry, but he doubted he could swallow another sip of water. "I don't know. Episodes, random crazy things. Just saying things that didn't make sense, mostly." His t-shirt clung to him in sweaty patches, and he scowled. Why had he told Laney any of this? It brought on the vivid memory of Kelly talking to herself, mumbling about "the melting man"…it popped into his head uninvited, unwanted. He had caught her uttering that phrase again just as she turned to notice him listening. In that one moment, his constrained panic had unleashed.

"Donavan?" Kelly's soft voice had pled with him. She was asking him to believe in her, to trust her, to let her tell whatever crazy scene her mind had concocted.

And he couldn't. He couldn't face what she had to say, knowing it would confirm every doubt he ever had about her sanity. He needed to remain in the dark more than he wanted to help her come to grips with the man in her imagination, repeated nightmares and visions of the "melting man."

Laney stared at him expectantly, waiting for him to finish. "And then the holidays came," he rushed on, deciding to skip ahead of some dark moments, "and everything went haywire. I hate to use the word crazy, but... Kelly went *crazy*. When I left the house, she was planting flowers in the backyard and then when I got home, she had cooked them all for dinner. Not just cooked them. Took them out of the oven and served them to us as if it were pot roast. Parker and I sat and watched her try to eat a plate of baked dirt and peonies. And she didn't snap out of it. She talked to herself about imaginary things, watched blank TV screens, put Jell-O in her hair to go to the store, slept by the mailbox so she could find where the mail would go. Just..." He searched for different words but came up empty. "Insanity. The lucid moments came farther and fewer between. Still, the doctors ruled out schizophrenia and a host of other stuff. "

Donavan kept his eyes on his glass. Had he played a part in it all? If he had just believed her. But by then it had been too late. She had died inside. Her eyes never again held the plea for acceptance, and he wished he could rewind time.

"She changed into someone...completely emotionless. Ice. There was no love for Parker or me. She knew who we were, could answer every question we asked but seemed entirely detached, and *that*...That was the worst. Crazy is one thing. But not feeling anything for her family—"

"But it wasn't her," Laney reassured him. She put her hand over his. "She wasn't herself."

"I know. That's what I tell myself. I started working with the doctors on a treatment plan when she took matters into her own hands. It's like she heard us plotting around her and snapped out of it just to stop us. On one of her lucid days, she packed her bags and checked herself into Barro's. It's a voluntary process, and during the psych evaluation, they determined they could admit her." He swallowed and sucked in his cheeks, remembering her note outlining her intentions that he had found too late. "When I got to Barro's and could see her, her first words to me were, 'I want a divorce,' as if we were discussing our next meal. Just like that. No emotion, no tears, no feeling."

"But that's—"

"I know. Everyone knows. It's not her. It's her mind. The only problem is that it doesn't matter. Every lucid, sane moment she's had since, every time I've talked to the staff or her, it's been the same. She never wavers. She filed for divorce and has told everyone she never wants to see me or Parker again."

He slugged down his water to put an end to the stream of words he had never intended to spill.

"Do you think she's just trying to protect you?"

"If she'd ever been that strong, that clever, that self-reliant, I'd say that's exactly why. But she's not. She has always... needed me. Wanted me. We were a team." *And I let her down.* "She's changed. And she doesn't want me in her life."

"That can't be true," Laney breathed, but Donavan kept silent. "Do you still see her?"

"Not since January. I brought Parker a couple of times and begged her not to close him out and...well, it didn't work. She made it clear it was over."

"Did the doctors agree that was best?"

"It didn't matter what the doctor said." His eyes met hers. "Laney, there was nothing left. I looked into her eyes so many times, hoping. I think I read people well—comes with the job—and I'm telling you, crazy or not, nowhere in her eyes, anywhere, was any indication she missed me, loved me, or wanted me. She had written us off, and I couldn't subject Parker to that anymore."

Laney's face registered sympathy, and she nodded. "I know what it's like to make those decisions. Not easy."

Voices interrupted and gave them both a second to compose themselves before the couples came in from the backyard. Laney gave bashful goodbyes before slipping back through the hall to check kids once more. Donavan let Gary and Eve take their time gathering their things along with Lance and Megan, trying to get his head back out of the funk he had put it in. He didn't regret sharing his hurt with Laney, but he hated the heaviness that came with the truth. He forced a smile now, his trademark casualness hard to sell as he said goodnight.

When Laney returned, the house was empty of guests.

"They're all asleep," Laney said sheepishly.

Donavan smiled. "They had a busy day." He paused, looking at Laney's unfinished drink. "If we have to wake them up anyway, does it matter when? Want to sit and finish that?"

Her *yes* came from a silent return to her barstool. Her bare shoulders relaxed as she picked up her glass. The lingering stress of the night had disappeared with the last of the guests. He had done it, despite his emotional dump on her. He had given her a night off, a night away from *her* weight.

She took a sip and froze. "Blondie? Is this *Funky Town*?"

Donavan groaned. "I swear to you, I just loaded up my CDs."

"You seriously need to trash the evidence."

"Don't do that," he mimicked. "Don't avoid the topic being about you."

She tried not to smile as he used her own words against her.

"Your turn. Rodney?" he asked.

"You called it a five-minute story. It's less than that. He's my neighbor. He is nice—or was nice—to the girls and me. Hmm, unemployed. Living with his sister and family. He always liked to hang out with us." She seemed to be thinking back then and silently took a drink. "Or maybe not. I don't know. I should have thought about it more. I just didn't want to come alone tonight, you know? It's hard when everyone else has someone and I'm alone."

"Michael came alone."

She squinted at him. "You know what I mean. I'm a single mom. There was no one else here tonight like that. I thought if I came with someone I'd... *blend.*" She glanced down at her borrowed clothing. "Boy, did I miss the mark on that one."

He couldn't help laughing with her. The trill of it stirred up the soft glow in her cheeks. His energy returned; the fatigue that had plagued him again all week— making him dread this party—left him. As late as it was, he didn't feel the least bit tired. A sudden notion struck him, and he spoke without thinking.

"Hey, the kids are crashed anyway, why not stay? You can crash in the spare room—it's yours. That way we can have another drink and let them sleep."

She cocked her head to the side as if contemplating. "If you're sure that it's okay," she said slowly, as if it weren't. Doubt crept up to her eyes at the same time he felt it himself.

"I'm fine with it, but if it makes you uncomfortable, I still don't mind driving you all home." He kept his tone casual, avoiding the implications of a "sleepover."

That seemed to ease her back into her seat. "No, it's a good idea. The kids will be thrilled... Dishwalla? Really?"

Donavan grabbed another bottle of wine to uncork. "I believe this is The Wallflowers, actually. And don't make me regret letting you stay."

"Get them out."

"What?"

"The CDs. Get them out. We're gonna have a CD trashing party."

"That's a thing?"

"Just get 'em."

They stood in front of three small storage containers, which Donovan had dragged into the dining room from their dusty home in the recesses of the master closet. Laney examined each with a painstaking meticulousness that was somehow adorable. "There are like two hundred CDs here."

"So explain the piles again?"

"These are classic keepers. Don't toss them. Marvin Gaye, Aretha, Elvis—"

"What if I—"

"Shh, shh! *Keep.* Now, these are the ones you want to throw into a deep hole and never, ever admit you owned. Put the one-hit-wonders in here, too. These you can keep if you want. Bon Jovi, Whitney Houston, Counting Crows—all solid so let's keep."

"I don't get why they're not 'bad' when all my other '90's music is in the trash pile."

"Because there is a difference between retro and retro classic. Don't worry; I'll teach you."

Darkness had engulfed the house except for the lamps glowing onto the piles of CDs. Amid the sorting and the wine, Laney sat with legs splayed to the right as if she had forgotten her makeshift clothing. Donavan watched her work in amusement, her legs tanned and smooth against the texture of the carpet, her face contorting every time another awful song played from Parker's iPod. She refused to turn it off solely to heighten her entertainment.

Donavan leaned against the empty armchair, probably the first time he'd touched it since Kelly left. The music and company had worked its magic for him, erasing memories and creating new ones.

"I can't believe it's after midnight," Laney said, finally noticing the clock. She yawned and stood. "We're so going to pay for this in the morning."

She wound her way between the stacks of CDs, nearly sending the keep pile scattering when she stumbled. Donavan caught her arm. "Steady."

"If I'd fallen into the trash pile, at least I would have had some cushion." She clung to his arm while he righted her. His hold lingered as she stepped over a pile, and for a moment they stood close, wreathed by decades of music silently awaiting their fate. "This is Extreme, isn't it?"

Donavan tucked his free arm around her waist. "I don't know. Seems rather natural to me—"

"The group," she laughed but didn't pull away. "This song playing. Isn't this Extreme? It is! This is my *favorite."*

"Oh. Right. Like I haven't heard that a hundred times tonight."

She sang over his teasing. *"...More than words...is all I need from you...."*

He pulled her closer, stepping backward as he guided her through the towers of CDs, letting his body sway just enough to encourage her. He hadn't lied when he said it felt natural, his hands on her waist, cheek on her temple. The warmth and smell of her were intoxicating.

"This might just be your real favorite," he softly laughed. "You know every word."

Laney smiled and opened her eyes, suddenly registering his nearness. Her hands, resting comfortably on his shoulders, tensed ever so slightly. "Donavan... this seems... a little dangerous."

"No, it's Extreme, remember?" She smiled at his joke but pulled back a fraction. "Laney, it's okay," he said. "I'm a cop, remember? Brave. Strong. No danger."

She hesitated for a moment, searching for something in his eyes, then folded into his arms again. "That's what they all say...."

They finished their dance around the room with no more need for words. And when the song led into the next and the next, it was quite some time before either of them noticed.

Chapter 9

3:32

Donavan thrashed the covers around him in retaliation to the clock's display. Four minutes since the last time he had looked. The room felt warm as if the shadows creeping in the widows tangibly filled up the room. He kicked at the blankets until a foot peeked out from underneath, letting in cooler air. His restless hands hooked behind his head, and a sigh escaped his troubled chest.

Insomnia, his nemesis, had returned. He focused on the ceiling, trying to shut his senses down, but it was no use. She slept in the next room, and he was far from tired.

Laney. Charlie's Laney. Correction: used-to-be-Charlie's Laney. Tonight she had become real. A person all her own. First, just someone he felt sorry for, someone he decided to build up and reassure. But now... now she was all Laney.

He hadn't meant to feel anything. He still had Kelly in his blood, he knew that, and he seriously doubted the year Laney gave him would be enough to get her out. But his wife was gone. Gone, gone. He shivered at every remembrance of her cold, loveless eyes. For a moment he tried to picture Kelly smiling, happy, playing with Parker or making a joke. But nothing came. Her ice had frosted even those memories.

She doesn't know, does she? Valentine's words haunted him. What in the world could he mean? What could that low-life vandal possibly know about his mentally-ill wife?

He sat up and scanned the darkness, letting the memories of tonight take over again. The dance had been spontaneous and... exhilarating. He held up his arms before him to remember how willingly they had held her. Traitors. It was crazy to allow her to stay. He groaned and covered his face with his hands. *I'm the strong one? Ha!*

There was something electric about her presence in the house that kept his heart beating at a higher tempo, his blood quickening. Slowly, he reached out a hand toward the wall between them just to see....

Instantly, he felt heated and alive, ready to sprint through the streets into the night and run miles and miles.

He dropped his hand, inhaled sharply, and held the breath a long time.

A soft light from his neighbor's back porch lent a glow to his backyard that pulled him out of bed, away from the dangerous shared wall. He stood next to the bay window where an alcove cupped the wall of his bedroom. The half-open blinds allowed his eyes to travel the length of the grass. Hours ago, it had held dozens of friends but now lay empty and surrounded by shadow. Something seemed out of place, as if....

There.

It had been quick. Just a flash out of the corner of his eye. The constant shadow that always eluded, that played tricks on his senses. It had been there, right there under the mesquite tree by the pool fence, in the corner... hadn't it?

Donavan stood still, his brow furrowed, and waited.

Nothing.

He tried squinting. Perhaps... just a trick of the light?

It's part of this insomnia, he thought, running a hand up and down his shirtless chest. A glint of something shiny distracted him: the rock Emilio had given him in the rock yard. He had dumped it onto his dresser when he'd returned home that day of the interview. He picked it up, rubbing his thumb over the green lines that ran through it. If he turned it just right, they seemed almost luminescent. Fascinating. Not enough to stay up for.

Flopping back into bed, Donavan's heart picked up its irregular rhythm as if it could sense the woman in the next room. He tossed the pillow over his head but could still hear his heartbeat as he chanted with it, *Be strong, be strong, be strong.*

§ § § § §

Laney skipped up the steps to her apartment, tired but happier than she'd ever been when handing the girls off to Charlie. The entire week had been one huge upswing since Donavan's party until the very moment she had given the girls back to their father.

She picked up her mail on the way in, neglected since last Thursday. Shuffling through the pile with a hum, her brain refused to concentrate on any of the envelopes. Images kept replaying themselves, mainly the one of Charlie with pure jealousy across his face as the girls recounted their party at Parker's house last weekend. They thankfully left out the sleepover part; it wouldn't be long, though, before they spilled that, too.

A giggle erupted as she remembered how he'd tried to fake an air of nonchalance. Clearly, he still wanted Donavan's friendship; they had been so close for years. It probably never occurred to him that his wife might make a better companion in the end.

Laney fumbled with her keys and dropped some mail as she opened her door. She re-collected the stash and threw it onto the island. Her sandals were off almost the same instant, and she flopped onto the couch with a satisfied sigh.

It had been one of the worst and best weeks since her divorce, and even though she never wished for an evening without her girls, she relished her silence now. She replayed the bad parts quickly—long rehearsals, paying a sitter for the performances, avoiding Rodney— and the good parts over and over—the successful play, happy moments with the kids, and mostly her one dance with Donavan, short and sweet, leaving her breathless and tingly. If he hadn't been such a gentleman....

Laney woke some time later to a soft click. She opened her eyes slowly, letting the foggy after-effects of her unexpected nap melt away. The day and time came back to her in pieces; an instant smile returned.

Gradually, the sound of the click registered, and she sat up and froze at the sight of her unlatched door open an inch in its frame. She scrambled to calm her overactive fears. Had she shut it when she came in? She had dropped the mail, so maybe it had distracted her? For the life of her, she couldn't remember closing it, but she'd never neglected to lock it in the past. Ever.

Forcing control over her alarm, Laney crept to the door. With a shaking hand, she pushed it quickly shut and swiftly turned the bolt. That's when it occurred to her that someone could have already come in while she slept.

Panic mounted to a crescendo as she looked down the short, dark hall to the bedrooms. Her hand covered her mouth to keep a whimper from escaping.

Don't be such a baby! You just left the door unlatched. That's all.

"Okay," her slightly braver inner self said out loud to her trembling body. "I can do this."

She raided the kitchen drawer first for the largest knife she could find. With a white-knuckle grip, she slid her back along the wall until she reached the bathroom across from the girls' room. Sweating buckets, she darted her head in and out quickly. Empty. She swooped in, knife high, checked behind the door then shower curtain with fast movements. Nothing.

The apartment held a dense silence that echoed Laney's breathing. She repeated her shaky investigation into the girls' room and then her own to find them void of intruders. Back in the living room, she scrutinized every corner, cabinet, and curtain to find nothing. Relief collapsed the tension in her shoulders, but her hands still shook as she put away the knife.

She attempted to return to normal by preparing a frozen dinner and camping in front of the fireplace, lit this time, and sinking down in her chair to grade papers. Her eyes darted now and then to the corners of the room where nothing stirred. She willed herself to act reasonable and concentrate.

Soon, the softer memories returned, and she began to doodle on her notebook behind the papers. Wayne's portfolio folder report peeked out at her from the stack of the others she required her seniors to keep. Wayne Radison. She picked it up and turned it over to examine his drawings and acronyms.

Along with other familiar doodles she'd seen, the large deeply scratched letters MEAN SPUR stood out. What the heck? Odd kid. So Jordan thought this could be an anagram. Her eyes narrowed and on a scrap of paper she began to rearrange.

MUNAPERS
PUN RAMES
RUN SPAME
SAPEMUNR
SUPERMAN!

She shouted out in victory just as the click came again. This time a very distinct sound, one of someone turning a doorknob. *Her* doorknob.

In a second, students' papers launched off her lap into the air like confetti, and Laney stood in the kitchen holding the knife with both hands over her head. Her breath came so quickly, she felt sure she'd hyperventilate.

Drama queen.

"Okay, think, Laney. No one can get in. It's bolted." She did Lamaze-stype breathing to control herself, but the knife stayed poised overhead.

"Who is it?" she called loudly, but her voice quaked. No one would be scared of that. "Who is it?" she tried again, more confident and in control, despite the weapon still frozen over her head in a death grip.

Nothing.

"Leave me alone, or I'm calling the police!"

Silence.

My imagination? Someone else's door opening?

She eyed her phone. Would she really call the police over a noise? What did she really hear? She had no one else to call except Charlie, and she groaned. She would rather die a thousand deaths than have him come to her rescue. Especially since she had thus far avoided his presence in her apartment.

Donavan? Almost equally embarrassing but even more impractical. He had Parker and couldn't jump on the freeway to get to her house like Charlie could.

The dilemma took so much of Laney's focus that a minute passed before she realized she'd stopped panting. She lowered the knife, gripped the island, and watched and listened.

Sounds from the stairs and landing muffled their way in, low and nondescript. Was that a voice?

Inching her way to the door, heart in throat, Laney peeked through the peephole. A figure stood outside Angela's door. The night grew dark enough that the landing lights revealed almost nothing. But Laney felt pretty sure it was Angela. The height and build looked right....

Angela had told her yesterday that Rodney left on a whim to ride down to Tucson with a "friend" he'd just met and stay who-knows-where for how long, another example of irratic behavior from a guy she had stupidly tried to pass off as date material. The woman across the hall put a key in her lock and disappeared inside. She sighed. Definitely Angela. Was that what she had heard? Her hand was so sweaty it slipped as she turned first the bolt and then the handle to ensure they held fast.

It was just your imagination. Drama. Queen.

Laney picked up her students' fallen papers and returned to her chair, but did little more than bite at her bottom lip and stare at the door. Eventually, she went back to the kitchen for the knife. It sat in front of her on the coffee table until she fell asleep in the chair and didn't wake until the sun streamed through her living room window the next morning.

§ § § § §

Monday had not brought the normal hum of routine and security for Donavan. The sun fought against the calendar as well, providing a heated backdrop to the miserable angst of the day. The gravel at the edge of the lot crunched under his feet as he hurried to put some distance between the station and his nerves. If he didn't beat it out of here soon, he'd take out his temper on someone nearby, and he was afraid that person might be Micheal. Michael, the only one left who could or would defend him.

Donavan ripped open his car door and put the vehicle in gear before waiting for the air conditioner to produce relief. He had played the game for a week, taking "time off," to Parker's delight, and giving Laney space in her busy theatre schedule, compartmentalizing his upcoming fate until the cowardly late afternoon Monday meeting had come. The news he had feared.

Suspended.

Donavan sped his car out the parking lot and cranked his radio at the first light. No matter how many times he told himself no one would ever believe *brutality* of him, there it was, on that damning videotape, the one that told a story from only one vantage point, so in-erasably "accurate" to the world. No amount of explanation could convince his captain otherwise.

His car stopped at the next light, relieved of the pressure to accelerate. Donavan trapped his phone into its dash holder to call his mother. He practiced what he'd say when he noticed a missed call. Laney.

She'd be at work today; this would be an odd time to call unless something was wrong. The light changed while the message played.

"Oh, hi, umm... I didn't hear the beep, so...." Donavan almost smiled despite himself. "But in case it did, and this is a message.... Oh, geez, just wanted to call because... well, I heard noises last night and, well... okay, long story short, I'm thinking about getting a weapon and don't even know where to begin. Charlie always—well, never mind. I just thought if you have a minute... I'm leaving work in about an hour, so could you call me? If you can?"

At the next red light, Donavan rang her back, but the call went straight to voicemail. He left a quick message and hung up.

A sigh escaped, and his earlier irritation became concern. Not what he bargained for. He had spent way too much time stressing over Kelly and had intended to break free from that. Now, whether or not Laney wanted it, he would worry about her. Good grief. Didn't she have anyone else to call?

Instantly, he felt ashamed. Of course she didn't. She was doing her best as a single mom, and here he was, annoyed that she had reached out to him, a friend and a cop, for help with home security. He was a jerk.

He turned the wheel right, into a dirt parking lot, and slammed the car to a halt. A cloud of dust billowed around his vehicle and slowly settled onto the hood.

A slow-building prickle, like the rising of goosebumps, spread over his body despite the heat. Donavan slowly emerged from his car and squinted through the falling dust cloud to the weathered shack with the broken, dirty sign that simply said *Jake's.*

How in the world had he ended up here?

For a full minute, he stood confused and slightly alarmed. When things got stressful, he sometimes went through the motions and found he did things without recollection. But never had he driven some place he hadn't intended to go.

He rubbed his chin and forced back the chilling sensation of subconscious manipulation. His laid-back nature pressed to the forefront, convincing him he could use a beer anyway. He might even be able to ask some questions about Vincent if that guy at the bar was hanging around. If nothing else, he'd avoid his life for a moment.

Curiosity won over trepidation. He pocketed his phone and moved toward the door.

Jake's remained, for the most part, exactly as Donavan had left it. The crowd varied, more men and a few women, there to watch Monday night football by the looks of the T-shirts they sported. Another TV emitted NFL pregame hype from the corner of the room in sync with the one behind the bar. The day still held its light, and the beams streaming through the dingy windows revealed its same dust trail as if the air hadn't moved in days.

It took him two steps into the door frame before his senses staggered with the same unidentifiable sensation he had first encountered. He rocked back on his heels the moment both feet cleared the doorway, and he could see and hear everything at once: the fan, the pool balls, and there—

Tick. Tick. Tick.

He turned toward the gigantic five-foot clock, rusty and ugly, marring the wall above the bottles. Ten minutes past six, same as before, stuck on a time that didn't yet exist.

Rufus tended bar, as plain and detached as before. Donavan spotted the solid black man, his clock-watching acquaintance from last time, sitting on the same stool. Two men, leaning on their elbows, flanked his right, hanging around the curve at the bar's end.

The giant man clamped a cigar butt between his teeth, his eyes glued on the screen when Donavan approached and ordered his drink from Rufus.

"Donavan, isn't it?" the giant spoke without looking at him.

"Right. Good memory. I'm sorry, I forget…"

A crooked smile pushed up the cigar. "No, you didn't."

Donavan slowly gave a smile of his own. "Harley. Right. Who's your team?"

"Football was never my thing. Now rugby—that's a whole 'nother ball of wax."

Donavan tried to picture him as a rugby player—couldn't see it. The men next to Harley seem to have no interest in football either. Their eyes pinned Donavan to his spot.

"Donavan," he introduced himself to the unfamiliar faces, sticking out his hand. All three men took in Donavan's hand with keen interest. The first man, taller and leaner than his giant friend, grasped it and met Donavan's gaze expectantly. He didn't exactly smile as he pumped the palm.

"Tag." The shake lasted a second too long, and Donavan felt himself fighting the same vibe as last time. He shouldn't be here. This place was uncanny. He had to go.

The man next to Tag equaled him in muscular build but was younger, shorter and fair. Tag's eyes reflected a dark, heated look, while this guy was all sunshine and light, a poster boy for a surfing Cal-i-forn-i-a with his boyish "hey, dude" grin.

"Brian," the blond said. He gave Donavan a quick shake and release to make up for Tag's awkward hold. Donavan recognized Brian as the pool player peering out from the backroom the last visit.

"Your team?" Brian asked, jerking a chin toward the TV.

"Sure," Donavan said noncommittally. "I was hoping for the news instead of the pre-game jabber, though."

"Nothing good on the news, anyway," Harley said. "Same 'ol depressing stuff, ain't that right, Rufus?" The expressionless blob behind the bar only eyed him, then passed the new arrival a drink.

"Just wondering if they had any more updates on the Valentine case. Last time I was here they reported catching the scumbag."

Tag and Brian seemed disinterested now and stared at the surrounding people. Harley sighed as if he dreaded the topic. "Yeah, a real *scumbag*. Sometimes people don't know what they are. It makes them distrustful of themselves. If you can't trust yourself, you sure can't trust anyone else."

It was Donavan's turn to keep his eyes on the screen and slowly sip at his beer. He tried to unravel Harley's rhetoric and turn it into his advantage.

"I don't think this guy can run from the depths of his scum."

"He'll be out in no time. Wait and see. But not before he takes some good folk down."

Donavan bristled. "What makes you say that?"

Harley seemed to think as he twisted the cigar around. "Sometimes you know someone without ever meeting them. You know what they are. Like you. I know you."

Tag seemed mildly curious at this line of conversation and tuned in. Brian ogled a girl in a mini-skirt until she turned to reveal a missing front tooth. His beer suddenly gained his undivided attention.

"You that guy," Harley said.

Donavan wished he had sat closer to the door. But the side of him that screamed *run* waned in this battle. The stool rooted him, and he had to ask, "What guy?"

"That guy who knows too much. He tries to act like he don't. But he knows." Harley's dark eyes twinkled. "At least, that who you seem to me. Valentine—he's that guy who thinks he smart. He's not so smart; he just greasy. Bad thing is he's gonna take good people down in his slime."

Donavan locked eyes with Harley, and for a minute he was sure the man knew everything. "You've met this guy, haven't you?"

"Don't need to. Told ya, I know the type."

"And what does his type want, exactly?" Perhaps this line of inquiry would be the backdoor to get Donavan what he wanted to know.

"Hard to say, but it's not construction materials. He's not crazy—that means he doesn't want to destroy things just to have fun."

"What's he after then?"

"He's looking for himself." Harley turned toward the TV again as if that ended the matter.

Tag coughed and shifted uncomfortably. Brian slammed down the rest of his beer and told them, "I'm up on the pool table. Anybody?"

Donavan wanted to try one time to get a decent answer from Harley, but the big man cut him off before the words formed. "Go on."

Donavan left his own drink unfinished and followed Brian and Tag in surrender. "Rack 'em."

Chapter 10

Laney climbed out of the car and stared into the bright sun as Donavan's ride pulled into the lot next to her at the Desert Ridge Shooting Range. It had been a week of phone tag, potential plans, and cancellations before she could pin Donavan down to coming out today. He agreed to combine his weekly target practice with a more detailed discussion of her protection concerns, bringing her both instant relief and nagging anticipation.

"Sorry," she felt the need to apologize when Donavan climbed out of the vehicle. "I'm sure you have better ideas on how to spend your weekend."

For some reason, being face to face after two weeks had past, left her nervous and sweaty about seeing her dance partner again. She tried to reassure herself that a busy schedule had kept them from interacting, nothing else.

"Not at all," he answered. "Doing okay?"

She wanted to ask him the same thing. His voice had sounded so strained on the phone. At first, she assumed she had called him at a bad time, that work-related whatever had him stressed out. But even now, the weight of his tone confused her. Where was the guy from the party? A sixth sense told her this wasn't the time to go into that, so she answered his question instead.

"Yeah, fine." Sunglasses concealed his eyes and the straight line of his lips gave nothing away. She hurried on with, "I'm just embarrassed that I freaked out, that I called you in the first place. I mean, it was probably nothing. I would just feel better...." Her voice trailed out, hoping he'd jump in with reassurances.

Michael got out of the driver's seat and joined them before an awkward silence clouded the moment. "Hey, Laney. Was thinking about running through the sprinklers after this. Wanna come?" His captivating smile helped produce one of her own.

"Ha, ha, very funny. You're lucky I don't have a weapon yet. And thanks for ditching me, by the way. I could have used a ride home that night."

He came over and lightly kissed her cheek. "Next time, you're my date."

"Promises, promises."

"Unless Rodney's available."

She gave him a deserved slug.

From where he stood, Donavan eyed the outdoor shooting range, detached from the joking. "You ready for this?"

She examined the range for herself and nodded more confidently than she felt. "Yep. Ready."

The weather behaved itself and without meaning to, Laney thoroughly enjoyed the outdoor activity and adult interaction of the afternoon. It reminded her yet again how her friendless, sheltered existence would need to change if she would survive being a single mom. But Donavan's cool distance also brought a new level of awareness that she actually cared what he thought. Was he enjoying the day too?

Donavan walked her through handling a weapon, but it was all just a refresher course for Laney. She listened patiently and fired the 9mm with moderate accuracy. Nothing worthy of headlines, but no shame either.

Both men nodded with acceptance after finishing their own rounds and gave her the lane one more time before calling it a day. She walked with them back to the lot, feeling accomplished, but Donavan's lack of conversation kept her elation at bay. Perhaps if they were alone…maybe then he'd open up to her about whatever nagged at him.

"Well, Laney," Michael said as he opened his car door, "with that aim I'd say you won't have to worry about being harassed by your dates anymore."

"Careful, Michael. That applies to wanna-be-dates, too."

"Ha, I'm too much man for you."

"Scared?"

"No, smart." He turned to Donavan. "Don't let her pull that helpless blonde routine on you. I got a feeling she could take a guy out, with or without a weapon. Good luck!" He disappeared inside the vehicle and waited for Donavan to say his goodbyes.

"Well? Still thinking you want a *gun*?" he asked her.

"Absolutely."

"You know tasers or mace are much more…" He stopped himself.

"Girly? Safe?"

"I was going to say 'female friendly'."

"Did it sound as stupid in your head as it did coming out of your mouth?"

A tug of a smile. "Also, less dangerous. But, if your mind's made up, here. Take this." He handed her the piece she had practiced with. "It's my personal weapon. You've shown you can handle it. Let's get you your own next week sometime, okay?"

"Yeah, sure. I have a lockbox already, so this will be...helpful. I mean, it'll keep me from freaking out again."

Donavan gave one quick nod and got into the passenger's seat. Donavan rolled down the window when Michael started the car.

"It's supposed to be nice tomorrow. My mom's having me and Parker over for a picnic dinner. You should come."

Laney hoped her sunglasses masked her arched eyebrows. His attitude today implied anything other than picnic-kind-of-mood. "Sounds good. I pick up the girls at three. We can come over right after that?"

"Good." Again, a curt nod. The tires backed out of the space and left nothing but a cloud of dust by the time she reached her car.

§ § § § §

The wind, wild and teasing, created a stir in the backyard that tugged at Nellie Peterson's attention. Laughing children and adult conversation did her a world of good, especially when she went more than a couple of days without human contact. True, she'd never been an extrovert *seeking* interaction, but old habits die hard, and a career in security had taught her to keep the ones you worried about close and engage with them once in a while.

Still, amid the camaraderie of her guests, her concentration waned as she stood in the corner of the yard surveying the meticulously kept mesquites and date palms, spreading lantana shrubs, and aggressively pink bougainvilleas, proud products of her gardening skills. The breeze rustled up stray, fallen blossoms and chased them around the outskirts of the yard; she decided it must be this uncommon movement of nature that had her distracted. Stray movement in the corner of her eye always made her wary, on guard, a remnant from her years in the Bureau.

Nellie redirected her attention to the grill and began unloading its odd array of goods—burgers, fish, and hot dogs.

"Here we go!" she called with genuine cheerfulness. She carried a laden serving platter over to the back porch table where her Sunday guests awaited their meaty complement to the bowls of chips and salads.

Laney eyed the platter and her focus landed on the large burgers, slimy with melted cheese. Nellie smiled with satisfaction.

I'm glad she came. It hadn't gone unnoticed that Donavan had visited with Laney at Parker's party, but it had taken a while for Nellie to remember that Laney was now single.

Must be slipping. Dang old age anyway.

Nellie tired of watching Donavan live out his pathetic attempts at a new life, one without Kelly, and it was time for her to step in. Parker practically lived at her house, putting her knee deep in this drama fest already. Might as well nudge Donavan in the right direction. If she didn't, that nauseating sack of blonde tresses, Kimberly, would move in to stir up trouble where trouble had just subsided, and a mother could only allow so much. She loved her only child to pieces, but like any man, no matter how cleverly observant she had raised him to be, he proved clueless at unveiling a woman's ulterior motives. He now looked at the fish and Laney with the same degree of interest, completely oblivious to his mother's match-making attempts—case in point.

The picnic had been all her idea; it was easy to make the excuse she would love to see Laney again. Nellie may not have been extremely close to the Whytes, but she had been friendly with them when Donavan and Kelly held their backyard parties. And she loved children. Well, the idea of them. No one need know that while their crazy, inane antics openly amused her, she found their rationale oddly cryptic. As an agent who had prided herself on her mastery of profiling, kids' random actions left her with a strange mixture of uneasiness and curiosity.

Parker, Urie, and Ella managed to stay in their seats to devour hot dogs, more from the promise of continued play time than actual hunger. Odd name, Urie. Someday she would get the nerve to ask Laney about it. Not today though, her hesitation having nothing to do with shyness. There was something in the way Donavan picked at his fish, only nodded and smiled at their conversations, at the way he hid his distraction with glances toward the kids now off playing chase-the-bug, that told her something brewed beneath. His normal slouch and unreadable eyes gave no helpful hints.

Man, she had taught him well.

A casual question thrown his way: "How's things?"

As the wind pulled at the paper plates and napkins, it toyed with Donavan's quiet mask. At first, Nellie soaked in his non-answer contentedly until the silence began to build in awkward premonition of something important yet not said. He cleared his throat and, finally, reluctantly, spoke up. "Lately…things have been a little…kind of rocky at work."

Nellie tensed, but Laney only furrowed her brow like she was trying to decipher a puzzle. "Oh?" the guest asked, setting down her burger with obvious regret. "What's going on?"

An odd tension spread as if caught on the breeze.

"You'll be hearing things on the news soon. About me. And it's…" he seemed to grapple with the right word, "it's not…good."

Nellie squeezed the metal arms of her patio chair. Not physically, of course. It had taken years of practice to control all outward signs of reaction. It helped if she pictured the things she wanted to do inside her mind and acted them out there. She pictured her hand, now, gripping the hard metal till her knuckles turned white. The mind exercise kept her exterior unruffled, hands light and loose on the rails.

"There's nothing I can say—that I can tell you to make it sound any better," Donavan continued. "It will possibly—probably—ruin my character, my integrity, my job," a quick arch of his eyebrow as if he thought of another one to add to the list, "most likely my entire career."

Nellie bristled at the realization that her clever boy had waited for the company of an outsider, however welcome, to drop this weight, hoping the fall of it could be lessened by landing on more than one set of shoulders.

"These *things* that they're saying," Nellie began, her voice controlled and even, "are they true?"

Laney remained still, her expression unsettled.

Donavan avoided eye contact, but he'd let his casual façade slip enough that small worry lines creased his mouth. "No," he spoke evenly, but looked down as he did. "But it doesn't matter. No one will believe it. Not even you."

She wasn't foolish enough to think the "you" meant her only. He meant Laney too. Laney's helpless expression indicated that she knew it as well.

Nellie continued to speak for both women. "Why wouldn't I believe you?"

Silence. Maddening silence.

The wind picked up and snatched the napkins from their fragile grip on the table, subversively aiding the delay of Donavan's story. All three scrambled to secure the paper goods again. If her son didn't spit out the rest of the story within the next five seconds, she would throttle him like her handful of napkins.

"Donavan," she spoke firmly once in her seat again, but Donavan remained standing. "You have never given anyone a reason not to believe you."

"Nevertheless..."

"Donavan—"

The children picked that exact moment, in their aggravating randomness, to appear from nowhere, drenched and caked with mud. In the solemn delivery of Donavan's news, no one had noticed their disappearance.

The adults stared for a moment, trying to switch their attention to the three giggling troublemakers.

Laney found her voice. "What. In. The. World."

"We're making mud pies," Urie chirped.

"Pies, pies, pies!" chanted her younger shadow.

Nellie brought her dropped jaw into action to snicker, "I doubt there's much mud *in* the pies by the looks of you."

"Where are you getting mud?" asked Donavan.

"The water thing," Parker pointed. "The black hose that gives the tree water? The top came off. It made a mud puddle!"

The three playmates danced in appreciation of the gift that the broken drip line had given them.

"Well, I'd say you found some fun!" Nellie said when no one else spoke. The other two adults turned as if to gauge her for honesty or sarcasm.

Donavan said, "Mom, I'll go check if the cap's came off and...."

"Don't you dare. You'll ruin their play."

Laney and Donavan exchanged looks.

"Let them make mud pies! What are you worried about a little dirt for?" *Sit down. Finish your story. Spill it....*

"And when Parker leaves muddy prints across your carpet?" he asked.

Mentally, her inner self narrowed her eyes at her son. Outwardly, she smiled good-naturedly, acting innocent to his intended diversion. *Dang it.* Well, might as well let him. Nellie couldn't speak her mind with Laney here regardless. Whose idiotic idea was this picnic anyway?

"I just had the carpets cleaned, so I guess you're right." She sighed. "Why don't you two run along to your house and get some things for the kids to change into? I'm sure something of Parker's will fit the girls. We'll let them play for a bit, and when they're all done, we'll clean them up with the garden hose and have ice cream." She added a laugh that seemed to fool at least Laney into thinking she felt right as rain, business as usual.

Nellie walked them through the house to the front door, leaving the excited bunch of mud slingers in the backyard. Laney slipped out the door, but Nellie caught Donavan by the bicep before he could follow. He registered no surprise at her firm grip. One look from him, his emotions now unguarded with Laney out of sight, gave Nellie all she needed. His expression held the struggle—the reality of the unspoken situation—she wanted to see. And something else she hadn't expected to find: an apology.

Her anger ebbed just enough for an unforeseen sympathy to surface. "We're not finished with this conversation," she said, not unkindly. She let her hand loosen on his arm.

He nodded in acceptance before he closed the door behind him.

§ § § § §

Confrontation had never been Laney's specialty. At best, she could assert herself when necessary, but she wished Nellie had been able to push Donavan into clarifying what the heck he'd been talking about. Nellie had kept a cool composure, not looking ruffled about Donavan's vague proclamation, while Laney remained a little freaked out. News... won't be good...*they wouldn't believe him*?

Of course she would believe him. This was Donavan. She knew him. She couldn't imagine something that would make her question his character if he told her it wasn't true. She trusted him. Was that being naïve?

Laney's brow furrowed as she considered every outrageous scenario she could think of that would result in the life-altering consequences Donavan alluded to.

Donavan walked down the sidewalk now, just a slight step ahead, a sign he didn't want to talk. Yet how could she possibly ignore the elephant he had dropped in the room?

"Donavan—"

"I'm sorry, Laney. That was poor timing on my part."

"I just want you to know...well, I'm here for you. Whatever it is."

Donavan stopped by his mailbox, this commonplace gesture silencing her again. "Forgot to pick it up yesterday." He sighed as he put in his key. He pulled out a stack of envelopes and sent a small patronizing smile her way that said he didn't think she could understand any further explanation. An insulted blush climbed to her cheeks. "I appreciate that, Laney. I really do."

Her tongue stuck to the roof of her mouth as she struggled to define her role. Was she only an acquaintance, then? A friend? This certainly explained his odd behavior yesterday at the range. But the memory of last Saturday further flamed her cheeks. Surely she was significant enough to know what was going on.

Only the wind continued to speak on their way three houses down to the Peterson's home. Donavan dumped the mail in the kitchen on his way down the hall. Laney could do nothing but follow. They found a t-shirt and elastic-waisted shorts for Urie, and an oversized t-shirt would work as a makeshift dress for Ella. The irony did not escape Laney that her daughters shared her wardrobe plight from just a short time ago.

Back down the hall, the two single parents stood at the apex of the house and together crammed the collected clothes into a bag, their fingers brushing as they both worked at holding and shoving. Eyes met and hands stilled.

Laney's gaze pled for him to explain, but his stare petitioned not to have to. Before either grew brave enough to speak, Donavan gave a slight double take at something over her shoulder.

She followed his line of vision. The mail.

Laney had never encountered this side of Donavan, the one with a dozen emotions filtering through his veiled expression. He dropped his side of the bag and moved to the island, lost in his own world.

He pulled an envelope from the top of the pile, its return address taking up a large portion of the space. He gripped it and stared. Hard.

Sweat gathered in the small of Laney's back, more uncomfortable with each passing second, but she kept still. She couldn't make out the address when Donavan finally ripped the seal open. Seconds later, he hurtled the entire stack of papers toward the small trash can just inside the back door with a suddenness that made Laney flinch. The papers smacked the wall, fanned out like flags of surrender, and slid helplessly to the edge of the receptacle, too awkward in their bulky bundle to fall completely in.

The man in the middle of the room, so different from the host of the party last weekend, threw his hands behind his head in a gesture of utter frustration. With his fingers locked together, he turned his vacant eyes to the ceiling. Laney opened her mouth to say something but ended up wrestling her bottom lip between her teeth instead. Was it better to just let him alone to process whatever was going on in his head? She swallowed her uncertainty.

A phone buzzed, reawakening Donavan from the distant place his mind had traveled to. He reached into his pocket, read a text, and replaced the phone out of sight.

"My mom," he said. "Looks like the kids are good and wet, so we should get going....Oh, shoes." His tone was expressionless as if his thoughts were one place and his body moved on autopilot.

"Shoes?"

"They'll need shoes," he said, looking randomly about.

"No, it's okay. I can just—"

"Parker has a couple of pairs of old flip-flops by the pool..." Donavan trailed off and headed out the back. As soon as the sliding glass door opened, the wind, eager for spectators, caught hold of the burnt-red curtains framing the glass and whipped them into a frenzy. The open front door, she realized, gave enough cross breeze through the screen to create a dramatic draft. Crazed vertical ribbons of drapery grabbed and snatched at the space before her. Laney took a step back so that the curtains failed to find a victim; the wind, however, did not. It ripped the papers from their loose hold on the trash can rim, the pages going airborne like giant, gangly snowflakes.

The frantic paper flight around the room began before Laney could react. She dropped the bag and grabbed a page headed for the sink, knocking the rest of the mail off the counter in the process. The wind had found a defenseless plaything and ramped up its efforts, giving Laney a full workout of jumps, squats, and lunges to retrieve every sheet and trap them against her body. She stood breathless afterward, curtains mocking her desperate motions.

She shouldn't look.

She couldn't look.

She didn't want to, but...

There was no need. The torn envelope she hadn't captured quivered pre-flight at her feet long enough for her to read the bold print without her having to glance at the pages in her arms.

She didn't mean to see; it was just there. *George Bennett, Atty.*

The envelope sailed away, its job done. George Bennett. She knew that name. George. An older man. His daughter, Brie, had been at the party even though he hadn't. Old family friends of Kelly's. An attorney.

A divorce attorney.

A small hammer pounded within Laney's chest. It nagged at her in a rhythm, pushing her to decide, to look, until her curiosity trumped character. She eased the papers away from her body and battled her will to read the top page.

She didn't notice the figure standing in the doorway at first, his body blurred by the long panels of fabric, but the moment she made eye contact, she thanked the flimsy veil that danced between them.

"What. Are. You. Doing?" Donavan's words, bitter and angry, should have sent her scurrying, but her own hurt and anger made her chin climb upward.

"What is this?"

"You're reading my mail?" Donavan slammed the door behind him and the room filled with a violent explosion. Laney screamed, the house filling with a simultaneous deafening blast beyond her comprehension. Something hit her hard and took her down so brutally, her teeth rattled violently when she hit the floor.

Donavan had tackled her as pieces of broken glass rained over them like giant, crystal hailstones. Seconds seemed like minutes—the collapsing back door echoed in a cacophony of broken high pitches around them. Laney would have filled the moment with more screams, but Donavan's heavy body made an unyielding shield on top of her, forcing the air out of her lungs.

"Stay down," he commanded.

She clutched at his shoulders, struggling against panic as the chaos continued a moment longer. The fall of glass and metal slowed to an odd chorus of tingling and creaking, and Laney's eyes sought the wall to make sense of the sounds.

The sliding door hung in shambles.

Donavan began to move when the wind pulled at a curtain rod that had loosened from its mounting. One end slipped from its support and crashed to the floor with a metallic bounce and resounding twang. Laney let out another involuntary shriek that Donavan shushed.

Then silence.

"It's okay." His eyes grabbed her attention only inches away as he slowly raised himself up on his toes and hands over her as if pausing mid push-up. She still clutched at his shirt, trying to get a grip on her reeling senses. Panic remained and made her wriggle under his protective frame.

"Don't," he ordered and she froze. "There's glass everywhere. Just...wait."

Meticulously, he rolled to his right until a shower of glasslets pealed off his back, pinging when they fell onto the tile. With more maddening slowness, he went from a plank to a crouch to a careful stand, letting the diamond-like shards fall from his clothing away from her. He made no effort to reach for her until he had surveyed the room for a full minute. He nodded his consent.

She stood and glass pellets slid off her head. She reached up to feel her hair, but Donavan caught her hands and sucked in a breath. His face again wore a mask of conflicted emotions she was at a loss to decode.

"Let me." He picked at her hair with quick nimble gestures while she examined the devastation. Her jaw dropped at the view, the back door twisted in its frame, mangled as if an invisible truck had hit it. Shattered glass covered the floor like pounds of crushed ice.

"*What happened*?"

"I'm not sure. I think I slammed the door too hard."

"It sounded like...I thought a bomb had gone off."

"It was just...the wind. It took the door out of my hands."

His words lacked sincerity, indicating that his uncertainty matched her own.

Small red dots appeared on Donavan's arms, sending a chill through Laney.

"Donavan, you're bleeding."

He looked down at his arms and then hers and nodded. "So are you." In a dozen little spots across their flesh, droplets of blood formed where exploding glass had found its mark. Laney's elbow had been sliced in a neat, red line where she had pushed herself off the floor. Shock kept her from registering any pain.

The remaining end of the curtain rod groaned from its mounting and let go with a crash. With it, the smoldering red material fluttered to its death. The wind, completely unbarricaded now, stormed the room without temperance, taking any rubble not buried under debris into flight once more.

Donavan knelt down to retrieve a crumpled paper before it could sail away and held it out to Laney like a smoking gun.

Her eyes challenged him back. "You told me you were divorced," she said, her voice shaking from...shock? Anger? She wasn't sure. "But those papers...Donavan, you haven't signed any divorce papers yet, have you?"

"Not now, Laney." His voice laced with warning, and he grabbed a paper towel to thrust at her bloody elbow.

"Are you kidding me? Yes, now! Why did you lie to me?"

"Laney—"

"Seriously, Donavan! Something 'bad' is happening at work? You're divorced, you're not divorced? I would like one modicum of truth today!"

His firm jaw wrestled out his words. "Technically I never told you I was divorced. Those were other people's words. I told you Kelly and I weren't together, that she *wanted* a...." He stopped as if it pained him to say the word a second time.

"How could you?" Her anger overshadowed compassion. "You let me—let everyone believe it was true!"

"Does it matter?" his voice rose above the gust that whined through the room in mocking triumph. "It was inevitable. Here it is!" He shook the crumbled paper at her. "She's done it; she's made it impossible to avoid. It doesn't matter if I divorced yesterday, today, next week—it's over!"

Pain grew in Laney's gut, watching the man before her, blood spotted and unapologetic of his unhinged emotions. All the news of the day slowly assembled into a clearer image of this man before her.

She had been wrong.

She had no idea who this guy was.

"It matters, Donavan," she said, the crack in her voice betraying her before she hurried out the front door and let the surfacing tears fall.

Chapter 11

From where Donavan lay across the couch, he could see the thick plastic haphazardly stapled around the broken back door. Would be best to get it more secure…after he figured out how to unwind. He needed rest, but his body remained rigid, muscles tense. For now, the makeshift cover would hold out the wind and impending rain.

He tried a big inhale and exhale. The afternoon blurred behind his closed lids. Laney's angry departure had left him alone to battle emotions. He couldn't remember what time his mother and Parker had found him cleaning up the destruction. Parker thrilled at how "wicked awesome" their demolished kitchen looked. Nellie showed less enthusiasm. She had asked cautious questions, and he sensed dissatisfaction with the answers. She was a hard one to fool, that one.

Laney had told Nellie about Donavan's cuts when she'd scooped up her girls and left. Typical mother, Nellie brought a small first aid kit with her. But Donavan had no scratches. Every bloody spot had disappeared from his skin.

Donavan had no explanation to give her.

Nellie packed a bag for Parker, declaring that her grandson was having a sleepover with Grandma. Parker wanted to cleanup with Daddy until Grandma cagily offered to let him stay up late with a pirate movie and have breakfast in bed the following morning.

Donavan hadn't argued with his mother. After securing the plastic sheet, the couch served as the only comfort to his state of confusion.

He had done this?

Again and again, he worked through what else could have caused this—some projectile, some trick of the wind, some flaw in the architecture. But he found no proof of any of that. The truth hinted at an implausible reality. The same sensation—could he even label it that?—that he felt each time he drove to Jake's, subconscious but persistent, nudged its way into the foreground.

He sat up and rubbed his arms. The evaporation of his injuries struck him again.

Miserable and fatigued, no rest of mind or body came. He grabbed the remote and turned the TV on low, hoping the murmur of voices could loll him to sleep. It may have worked if he hadn't flipped to local news.

There it was: that damning four seconds of footage played over and over again, that looked to be exactly what it wasn't, even to Donavan. It looked precisely like he had taken Valentine by the collar and slammed his head into the bars. His expression of utter disgust as he pulled himself off the crumbled victim didn't help his case. He shut the TV off without listening to the accompanying commentary, buried his face in his hands, and worked his fingers up through his ruffled hair.

Nellie would have seen it; she never missed the evening news. Parker would know soon. His dad, disgraced.

A cyclone of nameless reactions threatened to overwhelm him when his cell phone buzzed. His mother. Unconsciously, his jaw clenched. Not yet…he couldn't deal with her disappointment, her fear just yet. The tornado inside was unleashing, and his stubborn resistance gave way to the injustice of it all, the injury, the anger—he surrendered to it with reluctant permission until his body shook from its violence. He couldn't sit still; he had to do something.

Donavan found himself on his feet, keys in hand, answering a message his mind had told his body without sharing it with the rest of him until his feet were in motion. If there were any answers, an uncanny stirring told him it would be at Jake's.

Jake's alley parking held more cars than Donavan had ever seen there, and it was a Sunday night, no less. The door of the bar reawakened the familiar, ominous feeling; he ignored it and prepared himself for the guaranteed impact of entry. The assault on his senses met him straight away, joined by the heavy ticking of a broken clock and a slight, invisible push. He steadied himself and plowed forward through the crowd.

It was late. The room crawled with customers looking for a cheap drink, not an accurate clock. Crusty men and clingy ladies, full of attitude that itched for an outlet, came to listen to the jukebox and play darts or billiards. Their presence gave the space an odd blend of fun and caution, as if trouble, wrapped in disguise of a good time, would burst out if not handled with care.

Donavan headed to the next-to-last seat at the end of the bar. He forced his way through the loud bodies without seeing them until he hit shoulder to shoulder with a big guy in a mechanic's jumpsuit. A head taller than Donavan, he sported short, dirty hair and small, gray teeth. This guy's night already oozed trouble from beer-enriched breath. "Watch where you're going," he snarled.

Donavan donned an outward civility with subtle undertone of warning. It was a familiar on-the-job pose he often assumed. "Excuse me," he said, looking the offender squarely in the eye. The man growled something about being careful, but Donavan had already moved too far away to make it out.

Finding his spot, Donavan took the empty stool next to Harley, and Rufus delivered his drink in eerie foresight. As if on cue, Brian and Tag emerged from the darkened back room to lean on the bar's corner. Brian raised a glass to him, Tag nodded ever so slightly, and then motioned Rufus over. Had they expected him? Absolutely uncanny. Yet somehow, unexplainably… fulfilling.

"Saw you on the news," Harley spoke first. Harley gave no other indication that Donavan had arrived, gaze fixed forward.

"Camera adds ten pounds, don't you think?"

Brian laughed, and the corners of Harley's mouth curled. Only a grunt from Tag.

"Let me ask you something," Donavan began, unsure of what he would say. "You think I did that? That I took him down intentionally?"

"Who wouldn't?" Tag answered, his tone cold. Donavan eyed the speaker and made a rapid assessment; Tag might have some trust issues to go along with those dark looks.

Donavan directed his gaze to Harley. "What do you think?"

Harley took out the chewed-up cigar butt and had a swig of beer before he answered. "Seems to me, nothing is what it is."

Brian's grin grew as if cued in on an inside joke.

"Meaning?"

"Don't even try to figure him out," Brian interjected. "He'll just make your head hurt."

"I thought the saying was, 'It is what it is,'" Donavan persisted. "You're telling me nothing is what it is? How's that?"

Apparently engaging Harley in any meaningful conversation took work.

Harley took the bait. "Take this clock here for instance. Is it a clock?"

"Sure."

"Looks like a clock, has the arms and the numbers and the like, but does it tell time? Valentine's like that." Harley chuckled a little to himself, still watching the TV. "Yeah, Valentine's a broken clock. You know what he is, what he's supposed to be. But he isn't really what he's supposed to be under it all, is he?"

Donavan tried hard to follow along; Brian's headshake said *don't even try* from across the bar. "What he's supposed to be?" Donavan said. "He's supposed to be the bad guy. He proved himself right by framing me with this brutality charge. He is exactly what he is."

Harley eyed him now as if beaten by his own irrational philosophies. "What about you then? Are you what you are?"

"Oh, for crying out loud," Tag mumbled behind his raised mug.

"Sure. I'm one of the good guys."

"How do you prove that?"

"Well—"

"For Pete's sake!" Tag broke in. "Stop feeding him answers! Harley'll keep rambling nonsense if you encourage him. Of all the—"

Harley gave Tag a sharp glance that shut him up, though it did nothing to stop the glowering. The three men went back to staring at the TV, and Donavan stared at them. Really stared at them. He saw nothing extraordinary about them individually. Brian could be a lifeguard or student at UCLA. He'd easily fit in with his blond good looks and casual confidence. Give Tag an old button-down shirt with the sleeves ripped off and he could be any of the blue-collar guys in this crowd. Hard. Tough. Independent. Harley? Perfect blend of ex-military and life-learned experience. Unapproachable yet magnetic. And all three of them big as trees, Harley's bulging dark muscles and height edging ahead of the others a fraction.

It was during Donavan's unabashed surveillance that he sensed something unusual about them. He just didn't know what.

Everyone else milled around the bar on a different rotation of the earth, as if these three didn't belong here. Or maybe they did and everyone else didn't.

Crap. Now I'm thinking like Harley.

"What is this place?" Donavan breathed the question out loud for the first time, his gnawing apprehension full grown. Brian and Tag shifted their eyes to him and then at Harley, waiting. Seemed only Harley could answer. Or would.

"This is a strange and beautiful place here. Any place you want to hide out in can bury you with its secrets. And the very same place can free you with its revelations. Here, there's no place to hide, but things go undiscovered. You know when there's a part of yourself—"

"Harley," Donavan cut in and sighed. "I've had a very long day and an even longer week. I really need you to cut to the chase. Spit it out."

Harley emptied his mug and wiped his wide lips with the back of his hand. "Tag?"

Tag's mouth twisted, a hint at the fact he'd been eagerly awaiting this cue. He brought out two pool balls from somewhere and rolled them across the bar to Harley. Brian eyed the scene with intensity, his smile less friendly, more sympathetic. Donavan analyzed the balls and wondered if they would pop open and reveal the mysteries of the universe to him. Man, he hoped so. A talking pool ball might explain a lot.

Harley pivoted in his seat and jerked his head toward several rowdy men at the dart board. He handed a reluctant Donavan the cue ball and kept number 9 for himself.

"I could tell you what was about to happen, but you wouldn't believe me. Best you just live it. Now, pay attention."

With swift aim, Harley hurled the 9 ball at the back of one of the dart players, hitting him soundly between the shoulder blades. The force pitched the man forward, and he took out the drinks on the table in front of him. Shouts went up all around, and Donavan sucked in breath. The man regained his balance and spun around. That's when Donavan noticed he wore a blue mechanic's jumpsuit.

"What the—" Jumpsuit laid eyes on the foursome at the corner of the bar; Harley innocently jerked his head and eyes toward the pool ball in Donavan's hand.

"Are you crazy?" Donavan hissed.

"Uh-oh, boys," Harley drawled and added a sing-song, "Here... he... coooommmme!"

Donavan had no time to check Tag's and Brian's reactions. The towering figure in grease-monkey blue forced his way through tables and chairs, headed right for Donavan. Donavan put the ball down and jumped to his feet.

"Now wait a second—" he managed before the guy threw the first punch.

He dodged right, knowing he was too slow to miss the impact, when a deafening silence overtook him. The punch never came. The large man before him stood frozen. The face contorted in a menacing grimace, spit unmoving on his lip, arm outstretched, fist inches away from Donavan's face.

Donavan straightened in shock. His attacker wasn't the only thing stationary. The buddy at the dart board posed like a statue, frozen mid-step with the same ugly, fighting eyes as his friend. Terrified, Donavan looked around and saw that nothing moved. Not the fans, not a person, not the sound of a breath. Across the room, a dart had stopped in midair; drops of beer unflowed from a spilled bottle; a woman's hair remained curved, mid-swing. The silence, absolute and crushing, assaulted him, even the clock now quiet. He sucked in and tried to keep his heart from racing out of his chest when he realized Harley's hand clutched his forearm.

Harley's face shifted into a slow, deliberate grin. Not frozen. Behind him, Brian looked like a kid in line for Space Mountain, and Tag took a swig from his beer, doing his best to act nonchalant.

Before Donavan could find his voice, Harley said, "Umma let go of your arm now. But he ain't done swinging. I suggest you get busy."

Sound returned like a moving train just as Harley shoved Donavan to the side. The angry man's punch sailed forward, and the rest of his body followed when it met no resistance. Donavan turned himself over to instinct and sank his fist into the man's gut.

To Donavan's amazement, the man flew backward several yards, taking out the table behind him.

Nothing made sense. Donavan flexed his hand to find no pain.

Chaos broke out throughout the bar. The big guy had a lot of friends, and everyone celebrated the initiation of one last weekend ruckus. Trouble had come out of its wrapping and was received like an awaited present. Within minutes, chairs flew, bottles broke, women screeched, men roared, tables crashed.

For Donavan, it was like he'd stepped into an adrenaline machine. He hadn't used his fists in a long time, but surely it had never been this easy. Evading swings, hoping to put an end to the brawl, Donavan had no choice but to take on Jumpsuit's friend, seeking revenge for his spilled drink. Donovan ducked a thrown chair that almost took out Rufus. A server's tray shielded him from a flying bottle, but nothing could stop the blue suit now revived and coming directly toward him.

"Harley!" Donavan snarled. "When I get my hands on you—"

"Focus, boy! Here come a big one!" Harley cackled. In his peripheral vision, Donavan saw that Brian and Tag were having no trouble defending themselves. The guys charging them seemed to drop before they even reached their target. Jumpsuit, on the other hand, looked as if he wouldn't go down so easily.

"For the love of—," Donavan muttered when the assailant took another swing. He ducked under the first right hook, and a left jab grazed his shoulder. He cocked his left and let it fly, waiting for the crush of his hand, only to find his opponent gone. The punch had sent him shooting into the crowd.

Harley yelled and Donavan whirled to see a guy wielding a chair over his head. Instinctively, Donovan ducked and planted his shoulder into the fighter, sending him sailing into the upturned tables. A shot cracked into the crowd, and Donavan watched the crowd instantly sober up. He sprang to his feet to find Rufus with a pellet gun, dead-faced and detached as always.

"Everyone out," he said. Someone raised a bottle, and Rufus sent pellets into their backside. The person sent up a howl.

"Get. Out," Rufus commanded.

Awakened to reality, battered men with their protective women stumbled out the narrow doorway, still promising revenge. But both fun and trouble had drained from their voices.

Donavan's sides heaved, and he took stock. He saw nothing wrong with his hands. Not a scratch. Not a bruise. His arms looked fine. The shoulder where the only punch had landed didn't even ache. He felt insanely…alive.

He started back to the others as an unhappy couple brushed past him. They blocked his view of Harley for a second, but not before Donavan got a view of the exchange between him and Jumpsuit. Something passed from hand to hand between the men. More people blocked his line of vision, cursing their way to the door.

Jumpsuit followed behind them, passing Donavan without so much as a glance even as Donavan glared at him. Harley had returned to his drink, making as if nothing out of the ordinary had just ripped through the night. It seemed "get out" applied to everyone except Harley, Tag, and Brian; Rufus doled out refills to them while wearing his same stolid mask.

Anger engulfed Donavan. He grabbed the leg of a broken chair and swung it back, reaching to pull Harley off his stool by the front of his shirt with his free hand. Harley covered Donavan's hand as he stood, and the deafening silence returned. Rufus froze along with the beer caught mid-flow from the tap.

"You need to tell me right now what the hell is going on here!"

Harley didn't flinch. He brought his cigar butt up to his teeth with his other hand and eyed Donavan. "Can't tell you what you already know."

"What is that supposed to mean? No more psychobabble crap! How are you doing that?"

"How'd you throw that guy across the room?"

"You mean the guy you *paid* to fight me? I saw you just now. What's that about, Harley, huh? Answer me!" The noiselessness made his head swim, and he felt nauseated.

"How 'bout you put that stick down first."

Donavan's head reeled, and he dropped both hands; Harley released him at the same time. The train of sound whooshed past again. The clock regained its tick.

"Tell. Me." Donavan threw the chair leg far right, and it splintered in every direction when it made contact with the floor.

Brian and Tag looked on with grave anticipation. They were watching for something. Waiting.

"Tell me!" he repeated with an urgency that startled himself. "Are you trying to set me up? How did you—did everyone freeze like that?"

"Sometimes questions can't be answered with words."

"Oh, come on, Harley! There's always words! Just idiots who don't know how to use them."

"Really, Donavan?" Harley barked. He stepped up toe to toe with Donavan. "That's what you believe? Then answer me this: why are you here? Huh? Answer me that!"

Donavan recoiled. "I…I don't know."

"Really? Cuz only an idiot can't find the words. So tell me, genius, *why are you here?*"

"I don't know!"

"Well, you figure it out, boy, and then you can come back and ask me again."

Donavan closed his eyes and tried to think clearly, to return to the calm, confident police detective that could get resolution. "I…just…want…to understand. Please. How—who—"

Harley let out a huff. "You're trying too hard. Quit asking; start becoming. That's the best advice I can give. Don't think it, feel it, or analyze it. Just be it."

Frustration resurfaced and mixed with the beer and fatigue. "Goodbye, Harley. You know what you can do with your riddles." Donavan stormed toward the door with giant strides and heaved a fallen table from his path. It flew across the room and hit a window with a high-pitched shatter that sent fragments raining down. The table slid to the floor in helpless splinters. The sight made Donavan pull up short, trying to wrap his mind around his inexplicable strength.

"Ah, come on now," Rufus muttered, and Harley chuckled behind him.

"Don't worry, Rufus. You know Jacob's got it covered."

In his uncertainty, Donavan glanced at his hands and then to the men, but Harley and his friends had returned to TV viewing. "See ya later, Donavan," Harley muttered from around his cigar.

Later? Donavan fumed out the door. There wasn't going to be a later.

Chapter 12

Laney turned off the TV and threw down the remote as if it had bitten her. Lucky for her, the girls playing in the dining room had not seen the morning news nor their mother's reaction.

Wow.

If she'd had to predict the awful news Donavan had warned about, she would have never, ever guessed what she had seen. To watch him so callously throw a person around, unconcerned about the camera or the man's rights, so angry and hostile…

Flashes of yesterday mixed with images of the video. The mangled door frame, glass everywhere. He wasn't that kind of guy. He wasn't. Yet she had seen it twice now.

She shuddered and rubbed her arms where the scratches were still recovering. To occupy her runaway thoughts, she straightened the books and blankets and stuffed animals scattered over the couch.

It all added up to more than she had asked for, more than she could deal with right now. Seriously. She had never even planned on reestablishing a friendship with Donavan, never thought she'd see him after her divorce, never even gave him a thought! Then one day he bumps into her at the grocery store, and now here she was, scrambling to find a reason she would defend him, *could* defend him against the substantial evidence stacked against him.

Why did she feel the need to even *try* to make him into the good guy? Because she was falling for him? She wouldn't let that get in the way of what was right.

Was it because he was in a familiar place, the dry lands of a failed marriage? Well, he could find someone else to counsel him.

Or was it because her girls adored Parker, and she'd found a comfortable place they all fit into? That…that was an issue.

Laney punched a throw pillow a little harder than necessary as she fluffed it.

No, he was a liar. No need to analyze the video or the broken door. Whether he was truly a violent man or not—*how could he be? Donavan?*—the fact remained that he'd told her he was divorced when he wasn't.

He wasn't. Not yet.

"What does it matter?" His words echoed in her head, and her fist skidded off the pillow to knock over the lamp. The girls' heads popped up from their dollhouse.

"Oops. My bad." She smiled sheepishly, and they went back to playing with a giggle.

Laney grabbed her cell phone and took a deep breath. She needed to end this torture now. She slipped into the bedroom to keep the girls from hearing and paced the floor while punching at the buttons. It rang on the other end and with each tone, her sweat increased a little. Relief cooled her as Donavan's voicemail picked up instead of him.

"–and I'll get back to you–" Her throat went dry, but if she didn't do this now, in the spur of the moment, she'd never have the nerve.

"Hi, Donavan. It's me... Laney. I'm sorry about running out on you yesterday. No, that's not true... I'm not sorry. I know that things—that you have a lot going on right now. I want you to know all that other stuff doesn't matter to me. I would have been there for you to deal with that. I mean it. But if we're going to be friends..." Her throat froze and she switched the phone to the other ear as she fumbled through her thoughts.

"You lied to me, Donavan. It is a divorce, it will be a divorce—might be a little thing to you, but I really deserved the truth. No, that's not right either. You didn't owe me anything, did you? But the truth is what I wanted. So if it's all the same to you, I think it's best we not see each other anymore. Maybe around the holidays the kids could get together.... So, okay. Good luck... with everything. Bye."

Laney snapped her ancient cell phone shut and threw it on the bed. *Okay, that sucked.* Perhaps rehearsing wouldn't have been such a bad idea. The house phone rang the next second, and Laney's stomach flopped involuntarily.

He was calling her back?

Heart pounding, she forced herself out into the living room to answer the landline. Her heart settled back in rhythm when the Caller ID presented a welcomed name: Alice Whyte.

"Mom," she cooed in relief.

"Well, hi there!" Her mother's voice evoked images of sunny meadows, crystal blue streams, and big, puffy clouds. Her beautiful home in Cortez, Colorado, matched the matriarch's disposition perfectly. "Just calling to see how my girls are. Are you finally on fall break?"

"Thankfully, yes." But the idea of two weeks of endless days alone with the girls suddenly seemed daunting. "Mom, what if I came up for a quick visit?" Laney's heart beat wildly at the thought of a spontaneous road trip, going against her plan-ahead nature. "I could be packed up and headed out in like an hour."

"Well, of course I'm not going to say *no*! I can have your rooms ready in no time."

A mix of exhilaration and relief washed over Laney.

"Honey, it would be so nice to see you." Her mother's genuine excitement sealed the deal. "Start packing and we'll see you later this evening."

"Urie? Ella?" Small heads popped out of the hall bathroom, Ella pushing the way out with her unbuttoned jeans thrust forward in a wordless request for assistance. Laney reached down to fasten the clothing as unconsciously as Ella had expected the help.

"Who left the door open?" Laney asked them. She had followed the girls back in the house to use the bathroom before hitting the road. The SUV waited, packed and ready by the curb.

Urie looked back at the door and her eyebrows rose. "Not me!" she said defensively, throwing her hands up. They had a strict kids-don't-mess-with-the-door policy, and Urie wasn't going to catch the blame for being the negligent one. "You were the last one in, Mom. Remember?"

Ella gave her mother a wicked grin as Laney reconstructed the frizzy little ponytail on the back of the blonde head. "Bad, Mama! You weft the door open!"

Laney pulled her daughter's head in to touch it to her own forehead and gave her a wide-eyed look that made the little girl giggle. "Mama's sorry."

"We forgive you!" they chanted, their voices full of cheerful acceptance.

"Then let's go to Grandma's house!"

With squeals of exuberance, they flew out the door carrying their snack bags with them. Laney grabbed the cooler and locked the door behind her. She pulled on the knob several times to make sure it was secure. The latch seemed tight enough. Shrugging, she skipped to catch up with the girls.

They bustled with energy down the sidewalk, the last chance to move freely before the six-hour drive. Laney's eyes squinted to the view of the car ahead of them, and then widened in confusion. A sudden acid flare up laced her esophagus.

The back door of the SUV was wide open.

"Mom," Urie tssked. "We should ground you."

"Just let them sleep in front of the fireplace."

Laney's mother, much like Nellie, overindulged her grandchildren. They had made s'mores together in the den's fireplace and now snuggled deep in a blanket fort Grandpa had built them, listening to him read a story. Excited as they were, Laney could tell the trip had exhausted them, and suspected that Carl Whyte's deep monotonous voice would lull them to sleep before they could be drawn to bed.

"Are you sure?" Laney asked.

"Of course! They aren't hurting anything. Your room is right there if they need you tonight."

The room next door... her teenage bedroom she had shared with her sister for years: same wallpaper, same beds, the mirror and dresser still there. None of that bothered Laney, but the window always did. Memories of sneaking out at night made her blood run cold all these years later. Outside waited Zane and Hunter and a night that would change her sister Arie's life forever…so many years ago.

Laney shoved the memory into the furthest corner of her mind and focused on the two lumps behind the wall of blankets and cushions in the den. "They're growing so fast, Mom. It's hard to keep up with them."

Her mother smiled back and covered Laney's palm from across the kitchen table. Her mom's hand, wrinkled and warm, made Laney turn away, back toward the den, to hide surfacing tears. Age was catching up with the grandparents too; Alice Whyte appeared older and more tired than Laney ever remembered.

Alice sipped her tea. Her whitening hair still bobbed around her face in a style she had worn most of her life. She was attractive in her matronly way, her eyes kind and her voice like an elixir for Laney's soul. No one could hate Alice Whyte.

"Mom, I used to think you worried about such silly things when we were growing up. Like untied shoes and uncovered outlets, as if they were monsters that would somehow come up and grab us in our beds. Then I became a mom, and I'm even worse. I won't even let Urie open her juice box straw wrapper with her teeth because I'm afraid she'll suck in a small piece of plastic and choke."

Alice laughed. "Okay, that is bad."

"I know! I can't help myself, Mom! What's wrong with me?"

"There's nothing wrong with you, darling. It comes with the territory. Comes with being a mom."

Laney stared back at the fading firelight in the next room.

"Then what happened to Arie?" She felt her mother's hand stiffen over hers. "Why didn't she feel like this? She was their mom."

Laney prepared for her mother to get up and change the subject, as she so often did. No one liked to talk about Laney's twin. No one wanted to revisit the pain and disappointment her sudden disappearance had caused.

Alice stared at the fire, too, and Laney swallowed. She silently willed this evening to be different, for her mother to say something. Anything.

"I don't know, honey," her mother spoke hesitantly. "I really don't. The only thing I can tell you is that sometimes it... it happens to people. They somehow aren't born with that instinct to protect and...."

"Love?"

"I think she loved them; she just couldn't—"

"Mom, please, don't defend her." Laney floated tears again but this time as much from resentment as sorrow. "You always do that. You try to make her out to be less of a bad guy."

"She's not the bad guy, Laney, she's just...confused."

"Mom! *I'm* confused right now. I'm all alone, and I just lost a friend, a good friend—I think—and have to figure out how I will survive the next semester as a single parent on a tight budget. I have catatonic episodes in the grocery store, I'm forgetting to shut doors, and I have no place to wear my cool shoes." A tear finally overflowed the rim of its dam. "Mom, I'm overwhelmed, and scared, and unsure of everything—all the same excuses people give Arie for walking away. But I'm not going anywhere. I love them too much.

"Why didn't she love them like that?"

Alice gave a weak smile and kept hold of her own tears Laney saw pooling. "Honey, I make excuses because I don't have answers. People expect me to know—I was her mom. I should have seen her getting ready to bolt. I should know why she left, left us all, left you the girls. But I don't! I don't know why she didn't... didn't love them. I only know I'm glad she didn't."

"Mom!"

"Because then they wouldn't have gotten you."

"Oh... Mom. I don't know. I don't know if I'm ever doing anything right."

"You are. The girls are so healthy and happy. You should be proud of yourself and quit worrying."

Laney looked down at their hands for a minute. "Have you heard from her since—?"

Alice shook her head and got up, her standard way of closing the subject. "I made that baked oatmeal the girls like for breakfast. Unless you would rather go to the café?"

Laney sighed in resignation that this was as far as the conversation would get her. Her mother carried their tea mugs away from the table, and Laney buried her face in her hands to hide the torrent that began to flow in earnest.

"She's gone, Laney," a small, tired voice said at the sink. "That's what I know. Arie's gone, and she's not coming back."

A bitter truth that Laney had lived with all these years. She wiped her cheeks with a napkin and inhaled to regain the same composure Alice Whyte bore.

Gone.

If Laney were honest, that relieved her more than she would admit.

Chapter 13

With a soundless motion, Donavan eased the safety off his gun and breathed with trained patience. He kept his heart rate controlled, listening intently to sounds within the house, gun poised flat to his chest while he pinned himself to his living room wall. The plastic at the back door, ripped open by some unseen invader, flapped softly, creating a deep rippling echo, like the sound of water lapping against a boat's hull.

Nothing stirred for several long minutes; Donavan darted his head out for a quick scan. Gun leading, he performed a sweep of the kitchen, behind the island, all corners. He angled down the hall, back against the wall, tuned into the still night around him. He kept his weapon at the ready until he'd investigated each room, ending with his bedroom. A heavy sigh followed the safety clicking back in place.

He rubbed at his weary neck and wandered back through the house, still leery of the exposed rear entry.

Only two steps in the front door after a store run, Donavan's gaze had gone immediately to the heavy plastic sheet covering the gaping hole. An erratic, stretched jagged line opened the plastic, implying human hands had fought their way in without the use of a tool to cut an opening. He'd dropped his shopping bags with a too-loud clank on the entry tile and drawn his weapon.

Parker had been shopping with him for repair supplies all day; it was luck that Nellie had texted to invite Parker over for tacos before they had arrived home. As "cool" as Parker would think it was to see his dad in police mode now, the endless questions that followed would have been hard to deflect. And who knew what danger lurked.

But with no sign of an intruder, Donavan now leaned on the counter and stared at the fluttering plastic, his eyes searching for clues. His mind worked through his current cases—well, cases that *had* been his until the suspension—the situation concerning Valentine included, but there wasn't a motive for anyone to be playing games with him.

Did any of this have to do with the shattered door? Nosy neighbors? Vandals? Nothing logical connected. He retrieved the bags he'd abandoned, and on his return to the kitchen, he noticed it.

He examined all around the window to be sure. The rock had vanished. Parker had brought the green stone from Donavan's dresser after breakfast. Donavan had set it in the windowsill, he was certain, because he insisted Parker not carry it with them on errands.

Donavan checked the bedroom to be sure, knowing it wouldn't be there. He did another quick sweep of the house, ending back in his bedroom. No rock.

Who would want to steal a *rock*?

Hands on hips, he surveyed the area with meticulous care. A subtle difference in the closet made him cock his head to the side and study intensely. Every morning, the clear photo box on the top shelf revealed a sliver of a picture of Kelly and Parker together, a happy accident, but now, another random picture faced out from the box on the high shelf.

He reached up and pulled it down. The picture of Kelly and Parker was there, shuffled behind some others.

Who would be here looking at pictures? A crazy race of his heart screamed *Kelly!* But he dismissed the notion quickly. She could have just walked in the front door with the spare key if she came back. So who else would care about the closet contents?

A thought hit him with a chill. The photo box served as a front for his personal weapon safe, a small heavy lockbox hidden behind. No, *used* to. He'd given it to Laney. So... had he rearranged pictures as he'd moved stuff on the shelf? He was certain he hadn't. He just given the picture of Kelly a quick glance today, a solemn part of his morning ritual.

So best guess—someone had been looking for his gun and rifled through the shelf to look for it. Someone who knew right where to look for the gun. And someone who liked queer green rocks.

Why?

Donavan let his mind work through possibilities while he put his hands to work in the kitchen. Rain threatened, so stapling the plastic back together became his first priority. Next, he texted his mother and made an excuse for Parker staying the night with her. The weird events had him on edge, and he knew he wouldn't sleep a minute if he had Parker added to the mix.

He spread the results of his shopping trip out onto the counter and tried to focus on the repair, unsure he could even do it with the tools he owned. Within minutes, the puzzle worked its magic at engaging him in physical labor. He had attached the plastic to the outside of the frame giving him the ability to move around the inner frame and try to clean up around the edges so that installing a new door would be easier. Paying someone, he knew, would be a lot less hassle. But the week had dragged since his ban from work; watching DIY videos and chatting with the hardware store experts helped him make a plan for each day without having to think too far into the future.

As he watched his hands at work, a memory of his visit to Jake's seeped through from some closed window of his mind. The image of Harley's hand gripping him, the discovery that time could actually stop...Brian, Tag...so *strange*. Not to mention these hands of his had thrown objects—*people*—around as if weightless. What was that about?

To answer those questions seemed to take effort in unlocking something within he didn't want to touch. That he was afraid of? He didn't even want to pick at it and find out. Harley's infuriating, nebulous non-answers stubbornly kept him from seeking his own; he'd squished his brain's attempts all week.

He picked up a heavy screw from the cluster of tools he'd flung onto the table and rolled it in his fingers. Absently, he tossed it up and caught it overhand, over and over watching his fingers clutch and release in awe and bewilderment of what he'd seen these hands do.

Exhaustion forced its way between thoughts and actions, and a large sigh escaped him. He was so tired of being tired—all the time tired. When he woke, if he worked, when he lay down—always tired and still unable to sleep. Except when...

He caught the screw a final time and held it, mind restless. *Except when I am there.*

Frustration brewed and fought against the desire to understand, to *be*. All of Harley's veiled insinuations made Donovan believe he should have figured it out already. He closed his eyes and willed himself to relax against the counter, head in hands, to cave in to all the raw emotions that had confused him for days—actually for a very long time now—and focus, not on an answer, but on *being*. Isn't that what Harley had said? *Just be…*

But he didn't even know how to be himself anymore. Weeks—no, *months*—of a life off-kilter had him uncertain what a "normal" Donavan looked like. He had surrounded himself with activity to keep from mourning Kelly, to help him parent, to drive him to be productive despite fatigue and bitterness, sorrow and confusion.

Donavan stood up straight. For one split second, the emotional turmoil and intensity collided into clarifying perception. A solid beating in his chest verified what he'd been too obtuse to see from the start. His feet moved before his mind stopped, pausing only to grab his hooded sweatshirt when he flew out the door and into the coming rain.

His legs took off in a run before the hoodie came down over his head. He didn't understand why he was running, why he hadn't grabbed his car keys, but this felt *good.* Tiredness evaporated with the road behind him, the swift incomprehensive movement of his body consuming all weariness.

Miles passed like minutes, and Donavan's heart raced faster than his feet when he neared his destination. He sprinted over the sidewalks, empty this time of night, skidding on the dirt and gravel into the obscure, poorly lit parking lot. The sight before him stopped him short.

Jake's was gone.

The building was still there, looking more like a shack than ever, but the Jake's he'd known was just a shell—vacant, the front door wide open, unlit empty space within. The sign no longer hung in the window, not a soul in sight. It was as if time had rewound itself to before the owner had made the speculative decision to make this run-down spot an investment.

Still catching his breath, Donavan whipped wildly around. The slight wind picked up and he froze. He wasn't alone.

Two rusty, abandoned vehicles sat along the fence line, surrounded by debris and overgrown weeds to testify to their immobility. Something stirred there. Donavan recognized it more by instinct than proof.

"Hello?" he called, still struggling to breathe.

Three men stepped out of the shadows, and without seeing their faces, Donavan knew who they'd be. He moved closer to

Harley, Brian, and Tag until they formed an uncommitted circle in the semi-shadow of the light post. For a moment, Donavan felt so relieved he couldn't speak.

"I know why I'm here," Donavan said between gulps of air.

"Well?" Harley, barely visible, stood the furthest back in the depths of the shadow.

"Because," Donavan said, regaining breath. "Because I'm one of you."

The air held an odd quality around the empty walls of Jake's—what was formally Jake's. Without light, without Rufus, the broken windows and quiet bar gave no hint to its former patronage. In a matter of days, it had aged years...or regressed into its former state. Donavan couldn't determine which. He touched the door frame, in wonder of the way it used to make him react when he entered. A nothingness remained. The eerie transformation heightened his confusion that he so eagerly thought he'd been on the brink of unraveling.

With only the streetlight and the glow of Harley's cigar to illuminate them, the four men gathered inside, tense and serious. Donavan remained near the door, while Brian and Harley leaned against the bar, catching most of the light that beamed through a large gap in the wall that had once been a window. Tag chose to sit in a corner, shrouded in darkness.

"Now it's your turn," Donavan said. "Tell me...what exactly are we?"

"What do you think we are?" Harley asked. This time the question lacked its mocking tone. Brian didn't roll his eyes at the rhetoric; Tag remained silent. Donavan's answer felt important.

He frowned as he struggled for the answer. "We're... unnatural. Different. You were right, Harley. It's impossible to explain. But I feel it if I let myself." By their faces, he sensed the same was true for them. "What do you call us?"

"Superhuman," Tag answered.

"Extraordinary," Harley said.

"*Buttkicking*," Brian said comically, causing the others to smirk. "Superheroes."

"It all depends on how you look at it," Harley said. "How much do you know?"

Donavan inhaled and let go of his cauldron of emotions again, trying to let this unnatural self take over. He closed his eyes to describe it. "Not much. I have some kind of... strength. Crazy strength. But not all the time. I don't know what makes it come out. And I don't understand how to control it." He opened his eyes to find Harley nodding.

"It's like that at first. It's confusing. But now that you're acknowledging it, it will become clearer what your abilities are and how to manage them."

Abilities. He had so many questions, where to begin? "What happened to this place? Where'd it all go?"

Harley shook his head. "It happens like that. Something is there when we need it. Gone when we don't. Jake's was here for you to find us. Now you know. Now we don't need it."

"What happened last time we were here? How did everything... stop moving?"

Harley nodded to the figure beside him. "Brian." A hand rose to acknowledge credit. "That's his gift. He can stop time."

Donavan swallowed. "But that's... impossible."

Harley and Brian grinned but refrained from laughter. "Is it?"

"How...?"

"Can I explain it? Nah," Harley answered. "But what we can explain, it's time to tell ya. Better have a seat."

They moved to Tag's dim corner. Brian sat closer to the door as if lookout. Donavan wondered what he was looking out for, but didn't ask.

"Brian?" Harley said, giving him the floor.

Brian shrugged. "It's by touch only. If I touch someone, I can freeze time around us."

"But you didn't touch me last night—"

"Harley did. I was touching Harley and Tag when I did it. Harley was touching you both times. The effect travels."

"You can do that to anyone at any time?" Donavan asked in disbelief.

"I wish." He looked like a little kid for a minute. "Imagine all the things I could do if—" Harley scowled and Brian sobered. "It's a defensive move. I can only make it happen if I'm threatened. Or one of you is."

"Not... regular people?"

"Actually, I'm not sure. I know it doesn't work *without* touching. But if I ever tried on a regular person, it would blow my cover, if you know what I mean. They'd lock me up in some kind of loony bin, right? Or it'd freak the other person into insanity. It's nothing you can show off at a talent contest."

Donavan made a conscious effort to stop his head that slowly shook in disbelief. He examined Harley, who stared back at him as if waiting for the pieces to click.

"Harley, you sense what will happen ahead of time, don't you? You can predict others' moves?" That seemed the most logical explanation for what Donavan had seen during the fight.

Harley grinned a little and nodded.

"How? You know what they're thinking?"

"Like you all, my gift comes with limitations. I can tell when someone's planning to attack, not what they thinking exactly. More like a premonition."

His mind worked hard to wrap around this information. "How about…Tag?"

"Shock," Tag put in dryly. "Defensive."

"Shock? As in, you emit *an electric charge* on people?" An image of people inexplicably bouncing off Tag and Brian during the brawl replayed in his head.

Tag's voice sounded weary of this inquisition. "Only when attacked."

Harley clarified, "We all defensive people—"

"Superhumans," interjected Brian again.

"—who can only act when acted against. Our abilities are useless unless we're threatened. But *you*…"

All eyes fell on him now.

"You think I'm not?"

"Dunno. Have you ever been able to use your strength other than when endangered?"

His mind went back to the sensation of glass raining on him, on Laney, as the back door exploded out of its frame. He *had* demolished the door just by shutting it. He'd been angry, tied up with grief and confusion, but threatened by Laney's actions to invade his private pain?

"I'm not sure."

"Well, why don't you have a go at it?"

Donavan stared at the gang. He caught himself before he asked, "How?" He felt like an idiot with all questions and no answers. His feet stood, and his eyes surveyed the broken building around them. Nothing remained of Jake's except the long wooden bar, an eerie reminder of what had been. He walked over, put his hands on the top, and glanced back at Harley. Harley nodded encouragement.

Donavan took a deep breath and let his emotions collide. He had to find out. He was in this now, and it was too late to pretend he was something he wasn't anymore.

With surprising swiftness, he slammed his fist onto the top of the wood. A loud *crack* echoed around him, and he witnessed the smooth surface beneath his hand first create deep lines that traveled the length of the panel, down the sides, and then, when he smashed his second fist after, he eyed the hard planks splintering erratically, flying through the air like a startled flock.

In the same second, a hand gripped his wrist, and time stood still with a deafening nothingness. He found Brian beside him, grinning with approval.

"Better help me shield the other two or they're gonna get ticked when they get hit."

Donavan turned back to the frozen scene, the air consumed with broken, jagged pieces of wood. Some fragments, like sharpened stakes, headed toward Harley and Tag, frozen in their seated positions. Together, Donavan and Brian knocked the wood into new directions, the newest hero speechless with amazement. It was like walking inside an air bubble that floated through suspended space.

"What would happen if you let go of me?"

Brian shrugged and in the next second sound resumed in a huge *whoosh.* The spears flew harmlessly into the walls, floor, and windows, shaking the room with the force of their intensity. Donavan's eyes widened in Brian's direction.

"That."

"You let go?"

"Yep. You were iced while I moved the projectiles away."

"I never even—"

"None of these guys can. They don't even notice the time difference."

"But you weren't directly in harm's way."

"They were," Brian answered. "I can use it when I'm threatened or anyone in the group."

Tag gave a grunt, something close to admiration, surveying the now obliterated bar. Donavan swam in the awe of time control more than the evidence of his own ability.

"And you can hold them still in time for as long as you want?" he asked.

Brian smiled, looking wise beyond his youth. "Defensive, remember? Once the danger's gone, I can't hold time any more. I've tried. But it only works if I need to protect." His eyebrows shot up secretively, and he whispered, "Suuuppperr heeeroooo."

"Well, that answers that question," Harley said, ogling the wasted countertop with Tag. "Looks like another one of us finally has offense skills."

"Wait until we tell Jacob," Brian grinned, plopping himself on the floor in line with the door again.

"Hold on," Donavan said. "There's more of you—of us?"

"I was getting to that," Harley said, and Donavan sank back to his spot.

"How many?"

"Two... that we know of."

"Where are they?"

"They're coming," Harley informed him.

"Here?"

"Yes; they'll get the call."

"What's that mean, the call?"

Harley shifted, and his face glowed as he puffed his cigar. "You know how you knew to come here, but you didn't know how?"

Donavan paused to unravel another of Harley's weird-speak and nodded.

"We say that's getting called. You're not used to it yet. But soon you'll realize you go to certain places because you're... supposed to. And don't ask me why—" Harley stopped Donavan with his mouth half-open. "—Cuz I don't know why! I'm just like you. Don't know how it works. Well, the three of us got called here. We think it was to find you. The others are headed this way."

Donavan fell silent.

"You want to know why, don't you?"

"Don't you?" Donavan asked.

"It's like a mission," Brian chimed in. "Something we need to accomplish together."

"Who are the other two?"

"Jacob," Brian continued, "our leader. And RJ. He's our, umm..."

"Rock," Tag put in. "He's our rock."

Harley laughed in the cloud of his smoke.

Donavan tried not to let confusion get the better of him, afraid to speak and reveal his doubt.

"Until you, RJ was our only friend on offense. And he's strong... but in a different way. You'll meet him," Brian added, cutting off the next question. "We all met because of Jacob, which is basically why he's in charge."

"Where did you meet?"

"Different places and situations. But all of us—the Army. Everyone but you, that is. And we don't know why." They seemed to anticipate his next question. "You're the first person found by someone other than Jake. The first person without military background, come to think of it."

Donavan shuffled through a million more questions while he closed his eyes to sort through what he'd heard. His probing turned into an intense urge to fight in an instant, and he jumped to his feet as his eyes flew open. The others sprang to their feet after him, each tense and ready. Brian's gaze locked on the door, and Tag moved quickly to his side.

Harley eyeballed Donavan. "You felt it, too?"

He nodded in wonder.

"You getting connected to us fast. That's good. Real good."

"What exactly are we fi—defending ourselves against?"

Harley shook his head, and Donavan's urge subsided. It must have done likewise for the rest of them, because the tension evaporated into the room's shadows, and they all slid down to the floor again—everyone but Tag, who continued to scowl at the door.

"It's never the same. Right now, we still not sure who it is. We've fought against mobs, defused riots, taken out leaders aiming to overthrow governments, underground movements, revolts."

"Homeland Security has gotten a lot of help lately," Tag said tersely.

"I stopped an Iranian carrier from firing on a US plane once," Brian said, overtly proud. "Kept us from World War III."

"Like fun you did," Tag growled.

"How do you know? Were you there—oh, that's right. You were iced!"

"If you can't touch a speeding bullet when you're timelocked, how exactly did you divert a carrier?"

"Take a swing and let me show you!"

"Oh, like you'd last a second after I— "

"Harley, no one can touch a bullet except Jacob!" Tag cut off Brian in an attempt to get Harley on his side. "He's so full of— "

"That's enough!" Harley snapped, his cigar dancing from one end of his mouth to the other. "Let's focus."

"So you guys are defensive," Donavan said, aware that this may not be the first time Harley had played peacemaker between these two, "but not invincible, I take it."

Harley shook his head. "No. It's hard to take us down, but no, we're not invincible. Only Jake is bulletproof."

"He can't be killed?"

"Can't be shot. There's a difference."

"Who knows about you—us?" *Us*—what had he become?

The wind awakened a small patch of dust that scuttled across the floor toward the shattered wood. Brian shifted nervously as Tag stayed pinned to the door.

"Very few."

"Rufus," Donavan said, reflecting. "He knows. You told him?"

Harley shook his head, and for a moment Donavan thought he'd asked a forbidden question.

"He was one of us."

"Was?"

"An example of our vulnerability. When Jacob met him, it was too late. Whoever got to him first did that to him. Wiped his memory. Took his ability. He knows who we are somehow, but he's... not able to... help. He's a shell of who he was. Same can happen to any of us if we're not careful."

Donavan shuffled more questions through his mind, connecting pieces.

"So Vincent Valentine—I take it he has something to do with all this? Is he the reason we're called together? To take him down?"

"Oh, please," Tag grimaced. "If it were just Valentine, you think it would have taken so long to put him away? It's bigger than that."

"Okay, so what is it?" An uncomfortable silence followed, a slight stirring of the wind his only answer. "Well, it's hard to be careful when you don't know what you're up against. None of us know what we're called for? What we're up against? It all seems a little vague, doesn't it?"

"What do you know about the highway 'remote control' pileups?" Harley asked.

The question felt like it came from left field; it took a minute for Donavan to gather its relevance.

"Those vehicles—whatever they are—they are part of this? They're why we were 'called'?"

Before an answer came, the hairs on the back of Donovan's neck stood up, and he was pushing himself past Tag the next moment. He found himself in the parking lot, forming a circle with the three others, their backs to one another.

There was something out there, and it wasn't good. He sensed it, but could see or hear nothing but the faint wind, distant traffic, and dim lights' hum overhead.

As quickly as it came, the sensation subsided, and he turned to face the others. "Was that one of them? One of those...things?"

"We don't have all the answers yet, Peterson," Tag frowned at him.

"So what are we supposed to do?" The query now came more from an actual physical need to move, to do *something,* from a deep-rooted instinct that had finally awakened and been called forth. Donavan didn't need knowledge in this moment; he needed *action.*

"We need to get," Harley said in a low, urgent tone. "Move!" His troops obeyed and put themselves in motion.

"So what's the plan?" Donavan asked the retreating figures, confusion and frustration toppling over the excitement that had been building.

They broke into a jog, and in fear, Donavan grabbed onto Brian. "Hey!"

Brian grimaced in sympathy. "What do you feel? Let go and find out what you think you should do."

Donavan tried. "I don't know... nothing. There's some sort of gap in us? "

"Right. That means it's not time." The others called to Brian as they slipped into the shadows, but Donavan still clutched at him. "We don't work well until we're all together. Until then, we *wait*."

He broke from Donavan's hold and started jogging toward the others.

"Hold on! How do I get ahold of you? When do we meet again?"

Brian laughed and turned to jog backwards, facing Donavan. "You'll just know. Oh, and Donavan. Always come on foot, okay? That's important."

"Why? Hold on!"

They were gone. He stood alone in the lot with nothing but shadow and wind left to prickle the back of his neck.

This couldn't be it. There couldn't be just a sense of needing without an answer as to why. A hole. A gap. It twisted inside as he considered the two other members he'd yet to meet.

That wasn't it.

Still, instinct surging inside needed completion, definition. He wanted all the answers *now*!

He broke into a jog the opposite direction of his new-found group, an idea formulating as he moved.

Chapter 14

Laney snapped the long lighter switch with a precise *click*, rewarding her with an instant flame from her gas fireplace. She put the lighter far out of reach of the girls then chuckled at herself when she remembered they were miles away. She'd come home ahead of them, giving them a few uninterrupted Grandma-Grandpa days before her folks would deliver them back—before the Charlie handoff tomorrow, of course.

Colorado had been a wonderful break from reality, but tonight she craved the comfort of her chair and time alone to read a new best-seller her mother had given her. She snuggled in with a contented sigh and even toyed with permanently amending her wine rule to two glasses.

The warming liquid in her second glass coupled with the sound of rain brought a glowing satisfaction to the evening. If the girls had been here, she would have turned the couch to face her picture window. They would curl up with a blanket in their jammies to watch the drops roll down the glass with innocent fascination. She regretted they weren't here to see this unseasonal weather with her, but the huge heavy drops of the late summer monsoon hit the window with force and slid down the surface in a solid sheet, washing away any possible discontent.

A hard knock at the door startled her away from reading. It was after eight and dark out. Not too late for a visitor, but she wasn't ready to greet anyone in yoga pants and a loose t-shirt that hung off one shoulder around a comfy cami.

She moved toward the door and caught a glance of herself in the entryway mirror. She checked to make sure she didn't look noticeably braless. Nope, all good. However, tight curls responding to the humidity had escaped her clip and fuzzed all over her head. After re-clipping them back, the knock repeated with increased urgency.

"Who is it?" she called while trying to see out the peephole. The dark, hooded figure outside her door made her suck in her breath. *Please, please, don't let it be Rodney.*

No answer came. Perhaps the person hadn't heard her over the rain. Before she could call out again, a more persistent knock sent her stumbling backward.

Thoughts of her door recently unlatched or unlocked leapt to the front of her mind. Was someone stalking her? Her eyes flew to the hall closet where she kept her gun's lockbox. She hesitated, weighing rational thought against alarm, when the insistent pounding on the door sent her scurrying.

She opened the closet and reached high on her tiptoes to the shelf... nothing. Her hands groped around for a second as if trying to convince her mind of what her eyes could not see.

"Laney!" A familiar, muffled voice called from the landing. Her mind processed its way through panic to recognition.

"Donavan?" Dropping back to flat feet, she scrambled to the door. "Donavan?" she called above the rain. It drove hard enough to soak the second story landing. She peered through the peephole again. "Is that you?"

"You're home!" Donavan's voice sounded strange under his hood. "Can I come in?"

She ditched her glasses onto her entry table and let him in. A small puddle followed him, gathering slowly around his feet.

"Donavan. Why are you soaked?" The heavy dampness of his hoodie didn't belong to someone who'd walked from their car to the second floor. More like a kid who got pranked and thrown into the pool fully dressed.

"Sorry," he apologized. He removed his hood to reveal his hair darkened with moisture.

"What are you doing here?" Laney closed the door while her mind raced for an explanation.

His eyebrows arched as if unprepared for the question. "I went...running."

"From your house? Okay, wow." Not what she expected to hear. "Next time you plan a six-mile run, you might wanna check the weather forecast first."

A small drop ran off Donavan's nose, dangled there a moment, then plummeted into the puddle below. Another drop took its place, and another, but nothing could distract Laney from the intensity in Donavan's eyes. Something about his stare made her gut tighten and her senses sharpen. She could feel her blood rushing... everywhere.

"Let me grab you a towel," she murmured, trying to avoid her inward confusion. She turned toward the bedroom only to have him pull her back by her arm. He sucked in his breath like he'd been caught off guard as much as she was.

She hesitated, eyeing him in question, but he stepped closer without a word. He searched her face for something, though she couldn't think what. She had never seen him like this—flustered but imploring all at once. Needing something. Afraid of something.

Something was wrong.

"Donavan? What is it?"

He didn't answer her. Instead, he pulled her into him, his rain-soaked hoodie dampening her t-shirt when they met. She opened her mouth to protest just as his lips touched hers. Barely, softly. His hand released her arm and slid behind her, gathering her in a firm but soggy embrace, until all of her pressed against him. His lips didn't hurry. They drew her into a kiss with a slow deliberateness that gave her time to respond.

Laney wavered. But only a fraction of a second before her body blocked any logical objection. And she had plenty. But this...his kiss...it was everything she had expected and imaged it could be, and she caved.

When Laney thought she might melt into the puddle below them, Donavan pulled away and stepped back in the same soft motion.

The space between them was just enough room for Laney's senses to rush back home along with all the logical objections. She copied him, stepping back even further. "What... was *that*?" The breathiness of her voice made her blush.

He seemed to consider his answer and would have reached for her again if her upraised hand hadn't stopped him.

"You got my voicemail, right? I thought I made it clear we needed to give each other some time and space," she said, growing more in control of her words.

"Is ten days enough?" A small grin relaxed his face as if he knew how successful the kiss had been in making her innards go haywire. This time, though, the playful banter wasn't what she needed to hear on the heels of her let's-not-see-each-other-for-awhile request. His flippant attitude lit a fuse in her.

"Really? Is that what you thought?"

His face fell, and she guessed he'd caught on to his bad timing. "No, no. I mean, I didn't think—"

"You didn't think, what, Donavan? You didn't think about whether the girls were here or not? Didn't think it would matter if you showed up unannounced?" She searched his face trying to understand what the need had been, what the searching in his eyes had meant. But the intimate touch had produced a new crack in their fragile relationship. She couldn't have him assume what was broken could be so easily fixed. "You just 'happened' to show up all wet and adorable out of the blue, not even for a minute figuring, 'Hey, good time for a booty call!'?"

"No! It wasn't like that."

"No? 'Cause that's how it looks from here." She fumbled to cross her arms over her dampened t-shirt and glare at him, hoping that her quick, short breaths and burning cheeks wouldn't weaken her case.

Donavan froze, his deer-in-the-headlights expression fumbling with recovery. "Laney. I can explain. Just give me—"

"Save it." She turned on her heel out of the room and returned with a large bath towel that she tossed at him. "You need to dry yourself off, get back to running in the rain or call Uber, or whatever you need to do. But you need to *leave*."

His eyes held something beyond regret; they were panic-stricken. "Laney, no. I'm sorry—"

She ignored how his desperation pulled at her heartstrings.

"Spare me, okay?" she huffed. There was something vulnerable about his open-mouthed stare, palms up plea that rocked her emotions like a small boat caught in a current. In a fierce need for him to get out before she drowned in the wake, the words flowed in a rush: "What do you think—this is a game? That floating in and out of my life is a matter of convenience or—or depends on how you feel at the moment? That if you're confused or—or lonely, *hey*! Just go find *Laney*! She's lonely too. She'll be happy to hook up with me. Is that it?" Her voice grew louder and less controlled with each word. "I'm not the kind of girl who sits around and waits for *your* kind of guy."

"Laney." His eyes were frantic. "We have to talk."

"Donavan, there is no 'we.'" She moved to the door. "And I don't have to do anything I don't want to."

He pushed the door shut before she could open it more than an inch.

"Laney, please! Please, just listen."

"Don't do that!" her voice shrilled. "Don't you dare look at me like that and beg me to—to do anything." She was coming unglued and felt powerless to stop it as she jabbed a finger at him. "I have worked *too* hard for this life to allow someone to come and go as they wish, taking whatever part of me they want whenever they go."

"Right, I know," he nodded emphatically. "Because it would be like when Charlie left all over again. And that would be too painful. It would hurt *all over again.*"

She opened her mouth to spew more fury, but nothing came out except exasperated air. She sputtered and stalled until, reluctantly, she answered: "Yes. Exactly."

"Laney, you aren't the only one who felt cheated when you got left behind, left to deal with *unexpected* heartbreak." His voice, gentle and deep, held the same compassionate tone he used when they had poured out their grief over wine and music at his house so many nights ago. He had her attention, caught up in the memory, and she remained still, listening. "I mean, you hang on to a little thread of hope that it will all work out somehow. That you'll wake up one morning and everything will be fine again. You know down deep that's not gonna happen, but still, there it is—that crazy hope. And then when that thread disappears... man, the *pain*. I get it. You'd do anything not to be in that situation again."

An unexpected tear rimmed Laney's eye. "Yes," she whispered back.

He leaned against the back of her couch, the towel neglected in his hands. "That day I got the divorce papers—that was my thread of hope snapping." His eyes shot to the floor, the confession coming slowly. "I had thought I had prepared for it. I knew it was coming. I just..." He shook his head and shrugged. "Apparently, you're never ready for the end until it comes."

They were both silent, the hurt too thick for words. It was the Donavan she knew before her. Sincere, unselfish, open. Not the guy everyone saw on TV.

"Donavan," Laney spoke up, choosing her words with care. She'd let the brutality accusations go for the moment and deal with the issue of *them.* "Why did you let me believe—let everyone believe—that you were already divorced?"

His smile was grim. "Just easier. When people ask about your wife, you can only say 'She's fine' so many times before the questions about her illness become...invasive. Those looks and stares are far worse than any you ever experience saying you are divorced, trust me."

She didn't reply.

"Laney." His voice was pleading again. Sitting on the back frame of the couch, he was almost eye level with her. "I wasn't trying to trick you. I considered my marriage over; I moved on. I just didn't expect my reaction to seeing it in writing. And didn't expect you to be there to see it."

"I bet the back door didn't expect it either."

His lips tugged upward. "That's sorta the reason I'm here."

"You're here to talk to me about your back door?"

He rubbed his neck and shivered, revealing that the chill of his wet clothes had caught up with him. "It's complicated, Laney. I don't even know where to begin."

"That man...the one at the police station...."

He vehemently shook his head. "It's not what it looks like. I swear."

She sighed, her resolve to kick him out washed away with the rain. Compassion and curiosity had beaten down her resistance. "Let's start by drying you off." She took the towel from his hands and reached up to rub his head like she did the girls after their baths. He pushed back against the couch to widen the space between them and grabbed the end of the towel.

"I got it," he said quickly.

The air tensed a degree as she let him tug the towel from her fingers, avoiding her touch.

"Oooo-kaaay," she said, uncertain how to read this new behavior. Perhaps he wanted to show her his ability to keep his hands to himself. "How about I make you something hot to drink?" she asked, stepping back to give him room. "Coffee, tea, hot chocolate?"

"Coffee would be great," he said, rubbing his head vigorously.

"I'll find you something to put on, and we can throw your sweatshirt in the dryer."

She headed to the bedroom, kicking herself the whole way.

What are you doing? Making him coffee? Doing his laundry? Good grief....

He had to leave. He just had to. Nothing good would come out of this.

§ § § § §

Donavan watched the mug move to Laney's lips and forced himself to glance away. He only had one chance to find out. He couldn't blow it by letting those lips distract him.

When he'd left the abandoned Jake's behind with that gaping hole inside, his first thought was of Laney. He must see her *now,* his body told him. He had wrecked the door with her there, the only other time his strength had defied explanation. Something deep within told him there had to be a connection.

If she was one of *them*...then it wasn't his discovery to make. Like Harley and the others who had waited patiently for Donavan to acknowledge what he was, he'd have to nudge Laney toward her own discovery...*if* he was right. Laney hadn't busted up any doors or bars lately, so there was no telling what she felt.

That was first priority here—what she *felt.*

But the kiss?

Obviously, he should have formed a better plan. Any plan. She was right; suddenly showing up at her door reeked of desperation and diminished his chances of her discussing what she knew about *the call.* He needed her to be a willing participant in a conversation that involved questionable superheroes and unseen villains. How does one bring that subject up?

He began to understand Harley's tactics a little better now.

But the kiss had unintentionally done more than confirm she for *him.* Without explanation, an internal response awakened in every nerve in his body to a level of intensity he'd never felt before...no, that was inaccurate. That he hadn't felt since the night she slept so close to him, a wall apart in the guest room. That night, when he'd touched his bedroom wall between them, he had felt that an arch of electricity could overtake them. Tonight, that arch had met, and the kiss had almost undone him. He couldn't categorize it—it was unchartable. Beyond comprehension. He had had to back away from the sensation when it threatened to cross over from an acute stimulation to actual pain.

Conclusion: it could only be part of a supernatural bond... right?

Laney didn't seem to have the same reaction. She had been so ticked at him, maybe she missed it. Maybe she was trying to hide it from him.

He drank from his own mug and tried to wash the words forward from the back of his throat.

"I didn't come here to 'hook up'," he finally said, "—don't give me that look. I mean it. I actually wanted to make sure you understand why I have to go." He'd been thinking through this part, at least, during his run here. "I'm disappearing for a while, and I didn't want you to get the wrong idea. They're having me work undercover on the Valentine case."

"What? Why? I thought you were suspended?" They sat close on the hearth ledge, letting the weak flames warm his body and create sparks that danced across her troubled expression.

"Laney, that video you saw of me on the news... this will seem impossible, but it's not what it looks like. Valentine manipulated the situation to make it look like my doing. So yeah, well, it's complicated." He grimaced, in disbelief that he could so easily lie to her. "Anyway, I won't be around, Parker will be with my mom, and... I just thought you should know."

"So... you came to say goodbye?"

"Sort of." He groped for the next line and wished he'd asked for a drink stiffer than coffee. "Remember the back door?"

"Oh, my gosh, the door again?"

"No, wait, just listen. I need to explain about that. And it will sound crazy."

"I'm not sure I've heard *sane* yet."

He laughed a little and shook his head. "Yeah, well, hang on.... So here's the thing. There's something I need to ask you, something I need to find out. Well, actually it's a favor I need to ask. And I know it's going to seem... juvenile or, or stupid, but if you just, just this once, do this one thing—"

"Donavan, please. Ask already."

He put his mug down and took hers too, careful not to touch her. He tried to speak again, but after a study of her face, half-lit in the firelight, words abandoned him. Instead, he leaned forward and let the electricity of her nearness course through him once again. It thrilled him with painful ecstasy and sucked the breath from him, but still he leaned closer, letting it. Laney's eyes flashed first with confusion then disbelief.

"Donavan—"

"This is the favor—"

"You shouldn't—" she protested without confidence, and her sentence died out.

He reached forward and cupped her fire-warmed cheek with his hand. She grabbed his wrist, and it was all that he could do not to gasp from the flow of energy that overwhelmed him. A second passed while he tried to read her; her hold relaxed, and her thumb—intentionally?—stroked his pulse point. Her eyes closed, her lips parted.

He had to know.

His lips touched hers with only the lightest of pressure as the *something* surged with lightning speed through his veins. Still he lingered, until he thought he might die waiting for her to express the same.

When he could take the intensity no longer, Donavan put inches between them and dropped his hand. "Keep your eyes closed," he said in a low voice he fought to control. "Tell me what you feel."

"Donavan—"

"This is the favor. If you want to help me, answer the question honestly." Her breath came in small soft gasps so close to his. "How did that... feel?"

"Nice?" she asked.

"You're not sure?" he said harsher than he meant to.

"Sorry. Nice," she said with more certainty as her lashes pressed into her cheeks. "I meant... *nice*."

"Describe nice."

"Very, very nice?"

"What else? Laney, please."

"My... my heart is beating fast," she fumbled. "I'm warm. All over. And I'm thinking this is a very clever way of making me forgive you."

"Does it bother you? When I touch you?"

"Bother me?" Her eyes flickered open and their shine in the firelight held the question.

He moved further back to let his overwhelmed senses subside. He tried not to sound impatient, but hope was fleeing. "Nothing else? That's all?"

"Donavan? What's wrong? You asked me—"

"Thank you—yes. I asked and you told me exactly what you felt. I just needed to know that."

She pushed back curls that had escaped onto her forehead, and for the first time, Donavan noticed a long scab across her elbow. The cut from the shattered glass. It was just finishing its healing process. What had taken him minutes had taken her over a week. He hadn't thought to ask Harley about the phenomenon. Whatever it was, Laney didn't have it.

What was worse, he *needed* her in complicated ways that he still hadn't unraveled... but she didn't need him.

Tonight's events had taught him who he was and at the same time led him to this dead end. He would have to go, leave her, and finish whatever this "call" was without her.

Goodbye was necessary…yet very problematic.

The rain picked up and beat against the window with attitude. In the landing outside the door, the wind drummed the water wildly onto the exposed concrete. Laney raised herself up high enough to glance over the couch at the door before settling back.

"What is it?" Donavan asked.

"Just making sure I closed the door all the way. I've been having trouble with the latch lately."

"Your door comes open? Let me see it."

Together they crossed the room and examined the lock.

"I don't know if it's the door so much as me," Laney said, hugging herself against the chill that settled over them away from the fire. "I think I'm not being careful about shutting it. I turn my back, and it's suddenly open."

Donavan tensed. "It's happened before?"

She shrugged. "Two or three times."

"The night you said you 'freaked out' with the kitchen knife?"

Her eyes darted away, though a blush had no trouble staying. "Well...yeah."

"Ever see anyone? Anything missing?"

"No. I mean, I thought I heard stuff, but it was always something else. Look, I'm just being forgetful, Donavan. It's nothing."

"Where do you keep the gun?"

She looked startled as if remembering. "I was looking for it when you knocked... I think I pushed it too far back to reach. Here, on the closet shelf..."

Donavan made his way to where the gun should be and swiped the entire length and width. He came up empty. His face grew grim, his memory drawn to the gun's old hiding place in his own closet that had been shuffled around.

He moved past Laney, ordering, "Stay there," as he passed. He did a sweep of all the rooms and stopped by the dryer to retrieve his sweatshirt.

"You think someone broke in and stole it?" she asked him.

"Laney, you need to call the police and report the gun stolen. Right away." He moved to the door as he pulled the hoodie over the T-shirt she'd lent him.

"You're leaving me? *Now*?"

"I can't be here when they get here. I have to go."

"What is with you?" The heat in her voice had nothing to do with passion or an energy surge like he had. For sure, whatever he felt when they were together never happened for her. She threw her hand toward their abandoned mugs on the fireplace ledge. "What was *that*?"

"Lock the door behind me. Then call the police."

"You can't be serious? Donavan, what's going on?"

On the landing, the rain lashed at Donavan, bullying his hoodie once again. He couldn't stop himself from looking back at Laney, but he wasn't just unnerved by the missing gun. *The call* was coming on strong. It told him to find the others, to be with them. Laney's expression told him she definitely did not feel compelled to go anywhere he was going.

"You are seriously messed up, Donavan." Her simple clothes and frazzled hair never looked so inviting, even as her voice told him this was over. He wanted to stay and hold her by the fire till every circuit in his body fried his brain, hold her till she quit looking at him like a traitor.

She held the door between them. "Thanks for coming," she said, her voice raw with anger.

"I am so sorry, Laney," he said and stuffed his hands into his pockets. The words stung him as he told her, "I won't be bothering you again."

"You can bet on it." She slammed the door behind him, the echo chasing him down the stairs into the wet night.

Chapter 15

The driving rain did little to hamper Donavan's stride when he ran out of Laney's apartment complex. Drops pelted his face, an aggressive annoyance he sought to ignore along with the lump that had formed in his throat. His feet pounded out a rhythm that seemed to repeat the same thing with every footfall: She. Does. Not. Feel. It.

This evidence ripped through him and rearranged everything. Laney voiced anger and confusion at his stupid attempt to draw *it* out of her—how could he blame her?—and now little hope of their being together remained. His body told him to move on, but his heart wasn't so eager.

His destination, unsure but urgent, propelled him through another puddle and down an unfamiliar street. He forced himself to pause to a standing jog while considering if his feet moved toward somewhere by accident or design. A weight in his pocket made him pause. A clunky metal object joggled in the fabric—the screw from the broken back door; he'd absently pocketed it when he set out on his run. It felt wrong. Puzzled, he examined its molested shape in the shallow light of the streetlamp. Subconsciously he had gripped it the minute he had thrust his hand in his pocket outside Laney's door. Now it sat in his palm, a twisted knot of unusable metal.

He had done that?

His feet started again, off the sidewalk into the wet street, called to move. The mangled screw confirmed the truth, one he'd been waiting for Laney to verify. The incredible strength that came and went within him resurfaced around Laney. She might not cause his power, but she was more than just a source of the electricity that raced through him; her presence acted as an amplifier... sometimes. His brow creased as he considered all the times she *hadn't.*

He needed to talk to them. He needed to figure out what to do and, most of all, he needed to get on with it. With a rumble emerging from his throat, he pressed forward, running to who knows where, wondering how... when....

A housing development lay ahead. Still, Donavan didn't slow until he approached a playground in the middle of the community, which stretched out on a strip of grass, still dark green in the Arizona autumn. A jungle gym arched over wood chips on one side. Eerie, empty swings squeaked in the wind, their only audience the bushes that surrounded them. Beyond, a dark, open street lined itself with randomly lit houses, a few cars, and sidewalks de-peopled from the weather.

Donavan gripped the monkey bars above him and leaned on his arms to catch his breath; his shadow arched away from the glow of the light poles lining the edge of the empty lot.

A dark figure appeared across the park, black leather slick and shiny from the rain. Tag. He gave his head a cautious toss in Donavan's direction as Brian emerged from the shadows of the east side. Harley joined from the last end, eyes wide, damp cigar hanging from his lips. He tried to draw from it and then held it out for inspection as if just realizing its uselessness. The cigar went back between clamped lips anyway. They all studied Donavan expectantly from their different corners of the playground. The unrelenting rain brought tension even as they closed the gap and gathered around their newest member.

"Well?" Harley growled.

"There's seven of us," Donavan offered flatly. He knew no other reason they had gathered than for him to tell what he knew.

"Come again?"

"I'm number six, but I'm not the last one. There's a number seven."

"Oh, shut up," Tag said, rolling his eyes. No one else spoke up. Tag grunted in disgust as if their silence sickened him. "So where is he?" he challenged Donavan, but his confidence sounded watered down with the rain.

Donavan shook his head and ground the words out between clenched teeth. "No. No, it's a *she*, and she doesn't know. But I'm positive of her effect on us... well, on *me*. But there's no way on earth she's coming here."

The rain slowed, allowing this new information to soak in.

"It's a woman?" Tag spat out.

Brian's grin could be heard in his one-word response. "Sweet!"

A twitch of Harley's head in Brian's direction put an end to the joking. "There's never been," Harley said. Donavan had expected doubt and resistance, but underneath that, he had hoped they had "felt" Laney too.

"Well, there is now." As he said the words out loud, his confidence grew. It didn't matter what she *felt.* What he felt around her was all the proof he needed, that and the twisted hardware in his pocket. "She's not ready to join us yet, not with her history with me. But at least we know what the gap is."

Everyone quieted while they weighed Donavan's words in the disappearing drizzle.

"We need Jacob," Brian offered.

"I think we should talk to her ourselves," Tag countered.

"We're not going anywhere," Harley snapped.

"So we wait till she comes around?" Tag said, his volume increasing. His tone revived their tension, and in an instant everyone spoke at once, chests close, bodies rigid, each vying to be heard over the others.

"We aren't being called to do anything yet—"

"We all know it's time. If 'Seven' isn't joining us, what are we waiting for?"

"What's she look like?" —that from Brian.

"—stay put until—"

"—trying to convince her—"

"—never going to happen—"

"—without her powers—"

"And that's final!" Harley's voice carried the conversation to conclusion.

An invisible force grabbed the surrounding energy, and without communication, all four men turned outward, backs together. Donavan's strength rose and fell within him as if stretched by an unseen hand. The wind silenced, and all was still again.

"What. Was. That?"

The whites of Harley's eyes consumed his face as he turned toward Donavan. "They know we're here."

"Who?" Donavan asked, only to be ignored.

"How many?" Brian asked, a much easier question for Harley to answer. His gift.

"Three—no, four..."

His hesitation earned an angry glare from Tag.

Something rustled along the bushes at the edge of the park, and they all turned as one. Brian swiveled to watch behind them. "How'd they find us?"

"How'd you get here?" Harley asked Donavan suspiciously.

"I ran."

"Brian?"

"Same."

"Tag?"

A brooding silence.

"Tag!"

"I drove my bike, okay? But I parked it down the street."

"It doesn't matter, you fool!"

Brush vibrated further down the park; the group pivoted in unison. The glare of the streetlamps along the edges of the park revealed nothing but vacant play equipment in the green. Beyond that, the dark road held its secrets. The team moved closer to the center of the soggy grass in unspoken agreement. Every hair on Donavan's neck rose, but there was no way to see each direction at once. He prayed Tag had his back as well as Michael would have.

"I don't understand," Donavan said, and then the foliage erupted with a shower of leaves and water. A sleek, black machine shot across the grass, only it didn't move on wheels. It took Donavan a second to register it was running. That was his last thought before the world stood still at Brian's grasp. The metal contraption flew across the open space, back into the bushes, a victim of a quick zap from Tag.

The shock sent him reeling backward. "Metal," he cursed as he struggled to stay on his feet.

Brian had barely released them when a second machine slammed Donavan almost straight on. He never saw it coming. Someone shrieked, and he hoped it wasn't him. He scrambled for anything he could grab hold of and came up with some metal appendage on the contraption; it crumbled in his grasp and soared into the swings, where it twisted up in the chains with a crash. In the seconds it took to untangle itself, Donavan got his first real look at the assailant. The towering figure stood like a man, but all the parts were wrong. Arms and legs, made of slick black metal, unfolded as if a strange vehicle had come to life. Even though he saw no hands or feet, the pointed ends of its limbs could grasp and move objects, this evident as it pushed the chains away with dexterity. But most disproportionate to the body was an enormously long, narrow head, dark and reflective, silver slits carved out of the side of its angular shape.

A gasp filled Donavan's lungs, and then the figure fled into the darkness. Beside him, a creature sailed away from Brian, caught in his time trap while Harley growled at the sleek form about to slam him into the ground. Not a second too soon, Donavan's fist intervened and sent the black metal zinging back to the bushes.

Harley struggled to his feet behind Donavan without so much as a nod of gratitude. His powers of pre-knowledge only got him so far, but he didn't appear to appreciate the help in combat. Donavan ignored the slight and turned back to the others, waiting for another clash.

"They're gone," Harley said, his cigar lost in battle. "Not coming back."

"What were they after?" Donavan asked.

"Your motorcycle, idiot!" Brian hissed at Tag, his easy-going nature evaporating. "Us! They are after us because of your stupidity. You know better—"

"Would someone tell me what's going on?" Donavan insisted.

Harley didn't answer; he busied himself surveying the ground in what looked like a search for his cigar. Tag appeared visibly shaken. His trembling body convinced Donavan that shocking something made of metal gave Tag more pain than satisfaction. Brian sighed and simmered. Per usual, he offered Donavan the only spoken explanation.

"There's a reason I told you to come on foot. Remember? We don't know what these things are; in fact, that's the first time we've been face to face. All we know is they... sense us. They can track us. But only when we're in a vehicle."

"Why? The metal?"

"No. We think it's the fuel."

"Dang Oil Eaters," Tag muttered.

"Oil Eaters?"

Brian's lip twitched, humor returning to his eyes. "That's what Tag calls them. Sucked the oil and gas right out of his last motorcycle."

"How do you know if you never saw them before?"

Tag gave him the *idiot* glare that told him once again it was impossible to explain impossible things.

Harley moved to the edge of the grass and inspected the slick, wet asphalt. He put his hands on his hips and seemed lost in thought... or agitation.

"Those things. Same as the freeway robots on the news, you reckon?" He spat and wiped at his face. "We need Number Seven. Then we need to get to Jake."

No one argued. Donavan struck his fist into the side of the monkey bars and the side crumbled down, trapping Tag between its bars.

"Dude!" Tag scowled at the newcomer.

Donavan pretended not to hear him and turned away. The amusement on the others' face told him that he'd earned points.

"Serves you right," Brian said. "Next time leave your bike at home." He jogged alongside Donavan out of the playground, leaving his buddy to figure out a way to un-cage himself.

Chapter 16

"Mommy, have you been listening?" Urie's voice held the type of whine that reminded Laney of scraping her knuckles on a cheese grater.

The mommy in question unbuckled Ellie from her car seat and gathered her in her arms while turning toward the impatient sister to reply. "Yes, honey. Sounds great." The warm embrace from her youngest was short-lived, her wriggling body demanding release.

"So can we?" Urie implored.

"Can we what?" Laney shut the car door and hit the lock button on the fob twice to be sure.

Her eldest daughter sighed. "You weren't listening."

A headache furrowed Laney's brow as she moved the girls up the sidewalk to the apartment. Their morning of duck feeding and breakfast by the lake hadn't been the mood-lifter Laney had hoped for. "Let's go in, get some water, and relax on the couch; I'm sure I'll be a better listener then."

"No, no," Ellie pleaded with a tug on her mom's hand. "Cawtwheel! Cawtwheel, Mama!"

Laney hid an eye roll. Impressing her girls with her gymnastic skills remained a slight perk over the fabulous stepmother Victoria. But her pounding head informed her she wouldn't be intentionally turning herself upside down anytime soon, though.

"No, do that roundoff thingy," Urie interjected.

But Laney's mind had returned to a meeting Charlie had initiated the day before. He had excitedly thrust an envelope at her when she agreed to meet him at a coffee shop before Alice Whyte would deliver the kids back to Arizona.

"What's this?" She examined the envelope's contents and groaned.

"It's a ticket," he said, as if she didn't understand. "For you. It's good for any continental flight. Free!"

Her anger rose so quickly, it had been hard to get words out. "What are you trying to pull, Charlie?"

"I got my bonus, Ally—Laney. And I wanted to share. It's for you to go on a vacation of your own." His eyes held hope; his warm smile tried too hard.

"While you go to Hawaii." Laney said it as a statement, not a question.

"Sure," he winked. "Why not?"

She fought for control of her voice. "Your manipulation knows no bounds."

"No, really, Laney. No strings attached. Tori and I just want you to be happy, too."

And that did it. Just when she thought he could sink no lower or say anything more insulting than the last time. Be happy? Blood boiled in Laney's veins and took over her remaining self-control. She ripped the ticket in half and shoved it at Charlie's chest.

"What the—"

"Wanna make me happy, Charlie? Stop trying to fix me or use me or—or undermine me. You can't buy my kids away from me! They are not going to Hawaii with you! Go home to your cute little secretary and leave me alone. *That* would make me happy."

Her ego, exposed and bruised, had tangled Laney's emotions into a splitting headache that lingered into today. Though the lake had been moderately successful, she hated that at the moment occupying the girls felt like a draining chore instead of a pleasure.

A car approached, and the two girls squinted against the rising sun to see inside. It slowed to a stop and idled on the sidewalk beside them; a familiar voice called out cheerfully.

"Mr. Peter!" Urie squealed, not quite capturing the name. She ran to hug his legs when he climbed out of the car. Ellie followed close behind. "Did you bring Parker to play?"

Donavan smiled, but the tension in his shoulders said he wasn't any better than when Laney had the displeasure of his company in her apartment. Reflective sunglasses kept his eyes hidden; he wore a ball cap pulled low on his head, and a black jacket hung heavy on his shoulders. Laney bristled despite the small leap of her double-crossing heart.

The passenger door opened and a young female emerged to stand beside Donavan on the walkway. Laney's head constricted tighter in a rhythm of pain and weariness.

"Brie!" Urie squealed once more, reaching for the second set of legs. Ellie looked less sure but followed suit, her eyes wide. The girl with long, dark, poker-straight hair smiled wide and warmly greeted the little ones.

"Laney, you remember George and Callie's daughter, Brie? She was at my house for the Summer's End party."

"Oh, sorry. I don't think I got a chance to say hi then," Laney said, shaking the young woman's outstretched hand. Laney tried to hide her quizzical look behind her own shades. "What brings you here with this guy? I figured it'd be a long while before Donavan swung this way again." She only tried a little to hide her caustic tone.

"Brie is in her second year at ASU, majoring in early childhood development. Sometimes she watches Parker when she's not studying."

"I got to play with your girls at the party. They're so adorable," said the bright smile, both natural and mature. It lacked the hopped-up brightness of Victoria that made you want to reach for a dimmer switch.

"Well, it was good to see you again," Laney said cautiously and took the girls by the hand. "But if you'll excuse us—"

"Laney, I was wondering if we could speak for a minute," Donavan requested.

A small laugh bubbled in her throat. "You're joking, right? You can't be that forgetful. I think I was pretty clear about... when our next meeting would be."

"It'll only take a minute." He glanced to Brie as if to cue her, and, in turn, the young girl offered Laney's daughters each a hand.

"Hey, girls, wanna show me the doll house you were telling me about?"

"Yawh!" whooped Ellie.

Urie looked hopeful. "Can we, Mom? Can Brie come upstairs with us?"

Laney gripped the keys until her hand smarted, and with a set jaw she glared at Donavan. "Sure, girls. But only for a minute. We have a lot to do today."

They started as a group up the sidewalk when Donavan took the keys from her and handed them to Brie. "First door on the landing."

"Great," the cheerful girl responded, and her two companions bounced along contently beside her.

Something in Donavan's manner sent up red flags. He took Laney by the arm and led her toward the vehicle with all the casualness of a couple headed out on a date. She yanked her arm away when he reached to open the car door for her.

"What is going on?" She kept her voice loud and strong, masking the irrational alarm that grew inside.

"We need to talk."

"We do *not* need to talk, Donavan. There is absolutely nothing to say. How dare you bring someone here with you? You think because you brought Brie along I'm not going to freak out on you? That I'll make nice so that the girls won't think less of Parker's dad? You really have no idea—"

"For having nothing to say, you're doing a pretty good job." Donavan leaned back against the car and crossed his arms.

Laney shook all over. Her head pounded harder, and she bit her tongue to keep from rambling more. "I'm calling the cops."

"I am the cops."

"Correction. You *were* a cop. You may think you're fooling me with this undercover BS, but when the police came to take my report, they seemed very curious about your missing gun because *you* had gone missing, too. They were pretty nosy and very insistent that if I had any news of your whereabouts, I was to contact them as soon as possible. Truth is you're a wanted man, Donavan." She paused and squared her chin for effect. "Just not by me."

He stood stone still against the car for several, long seconds. Laney tried to hold her ground, but her nerves were fraying.

"It's time you knew what was going on," he finally spoke and opened the car door for her.

"Uh-uh. It's time for you to leave."

"This concerns you and the girls—their safety."

Laney thought she might explode from fury. "You leave them out of this, Donavan."

"Get in."

"Not gonna happen. Goodbye, Donavan."

She turned away and felt a vice grip on her arm. She gasped as he pulled her closer against him.

"There isn't time for this nonsense, Laney. What I need to discuss with you isn't about us. It's much more important." She heard him suck in his breath, and he let her go. The nagging question returned, the one that couldn't quite place why he pushed her away when she got too close. "But not here. Get in."

Laney stepped away, but found a hard object poking into her side. Alarm turned to horror as she envisioned a gun in his jacket pocket aimed right at her.

"I'm afraid I'm going to have to insist."

Laney froze for what seemed like an eternity, unable to move, unable to speak. She searched for something in Donavan's face, but his concealed eyes kept her clueless.

"Donavan," she whispered, finally finding a small voice. "What are you doing?"

"Get in," he repeated, and she cringed at the feelingless authoritative tone.

"Don't—" The object jabbed into her side, and she stifled a scream while she climbed into the car on the driver's side.

"Scoot over," he commanded, waving his pocket at her. She obeyed, climbing over the console, and he followed her in. "Buckle up."

She buckled, her mind racing for any means of escape.

"The girls…" she said in something close to a whimper.

Donavan buckled and stared ahead for a moment. Fear settled over Laney, and she whimpered again covering her mouth to keep the sound from escaping. It seemed to break him, and he turned to her, removing his glasses. She found the eyes of the Donavan she once knew looking at her. Soft with an edge of steely confidence.

"Please trust me, Laney. One last time." He shifted his face closer, and she recoiled, hand on the door handle. "One hour," he said. "That's all I ask. Give me one hour of your time to listen with an open mind, without judgment." She found it improbable that she could endure his company that long, and he seemed to read her mind; he swallowed hard. "One hour."

She remained silent for a moment, but he didn't move away. She swallowed hard too.

"Exactly one hour, Donavan. No guns, nothing crazy or stupid. We can talk for one hour, and you're going to let me hold your cell phone while you do. Any funny business and I call the cops." Somehow using his phone instead of hers made sense. "They'll... they can track your phone, you know."

A tug pulled the corner of his mouth. He fished into his pocket and handed her his phone. "Deal. Just one more thing." He reached behind her seat and pulled out a helmet. It was a smaller style, more for a skateboarder than someone on a motorcycle, but hard and durable looking. "Put this on."

"Huh?"

"In case the ride gets a little rough." Donavan jammed the car into gear and sped out of the lot with a screech of tires. He whipped the car out onto the street, moving well above the speed limit.

"Donavan!"

"Helmet."

She obeyed. "The girls! I can't leave them."

"They're with Brie."

"I don't even know her."

"I do. She's great with kids, and I've paid her for the afternoon."

"You what?"

The car barely slowed when it entered the on-ramp to the freeway and then picked up even greater speed as it neared the wide lanes ahead.

"Donavan, wait! Where are we going?"

"Away from here."

"This wasn't part of the deal—slow down!"

Donavan ignored her and zipped through the traffic. She glanced at his determined face and kept a tight grip on his phone.

"You have fifty-nine minutes left," she said when he didn't slow down. "Talk."

He tried to hide the smile that threatened to pull up the corners of his mouth and let it fade into sincerity before he spoke.

"What I have to say isn't easy. In fact, it isn't even believable. Just... just give me a chance."

She tensed but said, "I'm listening."

"How do you think the sliding door broke?"

"Un. Be. Lievable. You are obsessed with that—"

"Just answer me. How did it break?"

She threw her hands up in exasperation. "You—you slammed it. Hard."

"Have you ever heard of anyone slamming a sliding glass door so hard that they not only shattered it but also bent the frame out of the wall?" He suddenly swerved around a truck and ducked behind another one, producing a little cry from Laney.

"Have you?" Donavan's glasses returned to his face, and she couldn't read him, but his voice remained old, calm Donavan.

She clung to that one piece of sanity. "No. I guess not."

"Remember all the scratches we got from the glass? How I was spotted all over from the bleeding cuts?" He zipped away from the trucks and crossed three lanes to pull alongside a camper, as if playing hide and seek from something. "Remember?"

Laney kept a death grip on the door. "I remember, yes!"

"How long did it take for them to heal?"

"What?"

"Just answer."

"I don't understand what you're getting at, Donavan—watch the road!"

His smile was grim. "My hour, my questions."

"Fifty-six minutes and this pink mark right here is where my last scab fell off. The others are all healed up."

"So maybe ten days?"

"Sure." She glanced at the speedometer. Seventy-eight mph.

"Now think back. Ever remember seeing any on me?"

"I don't know! I—I guess not, maybe."

"I stopped bleeding after you left; within hours my wounds had vanished."

"Okaaaay... if you say so, I believe you. Now please, Donavan, slow down."

"Why do you think that is? How can you explain it?"

"I don't know! I'm not a doctor! You have incredible hemoglobin?"

"It's unnatural, Laney. All of it. To be strong enough to break the door like that, to have my cuts heal so quickly..." He trailed off as if expecting her to say something.

"Maybe... maybe someone tampered with the door? Maybe it was booby trapped to demolish like that."

He shook his head. He reached into his pocket and Laney froze again. Instead of a gun, he pulled a large bent screw from his pocket.

"What's that?"

"A screw."

"Donavan, I swear, if you turn this into a lame, high-school, 'Wanna screw?' joke, I'm going to—"

"Feel it."

Laney took it, weighed it and then grabbed the dash as Donavan swerved. Eighty-two mph.

"Nice. Does it do tricks?"

Did his jaw just tighten? He reached out his hand and took it back, only one hand on the wheel. Laney felt the sweat slide down her back, the throb in her head magnifying.

"Put your hand on mine."

She obeyed, hoping that the more she complied, the faster this would end.

Donavan's eyes never left the road while he squeezed his hand shut tight, quivering for a second while she covered his fist with her own shaking fingers. He opened his hand to reveal nothing more than a metallic powder in his palm.

Laney felt a strange lump in her throat. "Okay, okay. You're strong... like weird strong. I believe you," she whispered. "Now please tell me why we're speeding? Where are we going?"

But Donavan had tuned her out. His gaze at the rearview mirror sent him swerving once again. "Well, I'll be. They found us."

"Who—" The question turned to a scream as a vehicle in her blind spot slammed into the right side of the car. "Donavan!"

"Hang on. This is where it gets bumpy."

Donavan changed lanes without discretion, making it difficult for Laney to see who pursued them. They made it far left to the HOV lane—eighty-nine mph—for only a moment. Donavan pulled the wheel hard right and crossed all five lanes to the sound of horns and squealing tires, aiming for the off-ramp.

"Donavan Peterson! Tell me right now—" Another cry ended her sentence as the car lurched hard from another hit. Donavan course-corrected and barely made the exit. The light at the end of the ramp turned green, and he sped on through and straight back up the next on-ramp.

"Sorry, a bit busy. Hold on... Okay, look out your window... now!" Donavan slammed on the brakes and a sleek black figure, unable to brake as fast, flew by Laney's window. She gasped. The other vehicle—thing?—rushed smoothly around to head back toward them. Was this the remote control machine that had caused so much trouble throughout the city? It had no wheels Laney could see, only rapid motion underneath its shape with an oddly constructed helmet, so much ghastlier than any clip she'd seen on TV.

Donavan maneuvered the skidding car toward the next exit ramp where barriers warned CLOSED far before they reached it.

"Donavan—"

"Hang on."

The figure ahead came to a dead stop in front of them, its lifeless glare apparently analyzing what direction their car would take. This was *so* not remote controlled. It glared through humanless eye slits, a slight tilt of the head replicating a creature with thought, something able to make its own decisions. The soulless stare turned directly on Laney, and every part of her quaked.

The car picked up speed again, forcing the black machine to glide out of the way when they broke through the first construction barrier. A sudden impact on the car roof brought her voice to life again in a terrified scream. The roof dented under a second impact, and then another. The metal monster used its arms to pound the roof lower and lower until Donavan's fist pounded the roof back, dents protruding from each side. The car skidded down the half-constructed exit with Donavan keeping one hand on the steering. The whoever—whatever—on top of them refused to budge.

"Take the wheel," Donavan said.

Laney's protest lost itself in the noise of crunching metal and squealing tires. Unwillingly she gripped the abandoned wheel and the road rapidly evaporated into unpaved cement. The rough surface added a jarring rattle, even as Donavan's foot left the gas. He climbed onto his window frame, half in, half out, the flailing of his legs the only evidence Laney could see of the battle above her.

The robot fell from the roof and crashed onto the hood, latching on with its smooth, long claws.

"Donavan!"

Those eyeless slits turned directly toward her and paused. Was it looking at her? Hesitating? In a flash, it let go of the hood and brought its arm back. Laney stared in horror, the arm aiming right for her; she ducked as the car lurched her hard into the seatbelt. Donavan had swung back into his seat and hit the brakes before the creature could smash the window and grab her, then the wheel.

He hit the gas, sending them up and over the fallen metal heap in front of them. Laney's teeth clenched at the jarring crunch it produced when crushed; she gripped the dashboard, her eyes wide when they drew nearer to the dead end blockade with regained speed.

The next black machine appeared at her window. Donavan pulled the gun from his pocket; instinct stole the air from her lungs as Laney shoved herself back against her seat. She threw her hands under her helmet then covered her ears just in time as her window exploded from the assailant's arm that demolished it with a single punch.

As a shower of glass fell over her, Donavan flung his arm across her, pistol in hand. The bullet cracked from the gun and her chest reverberated from the kickback of his outstretched arm; their menace collapsed off just as the car found the last yards of the unfinished ramp. At the end, a twenty-foot drop.

Laney found her scream again.

The car plummeted off the end, the barriers no impedance to their speed. Hard ground rushed to meet them. Laney heard the click of Donavan's seat belt and then hers. The next second spun into a blur as strong arms pulled her like a ragdoll floating through space. Donavan jerked her on top of him and sailed out his open door. In freefall, the ground rose quickly and with a teeth-rattling thud they hit, his body under hers like a rock hard mattress. Fifty feet away, the car collided with the empty desert floor in the deafening sound of twisted metal and shattered glass.

The desert swallowed up the unwelcomed noise and wrapped them in its demanding silence. All fell still.

For a long painful minute, Laney lay on Donavan's torso, the breath knocked from her. Processing thought proved difficult, her headache compounded by shock. She struggled to sit up, a dust cloud engulfing them. They shouldn't be alive. There was no way. She slid off Donavan and realized for the first time he wasn't breathing.

"Oh, no, Donavan! Donavan?" Dust choked her. She fought against coughs as she pounded his chest. He didn't stir. She whipped off his sunglasses to find his eyes open, unblinking. "No, no! Donavan, no!" She drew her fists together, raised them high over her head, and swung down hard. They bounced off his motionless chest. She raised fists again when his firm hands stopped her before she made contact.

"Give me a second, will ya?" Donavan groaned.

"You're alive?" He released her and she sputtered and waved at the dust filling her vision. "How on earth—we fell from up there" cough "—and you just yanked me out and on top of you—and, and you're still alive—and those *things*! What were those things?"

Donavan grunted.

"What is it? Where are you hurt?" Her voice grew raspy from the effort to ignore the choking dust. "Oh, no, Donavan, there's blood!"

"Laney." Laney quieted to hear his choked voice. "Shhhhhh..." he said.

"Right." She held back the flood of words for approximately twenty seconds. "Just let me help you sit up." He didn't move when she tugged his arm. "No? Okay, just be still for a minute—"

"Hear that?"

Laney quieted herself again. She slid off him and sat alert. For the first time, she glanced around the large, barren field they had fallen into. Desert had been cleared of its sparse plant life to leave only small rock and dust around the bottom of the uncompleted underpass. Shrubs and cactus grew nearby, but showed no mobile signs of life. Distant traffic from the freeway echoed around them. Had anyone witnessed what they had? Had anyone seen them go off the road? Was help coming? The sound of a motor, a speeding vehicle—several—grew closer.

Donavan sat up and slowly got to his feet. Laney stepped back and stared while he looked for his sunglasses.

He found them and put them back on. "What?"

"You're... you're bleeding." She tapped the back of her head to mirror his injury.

Donavan felt the back of his head; his hand came back bloody. "We'll take care of it in a minute. Right now, run!"

"Wait—what?"

The roaring engines closed in on them. Donavan grabbed her hand and ran, but it took him a lot of effort. They headed toward the overpass and its huge concrete columns. With each step he groaned less, limped less, picked up speed. By the time they reached cover, he was running at full velocity, dragging Laney behind. He tucked her out of view just as engines whined into their vicinity. Every muscle in Laney protested, and she felt like her bones had all detached from one another. She kept a death grip on Donavan's hand while quick jerks of his head told her he was surveying their surroundings. She did the same and noticed several construction vehicles on the opposite side of the incomplete section of freeway.

"Come on, over here." Donavan pulled her forward, and together they sprinted into the mass of parked excavators, backhoes, and dump trucks—all centered around a small crane. In the midst of the machines, row upon row of large, empty cement tubes sat waiting to be put to use. For now, they would hide two desperate targets. The tubes' six-foot diameter made a clear running passage; Laney and Donovan ran the dozen feet of tunnel before zig-zagging into the next and then the next, trying to lose their pursuers.

They caught their breath and listened. Without warning, a black form leaped onto the gravel grater to their right and soared toward them. Laney flinched into a screaming ball as Donavan propelled himself higher to meet it. Its descending form took a single hit from Donovan that sent it sailing away with a metallic crunch.

"Of course," Donavan whispered. Before she could ask what he'd meant, Donavan pulled Laney through the maze of tubes again. They ended at the base of a large construction caterpillar. Before they could move out, another machine surprised them from above. This time it reached down into the hideaway for Laney before Donavan could react; its awful claw pulled her out of her hiding spot by the back of her shirt. Donavan turned to see her lifted, and his expression changed to rage. With two huge steps, he closed the gap and flew at the metal monster, sending it crashing backward, taking Laney with it. But she never hit the ground.

In the same second the machine lost its grip, Donavan propelled her into another tunnel, slamming her helmet into the side as he did. Her head reeled in pain. She crumpled inside to watch Donavan hit an approaching black machine, and then his body became a blur as he swung and punched and kicked. Another monster appeared at the opposite end of the tube, and Laney tried to call out, but she had no voice left in her. The thing stared at her as if not seeing her and moved away, above the tube and over onto Donavan. He shrugged it off and beat it down with ease, but flung it back over the construction vehicle for good measure. He struck another and another, but there seemed to be no end to them.

More engine noise filled the concrete hideaway, and Laney felt panic give way to hopelessness. The robots outnumbered them and, even as strong as Donavan appeared, he couldn't do this all day.

"Donavan?" She reached out to touch his leg; another assailant crumbled and sailed away from his fist. He stared down at her as if startled.

"Come here," he spoke in an eerie calm that made her quiver. He took her hand once more and pushed her into the sunlight, up onto the base of the nearby crane. She felt exposed, but climbed up toward the equipment's cab and leaned against the windshield on the front side. From the higher vantage point, she could see four—no, five—more robots headed toward them. Donavan scrambled next to her and awaited their approach. Though his body tensed and his fingers flexed, she caught a slight tug at the corner of his mouth.

"Ready?"

Laney stared incredulously. "No."

"Grab on." Donavan draped his left leg over to hers on the narrow lip of metal around the crane's cab, his back to her like a human shield.

She reached out tentatively and placed her hands on his shoulders as the first of the machines reached the base of the crane. "Donavan—"

"Don't let go. Not even for a second."

"Okay, okay! Do something!"

Donavan crouched lower with Laney clinging awkwardly to his back. He shuffled his feet onto the crane arm. His body quivered beneath her as he grabbed hold of the metal beams attaching the crane arm and pulled. Metal groaned in protest, and the crane began to sway.

"What the—what are you—"

The metal groaned, swayed, groaned, swayed, and snapped. The vehicle under them shuddered when the steel arm detached from its base. Laney gripped Donavan's shoulders tighter and spotted seven more creatures descending on the crane. When only yards remained between them, the stare from their helmet heads froze Laney's blood, but she didn't flinch this time. She kept her promise and held on tighter, even as a cry built up within her.

Donavan swung the massive tower of metal like a huge baseball bat and let it fly. It spun through the air across the open span of desert in front of them and with thunderous impact took out rows of the metallic monsters all at once. A rolling cloud of dust arose and brought an eerie silence with it.

Donavan turned slowly in a 360, surveying. They were alone. Quiet satisfaction filled his gaze, sunglasses flung aside somewhere in combat.

"You all right?" he asked. Laney trembled in convulsions and found she couldn't let his shoulders go. He shook some, too, despite his composure.

"What... are you?"

A full-on grin surfaced. "Superhuman."

"And those... things?"

"Not sure."

She looked about them. "Are they gone?"

"For now."

Relief enabled her to loosen her grip, but she shook so violently that her feet gave way. She crumbled down against the cab of the crane.

"Hey, it's okay," said Donavan, tone even. He knelt beside her. "But we can't stay here. It's too dangerous."

Her eyes widened, and he shook his head. "I promise, we're okay for now. We just need to move away from this equipment. That's how they find us." He glanced over his shoulder and then back. She pointed to his head in disbelief.

"What happened to your...?" She touched the back of her head; he mimicked her and then examined his un-bloody hand. "You're not... bleeding anymore," she said. "It's all gone."

He gave her an I-told-you-so shrug and straightened. He found his sunglasses, donned them, and motioned for her to stand too. "I believe I still have thirty-seven minutes left. How about we go finish that talk?"

Chapter 17

The hot coffee in a lidded cup snapped Laney back from her trance when Donavan slid it in front of her. He put his own cup down and sat in the chair opposite her with a half-sympathetic smile. She closed her eyes. Deep breaths. Under the table she clutched her helmet, working her fingers around the rim to keep them occupied.

When she opened her eyes again, a fast glance about the busy coffee shop did nothing to reassure her that she blended in. She had done her best to clean up in the restroom, but imagined her dusty jeans and not-so-white blouse drew attention. If they didn't, her wild hair would. Stuck under a helmet during a robotic assault had done nothing good to her sassy curls. A hair clip from her purse, salvaged from the car wreckage, did its best to wrestle the strands into submission.

"I may not know much about them," Donavan said, and as always, his calm, reassuring voice stilled her nerves. "But I know they don't like public places." His black leather jacket had survived their scuffle much better than she had. The mussed hair under his ball cap looked perfectly planned, with his recovered sunglasses sitting on top.

"Public places—what do you call the freeway?"

"And," he continued, "they can only find us if we're around vehicles."

"Why?"

"Don't know.

Laney's lips fluttered as she exhaled heavily, relaxing a little. "Why don't we start with what you do know? How did—"

"Uh, I believe you're still on my clock. Let me tell you a few things, and then I'll try to answer your questions."

She pulled her mouth into a troubled line and turned her cup around and around. Caffeine seemed like such a good idea for her throbbing head that she had almost cried with relief when they had spotted the café. The dead exit made crossing the freeway at the on-ramp relatively easy as Donavan hurried her into a strip mall less than half a mile from their crash site. A restroom, a chair, and a cup of coffee—as reassuring of a place as any for Donavan to finish the time she had promised him. It didn't work. She felt self-conscious, tired, and nauseated; putting the cup to her lips could be more than she could handle while she tried to concentrate on his words.

"First of all, I have a lot to apologize for. Forcing you to come. That was—"

"Drastic? Rude? Unsafe?"

"I couldn't just shove you into the car, but that's—that's something I'll explain later…" His eyes flashed with quick humor or annoyance—she suspected a bit of each. "Second, I didn't try to put you in danger back there. I couldn't calculate if they'd seek us out, and if they did... I thought it would go down differently." His brow furrowed, and he hurried on as if his list of apologies stretched longer than his time allotted. "And kissing you... I know you think I'm a jerk—"

"I get it. You're sorry. Please. Just tell me." Her voice broke, and she resorted to a whisper to control it. "What is going on?"

Donavan leaned forward on his elbows and studied her face, every inch of it. His eyes swept over her eyes, her mouth, her throat, until a blush came on, and she no longer cared about another soul in the room. It was just the two of them, the same two who had sorted old CDs in the middle of the night while they killed two bottles of wine.

"All this is new, this strength, this power," he began. "I'd no idea I could be this strong. There's never been signs; nothing like this has ever happened before. I can't even tell what brought the change. I've been so fatigued for so long, I thought it was just part of adjusting to my separation... from Kelly. But suddenly I had these moments when I came alive. Really alive again." His gaze moved to an invisible spot beyond her shoulder.

"When you come... alive," she asked, "do you— No, sorry. I won't interrupt."

"No, it's okay. Please. Ask."

"Do you... can you do anything else? I mean, other stuff?"

"No. Just become strong. Which includes a strength to heal myself." The back of his head showed no signs now of his earlier trauma. He looked down for a minute as if putting his next sentence together with care. "But sometimes, well, I'm stronger. At times, it's beyond super strength. It's—it's beyond words. I feel like nothing can stop me, like I'll never need sleep again. That's what I've been figuring out." He paused and an eerie premonition made her tremble all over.

"And? Did you figure it out?"

He nodded, not looking particularly thrilled. "It's you."

"Me?"

"Sometimes when we're together, I feel like I'm unstoppable. That crane. That wasn't me. That was *us.* I can pick up a grown man twice my size and throw him across the room on my own; I can turn a screw into a knot—but when I'm with you... I crush it to nothing." He took off his hat and ran fingers through his hair. "I rip cranes apart with my bare hands, for crying out loud. It's crazy." A hysterical chuckle rose from his throat, and he massaged the stubble around his mouth to subdue it.

Laney blushed. "You said sometimes. Sometimes when we're together?"

He nodded and leaned forward again. "I haven't figured it all out yet. I think it's mostly when we're alone... but I don't know. The night of the party, when you stayed over, I didn't notice anything different. Not when we were together in the same room, anyway." He averted his eyes as if that was all he would admit to.

"Oh." She swallowed and remained silent while a group passed close by to stand in line for their coffee. She tried to block out all else and match Donavan's intensity. "We're not alone now. Are you...? Do you feel it now?"

He nodded.

"You don't look happy about it."

"It's not just the strength, Laney." Donavan's voice dropped low. "It's an incredible awakening. It's like... like an electric buzz. Just touching you feels like getting shocked or like a super jolt of caffeine."

"I don't get... how?"

He shook his head and shrugged.

She looked at his fingers so near on the table and puzzled over them.

"That's why," she said slowly. "That's why you pull away, why you try not to touch me, isn't it?"

"I'm sorry, yes."

"Most of the time, you said."

"Yes."

"Now?"

"Yes."

"So it hurts to be near me?"

He remained silent, but his eyes didn't deny it.

"That night…when you ki—" she asked, not able to finish.

"That's when I began putting it all together. And I thought because the sense felt so strong…" He heaved a sigh. "I kissed you and thought if there would ever be a moment you would feel it too, that would do it. It was so strong for me then. But you felt nothing."

Well, I wouldn't say nothing, Laney thought but refrained from saying as she squirmed in her seat. "Can I ask about those things now? Who or what are they?"

"Again, I'm not really sure. Tag calls them Oil Eaters."

"Who?"

"Tag. He's one of us."

"Wait—Us? There's more of you?"

Donavan merely nodded as if this were no special revelation.

"How many?"

"Five—well, seven total, but I haven't met two of them yet."

"All like you? Super strong?"

"No. Super in other ways." He briefly explained Tag, Brian, and Harley, how they met at the mysterious Jake's and how they belonged together. He told her of their strange calling and the bond that united them. She stared in silent awe.

"So that's three others. You're four. Two you haven't met—five, six. So who's seven?"

"Laney…"

"What?"

"It's you."

She stared back into his serious eyes and let out a snicker. "Donavan, I may be a super mom and a pretty good teacher, but believe me, that's all the 'super' I got in me. I am not a... *you*... or any of those others."

"That's what makes this so hard. Trust me. If I didn't believe it were true, I would never have dragged you away."

"At gunpoint."

"It was actually the screw," he said sheepishly, "in my other pocket. I just let you believe—anyway, that wasn't intentional. I just couldn't *touch* you, and you weren't coming willingly."

"That's why? That's what this is all about?" She slid back and straightened in the chair. "You think because of the 'buzz' I give you, I'm one of you?" She processed that for a minute. "So you kidnapped me, put me in the middle of an apocalyptic battle, and hoped I would suddenly spawn into some sort of juggernaut?"

"Not at all," he said tersely. "That would be nuts." He reflected for a moment. "Yeah, okay, maybe."

"I could have been killed!" Someone in line turned at the sound of her rising hysteria. She gave sorry-about-that eyes to the customer. Leaning in close, she hissed at Donavan, "*I could have been killed*!"

"I wouldn't let them. Did you see them bounce off my fist like a tin can?"

"Do you remember pulling me from a falling car that could have crushed me?"

"You are number seven, and I wanted you to see how you fit in."

"Fit in? Like what? Join your superhuman club and—and we meet on Tuesdays for our weekly flex competition?" Her voice cracked as her heart rate climbed.

"Laney."

She crossed her arms and looked away.

"Laney?" There it was, that voice that sucked her in. "Laney, I am called to do this. It's impossible to explain if you don't experience it yourself. But I'm going to meet with the others, and together we'll figure out what these things are after. Right now, they seem only interested in us. We plan to draw them out of the city if we can."

He was crazy. She shook her head and rolled her eyes, unable to fathom how Donavan could be this—something other than an ordinary, single dad who threw BBQs in his backyard.

"Come with us."

Definitely crazy.

"Donavan," she said firmly. "The girls are my first priority. I won't leave them with some babysitter I barely know to follow a bunch of—"

Donavan held up his hand. "Laney, I wasn't kidding when I told you that I was doing this for their safety."

Laney went rigid and angled her ear toward him to make sure she'd heard him right.

"They will be fine," he said. "The Oil Eaters won't hurt them. In fact, I'm not even sure if they can see them. The only people those things seem to be interested in is us. Our gang. You being around the girls could actually put them in danger."

"So I have to go with you if I want my girls safe? Is that what you're telling me?" The panic rose in her throat again.

Donavan sighed. He slugged back the rest of his coffee, and his patience seemed to disappear with the last drop. He stood and zipped up his jacket.

"What about Parker?" Laney asked. "Aren't you at all worried about—"

"He's with his grandmother, and he's safe. I have nothing to worry about except missing the meetup with the others. Brie will stay with your girls until I tell her otherwise. They're safe. The girls love Brie, and she's reliable. Or you could call Nellie to watch them. Or Charlie. Your choice." Donavan pushed in his chair and leaned down on its back rail.

"My hour's up. What's it gonna be, Laney?"

Part II

Chapter 18

Laney gripped the dashboard to keep from being jostled out of her seat along the dusty, desert road. Road may have been too loose of a term, she decided, as the pavement ended and gave way to a broken stretch of cracked asphalt and cement. The bumpy ride gave little chance to talk, an appreciated silence as Laney's head continued to throb.

Laney called from her cell to make sure Brie had everything under control and would be available overnight. The possibility of not seeing the girls launched a round of acid reflex. She declined the chance to speak to her daughters, knowing she would probably freak out if she heard their voices. At least Brie's sweet reassurance gave her the boost she needed to make good on her promise to Donavan.

I must be out of my mind, she thought for the millionth time. The rugged path he chose didn't boost her confidence, either, but for the next twenty-four hours, Laney had committed herself to Donavan and his "call." Like it or not, here she was.

They hit a particularly large pothole, lurching the car. The noise and motion set off memories of their last car ride, and the fear of more robots made Laney whimper. "And you're sure they can't find us in this vehicle?" she asked for the second time.

Donavan nodded and kept his eyes glued ahead. "Alternative fuel."

She kept from asking about their destination again. His expression repeated what he'd told her: he felt what he had to do more than had exact direction. They had left the highway and turned onto a network of random roads leading into the Sonoran desert. Adjusting her helmet rekindled her headache, but it dawned on her that she had ibuprofen in her purse. She fished out two pills but had nothing to wash them down with. She worked at accumulating enough spit to force them down when the car halted. Her arm shot out to brace herself on the dashboard as a cloud of dust gathered around them, creating zero visibility.

A silence followed the cut engine. Laney gritted her teeth, steeling against whatever waited on the other side of the dust cloud.

Donavan remained stoic and un-reassuring behind his shades. "Let's go," he said when the air began to clear.

"Go where?"

"Out."

Laney scrambled out and swatted the floating dirt. Fifty yards away, she made out a large rectangular shape next to a man of generous proportions. A smirk of satisfaction crossed Donavan's lips, gone as quickly as it came. He locked the car and walked forward.

"Wait! My purse—"

"Leave it."

"Excuse me?"

"We can't risk being tracked. Keep the phone here."

"But my stuff—"

Donavan continued toward the figure, who remained arms crossed, unsmiling.

Terrified of being alone, Laney hurried to catch up, throwing the pills from her sweaty palm into her dry mouth along the way.

The stranger before them kept an odd stance, solid and unyielding, almost statuesque. His skin appeared so tan and rough, he could have camouflaged himself as part of the desert if not for his darker clothing. They stopped in front of him, and Laney drew in a breath and held it. He didn't just have a rocklike appearance; Laney could swear he *was* rock. The pores of his face pocked like tiny specks of sandstone, fine and gritty. His eyes sunk deep into his face with a nose that could only be detected by the shadow it cast. Lips, thin and brown, neatly carved a line above his chin like a natural crevice created by weathering.

Donavan's face showed no shock or disbelief; he simply held out his hand. "RJ, is it?"

The figure nodded and reached out his hand. "RJ" had all the makings of a statue brought to life, the stone skin shifting as if molecules rearranged themselves with movement, and yet he looked solid enough to withstand a hurricane. It was the most uncanny, terrifyingly beautiful thing Laney had ever witnessed. Unconsciously, she took a step back and inhaled deeply. RJ shot her a glance, and Laney instantly regretted her reaction. Years of dealing with kids in every shape and size, and balking at his appearance was her best greeting?

"Donavan," he returned, his voice deep and heavy, like the undertow of the ocean's roar. Laney opened her mouth, but nothing came out. Donavan nodded his confirmation and arched an eyebrow her way. She closed her mouth.

"This ours?" Donavan asked, smacking the side of the large rectangle, which turned out to be the trailer of a semi truck, minus the truck.

A nod.

"How'd you get it here?"

"Drove most of the way. Pulled it the rest."

Donavan grinned. "Well, whaddya know."

"It'll be easier with two of us." RJ eyed Laney, then Donavan.

"Oh, RJ, this is Laney. She's one of us."

RJ wrinkled his forehead, creasing the granite surface, but said nothing.

Donavan took a quick survey around the trailer with their new companion as Laney removed her wedged sandal to extract a stone. Her outfit wasn't what she would have chosen for a desert hike. She had donned a pair of old jeans and a white cotton blouse that morning to feed ducks with the girls. The thin layer of shirt ruffles along the buttons and small cap sleeve would provide no warmth once the sun set, despite the white camisole underneath. *The problem with being kidnapped,* she thought sardonically, *is that one never has a chance to grab a sweater.*

Donavan pointed to something in the distance, and RJ nodded agreement. Fear struck a chord in Laney again, and hastily she put on her shoe, nearly tripping on her way to join them.

"What? What is it?"

"We're headed that way," Donavan told her.

"Why? What's there?"

"The others."

"Are we... driving?" she asked, looking beyond to the half-hearted road that disappeared into the landscape.

"No. We're hauling the trailer there." RJ already stood at the head of the trailer, rattling chains at the hitch.

"Okay, but wait. How are we doing that? Exactly?"

His grin returned and Laney marveled again at this blend of Donavans that she didn't yet understand. Caution and confidence combined, stimulating and alarming her.

"Come on. I'll show you.

Chapter 19

The sky streaked by, blue and white, rain erased from the memory of the lingering clouds. The sparse landscape blurred before Donavan's eyes, flashes of flat scrubby desert everywhere with the mere hint of mountains ahead. Water streamed from his tear ducts as the wind caught him full in the face, complicating the deep breaths he needed to charge ahead. Still, exhilaration and adrenaline drove him forward.

The superhero thing didn't hurt either.

Energized by Laney, Donavan scarcely noticed the makeshift chain harness that cut deep grooves into his jacket after he had shouldered the weight of the trailer and sprinted along the broken road. RJ pushed the trailer from behind while Laney clung to Donavan's back for dear life. She could sit on the hitch near his waist, but to touch him and give him strength, she had to lean precariously onto him. Laney obeyed his order to hang on tight and clung to him like an oversized papoose, all he needed to have his strength soar to monstrous proportions even while his nerves came undone.

His reckless speed pushed back the questions that nagged him. He could only imagine what ran through Laney's head. There was no way to stop and comfort her now. Even if they could speak, try as he might, there was no way to explain the call that led him and RJ where they needed to be.

And he had no idea where that was.

Why a road? Okay, that was a question to consider. Obviously, the pavement had served a purpose. It stood out in the rugged desert, its age and color out of place, the asphalt too black. New road? But the cracks and weathering, along with the side brush and dust, implied abandonment. New and unused?

A faded metal sign came into view. It read something about county property. Donavan felt Laney pop her head up off his back, but he sped by too quickly to read the lettering. Another sign angled so there was no missing it: *NO TRESPASSING under penalty of law.* The tension in Laney's grip meant she'd read that sign and its connotation worried her. One more thing to increase her distrust.

What am I doing bringing her here?

Donavan swallowed a new wave of doubt and pulled on.

In a miraculously short time, the odd crew of three closed in on the base of the mountain. The road rose and curved, branched and narrowed. Around their path, rock climbed higher through the thickening cactus, creosote brush, and tumbleweed. The road straightened and then began its ascent once more until the rock walls and curvy turns blocked a view of where they'd been. No turning back, the closed-in trail seemed to say.

Over a rise, a small plateau opened, and a peculiar sight interrupted the otherwise wild landscape. It brought Donavan to a quick walk; two deep breaths and his breathing returned to normal, as if he'd never run. Laney loosened her hold as RJ helped him bring the trailer forward. Before them, a series of partially built homes.

Row upon row of house frames faced them, nothing more than wooden skeletons on cement bases. The two men rumbled the engineless trailer down an empty street until it made it to the far end of what could have been a neighborhood. But no one lived there, present or past. Broken pipes and blank window cut-outs spoke of a modern community stopped mid-construction.

Donavan moved into a large area. To their left sat one of the unfinished structures; to the right, a curious canyon on the mountainside. Interrupting the upward rise of the land sat a deep depression that cradled a lake—more of a pond, really—a green pool of stagnation surrounded by contrived rock formations and organized saguaro cactus clusters. The water feature sat out of place, lovely and strange while the hill rose behind it and disappeared into the sunlit horizon.

As his adrenaline diminished, an awareness of the woman on his back returned.

"Laney."

Laney mumbled an apology and slid off. RJ rounded the front of the trailer, and Donavan joined Laney in staring at his size. He had grown several inches taller and broader, his arms more like boulders stacked together than muscles. Donavan grinned and reached up to clap him on the back with a laugh, exhilarated by their success. RJ nodded, expressionless, but under the granite features Donavan sensed his satisfaction too.

Donavan shifted his glance to Laney and caught her in an open-mouthed, wide-eyed stare. He cleared his throat; she got the message. Blushing, she looked away and shoved her hands deep into her jean pockets.

Around the side of the trailer, four large figures appeared, dressed in military desert camouflage. Donavan's pulse quickened and an overwhelming sense of belonging took over. He moved forward to meet them, but Laney seemed more reluctant. "It's okay," he said. "Time to meet the gang."

Donavan had hoped to ease Laney's nerves with an introduction, but the lineup that greeted them didn't say "welcome wagon." Four men, formidable in size and expression, stood before them like a firing squad, and for a moment Donavan could only see them through Laney's eyes: a cigar-chomping black man, a surly-looking Latino, and an overconfident white boy, every one of them larger than Donavan, intimidating and unapologetic for it. He prayed they didn't send Laney hightailing into the desert.

Beside them stood the tall, serene leader that should help ease Laney's tension. Donavan himself had looked forward to this meeting. First things first, though, for Laney's sake.

"This is Harley." Donavan nodded to the man who couldn't relax the hold on his cigar butt long enough to smile. Laney stiffly nodded back.

"Tag." A quick nod and impatient scowl came from under a ball cap pulled too low. Laney's return nod was even smaller this time.

"Brian." The blond with his arms akimbo beamed at her and said, "Well, alright," a bit too loudly. Donavan had no idea if that was good or not; Laney gave a smileless nod, indicating she didn't know either.

"Jacob." Donavan turned to the man on the far left with unabashed curiosity. Jacob wasn't as muscular as Harley or fierce looking as Tag, but something about him commanded attention. His face was pleasant, with small, sharp eyes that spoke of knowledge and patience. He shouldered an air of unmistakable confidence. Of the four, he alone stepped forward to shake hands with the newest recruits, Laney first.

"Hello," Jacob said. Laney visibly relaxed as she shook his hand and returned his small smile.

"Hi. I'm Laney," she answered.

Donavan realized his own tension decreased at her response. Behind Jacob, Tag inhaled and sighed; the others shifted uncomfortably.

"Welcome," Jacob said, truth evident in his tone. The leader turned his gaze to Donavan with even more interest. "And Donavan. Good to meet you."

"Ditto." The two men shook hands firmly. "Where are we exactly?" Donavan asked with a quizzical squint.

"Boulder Vista, I think was the name before they abandoned it."

"Abandoned," Laney echoed, surveying the empty street of semi-houses.

"Left behind by the builders—contractors. They started the building in the height of the real estate boom. Put them up fast to get a jump on demand. Thirty slabs here that I counted. Most of them have frames, some are empty. Market dried up though. Ran outta buyers. Cheaper to leave it all unfinished than tear it down."

"Modern ghost towns," murmured Laney. "I read about them. There was one in Gilbert. I can't believe this is still here."

"Still wondering," Donavan spoke up, "why we're here."

A silence fell over the group as if they were all waiting for someone else to confess the answer. A turkey vulture cast a shadow as it circled overhead, and nothing but the sound of the wind in the canyon spoke for a time.

"No black bots if that's whatcha mean," Harley finally answered.

Donavan reminded Laney of the sense Harley had about impending attacks.

"We got here on foot a few hours before you. Haven't seen or heard anything yet. We hoped you'd show up with this." Jacob nodded to the trailer behind Donavan.

"What's in there?"

"Supplies, I'm guessing."

"Firepower?" Brian asked hopefully, like a kid awaiting a promised present.

Jacob held up his hand. "Let's take care of other matters first."

Tag nodded in agreement and stepped forward. "Exactly. Let's hear what she's doing here."

Harley growled something to Tag between his teeth before Donavan could. Tag quieted, but refused to back down. He removed his ball cap and approached Laney, scanning her from head to toe.

"No, I was going to say that first we need to do a little reconnaissance," Jacob interjected smoothly. "We may not sense a presence now, but we've all been called here for a reason. Let's scout the area, see what's around us. We need a handle on where we are."

"Without weapons?" Brian whined.

"We have our pistols. That's enough for now. None of us saw anything coming in, and Harley isn't sensing any danger."

Donavan wide-eyed the trailer and wondered just what kind of firepower to expect.

§ § § § §

Laney gawked at the four men before her. Not one of them looked as if they'd ever skipped a day at the gym. Each set of biceps bulged under T-shirt sleeves so impressively that Laney forgot about RJ's astonishing growth spurt. The capped, ruffled sleeves over her own puny muscles were woefully out of place. She suppressed the urge to drop and do a quick set of pushups.

"The four of us came from the north and skirted the mountain on the east," Jacob was saying. "On that side of the mountain is just more open desert. We saw no signs of disturbance, so we circled south and came in on the same road as you. Let's clear the west side. Harley, take Tag and RJ to the backside and circle around. We only have a few hours of daylight, so get moving."

Laney tried to look as casual as Jacob. Tag, scowling at her like a schoolyard bully, recapped his head and obeyed Jacob without complaint, jogging away with Harley by his side. RJ reappeared from behind the trailer. The immense rock of a man joined Tag and Harley, and together they disappeared up the road. Was it her imagination or was RJ larger still?

Jacob continued his orders: "I'm taking Donavan to the top of the ridge with me on the other side of the canyon. We have some things to discuss."

Laney forecasted Jacob's next words and opened her mouth too late to protest. "Brian, take Laney with you. Follow the base around to the north."

"But—" Laney forced out.

Donavan held up a hand to refrain her. "Laney, it's okay."

Seriously? "What's okay, Donavan? We don't know why we're here. I don't know any of these guys—and you barely do either—and you think it's a good idea to split up and look around? I think we all need to stay here. It's safer, don't you think?"

Jacob moved away, checking his weapon, as if she hadn't even spoken. "Donavan?" he called back over his shoulder. Brian impatiently waited on Laney, seemingly unconcerned with eavesdropping.

"We're all on the same team, Laney." Donavan used his *there-there* voice that needled her nerves just a little. "I told you, Harley has this sense; it gives us a pretty good idea if we're safe, but we need to get a lay of the land before dark." Brian cleared his throat, but Donavan proceeded. "So go with Brian and let me get some answers from Jacob. Brian's a good guy. He's not gonna let anything happen to you." He gave a quick dismissive nod before hurrying after Jacob.

"Oooookaaaaay," Laney managed. Brian drew his weapon in a swift motion and snapped on the safety with an expectant glance in her direction.

"Uh, I don't have one of those," she pointed.

"No problem. I got us. Ready?"

"Is it really necessary to have it drawn?"

Brian shrugged and tucked the pistol in his belt at the small of his back. "Better?"

Laney nodded and numbly followed Brian through the wooden frames until he found a weak trail in the boulders to follow. High above them, the dust-colored rocks stacked themselves into natural works of art. Saguaros reached their spiky arms in majestic grandeur and mystery. Most days they reminded Laney of centennials, standing guard over the desert. Today she imagined them as mocking spectators. She stumbled several times trying to take in the ridge above them, waiting for another attack of machines. She finally gave up and concentrated on her feet to keep from twisting an ankle.

"This looks like an animal trail," Brian observed, once they had made their way out of the scruff.

"Probably Javelina."

"Have-a-what-now?"

"Javelina. It's kinda like a wild boar, a peccary that lives in the desert. You're not from around here?" Laney asked.

"Nope. Never been a desert kind of guy." He smiled. "The sun I like comes with ocean waves. Florida. Why have sand if there's no water..." His voice trailed off with a shake of his head as his eyes scoured the terrain they walked. "You live in this. You like it?"

"I'd like to move back to Colorado someday, but it's okay."

"So what's your story?" asked Brian.

"I've lived in Arizona almost ten years." The path grew rockier. It would be nice to have sensible hiking boots like Brian. Her wedges weren't going to cut it.

"Not what I meant." Brian grabbed her elbow and helped her over a larger rock that blocked the path that only small animals could sidle around. "You and Donavan a thing?"

"What?" Her cheeks grew warm. "No. I mean, we... we kind of—"

Brian laughed easily. "It wasn't a trick question."

"No, we aren't. But he needs me for his strength. I assume he explained that."

"Interesting. No. We don't know much about you, and, may I say, we're preeeety curious. Never had someone that accentuated someone else's ability; never had a girl one of us, either."

Something about the way he said *girl* didn't sound like a compliment.

A large bird appeared from nowhere and circled low and silent over them. Laney flinched at its shadow and checked behind her. Did she hear rock scatter? "Aren't we supposed to be scouting or something?"

"We are."

"Really? What exactly have you been discovering other than ways to make me feel awkwardly out of place?"

"Not all the boulders on this side have the same makeup as the other side of the mountain. Many are darker brown. Fewer cactus, less growth, but nothing recently disturbed." He pointed up the side of the mountain that rose several hundred yards above them. He focused on a collection of rocks that looked like any other to Laney. "See that? I like the way the rocks dimple in there. Possible cave. Remember that. It's close to the funky-looking cactus with the broken arm and holes in the side. Could be a really good place to hide."

"You think something could be up there?"

"No. I meant if *you* need a good place to hide."

"Oh. What else?"

He eyed her. "Say we're being followed." Laney whipped around to check the trail behind them, earning another laugh. "We're not, but if suddenly—wham!—we get sneak attacked, or here comes an Indiana Jones boulder— what would you do?"

"Go to that hiding spot?"

"It's not a test. Just wanna know what your instincts are. Bam!" he smacked his hands together and pointed at her. "A bad guy is up ahead on the trail! You—do what?"

"Um, I would...I don't know, duck behind that rock there."

"Good. Even though everything is low here in the desert, you get lower. It still helps conceal you. Don't run unless you have to; and absolutely stay with one of us. Grab onto me if you can."

"Okay," Laney inhaled, taking it all in. Perhaps this was constructive after all. "Anything else?"

"Rattlesnake to your right."

"What! Where?"

Brian threw his chin in the direction of a rock ten feet away, and sure enough, a diamondback coiled itself on the surface, silent and camouflaged with its dusty patterned back.

"You didn't grab onto me." Brian tsked. "But you didn't run, either. That's good. Staying still is your best defense when it comes to wildlife encounters."

"Oh." Laney followed thoughtfully as Brian led on. The trail narrowed, and Laney walked a little behind, trying to observe her mentor undetected for a moment. He was younger than the others, mid-twenties, and very self-assured in his gait. Laney had written his swagger off to youth at first but realized there was probably much more to her youthful guardian.

"So...what's your story?" she asked.

Brian glanced back from under a strand of sunlit hair and smiled with perfect white teeth. "I can't wait to show you."

§ § § § §

Donavan's stride fell in sync with Jacob's in unconscious agreement. They took the path to the northeast, and before Donavan asked the first question, Jacob was answering it. "Lots of missions under our belt; never been like this before."

For whatever reason, the simple acknowledgement that his leader was in tune with his concerns eased tension from his shoulders. "How so?" Donavan asked.

Jacob nodded to the trail that would take them higher up the side of the mountain, but Donavan had already moved himself in that direction intuitively.

"So many unknowns," Jacob answered. He gave Donavan a half-hearted grin. "Never saw you coming."

Donavan considered that and watched the trail for several quiet minutes. "I can't put my finger on it—the moment that brought me to Jake's. When I knew, when I felt... It's still unreal."

"Was hoping you came with a few answers for *us*." Donavan glanced over at Jacob, different from the others. There was something about the square of his shoulders, his keen eyes, that made him easy to follow, to confide in. Jacob jerked his chin to the ridge before them. "Why this place? Those monster machines? Any clues about them other than their desire to eat oil and rip us apart?"

"Sorry," Donavan exhaled and continued his climb. "Nothing else I can tell you. I'd hoped you'd have some answers for me about why I'm like this, why Jake's appeared and then disappeared, how the construction sites got 'unrobbed.'"

"There's two pieces of us you need to know," Jacob surprised Donavan by answering right away. "There's the biology of us and then the mystery of us. We are working on figuring out the biology, but the ways things appear and the call—so much of that is just a mystery we've had to live with."

Donavan let that sink in for a minute. "Tell me about your other missions. Why are they so different?"

Jacob squinted against the sun. "Drug rings. Illegal weapon sales. Kidnapping. Human trafficking..." His face sobered. "We had just stumbled on a trailer full of girls shipped up from Mexico when the first Oil Eater found Tag's bike."

"Don't you report that kind of activity?" Donavan's brow furrowed. "The FBI, ICE, or— I don't know— the police?"

"It's not like we get to the scene in time for that, in most cases. Within hours of us meeting up, we're thrown into impossible situations. So, yes, we eventually report what we need to. But we take care of the immediate danger. Sometimes we're there because the situation is beyond what authorities can handle."

"How do you even know where to go? That's beyond the call I feel."

"The guys haven't told you much, then. We have someone on the outside, Leon, that gets us into the action most of the time. Other times, we end up finding missions on our own. I'm not sure if we just happen to be in the right places at the right time or if this call is the real deal. But this time...I'm not sure what this is."

Donavan gave it thought.

"There was this rock. A odd green stone..." He told Jacob about what he found at Dickerson's rock yard and how it had disappeared from his house. "I can't find a connection to these robots, but there has to be a connection to Valentine, the guy who broke into all the supply yards."

Jacob nodded, confirming that he, like Harley, knew all about the role Valentine had played in ruining Donavan's life. "Harley seems to think Valentine is some sort of distraction, a patsy for someone."

"Harley seems to think a lot of things. I just don't understand most of them."

Jacob's face broke into a genuine grin then as they topped the ridge. Together they scoped out the desert below, Donavan hoping and dreading they would find something new.

Chapter 20

The weary hikers returned to the pseudo-neighborhood nestled on the mountainside. At least Laney was weary. Her feet were killing her, and her resentment mounted. No one else seemed to notice or care. Ready for a fight yet to come, the men turned from frustrated to restless. Jacob debriefed each party; all told similar reports. No one had seen or sensed a thing.

"Now what?" Tag said impatiently, and Laney made a note to keep at least one person between him and herself.

"Now we open the box!" Brian grinned, clapping him on the back. Tag seemed annoyed at the gesture but hurried after Brian when Jacob gave the go-ahead. They moved to the trailer as one, Laney seeking Donavan's side. A large door on the side of the trailer slid open after the push and pull of several levers. Inside, boxes and crates of various sizes stacked high and deep, blocking a view to the back wall. Jacob and Harley vaulted themselves up as if on a springboard and began handing down containers to those on the ground. No one asked Laney to help. She sighed and took a step back, surveying their surroundings and noting RJ's absence. She hadn't seen him at the debriefing either.

They found a crowbar with some of the first crates and the three men below pried off the tops and tossed the tool to one another as if it were a pencil and not a skull-crushing tool. Most boxes contained food stuff, cans and metal containers, a water filtration system, bedding.

"Weapons," Harley called from deep within the trailer. Brian gave a cheer and jumped in to join him. Laney just stared at the rows of canned beans in one box with a slow growing dread. She caught Donavan's eye; he'd just opened a crate that held camping tools, flashlights, and tins then scowled.

"Are you thinking what I'm thinking?" she whispered.

"Yeah," he mumbled, putting the lid back on a crate. "Someone thinks we will be here a while."

It didn't seem like the time to remind him she was on loan for twenty-four hours only.

The campfire sparked and Laney jumped for what she insisted to her inner coward would be the last time. The glow of tightly clustered logs sparked within a ring of rocks the men had assembled. Around the logs, a ring of large stones created a resting place for the bedraggled bunch. Brian, with a bedroll used like a small pillow, settled against the rock across from Laney and looked as if he could fall asleep as easily as if he were in a La-Z-Boy. RJ, an almost unrecognizable mound of boulders, had moved off to be the watch. His incredible growing size distressed Laney, but she kept her thoughts to herself. She cradled her knees tightly up under her chin, an old army jacket pulled around her for added warmth. The canyon provided no light after the sun went down. The clouds had returned, obstructing the moon and stars, leaving the fire as the only light for miles.

Donavan sat right beside her but seemed miles away. Harley, to her left, unnerved her with his dismissal of her, only slightly less intimidating than Tag's disdain, which seemed to carry over to being irrationally pissed at the world in general. But particularly her. She decided she'd take Harley's indifference over Tag's attitude any day.

"Any word from Rheinland?" Harley spoke into the darkness.

Jacob's eyes reflected the flames as he drew in one outstretched leg and replaced it with the other. "You mean about what he found? Yes. There's been some recent…discoveries."

A new wave of tension from the men; more uncertainty for Laney. This didn't seem like good news.

"How long were you going to sit on that?" Harley growled.

Donavan glanced at each member. "Who's Rheinland?"

"Leon. Our outside man I told you about," came Jacob's answer. Donavan kept silent and Laney followed his lead, waiting for an explanation. Somewhere in the dark, Laney heard RJ shift his massive size.

"Our *origins* have been a mystery since we met." Jacob kept his eyes ahead, the fire drawing him into a conversation he seemed reluctant to participate in. "We met—various places and ways. By accident or design. I was in Harley's squad for quite a while. We found out about each other's power through circumstances."

"Shhheeeesh," Harley said, shaking his head at the memory. He clasped his hands behind his neck to stare up at the starless night.

"I ended up as Tag's platoon sergeant, and together we ran into Brian in the field." Tag said nothing but appeared to have emotions rolling under his crusty exterior when Brian slapped him in the chest with the back of his hand. The depths of their attachment grew almost tangible. "RJ—he tracked me down in Florida," Jacob continued. "So you could say we were all destined to meet.

"I met Leon Rheinland during some medical training. He'd worked on Rufus after his, well, accident. He realized what Rufus was, as hard as it was to believe, but could do nothing to save his power."

Laney's mind rolled through the names and places Donavan had dumped on her. Rufus: the barkeep at Jake's.

"What accident?" Donavan asked. "What was his power?"

"Transparent vision, we think. Rufus had a truck flip over on him. According to Rheinland, Rufus might have been able to see through objects. That was the first time Leon— Rheinland—knew we existed. He tried to help Rufus recover his gift, but the guy...he was in bad shape. His concussion worsened until it left him like he is."

"Still a darn good man," Harley said, his affection for the man apparent. "Wish he'd warned us about Jake's though," he added under his breath. "Showed up to an empty lot."

"Rheinland keeps a lot hush hush. Jake's and Rufus are examples of the things Leon helps orchestrate for us, but doesn't talk much about."

"So spill it," Tag said. "What'd he find out about us?"

Again Jacob turned to Donavan and Laney to include them in the conversation.

"The call—the energy or force that works with us—" He eyed Donavan seriously. "As a man of science, Rheinland has spent a lot of time and money helping us figure out why we've become..."

"Superheroes," Brian jumped in with obvious self-infatuation.

"Super human," Jacob filled in.

"Freaks," Tag mumbled and tossed a stick into the fire a bit harder than necessary. A spray of sparks scrambled upward, and Laney barely winced this time.

"Being abnormal ain't exactly like winning the spelling bee," Harley commented. Laney looked quizzically at Donavan for an explanation, but he just shook his head to say *don't ask.* "Which is why Rheinland was helping us get answers," Harley added.

All eyes turned to Jacob. "From a scientific standpoint, Rheinland is convinced that our powers have a biological reason, not a supernatural one. If Rufus lost his powers because of physical trauma, it stands to reason that our traits have an organic explanation. He took blood and DNA samples from each of us, but none of us have much in common. He's made it his life pursuit to find out what makes us tick. Up until now, he's had nothing."

"So you mean he found something this time?" Brian asked, sitting up.

"Have any of you heard of Landon Biometrics?" Nobody had. "Rheinland started his search for commonality with Rufus. We already know he's been over our medical backgrounds a million times with no significant common thread. So he traced back everywhere Rufus ever lived, his family, friends, career—everything that could possibly influence his biology. When he found no links there, he moved up the family tree. He started digging into Rufus' mother and father's past. Again, nothing, not for the longest time. He found out that for one brief summer Rufus' mom worked as an assistant at a lab in Georgia. It was only because of his diligence to the project that he finally found his first clue.

"When Rheinland started looking into our past with the same scrutiny, RJ's family let him go through personal things RJ's mother left behind. She died of cancer a number of years ago." A shuffle in the dark outside the ring of men meant RJ was listening in. "In a box of old memorabilia was a medical wrist band, the kind you get at a hospital. It read 'Landon Biometrics.'"

"Two of us have family who visited the same hospital?" Harley grunted. "So what's that mean?"

"Lab," Jacob corrected him.

"What about the rest of us?" Tag said. "My family is from New York, and I've never even heard of this Biometrics place."

Jacob held up his hand to steel off more questions. "Leon's still searching through family records. He's investigating the lab, too. It's closed now, been closed for a long time. In fact, finding the facility itself was near impossible. It was destroyed in a flood."

"My mom had tuberculosis." Brian's voice sounded distant. "She got it working in South America for the Peace Corp. We know she went to Landon for treatment or testing or something."

Jacob nodded in agreement. "Rheinland spent almost a year finding people who knew the facility's location and purpose. Mostly research. Cancer research specifically. Independently owned and operated. RJ's mother died of cancer, so that started him down a trail. Rufus' mom had hepatitis C, though, not cancer. And she was an employee there, as far as we know, not a patient."

"My dad—he had cancer. But sounds like we following the mom parade. She had some kind of eating disorder. Not the throwing up kind. She had trouble digesting food. Something with her esophagus." Harley stared hard into the fire. "Alaska disease. No, wait…that ain't right. Give me a minute; it'll come to me."

Tag remained silent, but his jaw worked and his body squirmed.

"My mother never told me," Jacob continued, "until I really pressed her, that she had been treated for an enlarged pancreas that threatened her life. She didn't want to talk about it, but she's never heard of Landon Biometrics. So our only thread is that all our mothers were sick and treated before we were even born."

"So is Landon labs involved or not?" Tag asked, shaking his head. "My mom's never set foot out of New York her whole life—never been to Georgia."

"Achalasia!" Harley called out. "That's it! Got it."

Tag huffed. "Rheinland hasn't got us any closer to an answer of who we are then before!"

"It's the closest connection we've made," Jacob insisted. "Rheinland's not giving up. He'll keep working till he knows what the testing was and whose mom had contact with them."

"Donavan? Laney? Has your family ever been to Georgia?"

Donavan pondered for a minute. "My mother traveled a lot for work. There's a good chance. But as far as I know, she was never seriously ill."

"Laney?"

"I don't…" She racked her brain to sort through her mother's past. Before she was a housewife, she'd worked in payroll.

Previous to Colorado, all their family had lived in the Chicago area. She never knew of her mother going South or being ill. "Sorry. I've got nothing."

"Well, with your permission, Rheinland has added you to the list. He'll see if there's something that connects you to us."

"Which brings up an interesting question." Tag's voice revealed that the fire had done nothing to warm him to Laney's presence. He leaned forward to where the shadows danced in creepy patterns across his features. "How are you connected to us? Why didn't you get the call? No one has ever joined us who we didn't sense first."

"I did," Donavan insisted.

"—and didn't feel it themselves," Harley chimed in. "If you sensed her, Peterson, how come she didn't feel it, too?"

"Not to mention no one has ever joined without a power of their own," Tag persisted.

Brian added, "Or was a girl," with more enthusiasm than the others expressed.

A thick silence wrapped around them, and Laney's tongue couldn't loosen from its hold.

Jacob spoke in her place. "We've always known there was a sixth one of us somewhere. Does anyone doubt Donavan's calling?" No one spoke. "Well, if you believe he belongs here, then you have to believe Laney does. There's no way to deny that if she affects his powers, she belongs. Objections?"

More awkward silence followed, and Laney hated herself for not being strong enough to speak up. But truly, what did she know? This morning she had no idea that this band of superhumans even existed. It was impossible to know how she fit in other than a super-supplement for Donavan.

Tag spoke with the same mistrustful undertone. "A demonstration would be nice."

"Tomorrow," Donavan agreed.

"Our priority right now is safety," Jacob said, taking command of the conversation again. "Someone needs to take watch after RJ."

A million and one unanswered questions jumbled in Laney's mouth; it took her considerable effort to swallow them before they spilled out. Donavan didn't even give her a glance as he stood to volunteer. "I'll take next watch."

§ § § § §

"So it's you and me, Buttercup."

Like Laney needed a reminder that the straw she'd drawn for the watch following Donavan was with Harley. Somehow Donavan and Jacob got to be together again. It seemed their leader wanted a handle on who or what Donavan was—that he liked the newcomer, too. The others paired up to sleep a slight distance from one another. RJ remained at a distance. His detachment from the others and their acceptance of it was at the top of her list of questions.

"Could we at least have an extra blanket?" Laney mumbled. They perched high up the hillside with a view of each side of the ridge, a place Donavan and Jacob had scouted earlier. The glimmer of the dying campfire flickered below. The watch crew had flashlights, walkie talkies, and a weapon as their resources. If black robots picked this moment to reappear, Laney hoped Harley's intuition would be enough to give them the advantage because she was sure she would turn into useless bait.

Harley chuckled as Laney shivered. "We'll only be a couple hours. It's good to have the cold keep you awake." He lit his cigar from behind a shielding hand and took a few puffs.

Laney gagged. "Any chance you could do that elsewhere?"

"Any chance you—ahhh, fine." The glowing tip disappeared, and the two sat in dark silence for a moment. "So you and Donavan, huh?"

"What is with everyone's obsession with our relationship?"

"Is there one?"

"One what?"

"A relationship."

"We…have…it's not that simple."

"Meaning?"

"Could we talk about something else?"

"Sometimes the thing right in fronna us is the one we most don't wanna see."

"Huh?"

Laney thought she saw a flash of white teeth in the sparse moonlight as Harley leaned back with the unlit cigar clamped in a grin, but he didn't answer her.

"There's still some things I don't get," she changed the subject before he spoke again. "Everyone being super and all—that's freaky enough. I get that this guy Rheinland is trying to find a plausible reason, but what about Jake's? It's a place. How can it just magically appear and disappear like Donavan said?"

Harley didn't answer, and Laney wondered if she had said something wrong.

"Some things are hard to explain. Some things we can't." A pause. Harley shifted on his rock and started eyeballing her again. "Your boyfriend, for example." A purposeful subject change, no doubt, given away by his tone. "How do you explain how you two…work? You two gettin' serious?"

She rolled her eyes and gave in to the topic. "Okay, listen. We tried to date, sort of. It didn't work out so well."

"How come?"

"It just got complicated." How? When? It had felt easy to start. She tried to hold her ground even as her thoughts betrayed her. "He was divorced, then he wasn't. He got kicked off the force, started acting erratic… it was all too much. We had to give it up."

"But now you here."

"Well, yeah, because he showed me what he can do. And those things," she waved her hands around in the darkness. "They're out there. He told me it isn't even safe for me to be at home with my kids. How could I do anything but help?"

"So are things still complicated, I mean, seeing that you followed him here?"

"Are you kidding me? I'm sitting on a rock in the middle of nowhere with you, a complete stranger, to be night watch for a band of, of—whatever we are—wearing shoes that gave me blisters from hiking a mile with golden boy, while *my* guy voluntarily hiked in the opposite direction. I can't step closer than twelve inches to him without zapping him or something, so I'd say, yeah, things are a little complicated.

"But right now I'm more worried about doing my business in a prickly bush in the morning than if my boyfriend likes me or *like* likes me… so could we just talk about something else?"

A low chuckle rumbled from Harley's throat. "I dunno if you belong here or not," he said. "But we sure gonna have fun finding out."

Chapter 21

"Nothing!" Brian reported much too loudly. The rest of the group had just begun to stretch themselves out of sleep when he walked into camp and announced the results of his dawn shift. This observation did not sit well with him despite the fact it matched every other report of the night. He punched his fists onto his hips and huffed. "Harley? Still no tinglys?"

"No." Harley looked more in need of a cup of coffee than most. "Nothing. If they planning anything, it's far from here."

"Great," Tag grumbled. "If there's no threat, what are we doing here?"

Jacob held up his hand. Spending the night—or part of one—on a blanket in the dirt apparently hadn't affected Jacob the way it had Laney. His stepped forward refueled and alert. "We've been in plenty of situations that have taken time to unfold. We'll know soon enough."

"We've always known more than this," Tag countered. "What are we doing in the god-forsaken desert, miles from—"

"Tag!" Harley barked. Tag sat down heavily and quieted.

"But he's right," Brian spoke up. Both men eyed the speaker cautiously. No one was used to Brian speaking out; that was Tag's role. "By the time we're in danger, we've always had a pretty good idea of who and why. This time they're on us before we know a thing; and it's from a what not a who."

"Well, it makes no sense that someone or something is out to get our group," Harley said. "We don't make enemies; we find other people's enemies, bury them, and get out before anyone's the wiser. We're called, just to something bigger this time. Usually we grab the tail and kick the tiger's butt when it turns on us. In this case, the tiger found us first."

"What tiger, Harley?" Tag asked. "These robots? They are the tail; for Pete's sake, who exactly is the tiger in your dysfunctional scenario? A delinquent property manager who didn't clean up his mess in this rotting neighborhood? Ooooo, scary."

Laney gripped her head, trying hard to decipher the tiger metaphor, but Donavan's eye roll encouraged her to give up.

"Hey, Tag, your mamma called," Harley badgered, not ready let go. "She want her purse back. Either man up or move out, ya pile of--"

"Go ahead," Tag sneered. "Say it."

"Aw, beat it."

Brian laughed, but Laney gave him a "huh?" with her arched eyebrow.

"We had a swear jar for years," Brian grinned. "Harley lost a fortune—fifty bucks once in a single day. He's had a sissy mouth ever since."

"Okay, boys, enough." Jacob didn't need to raise his voice to get attention. "We'll make use of this time while the danger isn't imminent. Let's see how well we work together with our new members."

"Does this mean we get to play with artillery?" Brian beamed.

"Among other things," Jacob said, dumping dirt onto the fire.

"I believe there's still one mystery we can clear up right now," Tag said. Everyone followed his gaze to Laney.

"What? Me?"

"It remains to be seen how you fit in with the rest of us," Harley explained.

Brian grinned. "It'd be nice to know if that magnification effect you have on Donavan works on me—on us, I mean."

"Oh."

Jacob looked dubious, but relented. "Donavan explained to you about the rest of us being defensive or offensive? You're kind of new territory for us. If you give Donavan the strength he says you do, clearly you're part of the offensive team. But we don't know if our skills can help protect you in the way it does the others in the group."

"Well, don't you all...mesh with Donavan? Why would I be different?"

"We can't feel you," Jacob said. "None of us detected you as one of us. Only Donavan."

"That's never happened before," Harley reminded her.

"Right. Okay. So what do you want me to do?"

Jacob gave Tag a nod; a smile spread across Tag's face, one that gave Laney goose bumps.

"Just a few tests. Nothing major." Tag picked up a piece of firewood. "Brian first."

Brian walked over to Laney and grabbed her hand a little too comfortably. "Don't worry," he whispered, though she was sure the rest of the crew could hear him. "I've never failed at this...yet."

"Ready?" Tag asked, and before she could protest, he pulled the board back in a whistling arch. "Let me know if this tickles."

"Hang on—" Donavan started, but the board was in motion before he finished.

Laney flinched and shrieked as Tag showed no sign of holding back his swing toward her. The next moment her ears filled with a wind that sucked the air away from her, and everything stilled. Brian had an iron grip on her wrist as she had tried to wriggle away in panic.

"Easy," he said. "You don't want to lose me."

She stared at him in disbelief. "You—you really can stop time. None of them can see or hear us?" The group had become motionless in an unworldly haze around her.

"Nope."

Laney viewed the mountain, the ground, her body, the others—all exactly the same, but not inside the world where she stood; a surreal sense of being part of something extraordinary made her insides quiver.

"And if you let go?"

"A world of hurt awaits you." He nodded toward Tag, frozen mid-swing. The sneer on his lips told her he might actually want to make contact.

"Now what?"

"Now we move." They took a small step to the right with wavy lines of quivering air parting as if their footfalls were moving their time bubble.

"My ears," she said. "The sound's coming back."

"That's because we're moving away from the danger. Once there's no threat to us, the time restarts rather quickly. Get ready. One more step."

"I have a better idea," Laney said, narrowing her gaze at her assailant.

In seconds, time rushed back to normal, and not only did Tag's bat beat the empty air before him, but he received a whack on the back of the head at precisely the same moment.

He spun around to find Laney behind him.

"Brian," Tag growled. "You promised never to do that."

"Wasn't me," Brian answered, holding up his hands. "All Laney." But Tag's glower aimed itself at the person who had made Laney's trick possible.

"And what exactly was the plan if the shield hadn't worked? If the board had made contact with her?" Donavan asked, deep grooves dug in his brow. Laney's heart pattered a little at his vocal concern.

"Aww, I wasn't going to hit her that hard," Tag smirked.

"So she can be trapped in Brian's force," Jacob noted. He smiled slightly in Laney's direction. "Nice *move,* Laney. So any training?"

Laney shrugged. "Self-defense classes in college. Gymnastics. Does that count?"

"Brian, how about you? Any difference with Laney holding on?"

Brian shook his head. "Nah. Her skin's softer than any of yours, so that's a bonus. But no; there wasn't any extra intensity or anything like that."

"Harley, how'd you feel?"

"Felt it coming."

Brian picked up the board and joggled it in his hand. "Tag's up. Jacob, wanna do the honors?"

Brian tossed Jacob the beam, which he caught with the ease of a batter coming out of the dugout. Tag came near Laney and Brian. Jacob didn't look apologetic as he swung the testing tool toward Laney, but he also didn't seem to share Tag's delight at the task. Laney instinctively flinched but managed to hold it together as Brian grabbed one hand and Tag grabbed her other. The board whipped forward, and Tag threw his free hand out fast while a blinding blue light filled the small, timeless world the three figures inhabited. The bolt of electricity headed straight toward the board and its batter. Within the same second, the sizzling light splintered and traveled toward Laney, encircling her without warning.

It was the last thing she remembered before her back hit the ground, darkness wrapping her up in a tight cocoon.

"Are you crazy?" were the first words she heard as consciousness returned. "You could have killed her!" The voice very definitely Donavan's—definitely an unhappy Donavan.

"How should I know that would happen? She was in the time lock with us. In theory, that should have protected her," Tag's voice protested.

"Did you not even consider holding Brian's other hand instead of hers?"

"How would that prove anything?"

"Please," she moaned. Someone knelt by her side while she wrestled one eyelid open. "Stop fighting, you two."

"You okay?" Donavan said close to her ear. His hand held her shoulder for the briefest of moments, but it gave Laney comfort.

"Oh, yeah. Just peachy."

Donavan helped her up, the smell of singed hair in the air. "And for the record," she told her onlookers, "I failed that one."

A few laughs erupted. Jacob smiled slightly, and he came to stand in front of her. "Let's have a look." He cupped her chin in his fingers and examined her eyes, slowly turning her head first one way and then the other. "Seeing any spots?"

"Does red count?"

His smile widened. "Keep that anger in check. You can use it later. Squeeze my hands…harder. Any pain?"

She shook her head. Her fingers and toes tingled, her legs felt wobbly like Jell-O. With all eyes on her, she decided it was no time to show weakness. "Not really. Just like the wind got knocked out of me." She gave Jacob a once-over and realized he was unscathed. "How come Tag didn't take you out? You weren't in the time lock, and he electro-zapperated you too."

"My gift. No bullets, no shocks, no radiation affects me."

"So the zap bounced off you?" Anger still lingered in Donavan's tone.

"No, the shock reached me, just didn't hurt. Now we know that Laney isn't…zap-proof. Grabbing her hand was definitely a bad move. Tag, use more caution. We aren't out to maim anyone."

Jacob's simple admonishment hit its mark; Tag dug his boot heel into the ground while his hands found his back pockets.

"But what about us?" Donavan asked. "If Tag wanted to hit us, would it take us down?"

"It hurts," Harley confessed. "But unless he unleashes all he's got, we good."

"Tag, you feel any difference in your powers?" Jacob asked.

He answered no.

Jacob continued calculating what Laney's inabilities meant. "Okay. So Harley and Brian have you on radar, but not Tag. That's…unusual."

"Why do you think that is?" Donavan wondered out loud.

Jacob's eyes narrowed in thought. "She's us, but not completely. Like she's not finished yet maybe."

"So I still have a chance of developing the power to fly?" Laney joked since it didn't seem like her legs would cooperate anytime soon.

Jacob half grinned and cuffed her arm. "Let's hope. It'd be great if one of us could get off the ground."

"Now we get to play, right?" Brian's undeterred enthusiasm broke up the musings.

Jacob nodded, and Harley signaled everyone over to the trailer. Brian gave a whoop, sprinting ahead. Several large plastic tubs were handed down from Harley to Brian, and they removed protective vests and several guns Laney didn't immediately recognize. Each weapon housed a long, thin metal tank beneath the barrel.

Laney's comprehension dawned once she spotted the small bags of round pellets, and she scrunched up her nose. "Airsoft guns?"

"Yep," Brian grinned. "You can be on my team."

"Thanks," said Laney, "but I'm a horrible shot."

"Yeah, but I'm not."

Once everyone geared up, Jacob called out directions. "It's important that we know how we work together, and this is the best way to do that."

"Nah," Brian winked at her. "That's what he always says, but really we just do it for fun."

"Our defensive team is useless unless attacked, so we need to simulate that," Jacob went on. "Harley, you take Tag and Brian." Brian shrugged regrets to Laney and joined his team. "I'll take Donavan, Laney, and RJ," Jacob said. Laney had all but forgotten about RJ. She couldn't locate him anywhere in the open, but she was pretty certain he'd be just fine without safety gear. Jacob finished out his orders with, "Harley, take the houses on the west side of the street and we'll take the east side."

"Last man standing?" Brian asked.

"Yes."

"Any rules?" Harley asked, fishing in his pocket for a cigar.

"Tag, no tasing the others. Only objects. Donavan, we'd like to see what you've got with Laney by you, but go easy. I'll let RJ know he can't simply disarm the other team. Way too easy for him. Questions?"

"Yep," Laney volunteered, shooting her hand straight up.

"Laney?"

"Sorry I didn't get the wardrobe memo before I got dragged into this, but there's no way it's fair if I'm running around in these shoes. Suggestions?"

Jacob jerked his head at Harley who then bounced back into the trailer. He slid out another storage tub full of army apparel. Laney rummaged through until she found three pairs of boots at the bottom. One pair was close enough to her size; the green socks looked itchy, but Laney welcomed them in trade of more possible blisters. She donned the helmet Donavan had given her and a protective vest. No one else seemed concerned with eye wear. She readily put on a pair of goggles, not caring how she looked in her thin cotton blouse under an oversized vest, large awkward army boots and headgear.

"Better?" Jacob asked. His down-to-earth approach to everything made it easy to see why Donavan had trusted him so quickly. It helped Laney feel empowered despite her grunge attire.

"Good to go."

"Ever shot one of these before?" he handed her a weapon.

"No. Had a Master Blaster squirt gun that looked something like it."

"You don't get wet with these things, honey," Tag pointed out.

The teams split up, and Laney quickly jogged up to Donavan. "Okay, a little help here. We're really going to shoot these things at each other?"

"It's airsoft, Laney," he smiled. "They're low gauge. You'll be alright."

"I hear they hurt."

"A little."

"So what's our plan?"

"Don't get hit."

Behind a wooden beam that only partially concealed her body, Laney slid to the floor with her weapon held high, her breath coming in short gasps. Despite being tagged in the back several times already, the game continued. Since they considered her teamed with Donavan, no one wanted to concede she was out until they'd hit Donavan too. Donavan stood around the partially formed wall, back to back with Laney. His gun balanced through an empty window frame, and Laney didn't need to see his face to know it held confidence and determination.

She had neither. Each time a pellet whizzed her way, her heart screamed retreat while her limbs became uncontrollable conduits of fear. Her years of competitive sports hadn't prepared her for the kind of panic this simulation evoked. And she sucked at it.

Letting defeat overwhelm her, she lowered the gun and glanced at RJ crouched just outside the house, his monstrous form obvious through the breaks in the wall. He no longer looked human. She wasn't sure how turning into rock form came about, but in the face of a simulated battle, RJ had become almost completely stone and grown another foot in height. Solid mobile rock. No vest needed. His eyes, mere slits in a rounded boulder on top of sandy, squared shoulders, held fast to the horizon. The airsoft gun looked like a toy in his massive hands—seemed doubtful that his fingers could even squeeze the trigger. His movements drew so much attention that he intentionally kept frozen until needed.

Jacob backed himself into the room and barely glanced at Laney.

"On your feet, soldier," he said, not unkindly. Like Donavan, Jacob treated her like a kid sister only there to make a game with the big kids even. They tolerated her bumbling around by their sides, her mistakes forgiven quickly, her orders given patiently. Laney could see no game plan and had no idea where the others were. It didn't matter; no one could match Brian's defensive skill. Twice Jacob and Donavan closed in on the other team—Laney trailing behind, RJ on the outskirts—but the others would disappear, thanks to Brian's time warp. Their quickness pleased

Jacob, but as their leader, he also was determined to think like the enemy and find a way around the warp. The key was to separate the players on the other team. Without Harley detecting the advance for Brian, they could hit Brian by surprise. Without Brian in the game, Harley and Tag would become easier targets. That much Laney understood.

She stumbled to her feet and tried to put on her war face, but Jacob's slight grin told her she couldn't pull it off. A rumble from RJ caught their attention, and with an oversized hand, he gave a signal. Their leader nodded and pulled Laney around the wall where they stood with Donavan. After more rapid hand signals, Donavan pulled her down a hallway while Jacob stayed put.

The roofless hallway had no wall at its end and led straight out the side of the house. RJ moved outside the wall to their right. Before Donavan could poke his head around to check, Tag appeared and fired a round. Laney screamed while Donavan instinctively flattened himself to the wall, allowing the pellet to speed past him. As Laney turned, a *thwunk* hit her left buttock and sent a smashing pain through her muscle. She sank to the floor with a cry, her weapon forgotten, her throbbing backside the only thing she cared about. Commotion around her vaguely registered. Harley assaulted Jacob, and Brian had RJ in his sights. After much shouting, shuffling, and a few curses, her team surrendered—game over.

Donavan offered Laney a hand up, but she swatted it away.

"Don't be a sore loser," Donavan said, pulling her up anyway.

"Says the guy who didn't take a bullet in the rump. Dang, that hurts! Are we done now?"

"Let's switch up the teams," Jacob called out.

"Oh, for crying out loud. No." Laney threw down her gun and held up her hands in defeat. "Time out, okay? I need a time out."

Jacob made his way to Donavan and Laney while the rest of the guys rallied around RJ to include him in their next game plan. Jacob jerked his chin at Donavan, which seemed to be a signal to recap.

"It's difficult," Donavan said, shaking his head. "I can't really unleash or I'd hurt someone. When Tag was on us I had no time to block him with, say a piece of the plywood, which would have been easy enough for me to rip from the wall. All I could have done was hand to hand, and then I would have damaged him, I'm guessing. Perhaps you need to let Tag be able to shock me so I can defend—I don't know. Simulation is just not realistic for me."

"I'm thinking you could have taken the bullet for me," Laney chimed in.

"Suggestions?" Jacob asked, as if she hadn't spoken.

"Pair me up with Harley. If I know they're coming, I can play defense without harming anyone."

"Worth a try. Tag and Brian have already proven they're pretty invincible paired with Harley. Let's see what they do without him."

"Excuse me," Laney interjected, "but I don't see the need for me to do this. I am useless and also injured. Can I just sit this one out?"

Harley called out to them, and Jacob nodded at Donavan.

"Form the new teams and reload. Let me talk to Laney a minute."

Donavan hesitated, but like everyone else, he obeyed without complaint, giving Laney a *be-good* look as he jogged out through the wall frames.

"How'd you feel during the simulation?" Jacob asked her.

"Confused. Scared. Utterly helpless."

"Good. We can work with that."

"How could any of that possibly be good?"

"When we're attacked, it's never neat and organized. Nothing ever goes as practiced or planned. We work inside the realm of confusion."

"How?"

"Tell me why you're scared."

"Because I don't want to get shot! Do those metal machine freaks have bullets?"

"It doesn't appear so…" Something in his voice caught Laney's attention.

"But?"

"Who knows. They could."

Laney let that sink in, swallowed, and nodded.

"Right now we're in a simulation, Laney. I need you to use that confusion and fear to practice. What are you going to do when the bullets are real? Are you going to scream and slide to the floor? Wait for one of the guys to pull you to safety?"

Laney chewed her bottom lip. She was going to gnaw a hole by the end of the day.

"Figure it out. Create a goal for yourself. Do it as if you're saving your children. Think on your feet and don't worry about getting tagged. It's gonna happen at first, but you'll get better if you think through it and decide what you're going to do with your fear and panic."

"It's easy for you to say," she said. "You've got skills."

"You're athletic. You're smart. And Laney, you're not useless. Donavan needs you and will use you. Figure out how to use him."

"Okay."

"Don't give up; get better."

With an exhale, she nodded and walked with him toward the group. *You're saving your children* was the only thing she let run through her weary mind. She couldn't quite work up an image of her children in danger, so she let the words be enough.

The next round went no better. Laney got tagged with embarrassing speed, despite her determination to stay low and alert. Instead of fearing failure, she let her frustration fuel her as Jacob had suggested. Jacob was on her team the round that followed, along with Tag and Donavan. This time she worked hard at using Donavan. She used him as her weapon while she worked as the eyes in the back of his head.

The next time the others cornered them, Laney broke away from Donavan. Harley approached, hid behind a wall, and the two aimed shot after shot at each other. Harley never detected her and continued down along the frame of the house. With adrenaline coursing through her, Laney peered out from behind the wall and took shaky aim at Harley's back just as a force behind her swept her off her feet. She tried not to squeal as RJ lifted her over the wall and set her next to Donavan, proof that she was a casualty. But it cost him. With RJ exposed, Jacob quickly tagged him. When Harley circled back, he received a shot to the chest. Laney finally had a team win despite her takedown.

"Feels like lunch time," Tag said when they all reconvened. "What we got to eat around here?"

"Not yet," said Laney, a bit too harshly, drawing curious looks. "Let's go one more time."

Tag looked like he would protest, but Jacob nodded consent, and it was a done deal. Laney found a rubber band among the supplies and whipped her hair into a messy bun. The helmet no longer fit well with the knot, so she ditched both it and the goggles. Her blouse, no longer white, she abandoned in favor of only the cami underneath.

Jacob put Laney and Donavan on his team but with RJ, the original four. They all reloaded—except Laney who hadn't fired a shot—and split up to take their places.

Donavan jogged next to Laney as they took advantage of their sixty-second countdown. "You sure about this?"

"Of course not," she panted. "But I have to keep trying."

"You're doing great."

"I'm slowing you down and getting you tagged every time. Let's split up this time so you can feel unencumbered. I wanna see how I do."

They found a house they hadn't yet used and spread around its perimeter by Jacob's direction. "Laney," Donavan said, checking his weapon, "I'm not going to leave you in a real— "

Something stirred in Laney, but she ignored it and she cut him off. "Just this round. Every man for himself. Come on; it's just airsoft."

Donavan stopped and searched her face until she almost blushed. "Okay. This round only. Just...shadow me. Can you do that?"

She had seen Tag and Brian do this well. "You got it."

Donavan headed out along the south side of the house. Laney waited until he made it to the end, checked around the corner, and disappeared. At the corner, she did the same thing and began the hunt in earnest. She listened hard and paused even when Donavan went ahead. She thought about the pattern of the houses, how Tag and Brian operated, and tried to guess where they would most likely attack. But, by Jacob and Donavan's quick advances, she could tell they only had winning on their mind, not defense. Laney inwardly sighed and followed. She still limped from the shot in her backside while the others healed already from any shots they'd received.

Light footfall at the house to the right made her pause and backtrack for cover. Whoever it was would approach soon, and her chosen hideout contained too many unfinished walls to conceal her. Her only hope was to backtrack into the house she'd just passed. It also would take her further from Donavan, but maybe she could come around back of the other team. The thought excited her and simultaneously made her break into a sweat. She ran to the more-constructed house and found a wall to hug just as Harley and Brian came sliding against the houses across the street. She tucked back and waited several long seconds.

Just as she moved forward to peek, the faintest of footsteps caught her ear, the telltale of someone on the other side of the wall. They'd seen her. Laney broke into a run through the house, her pursuer following. A pelt hit the wood next to her, but Laney weaved between empty walls, her heart ready to pound out of her chest. Fear and confusion—yeah, that's what she had, and she had to use it. If she could just make it around the outer wall... but then what?

With serpentine steps, Laney focused on the backdoor, framed by a completed wall. A simple silver pipe running across the open ceiling caught her attention. Not knowing if it would do her any good, she lunged forward at the last second, grabbed the pipe, and swung her feet up in front of her. The pursuer—who turned out to be Brian—skidded under her upraised legs before he could stop himself. Too late, he turned and raised his gun, but Laney dropped forcefully down on him. She landed heavily on his chest, disarming him in the process.

Donavan had been right—catch him by surprise, and Brian didn't have a chance to timelock himself.

Laney, straddling her captive, aimed her gun at his vest, ready for her first shot of the game. Brian grinned and held up his hands in surrender. She took her finger off the trigger and tried to breathe past the ache in her lungs. Before either of them could speak, more footsteps approached. She righted herself and listened.

Someone was obviously running in their direction. Every instinct told her to flee, but she refused, pushing past the thought of another battered body part. She readied for a shot. Fear said she'd tag the wrong person, that she would get tagged first, or that she would miss altogether. Despite the swimming doubt, Laney held her ground when the figure charged around the corner.

Harley.

Her shot made it off before his, and curses exploded from him as he went down. Laney exhaled hard, sweat pouring down her temples. Harley sat up and rescued the cigar that had fallen into the dirt.

Laney glanced at Brian, still flat on the ground between her thighs and grinning like an idiot.

"Well, alright," he said.

When Laney looked back at Harley, something in his posture told her he wasn't alone. He was trying too hard not to look back at the corner he'd just rounded. According to rules, he and Brian were "dead" and unable to say a word.

Slipping to her doorframe, Laney caught a glimpse of Tag through the half-naked perpendicular wall, sneaking toward Harley. Squashed invisible in the doorway, Laney considered her options but felt trapped either going forward or back. So she went up. Using the pipe again, she swung herself as silently as possible on top of the roofless wall and lowered herself to lay flat across its width.

The effort made her butt ache, but she bit her lip and pushed through the pain. Brian stared straight up at her with his wide smile until she scowled back at him. Obediently, he shut his eyes and let his tongue hang out to indicate death as Tag crept around the corner. If Tag saw her in the next few steps, she'd have no way to position her weapon in time. She had to hope... just two more steps... and he was walking below her. Unable to hide her own grin, Laney tapped his head with her muzzle, and he froze.

"Bang," she said.

Shoulders slumped and head down, Tag slowly raised his hands. Brian called out the end of game as he popped back up.

But like a sudden change in weather, Laney knew something was wrong. Harley bolted upright in panic, and Tag shouldered his weapon, tensely. Brian leapt for her. She stifled a cry when his hand closed onto her ankle and the sound of stopped time rushed in her ears.

"What's going on—" she tried to speak while Brian awkwardly pulled at her to stand beside him in his timelock. "I don't know," he said, all signs of humor gone from his face. "Something's out there." Tag and Harley stood frozen.

Brian pulled her forward around the corner. "Follow me," he said needlessly, his hand tightly clasped on her arm. Laney scanned to the left and right for Donavan and the others, but Brian didn't seem to care. She expected time to come crashing back around them as soon as they cleared themselves from potential danger, but they jogged beyond the houses and to the trailer still in his lock.

"Keep hold of me. No matter what."

She grabbed his shirt and nodded. At the trailer, Brian opened the weapon's locker and drew out ammo. He shoved a large long gun at her.

"Take this."

Sounds collapsed around her, and Laney sensed they were no longer shielded. Did that mean they were no longer in danger?

"I can let go?"

"Yes, but stay with me." Brian slung three extra rifles onto his back, and two onto Laney's. "Let's go." Apparently, Brian wasn't taking any chances.

They backtracked toward the others when Harley and Tag appeared at the end of the road, running towards them. Jacob appeared from a side street, his stride swift and purposeful.

Fear and confusion, fear and confusion…use them.

Laney swallowed and tried. But Donavan was nowhere to be seen.

Chapter 22

The dawning within Donavan happened quickly. Instantly. One moment he hid behind a wooden beam, controlling his breathing, deep in combat simulation mode—the next, his heart was pounding, his feet moving, a snag of a missing second in his conscious: Brian's time stop.

Laney.

More powerful than the sudden danger that awakened his body was the need to find Laney. To protect her. At first, he fought the impulse drawing him out of hiding, but Jacob streaked past, and in a moment RJ rumbled into the street with them. *They* sensed it, too. Feet moved toward camp, the same intense alert driving them without knowing why or where.

Laney.

Donavan had kept her within his peripheral during training, but now he had no idea where she'd gone, a good indication that Brian had swept her up in his protective time shield. Somehow that didn't matter. His body still screamed for her, needed her with him.

Laney, Laney, Laney….

There she was, standing at the end of the street with Brian. Harley and Tag rounded another corner the same second Laney turned her head Donavan's way. She called his name with a desperation that constricted his own throat. Yet his sprint slowed to a jog when, just as it had enveloped him, the alarm within subsided. Danger passed, a fight no longer imminent, an enemy gone or unfounded. Somehow he knew this, but one look at his comrades confirmed its truth.

The men unloaded the weapons from Brian's and Laney's shoulders to arm themselves, though it seemed obvious they were no longer needed. To everyone except Laney, that is. She shrugged off the rifles to the nearest hands, ridding herself of the clunky metal. In a wild charge, she flung herself into Donovan's arms.

The force nearly knocked him off his feet, and his teeth set against the shock. He embraced her in return then moved away to bring his limbs back into control. She noticed; her expression of concern and need turned to disappointment. Her shoulders slumped as she moved to his side, but she said nothing.

"What was that?" Jacob looked at each of them for any explanation.

"It's gone," Brian said.

"How is that?" Tag asked. "How did something get that close to us and get away? Harley?"

All eyes went to their human early-alert system.

Harley shook his head. "Nothin. I got no sign till like a second before the rest of you. It come in fast and then gone...." He continued to shake his head and scowl, looking no one in the eye.

A raw suspicion needled at Donavan, and not for the first time. He worked his jaw, surveying Jacob's face for signs of similar misgivings but found the closed look unreadable.

"Tell them." The words came from Donavan before he realized he would say them.

All eyes came his way, and he nodded in Harley's direction. "Level with us, Harley."

"What garbage you talkin 'bout?" Harley's chin jerked back at Donavan.

"Tell them. Tell them that you can't feel a thing." Their eyes locked and everyone got quiet. "Tell them you haven't felt a thing since we've been here."

Harley growled something under his breath and chomped at his cigar. Glances moved around the circle.

"How did Laney get the drop on you just now?" Donavan continued, more certain now in his hunch. "You came around the corner, right into her line of fire. Why didn't you know she was there?"

Laney snapped her head in Donavan's direction. "You saw that?"

He nodded and realized he'd inadvertently admitted to babysitting her, exactly what she'd asked him not to do. But this was more important, and he kept his eyes on Harley, waiting for a reply.

"Laney's different," Harley finally growled. "She's like a tamed Labradoodle mixed in with junkyard dogs. No one would notice her unless they lifted her tail."

Brian squinted hard at Harley's absurdity and thrust his palms out. "What does that even mean?"

"Harley," Jacob said with measured patience.

Harley's eyes fired daggers of hatred toward Donavan, the kind that years of police work taught him to ignore. "Alright, alright," Harley said. "I ha'n't been able to... exactly... detect much lately."

"Since when?" Jacob asked.

"Since the Oil Eaters surrounded us at that park a week ago. That night I could tell they were coming seconds before they appeared. But here... nothin'. I thought it was cuz they're far away from this spot, off in the desert or somethin." He paused before he ground out the last part of his admission. "But just now... I feel what ya'll felt, like we being watched or something. That's all though."

"What feeling?" Laney asked.

Donavan shrugged his inability to explain. No one else answered, so he tried his best. "I told you, just a sensation. Like goose bumps right before something happens. An urge to fight. We get it right before the Oil Eaters appear. But Harley, he's supposed to get the jump on us. He doesn't just get the willies, he senses what the enemy is going to do before they do it."

"This is crazy," Tag broke in. "Harley, you helped us—you knew every time the other team was going to strike, didn't you? I saw it!"

Harley shook his head in defeat and rubbed its smooth surface as he spoke. "Not really, no. Just going on observation and instinct. You just assumed I was helpin' more than I really was."

Everyone soaked in this new information in an uncomfortable silence.

"So do you sense *anything*?" Brian turned toward Laney, eyes wide with curiosity.

She shook her head grimly, and Donavan bristled when the attention turned once again to his hesitant counterpart.

"I'm tellin' ya, she doesn't fit with us—no offense, Donavan," Harley said.

RJ grunted a dissension, which made Donovan appreciate his rock partner even more.

"Harley!" Brian hissed, joining RJ's disapproval. Points for Brian: another one sticking up for Laney.

"Well, someone's gotta speak up! She makes Donavan better? I don't see it. Tagged him several times myself today. She's got no power, can't sense a thing, and s'got no training. Tag can shock her, for harmony's sake! For all I know, she's the reason I can't feel nothin."

"Excuse me," Tag spat, "but since when did Curly Top become the focus of this conversation? We were talking about you, Harley." Tag untangled himself from his vest and gear as if suddenly claustrophobic. "You, who are supposed to be one of us, leading us to believe—never thought to mention you have no power to—" the equipment flung into the crowd, narrowly missing Brian. "Come on, man," Tag said, "you've been lying to us! Let's deal with that!"

Harley came at Tag; Brian jumped between them to straight-arm them apart.

"Everyone settle down," Jacob said in one sharp clip. "This is new territory for all us. We were brought here without much to go on. Harley, it's not going to do any of us any good if you're hiding information. If you've lost your sense, well, we'll deal with that. But together. Laney included—let's have no more talk about her fitting in."

Harley didn't let it go that easily. "If you wanna point fingers at someone for not feeling nothin—"

"Let's not forget who just took your team out single-handedly," Laney spoke up, surprising Donavan with her boldness. She put her hands on her hips and glared at Harley and Tag, making her look more like an angry girlfriend than a soldier, but Donavan stayed silent.

Harley's jaw worked, but whatever come back he intended came out as submission. "Duly noted."

Tag's sigh held more frustration than acceptance. "That still doesn't mean..." his voice trailed off under Jacob's glare.

Experience told Donavan to act now, within the calm of the storm, rather than wait for the same argument to erupt all over again. He turned to Laney and thinned out his smile. "Time we gave them a little show."

Understanding crossed her features, and Laney returned his nod.

"Gentlemen." Donavan led the gang over to the nearest structure and examined the hollow house in front of them. It was free of pipes or obstacles in its incomplete state. Gripping one of the supports, he nodded to Laney who placed her hand on his back. With swift motion, Donavan pulled the beam from its mounting, causing half the house to crumble. Before the crashing wood hit the ground, he stepped forward, Laney still gripping him as he swung twice and collapsed the rest of the frame using his beam like a wrecking ball until it was nothing more than a splintered bat. The destruction felt satisfying and, impromptu, he leaped and landed on a knee, burying his fist into the concrete foundation, Laney clutching his back. The floor cracked and broke like a plate of glass, almost taking his companion off her feet when the slab settled in big uneven chunks.

The violent disruption of the base caused the triangular rooftop beams to bounce off the house beside them and plummet unexpectedly toward Donavan and Laney. Laney's grip tightened, and the adrenaline surged until he thought it might shoot out his veins. He rose to his feet, but held back the urge to lash out. When only inches separated them from the free-falling boards, Donavan's fist shot into the air and a thousand shards of wood showered around them. With one more quick motion, he twisted so that his arms encircled Laney and her head tucked deep into his chest.

The remnants of the structure whined a bit, then settled with an exhausted sign. Donavan slowly unwrapped his arms. He held Laney's shoulders and looked down at her amid the massive pile of rubble.

"You okay?"

It seemed forever ago since he had intentionally embraced her, and for all the inner turmoil it caused him, at the moment, he didn't want to let go.

"Yeah. How about you?"

He gave a small smile and released her. "A little sizzly, but okay."

Together they turned to their onlookers.

Harley's cigar fell from his lips. Jacob's eyebrows arched in admiration. Tag grunted, and RJ gave the first semi-smile Donavan had seen on the rock giant.

Only Brian, his face lit up like a neon sign, spoke up. "Well, alright then!"

§§§§§

A new unrest stirred the camp into action. Anxiety had infiltrated like a slow gas leak, altering personalities and thickening the air with uncertainty. The ghost town hummed with men grouped into motion as if disengagement came with a strategy all its own.

The men paired off and excluded Laney. She had proven her worth to stay with Donavan, but everyone was set on edge, an attack looming like a certainty. If they weren't going to include her, then she might as well go back home, whatever that meant. Now just didn't seem like the time to bring it up.

Begrudgingly, she decided to win them back by preparing the food, seeing as she had postponed their lunch for another round in the game. Beans and some pan cornbread that smelled far better than it looked was the best she could do. She delivered it with cheer but received vague appreciation in response.

It took some time to find Donavan and Jacob. As the mountain sloped down on the southeast side, into the desert, more rugged rock and cactus formations littered the hill. The two men stood in a tucked away blind not far from the trailer. She heard their voices before seeing them. She rounded the corner and stopped unobserved, reluctant to interrupt their deep conversation.

Several leveled stones served as a makeshift table. Jacob gestured to several black and white photos strewn across the surface. He put names to the faces, his voice rapid and smooth.

"Tag and Brian gather intel before each mission," he was saying. "Those coyotes—the human traffickers—were our main focus when these metal monsters started popping up. But, I don't know. Considering the high level of technology, I don't see what that would have to do with some low level bandits out to make a buck. I don't think these missions are connected.

"So we went to work on old cases, possible enemies. The problem is, we don't really leave many loose ends. We make problems go away. Not many people get to see our powers in action, and when they do, we do our best to make them believe a different reality. That makes our suspect list rather short.

"Players you should be aware of." Jacob indicated three photos Laney couldn't see, so she vied for a better view. The first photo was a mug shot of a man with oily hair and sinister features. His grin showed gaps in his teeth.

"Vince Valentine," Donavan said.

"I know you're familiar with him. We're certain he's not the main brain behind these robots. In fact, the guys found nothing that tied him to this. But the way he made his way in and out of the rock yards definitely has our attention."

"Ours too," Donavan nodded. Laney realized he had spoken as if still part of the police force.

"He's the one," Laney said out loud. "The one from the video..." Eyes turned toward her, and she wished she'd remained quiet. Still, it unnerved her to see a clear shot of the man Donavan had reportedly assaulted.

"We don't have any information about the rocks you mentioned, the ones taken from the rock yard—from your house," Jacob continued as if Laney hadn't spoken, his words rushed. Perhaps he was as nervous as the rest of them; did he think an attack imminent? "Brian's our science guy. Give him all the info you have on that when we're done here. We can't find any reason he'd want the stones. Still, there's something not right about Valentine; we just can't place it. At any rate, he's in jail now, somewhere we can keep an eye on him."

Jacob shuffled to other pictures.

"Faces you should familiarize yourself with. Leon Rheinland I've told you about." Jacob held up a photo of an unassuming man who could be anyone's friend. His lab coat gave him an intelligent air, but his eyes conveyed common sense and lack of prejudice. Laney remembered the group's campfire chat; he was the man working to find out clues to their identity.

Jacob picked up two more photos. "Ozegovich and Calloway."

Laney stepped closer. Unlike grainy, unflattering Valentine photos or the business directory shot of Rheinland, one figure stood out, very postured with a confident smirk in glossy color. "Wow, he's a looker," Laney said. Jacob paused patiently, and when she bit her lips to keep from speaking further, he went on, first explaining the non-glossy figure.

"This is Nicholas Ozegovich. Rheinland gets funding for biological research from several sources. One of them is

Ozegovich, who has pretty deep pockets." The man in the black-and-white shot sported a neat mustache and tie. "Ozegovich is a philanthropist who throws money at all kinds of scientific research. He's tight with Rheinland, trusts him, and has given plenty to Rheinland's pursuit to our origins, except without Nick's knowledge. Rheinland hid us in with his DNA research so that Nick doesn't know anything about us. Decided it would be better that way."

"So he's a good guy. . . right?" Laney said. "I mean, indirectly he's helping us."

"That leads us to Maxwell Calloway," Jacob said in answer to her interruption. He pointed back to the glossies that were obviously from a photo shoot.

"Max Calloway is a bit of an annoyance; he's good friends with Ozegovich for no other reason than to feed his wild side. Girls, parties, extravagant trips. Rheinland is close to Ozegovich, but he keeps his distance from Calloway. Lately Rheinland has detected Calloway's curiosity about his relationship with Nick O. We've got nothing on him, no connection to us. He's not into anything nefarious that we can tell. Just a notorious playboy, heartbreaker. Lots of international travel. Hard to keep tabs on. "

"Does he model?" Laney couldn't help but ask as they shuffled through a rather thick stack of vanity shots.

The man in the photo eyed her back with a naughty little smile that spoke of charm and dishonesty. The blondes in the photo, one on each arm, didn't seem to mind. In one picture, he leaned back against a sports car, revealing that he was neither tall nor built but could wear a suit particularly well. In another shot, much closer, his shock of cropped, white-blond hair highlighted his pale skin and a set of piercing blue eyes. The next photo, an action shot, followed him as he strolled with purpose down a street. The girl on his arm wore an elegant red, drapy coat and black heels while he sported a bowler hat and dark jacket. All the photos showed taste and style, as if taken for a cologne ad or magazine layout. Cocky, arrogant, handsome. He oozed opulence from his second dimension.

"And neither Ozegovich nor Calloway has a connection to these machines?" Donavan asked.

"Nothing so far. We don't know what those machines are, where they came from, or what they want. I'm working backwards, seeing if any of these people somehow connect. Rheinland is confident our identity is still a secret. But if we're looking for a money source, these two are good for that. The fact that Calloway has been nosy doesn't sit well with me, either, but other than appearing to be a bit greedy..." He shrugged. "Ozegovich has his hand in a lot of speculative science projects. It wouldn't surprise me if these machines interested him. There's just no proof of his involvement."

Laney set down their lunch and picked up the close shot of Maxwell Calloway. The intensity of his blue eyes made her quiver inside. "Wonder who took these pictures. I mean, seriously, this looks like a magazine cover. If I had to guess, I'd say he's wearing designer from hat to shoes."

Two patronizing smiles met her glance.

"I brought lunch. You want me to... " but she couldn't think of a single other thing to say to break the awkward silence. "So... I'll just be going."

"This should only take a minute," Jacob answered in the same patient tone Donavan used on her, but she felt dismissed anyway.

Laney dropped the photo onto the pile. Calloway smiled up in victory at her. "Right then."

With cheeks on fire, Laney marched over to the trailer. Twice she almost turned back to give them a piece of her mind, but since Donavan hadn't spoken up for her, she lost the nerve each time. How on earth could a photo show be helpful at a moment like this? Couldn't Jacob pick a less hectic time to debrief? Nevermind. She'd find something more useful to do than concocting theories.

The back end of the large storage container had been thrown open. Inside, Tag and Harley huddled in a small makeshift booth separated from the rest of the trailer. Curiosity mollified her anger. Tension drove their movements as the two men clicked buttons and turned knobs on panels filled with dusty electronic boards, odd archaic technology from eons past. Laney understood none of the clipped words the pair shot back and forth. Tag flipped a switch and kicked off a loud humming. She hadn't seen a generator come out of the trailer, but there it sat.

"What do we need all this stuff for?" The second the question left her mouth, Laney wished she could take it back. No one was in the mood for interruptions and explanations.

"We're surrounded by rock and abandoned houses," came Tag's impatient answer as he placed a pair of headphones on. "This equipment helps us scope out the territory."

"Like what kind of equipment?"

Harley glared at her.

"Legit question," she persisted. "What exactly are these gadgets going to do for us?"

"Electromagnetic pulsar," Tag pointed out a rod connected to a bungee cord. "Sonar," he pointed to a screen, "electron scanner, neutron reader, X-ray, Geiger counter—want me to keep going?"

"How on earth did you get all this stuff?"

"Left over from last year's rescue of an Iranian princess from a kasbah hidden in a cliff in Algiers. Useful in finding a vein of gold that trip, too."

She couldn't tell if he were joking. "For real? So how often…?" The glare blazing from both men made her question fall flat. She got the intended message: unwanted here too.

Laney made sure lunch had been cleaned up and watched the others buzz around her. No one took lightly this latest indication that something lurked around them. She had to find something constructive to do to help prepare. Brian busied himself organizing packs of food, medical supplies, and ammo. She joined him until he realized she kept taking supplies from piles he had already sorted and organized for another purpose. He smiled in his condescending way and enthusiastically suggested she help RJ gather firewood and serve as a lookout from up the hill. She glanced at the rock-man, who was walking over to the house she had helped demolish and sighed. His silent company was better than nothing.

RJ barely glanced at her when she caught up to him. Laney swallowed her uneasiness and focused on the mangled frame before them. The collapsed structure provided easy pickings and was high enough on the hill that they could spot uninvited guests before anyone else in the camp. RJ surveyed the perimeter first, and Laney understood from his movements what he was investigating.

Were they close? Hidden among the structures? Laney had a mental image of the metal monsters circling the camp, looking for a way to get the upper hand, to surprise them all at once. Maybe it was better when they split up. Maybe the machines were waiting for one group shot. Or maybe they wanted the group to break up, take them out one by one. From her vantage point, she could see that none of the guys in camp were looking over their shoulders. They relied heavily on the sixth sense of theirs.

Nothing could approach RJ and Laney without their knowledge if they worked in the center of the house. That seemed to be the unspoken plan. RJ began his work of making the debris into usable firewood, his huge granite back to Laney as if she didn't exist.

Alone and dejected, Laney pondered any topic that might break the ice.

"So you're from Florida?"

No response.

"I've always wanted to go there. Never had the chance. You've always lived there?"

The brown head may have given a slightest nod, but Laney detected no friendliness in it. Still better than nothing, so she prattled on.

"RJ... what's that stand for? Are they the initials or is that your real name, RJ?"

Silence answered.

"Laney isn't my real name. It's Alexandria. I know, I know, it's nothing like Laney, but my dad used to give me all kinds of nicknames growing up. Just trying them out. Like Alex and Alexa and Lexi and Andria and Andi. My sister—she was only three or four—she played along with him. She came up with Laney, and I don't know, it just stuck. My dad liked it because Arie had invented it, and he thought it was cute how it made no sense.

"I grew up in Illinois myself until I was in junior high. Then my folks moved to Colorado, which was so much better. Ever been there?"

Only the low grind of rock against rock answered her as RJ's enlarged thighs moved him through the rubble. Massive hands snapped boards, creating smaller, manageable pieces.

"The mountains are incredible. So different from here. Not all sandy and—"

"Here." RJ handed Laney a hammer. He nodded toward the pile of broken lumber nailed together to her left.

"Oh. Right."

The claws of the hammer proved to be of little use to Laney against the thick boards with long nails. RJ, on the other hand, worked effortlessly. He looked more human-like now, like at their first meeting. His enormous size had diminished, so he had become more of a human in a rock suit instead of the other way around. Perhaps his proximity to danger caused his earlier growth.

He turned and caught her staring.

Embarrassed, she tried to look away but couldn't stop herself from asking, "So how long have you... been... you know, like that?"

She wasn't sure he would answer, breaking her stare and returning to his work. "Six years." The sound and quality of his voice surprised her; it differed greatly from his former rocky self, more rich and full. His tone changed with his size.

"Does your family know?"

He continued to stack without speaking until she opened her mouth to ask the next question. "Listen," he said, cutting her off. "Listen for them. They could be coming."

"But that's gotta be hard," she said, ignoring the ploy to silence her. "Does that mean you haven't seen your family in six years? Do you always... look this way?"

RJ stood and moved toward Laney so quickly that she stepped involuntarily backward. His large frame came to stand over her with the crowbar. "Here," he said and thrust the tool in her hand.

"Th-thanks." She clung to the thick iron bar. "So... how does this work? Same idea as the hammer, right?"

RJ grunted. Taking the bar in his oversized hands, he placed it between two securely nailed boards and braced his feet around them. With a mere tug, he separated them and handed the tool back to her. She took it and weighed it her hands, hoping RJ would return to his own business. He waited for her to start.

"Okay. Right." Laney imitated RJ's actions on a board of her own but slipped several times before she secured the claw properly. RJ never offered help but didn't grunt either. She continued prying until after several long minutes and visible sweat, she managed to ease the boards apart. RJ moved off to his own pile, satisfied.

Laney sighed and focused on her work long enough to forget about metal monsters. "You know at first I thought Brian was just giving me an easy job to get me out of the way. Get the girl out of here, you know? That way you become the lucky one who gets to babysit. But now I have splinters, I'm hot, tired, and starting to think... they just gave me the Tom Sawyer treatment."

RJ gave her a quizzical stare as he kept working.

"You know. Tom Sawyer? Got all his buddies to paint the fence for him because he made them believe that it was fun, not work." He turned toward her with surprising interest so she recounted the Mark Twain classic tale, and he quietly listened with small nods of acknowledgement. She jerked her head toward camp. "Bet they're all sitting around eating the rest of the beans and laughing it up while we bring in the wood."

His grunt sounded like agreement.

"Sorry you got stuck with me." Laney dug the crowbar in tight and rocked it back and forth without much success. A pair of rough hands stopped her and finished the action. "Oh, thanks, RJ... Robert? Richard? Raymond?"

"I'd rather you be here," he said and nodded to some separated wood without recognizing her name conjectures. "I'll break it up. You stack."

A moment of clarity stopped Laney, and she watched as RJ's muscles almost shimmered in the midday sun, like smooth, polished stone. If she squinted a little, he wasn't rock at all, but a sweaty, shirtless construction worker sans the hard hat and steel-toed boots... just another guy.

"*They* make you become so huge, don't they?" she blurted out loud. "I thought it was because of our attacks, like a protective response, but... you're only like that when the other guys are close by, aren't you?"

A dark shadow crossed his face, and Laney was sorry she asked. No wonder he stayed away as much as possible. She could only guess how uncomfortable it would be to undergo such a constant, rapid metamorphosis.

"But not around me," she finished. "The others make you bigger, but I make you normal again. Well, at least there's a little plus in my being here for you, right... Ronald?"

As her firewood stack grew to admirable size, the labor helped her work out a few things. For starters, it wasn't she alone who struggled with these inexplicable abilities. Harley was losing his touch; Donavan was incomplete without her; RJ struggled with his incredulous size and shape. A slight comfort to know that she wasn't the only one with unanswered questions.

Without warning, a sudden blow swept Laney off her feet. The air crushed from her lungs as RJ's massive arm encircled her and propelled her away from the stacks of wood. She scrambled for breath and a foothold, but RJ juggled her like a rag doll. His long, cumbersome strides took them behind a concrete wall around the back of another house. He crouched low to conceal himself and loosened his hold to give her a chance to breathe.

"They're here," was all he said. She gave no reply and tried to refill her lungs and look about. For an eternal minute they knelt and waited. A flick of her guardian's chin told Laney which direction to keep her eyes.

Before she had her bearings, he pulled her into motion again; this time Laney stumbled up onto her own feet with RJ's hand tightly encasing hers. They moved over rock and unpolished ground with such swiftness Laney wondered if she would end up flying behind him like a kite. Her inferior human legs couldn't keep up.

The threat must have come from the right because RJ quickly shoved her left, toward a well-framed house and rumbled, "Go!"

Laney obeyed out of numb confusion, but barely made it to the doorway when the sound of demolition jerked her body back around. She tried to look behind her while running and ended up with tangled results.

Her feet snagged, and, with a thud, she fell hard over the frame at the doorway, just missing the actual entrance. She pinged around like a pinball as panic and momentum drove her forward. Collapsing to her hands and knees, she scuttled to safety, not stopping till she had crawled around the corner. Huddled against the wall, she discovered blood on the front of her shirt. It freaked her out a little, but her body surged with energy. She tried to stand when an arrow of pain stabbed her ankle.

A rumble like thunder engulfed the camp, and the ground shook. Her brain shamed her while her body hesitated; she should be out there. If there was a fight, she wanted in. The realization scared her even more than what waited around the corner.

The ground settled, the chaos outside subsided. With considerable effort, she stood, feeling the full effect of the damaged ankle. The blood might have come from her head, she decided, but it neither hurt nor distracted her enough to keep her hunkered down. A board nearby became her weapon of choice. Heart pounding, she prepared to burst out the door into the fray just as a figure closed in.

Her lungs let out a warrior's cry as she swung the board with all her might only to be jolted mid-swing by Donavan. Her leg was up in an unplanned back-up kick, but the damaged ankle collapsed and dropped her to the floor at his feet.

"Laney! What the—what are you doing?"

"I thought you were one of them. What's happening?"

"They were here." He reached down to help her up, but she waved his hand away, still mindful of the discomfort she caused him. "We all felt them; I didn't see any of them, though."

She nodded as she rose, biting back the pain. "I heard them. Are they...?"

"Gone."

"I was going to say 'ghosts'?"

A slight smile tugged his lips as he shook his head. "Doubtful. RJ made contact with them. I don't know about the others yet. Come on."

She balanced herself on her feet as best she could.

"Did you feel the ground move?" he asked, and she nodded. "That was everywhere—an earthquake of some kind or they disrupted the ground—"

Shouts interrupted him, and Harley jogged into view.

"That lake moved," Harley reported. "The earthquake sent it rockin'— thought it would flood camp. Now it's half the size it was."

Jacob and Tag jogged up from the direction of the camp. They had seen RJ's scuffle and pursued what they thought had been a small army of the bots. But they disappeared as quickly as they had shown up.

Brian ran up last. "Where did they go? It's like they vanished!" He wiped at his brow and revealed something tucked in his hand. "After the quake stopped, I found this." He opened his palm to reveal a brilliant green rock, curiously out of place in its texture and shine amid the desert terrain.

"That's the rock," Donavan nodded. "The same kind stolen from my house."

"Also," Brian continued with squinted eyes, "a house over there just collapsed for no reason. Know anything about that?"

Donavan spoke up, his voice sheepish. "I may or may not have taken down another building looking for those things."

Raised eyebrows and nods of approval all around.

Laney tried to take a step forward and had to reach for the frame for support. "*Also,* I may or may not have sprained my ankle running away from those things."

"Plus your head is bleeding," Harley added.

Tag ignored the banter and pivoted slowly in his place. "I'm next lookout. I'm going to get RJ to show me what happened up here. They can't be far." The others offered similar support.

Laney could swear Donavan stifled a frustrated sigh beneath the patient smile turned her way. "Let's get you down the hill."

Chapter 23

The pain in Laney's ankle did not provide an adequate distraction from a revelation that had suddenly burst to the forefront of her brain. Somehow all fear and anxiety had turned irrationally into something else. Exhilaration? The latest impending attack had made her fearful only to a point. Mostly it left her breathless. Like an unexpected roller coaster you wanted to ride one more time just to make sure you were as tough as you thought you were. She kept silent and avoided eye contact as she sorted this developing rapture out. Unfortunately, she couldn't bring her ankle on board.

Jacob quickly accessed no broken bones, but the slow coloring and swelling indicated damage below the surface. She told herself that the injury wasn't that painful. But after a bad attempt to walk unaided, RJ pushed through the group, and without a word, picked her up like an overprotected kid with a skinned knee.

Childishly braced against RJ's huge hip, her puny arms around his thick neck, Laney got her chance to be up close and personal with RJ for the first time. The texture of his skin remained a source of undeniable fascination. His body, which looked so gritty and sandy from a distance, felt surprisingly soft and flexible up close, like a good pair of yoga pants. He became more human in feature, form, and feel than she would have suspected, being snuggled up so close; she tried not to squirm or stare too much.

RJ deposited Laney into the "bedroom" of their camp house and stayed by her side until Jacob brought in the medical kit. Donavan hovered, but his crossed arms didn't give Laney much comfort. She knew his mind must be revved up as much as hers.

"Should be good as new in a few days," Jacob reassured her. He bandaged the swelling flesh and its surrounding cuts. "Wanna talk about it?"

"Talk about what?"

He gave a little knowing smile. "What are you thinking?"

"That it sucks that I actually did okay in our little war game and then got hurt running away from something I can't see. And I wish..."

"What?"

"I don't know," she shrugged. "That I knew more."

"Don't let these guys intimidate you," he said. "None of us knew what we were doing when we first got called."

She considered telling him of the urge to fight, the glimmer of a spark within, but remained silent, remembering how excluded he'd made her feel earlier.

He said, "Get some rest," before exiting.

She arranged herself so that the shade of the wall protected her from the descending sun. Propped up, she felt ready to fly to her feet—well, limp anyway—at a moment's notice if the threat returned. Donavan gave her aspirin from the kit and left to join the others, promising to be right back.

A twinge of hurt followed; he never glanced back on his way out. RJ, her remaining companion, kept to the corner where she witnessed his vulnerable change from giant back to man. The others gone, just the two of them here, brought him down to the size she had first met. The miracle of it struck her all over again, and she wished she could move in closer.

"Could you bring me something to prop my ankle up higher, um... is it Roger?"

She hoped her humor might produce a smile, but he disappointed her with stone-faced silence as he retrieved a rolled-up blanket to add to the pile under her injured foot.

"RJ," he corrected her and returned to the far wall. He, too, seemed ready, waiting for the unwanted presence to return.

Shouts. Laney raised herself up, and RJ answered them back. Only directions, coordinating their efforts. RJ gathered some things and left her. She slumped back into her pathetic prone position.

Long minutes moved into an hour and headed toward another. No word. She closed her eyes and pictured the details of this stress-filled day. Donavan's face appeared many times with that something in his eyes that stirred her. How had she let herself be talked into doing all this for a man? Or was it for the kids? The reasoning seemed cloudy. She pushed those ideas aside and reflected on the "fear and confusion" she had suppressed. She pictured all her battles, the first physical confrontations of her life, and rallied at her response. She had taken down a few guys, used her brain, and hadn't sucked too bad. Not only that, but she felt... alive.

Before she'd tripped over her own feet and ended up here that is. *Sigh.*

She should call it a day—tell Donavan it was time to go. Experiment over. Even if she put her kids at risk being near them, she couldn't live without them forever. She should go back.

Still... she wanted to stay.

An oddly familiar stirring came within, this new self seeming not so new at all.

She yanked herself up with a start and found she could stand okay. Memories were coming to her in a rush that made her breath catch between her teeth. A part of her long ago put away...

A single step on her injury forced her back against the wall. She wasn't going anywhere soon. With eyes shut, she did the next best thing.

"Donavan!"

§ § § § §

Panic, fresh and sentient, prickled the back of Donavan's neck and kept him focused on his mission. They had split up to scout; he had taken the inner circle closest to camp and scoured every bush and scrub, but as the light began to fade, he had seen only vague marks that could be tracks, but were too scrambled and slight to be sure. It was difficult to know when he had never really seen the tracks their terrorizers could make in desert dust before.

But nowhere, high or low, was any sign of a machine.

Thus, the panic.

He hadn't really expected an easy answer to this mayhem, but he hadn't thought they'd all be so clueless either.

Laney called. He whipped his head in her direction, surprised by the urgency in her voice. A lump rose in his throat, his thoughts on her vulnerability. Tag had been in his ear for a long lecture on the implications of her quick injury. He pushed those thoughts aside; her safety was priority at the moment and his feet made quick work of the ground between them.

He found Laney leaning against the wall standing over the bedrolls he'd left her on. His gaze wildly took in the space around to find no threat of robots.

"You came," she said, her breathing irregular. "We need to talk."

Donavan's muscles eased a bit, and he lowered his weapon.

"Laney. Now might not be the best time. We're trying—"

"No," she insisted. "This is important, please."

He hesitated. A glance over his shoulder told him no menaces had appeared and that the others in the distance continued their harried search for signs.

He caved and came to sit next to her on an upturned bucket.

"Yes," he agreed. "We do need to talk."

She looked hopeful as she turned her face toward his.

"Laney, I'm not sure bringing you here was the right call."

"What do you mean?" she asked.

He remained silent, struggling with words. As much as he needed her, and yes, wanted her, the truth couldn't be ignored.

"I know I led you to believe I couldn't do this without you. That's partially true," he said. "We know I'm not as complete without you, but I can still hold my own with the other guys. I collapsed a house just now without you. I'm beginning to think that maybe I've put you at unnecessary risk."

She snorted a laugh. "Really. *Now* you think that."

"Laney—"

"No, wait. *My* turn. Didn't you tell me these things would find me and track my family if I didn't come?"

"I'm not entirely sure that's true, either."

"So you said what you needed to say to get me here. And now that you've seen how much I *can't* do to help you, you're full of regrets."

Her back straightened when she spoke. He cleared his throat and picked his next words carefully.

"You have to cut me a little slack," he said. "I had no idea what to expect. We all thought—well, I thought that we'd know what to do when we got here, and the fight would be quick. We're all just operating on feelings that pulse through us. Instincts that don't give us many clues as to why we do what we do. I pulled you here believing this was your fate, too. That with me beside you, nothing bad would happen. Now...." He gestured toward her damaged leg, and for a moment he thought she might explode into a tirade that would shatter the surrounding silence. Instead, she clapped her mouth shut and her shoulders drooped a little more each second. She seemed more disappointed than angry.

"I get it. They think I'm a wimp," were her next words. She limped over to a bucket of her own to sit on next to him, a gesture likely designed to prove them all wrong. "They look at me and see a mom of two with little in the way of tactical skills, but...." Her pause contained a potency that made him take notice. "Lately, it's as if I feel my past rising up." Her words were sharp, clear. "There is another side of me. You don't really know me. Not... all of me."

"Laney—"

"No, listen, Donavan. I need to tell you about... how I used to be. I think it's important to all this. Maybe. So could you just listen a minute?"

Donavan tried to find a way to put her off, but her eyes implored him with an intensity that melted him. *Dang it all anyway.*

He put his weapon down and leaned his forearms on his knees, trying to convey his full attention that he had trouble giving.

"I should tell you a little about me and Arie," she rushed on as if she sensed his divided focus. "How we used to live. And how I lost my sister."

Arie? Curious, Donavan nodded, patiently allowing her the courage to begin her story.

Chapter 24

Showers were in the forecast that morning. I woke and frowned at the unwelcome news blaring from the TV. Arie always had the TV on in the morning. One of the huge inconveniences of sharing a room with my sister.

"Rain?" I asked stupidly. Arie smirked in return. Rain could ruin our evening plans, which appeared to secretly delight her, like the obstacle added dimension to our adventure. Looking back, it was an omen I blatantly ignored. I should have paid more attention to my own instincts. Instead, I relied on Arie to direct us.

For as long as I can remember, the two of us were the most tenacious of twins. We had no other siblings, just the two of us, wearing our parents out with our endless activity. Any club or sport you could name, we tried—the routine monotony of piano lessons, Girl Scouts, and dance classes. But when junior high came, sports dominated our time. The more off the grid, the better. Bike racing, trapeze school, snorkeling. By the time we reached high school, we were living our best life. We didn't just live sports; we excelled in them. Nothing stopped us from doing more, growing competitive—that amazing unstoppable feeling of youth. To become the best took a lot of devotion, so we narrowed our focus to fit our gifts. I chose gymnastics; Arie, swimming.

Academically we rose to the top of our class, bound for college on a wave of scholarships. Everything came so easy to us—friends, trophies, grades. Our future looked radiant... if it hadn't been for one thing. We were bored.

"Don't forget to come straight home," Arie told me as I listened to the distant thunder. Her eyes glowed with the secret we shared while she dressed for school.

"After Debate Club, remember?" I reminded her, jumping out of bed, but I was excited too.

"Ugh, when are you going to quit the debate team?"

"After I get a full-ride college scholarship," I joked. We giggled at that because we had several colleges hounding us already. But none of those schools had seen our current semester grades....

"Well, just get here as quick as you can for dinner."

Eating dinner with our folks was an important part of the scheme. The ruse of a family night gave us the chance to sneak out later. We'd wear our parents out with our rowdy recounts of the week, a Friday night tradition, until they gladly let us excuse ourselves to our room for the night.

I wished I had appreciated dinner that night, that I had understood that we were a great family. That wasn't a ruse. The way Arie made everyone laugh. How her eyes sparkled when she was on a roll. If I could only remember the story she told, using the salt and pepper shakers as players in some animated tale she told to make my parents laugh until they cried. She was on her feet, arms flailing, the all-consuming bright and shiny force in our home. No one hated Arie. No one. To meet her, even with her thick self-confidence and no-nonsense attitude, was to fall in love with her instantly.

The plan worked perfectly. Arie wore them out with her non-stop chatter and constant movement, even knocking over the sugar bowl for added assurance that we would easily be excused to our room for the rest of the evening. The gentle, quiet voices of my folks in front of the fireplace sealed the deal. We turned our music on, just loud enough to drawn out the noise of our movements around the room. Changing clothes to go out, I eagerly donned my new leather jacket until I heard the thunder approach, no longer a distant threat. I stopped mid-dress and looked at Arie.

"Oh, stop worrying, baby," she said. "A little rain won't kill you."

"Yeah, well, it's not the way I wanted to break in my jacket. Think I should wear my old one?" I didn't want her to know I was nervous.

Arie shrugged. "You know me. I'd wear it anyway."

That was Arie. Always ignoring boundaries, taking things too far. Our breakout into extreme sports had been the first step in combating boredom. For our entire junior year, we used every extra moment—which wasn't many—to discover rock climbing, whitewater rafting, speed skating. One rare moment we both were free from practice, we hiked our way to a cave to spelunk.

On the trail, we met several girls going our way. They seemed like the fun, spontaneous sort, so we stuck on the trail with them for a while. Eventually, the trail branched, and they took a separate route. We noticed they didn't have any gear with them, not even backpacks, which seemed odd, but we were too set on our own adventure to be too inquisitive.

After our cave exploration, Arie and I stayed out later than we planned and ended up coming down the trail at twilight. The glow of a campfire led us to a group of teens camping on their own. They were all from a neighboring high school, and we would have been outsiders if not for the girls we had befriended on the trail earlier. No wonder they'd had no packs: they had dug in for the weekend and set up camp.

That was how we came to know Corie, Hunter, Rachel... and Zane. These kids weren't like any of our friends. They were free-spirited and alive, and I'll admit, rebellious. Half of them had snuck out, lied about staying at a friend's house, and came camping with an expired license. Couples disappeared into the shadows to hook up, the occasional breath of pot overpowering the thick smell of the campfire. They offered us alcohol, which we turned down. Arie and I had been the golden girls our whole lives, pure and perfect. We just hung out at the fire and soaked in a kind of unwound freedom we had never experienced before.

Boredom disappeared from that night on.

Months later, on this Friday night, we had particularly exciting plans that would push the bounds of that freedom.

We yelled goodnight to our folks and turned down the lights and music. In the hushed darkness, we waited for Zane and Hunter to come. Raindrops began to click on the window long before Zane's pebble did.

Climbing out of the window and down the side of the porch thrilled me; if Arie weren't so persuasive to lead me into trouble, that feeling might have been enough. I took my helmet from Hunter and gave him a quick hug in thanks. Hunter was a good guy, but not my type. He knew it and didn't care. His goal was much like mine and Arie's. To find something to take him away from the tedium of life. Like us, he found the one person who could do that.

Zane.

He was pretty much the reason our senior year spiraled into a series of ditched classes and excuses. Our parents hadn't caught on yet; we knew it was a matter of time, but accepted the challenge of concealing it as long as possible. Grades were plummeting fast, our scholarships hanging precariously in the balance, and we were running out of plausible excuses for our erratic behaviors. All our friends at school noticed the change, but Corie and Rachel and their friends became our inner circle. This new crowd wasn't the kind you brought home to meet your folks. Zane had two tattoos—and plans for a third—multiple piercings and sported the beginnings of a beard. Arie was crazy about him, but he wouldn't be coming over for dinner anytime soon. I often wondered if that was exactly what appealed to her.

I put on my helmet and climbed on Hunter's motorcycle behind him, my heart racing as the rain whipped in lashes at us in the darkness. I tried to catch Arie's attention to give her an excited thumbs up, more to reassure myself of my bravery than form camaraderie with her, but she only had eyes for Zane. I think maybe she knew... that under all the adrenaline, I was nervous that night. This was a bigger risk than we'd ever taken. If anyone was going to put the brakes on this massively reckless plan, it would be me, and she knew it. She sped off with Zane without a glance back at me.

The wet road before us glistened like a sea serpent slithering up the mountain, bending in complicated switchbacks that any sane driver would shrink from in the best of weather. I don't ever remember a more terrifyingly exquisite evening. The taste of it lingers still, like a bitter, intoxicating drink you tried to turn down, but that taste.... It calls to you. You can't stop yourself.

Hunter took the turns with careful, calculated maneuvers at first, but when Zane picked up the pace, Hunter didn't hesitate. These boys knew how to give us the thrill factor we so desperately sought. The adrenaline rush—sliding around turns, barely in our own lane to right ourselves—trumped anything else in my young life. I trembled from head to toe and stopped praying after about the third curve. The exhilaration awakened something in me. Something awful; something wonderful.

As Zane's engine whined louder ahead of us, I peered around to see his bike taking a curve too fast. Arie raised her hands like she was on a roller coaster, and then their taillight disappeared over the shoulder. My blood turned to ice, and complete terror pierced my ecstasy.

When we reached the cabin, she was there. I nearly fell off the bike to run to her. I found myself shaking, whether from the cold or the ride I don't know. We were all soaked through. Arie didn't seem to care, and it was clear her ride had not terrified her, only amped her excitement. She grabbed Zane's hand and followed him into the cabin, broadcasting her unbridled freedom with a loud whoop as she went. Hunter gave me a huge grin, grabbed my hand, and followed.

I wasn't in the door five seconds before someone put a drink in my hand. We had long ago abandoned the discipline that athletics had always held us to. The room, warm and tight, held two dozen teens in a hunting lodge built for half that. Someone's uncle was our unsuspecting absent host. Our friends who didn't have to play the wait game with their parents had arrived before the rain and set the party into motion.

This part of the night unfolded like many before had: same faces, loud music, convenient store food, plans for love and mischief. And somehow that was the very reason I felt uncomfortable. Truth slowly found its way through the depravity that night. A truth opening like a package wrapped inside another package inside another that you can't rip through all at once.

Amid the couples, the dancers, the laughers, the arguers, there was Zane. This was the world he had created. Not one of us would be here if he hadn't told us to be. The realization alarmed me. Arie and I had always been so independent, so in charge. We were used to people taking notice of us, gravitating toward us, and now... now *we* were the sheep.

All for the sake of that feeling. That thrill. One dangerous stunt traded up for the next that would send our hearts into a new kind of arrhythmia. Zane was all that to the enth degree.

I squirmed my way back into the throng, but another truth was unwrapping. The bike ride had scared the crap out of me; from the moment I had come into the cabin, I had been trying to keep it together and pretend it was all part of the crazy life I enjoyed. But in the split second I'd thought Zane's bike had gone off the side of the mountain, I realized I longed to protect my sister with an intensity stronger than any thrill I chased.

I spotted my sister across the room just as she swallowed something Zane handed her. My heart began to beat against my chest like a caged animal. I jumped when Hunter popped up next to my elbow with a box in his hand. His crooked grin told me he'd partied quickly to make up for lost time. The pills in front of me bounced in the box as he shook them in rhythm with the music. "Try a pink one," he yelled above the din. "They're awesome."

The box held a destiny of Zane's choosing. Across the room, Zane's stare met mine. Waiting. I looked down at the box. "No, thanks." I gripped my cup and tried to squelch the uneasiness that threatened to overtake the night.

Zane moved toward me, and I brushed past Hunter only to get blocked in by a group of girls singing unbearable karaoke, arms locked to keep themselves upright. Hunter said something I couldn't hear so I leaned closer. "Nice jacket," he smiled just as Zane reached our side.

"Thanks," I smiled back. I sensed that if I gave in, Zane would leave me alone. I grabbed a pink pill and pretended to throw it back. "Changed my mind." I planted a pity kiss on Hunter's cheek before moving away.

The night went downhill from there. Apparently no one else said no to the pink pill. A moody desperate angst seeped its way through the darkness until eyes glazed and conversation dulled. I watched Arie slide into a drugged stooper; I begged her to come home with me. That's when Zane decided we all needed to play a game.

He produced a revolver and explained the rules. My hands grew clammy as he told his captive crowd that the gun held only one bullet, and he would spin the chamber each time before handing it to the next person. He demonstrated, holding the barrel to his temple and pulling the trigger. We were playing roulette. Russian roulette.

A roar rose up when an empty click came after.

I dug my nails into Arie's arm. "Let's go."

The girl that looked at me was barely recognizable. She slapped my hand away with such violence it knocked me back.

"You go," my sister said in disgust laced with insanity. "I'm staying."

I couldn't believe this was my sister. I couldn't believe that I had ever let myself get here, that all these people, people I thought were my friends, were willing to end it all on some stupid game Zane set up to amuse himself. This wasn't about courage or thrill seeking; this was about everyone's blind devotion to Zane, the center package in the truth bundle. I stared it in the ugly face when I looked at Arie.

"Arie, listen to me, please. You don't know what you're saying. Zane's gonna get us killed. He's not safe."

Arie laughed in my face. "Safe? Who wants safe?"

"We do," I insisted and tried to pull her again, only to get the same vicious reaction.

"Maybe you do, Laney. Maybe you're the one who wants to have a life with dinners at home, doing your tumbling routine, wearing department store clothes, dating pretty, clean-shaven boys—"

"What are you talking about?"

"—but I intend to live with the wind in my hair, wearing whatever jacket I feel like, riding in convertibles with men in bowler hats, eating exotic foods out of coconut shells—"

"Arie, you're not making any sense! Listen, I think the rain's letting up. We can walk back—it's not that far."

"I'm not going anywhere."

"And I'm not leaving without you."

Zane suddenly appeared by Arie's side, and a tense silence shrouded us amid the groupies preparing for the game of their life.

"As a matter of fact," Arie said, taking the revolver from Zane's hand, "you are."

In that moment, everything I ever thought I wanted out of life evaporated. The Laney I had become, or was pretending to be, didn't want to exist. It all felt wrong, horribly wrong, and I wanted out.

I stumbled blindly out into the storm that hadn't given up its force yet, torn to the core about leaving my sister but knowing there was no way I could stay. I sobbed the whole four-mile walk back home, alone, in the pitch black.

It was the last time I ever saw my sister.

Chapter 25

Donavan wished he could do more than sit like an idiot as tears carved streaks down Laney's cheeks. He braced himself and leaned forward, but she waved him away.

"I'm fine, I'm fine. I just hadn't thought about that in a long time."

"I didn't know."

She smiled weakly and wiped her nose. "We're learning a lot about each other lately."

He thought of Kelly and grimaced. "I'm confused, though. You never saw her again? But you adopted Arie's daughters."

Laney nodded. "She never came back that night. After I walked all that way home in the rain, I fell into my bed and cried myself to sleep, soaked to the bone—I remember thinking I would shiver myself to death. But I couldn't make myself get up, couldn't tell on her. I didn't want to get Arie in trouble.

"When they came to my room in the morning, I was crippled with fever. Predictably, I had gotten sick from the cold. Arie didn't come home for two days. Drove my parents crazy with worry looking for her and trying to take care of me. I ended up in the hospital with pneumonia, so I wasn't even there when Arie finally showed up. She packed her stuff and said she was taking off with Zane. And just like that, she was gone."

The pain in Laney's voice was raw, real. Donovan tried to speak up, but Laney lifted her chin and continued. "I knew none of Arie's plans; I stayed four days in the hospital—the longest I'd ever been separated from my sister—and she never even said goodbye. Just…gone.

"My dad spent the next six months trying to track her down. Zane had been living with his step-dad, who didn't seem keen on finding out where Zane had disappeared to. If he knew, he wouldn't let on. We finally got a letter from Arie postmarked Vegas saying she was doing fine, not much more. By then she was eighteen, and there was nothing my parents could do to bring her home.

"She never contacted me." The emotion in Laney's words had come under control, like she was determined to get it all out before he interrupted. "While I was away at college, she showed up at my parents' place a couple of times, riding a motorcycle, dressed like a tramp—Mom's words, not mine—still wildly independent. I mean, she didn't even try to see me. It hurt more than you can imagine. She missed my wedding. My *wedding!*" Her eyes widened, remembering the cruel snub. Donavan nodded sympathetically. "Not long after we married, I discovered... we found out I couldn't...."

"Couldn't have children," Donavan added the words delicately when she could not finish.

"Right." Laney paused as if sorting through the painful memories to select just the right ones. "And then Arie shows up at my mom's door with Urie. She didn't even know who the father was. We assumed Zane. Arie tried to be a mom for a little bit, but I don't know, she just couldn't do it. She bolted. One thing led to another, and Urie became ours. Can you believe you can just give your kid to someone else, all with just the stroke of a pen, a pile of paperwork, without even being in the same room together? My heart broke to see how much Urie resembled her mom and know her mom could just...." A shudder jerked at Laney's shoulders, and Donavan clenched fists to keep from reaching out to her.

"Well, anyway… " Laney drew in a deep breath. "The adoption had barely settled when we heard she was pregnant again. This time she helped us make adoption arrangements immediately."

Laney shifted her weight on her seat and winced when she repositioned her leg.

"You should elevate that."

"I will, just let me finish. I think now... I've figured something out. Today, out there…the danger, the—the adrenaline. It all felt so…good? So normal—no, not normal but familiar. Like I had lived it before. And I realize that all those years, all that thrill seeking I did—maybe it prepared me for this. Maybe I'm more ready for this than I thought. Maybe I *am* one of you guys."

"Lan—"

"No, listen. I may not have any super powers or anything, but I'm not afraid. I'm not scared to move beside you and be your added strength. I don't think I feel torn anymore. I'm okay with being here. I want to be here."

"Laney," Donavan , more conflicted than ever about the tangled mess he'd exposed her to. "I can't tell you what I felt when I thought those things had gotten you—"

"But they didn't!"

"—with me unable to help you. Unable to control...look, I appreciate that you trusted me enough to come out here with me and try. It's all my fault you're here. But we have to go on without you. There's no way I can risk your safety—"

"You're not risking it, I am. It's my choice. We need to find these things." She stood on shaky legs and balanced her height over his seat. "Who else can stop them?"

Donavan hesitated. It was late, they were tired, and the aggravation of the day weighed on them all. He turned to see the weary men slowly returning to camp. The rush was over. Their enemy had disappeared again and left them with more questions than before.

His shoulders dropped. "Okay. Okay for now. Let's get you lying down and get that leg up," he said and carefully helped her lie back down.

§§§§§

Okay for now was not the conclusion to the subject that Laney had hoped for. But her ankle was aching again, silencing her from badgering Donavan any longer. He helped her to "bed" where pain set in at new levels. She dare not ask for some more medical care, not after her little speech.

As the moon and stars made their appearance in the darkening sky, RJ came with a plate of dinner—more beans with rice—that she did her best to choke down. With night closing in, RJ rose to make a fire for Laney in a barrel centered in the room, but she begged him not to. It would diminish the star shine. Besides, who knew if fire would bring the robots back? The thought made her shiver.

"Stars are so bright out here," she said later when the sky had mapped out its glory. No reply. She had been brooding ever since Donavan left and had to find a way to take her mind off of it so she hurried on. "Don't know that I've ever seen Cassiopeia so easily before. See Orion? I would always look for his belt when I was a kid—the only thing I could pick out. It's those three bright stars in a row right there."

She pointed upward and was pleased to see RJ's head turn slightly in the direction of her finger. Since she had his attention, she continued, taking her mind off her ankle, her man problems, and robots. "Some say he was an orphan. He fell in love with Diana, but her brother wasn't having it. Apollo, her brother, tricked her into shooting Orion with an arrow when she didn't know it was him. So many characters up there like that. I never got why they couldn't all get along. I mean, they all share this crowded patch of sky—that's how I thought of it when I was little. Why wouldn't they team up? Be on each other's side?"

RJ nodded and listened, taking in the stars as she spoke. His interest in her stories warmed her.

"Maybe because I got along with my sister so well, I just didn't understand..." Laney's voice trailed off. Thinking about Arie was never good. "Have any brothers or sisters?" she asked. "Any close family?"

"No," the reply came harsh and quick. She frowned.

"Well, that's the good thing about this group, really," Laney rushed on, indicating the men outside the house frame. She didn't want to lose the ground she had gained with RJ this morning. "We're like a make-shift family, don't you think? A dysfunctional one, I'll give you that—a little better than the constellations, though. Everyone has everyone's back here."

RJ stood with all the grace that granite might, dark and unreadable against the night sky. "I don't need family. Or anyone else."

The sheer size of his silhouette took Laney back for a second. "Everyone needs someone—"

But RJ had already moved, climbing over the wall instead of squeezing through the doorframe; just like that, he disappeared into the dark desert.

Laney lay back again. *Great.* Her only companion was gone, and she was alone with her throbbing body and antsy thoughts.

At some point, she must have fallen asleep, but she tossed and turned. Dreams tortured her, images of a giant rock rolling into camp and landing in a pool of oil that splashed over them and trapped them with its weight and slickness. She crawled and grasped against the ooze enveloping her, but she had no traction, couldn't speak. The oil turned to tar and sealed her mouth, trapped her limbs; the black sludge pushed her eyes closed, sucked her breath away, the pain in her ankle tying her back to reality....

She startled awake. She stood beside the useless house frame, looking out to the campfire, free from the awful sucking goo.

No, dreaming still, she realized as she moved effortlessly across the sandy desert floor, free of pain. Crazy how she felt unnaturally alert in her sleep. Laney stretched her hands out around her to feel the air that seemed so real, so cool and palpable, and wondered for a moment if flying were possible. She imagined her dream body gliding over toward the fire pit, but in actuality, it walked. The small blaze mesmerized her with an aura of images Laney couldn't make out. Motionless lumps turned out to be just logs and stones.

"What do you need?"

Tag's voice startled her, and Laney shivered despite the little warmth. Slowly the form on a rock shifted and revealed Tag's body slouched forward, hands tucked under his armpits, legs outstretched and crossed at the ankles.

"Nothing." The sound of her own voice startled her more. Her dream-self sounded lucid. "What are you doing up?"

"On guard."

"Don't you need to be awake for that?"

"I'm awake," he growled. "No one's sneaking up on me without getting a serious jolt."

"You're not afraid?"

"Afraid of what?

"I don't know," Laney shrugged. "Getting shot? Falling asleep and rolling into the fire? Oil Eaters?"

"No, no, and yes."

"Why the Oil Eaters?"

"Dumb question."

"Is it?"

"Yes," Tag huffed. "Now go back to sleep."

"You angry at the Oil Eaters, or do you just hate me for being here?" she asked.

"Both?" He smirked at that.

"Why?"

He heaved an exasperated sigh and eyed her from across the ebbing embers. "Oil Eaters don't have an agenda. We can't even find one, but we know they're out there. That makes them unpredictable. The most dangerous opponent is the one that can't be calculated. You? I've said it before—you're a liability. I don't care how many houses you can smash to bits with Pete."

"Pete? Oh, as in Peterson. Got it." She rubbed her eyes and looked at her hands. They glowed red from the backdrop of the fire. Maybe she was awake after all, though she felt a bit groggy and out of place now, her alertness fading. She wiggled her foot and found her ankle still worked fine. Nope, a dream.

"Why should I be a liability to you if you got the jolt magic on your side?"

His sneer turned slightly sinister. An uncomfortable lump rose in her throat as he leaned in closer. "Say we meet up with Oil Eaters. You're tagging along with Pete, doing your thing, and then the two of you need help. I give a zap and you're in the way. ZZZZttttt!" He lurched at her, hands up, and she jumped backward. "You're toast!"

The darkness seemed to pull at her from behind, drawing her back to bed; she tried to steady herself and decided to sit on one of the stone seats before her legs collapsed.

"Well, it's my hide. If I get in the way of your zap, that's my problem, not yours. You seem like you'd enjoy another chance to shock me."

"Don't think I wouldn't. But I don't need the rest of them breathing down my back about it."

"So they're forcing you to care, is that it? Without them, you'd have no soul?"

He lunged forward, and she recoiled, gripping the stone beneath her for balance.

"*Listen*, Laney. We've seen more, done more, lived more than you and your fairy tale life could ever imagine. I know what it's like to care. I know what it's like to have that ripped away from you and not have anyone give a crap about making it right. It sucks being *super* and having no one to share it with. You're here because Pete wants you here; he doesn't need you. He's got a thing for you, and that means he cares too much. That means you are a li-a-bil-i-ty," he said, stabbing a finger at her with each syllable. "To him. To me. To all of us!"

The sparks that rose from their dying campfire couldn't compete with the heat in Tag's eyes, causing Laney to quake from head to toe. Tag resumed his slouch, arms crossed, his words hanging like a taut curtain between them.

It proved difficult to move again, but heading back to her makeshift bed seemed like a safer place to continue this dream. The desert floor slanted and buckled beneath her. She was slipping into distorted reality again as ahead she made out Jacob walking toward her bed. He bent over her sleeping body and spoke.

"Laney? Laney, open up."

"Hmm?

"Laney, it's Jacob. You're dreaming. Time for more meds."

Laney woke in a sweat, pain ripping through her ankle again. "What?"

"You've been tossing and turning. Bad dream?"

"N-no," she answered in confusion. Was it?

"Take this."

She finally accepted the pill he held at her mouth, something different from aspirin, and dutifully swallowed it with water from his canteen. "Donavan?" she asked.

"He's sleeping. He'll be next watch."

Disappointment weaved itself into her troubled dreams filled with underground creatures, a long red curtain separating her from Donavan's outstretched hand and Tag's mocking laughter.

Chapter 26

Morning brought a foggy haze, not in its sparse clouds and slight chilled air, but seeping from the corners of Donavan's brain. Sleep, broken up by his rotation on night watch, had not benefited him much. A deep irritation had firmly rooted itself after the appearance of *them.* It drove him forward, had him stuffing tired feet into stiff boots before the others stirred.

Or so he thought.

Brian met him at the fire, tugging on a clean shirt and shoving it down the waist of his still-dirty cargo pants. They nodded a greeting and discussed options in hushed tones, till one by one the others joined them with the exception of Harley who had early morning watch. Subtle glances made their way toward the house where Laney slept. The conversation shifted, a decision made, RJ being the last to assent.

"I'll go tell her," Donavan said darkly, having been the first to insist on the only way he knew to keep Laney safe.

§ § § § §

The oversized wheelbarrow jarred its way across the rough desert floor, its "driver" apparently unconcerned for the welfare of its cargo. Laney, the said cargo, had to clutch at the sides for dear life which kept her from reaching back to attack her friend-turned-traitor.

When Donavan told her of his plan to have RJ push her in the rickety contraption the whole way back to their car, she had laughed. Outright and in his face. He wouldn't!

At yet here they were, RJ propelling the one-wheeled cart from behind, her head wrapped up in a pair of corroded goggles and dented helmet, zooming toward the car that grew larger on the horizon.

RJ unceremoniously spilled her out next to the vehicle as the cloud of dust caught up with them and settled around them. Laney removed her headgear and rinsed out the dirt buildup on her teeth with canteen water before turning to glare.

"RJ, this is stupid. You know that?" He looked blankly back at her. His back-stabbing stung her; his silence produced rage. "So I'm supposed to jump into the car and drive back home? Just like that? No one thinks they could attack me?" No response. "What's stopping me from driving myself to camp?"

"Me."

"So you're on their side, huh? I thought you didn't believe in this *we-are-fam-i-ly* business."

"It's for your own good. Get going."

Laney huffed and plopped down on the ground. "No."

RJ revealed nothing in his stone cold stare. He simply took hold of the cart and ran off in the camp's direction with a wake of dust trailing.

A slow panic rose; she started to cry out to RJ despite herself, but it was too late. He was gone. She popped up, shielded her eyes, spun left then right. All alone in a vast desert. Alone *and* vulnerable. Unprotected.

§ § § § §

The temperature cooperated, while the terrain did not, as Donavan scrambled a precarious rock formation on the mountainside. Despite the fact that the sun hadn't worn off the chill of the morning just yet, sweat beaded his brow from exertion and anticipation.

He had spotted this location through binoculars, and something tingly had his hopes up high. The way the crest had a divot, and the rocks sloped...it could hide something just on the other side.

With nothing else to go on but a hunch, Donavan persuaded Brian to follow him up the incline and boost him over the last obstacle, an outward facing rock that jutted its lip away from the mountain. Donavan stood atop and faced one more boulder.

"Anything?" Brian called from below.

"Not yet," he called back. The whisper of soft rock slide beside him made Donavan whip his head right. A ground squirrel scampered out of sight. "There's one more rock," he breathed with heart racing. "I'm going over."

§ § § § §

In the long minutes of paralysis after RJ disappeared, Laney kept her sight on the last spot of dust clinging to the air, watching it fade along with her hope. He had left her.

A hawk circled, and Laney swallowed. What were her options? If she waited till night, could she drive into camp without them seeing her approach? She realized with alarm that she wasn't entirely sure she *could* find her way back. The dirt road branched off several places and wasn't exactly clear cut to begin with. If she waited until night and got lost, she multiplied her chances of ending up on a coyote's menu. Some of the rock formations would help guide her, surely, and she knew what their mountain looked like…right?

She ran a hand through her troubled hair and looked over at the car. Returning home was another option. She would be with her girls within hours; she could return to a normal life; she could forget this crazy, misguided adventure Donavan had sucked her into. He could find someone else to be *the one.* Jerk.

Her boot toes dug into the ground in protest and anger as she made her way to the vehicle, stopping short at the reflection that met her at the window. Wild hair, no makeup, dust streaked skin, dirty camisole, slight sun-burn, ripped jeans… she didn't recognize the person before her. The reflection grabbed a handful of fly-away curls and solidified its identity. It was her. A new her.

Reality set in as she faced this new person. This wasn't a game; this wasn't about her and Donavan. She had come with him because some big black monsters threatened her. Her children. Potentially their city. Wasn't that something she still cared about?

Of course, the black robots had never personally attacked her with the girls in the city. Hadn't she been close to their appearance on the freeway after her grocery run? They hadn't sensed her or come after her then. And the only time Donavan had seen them was when he was with her, with the others.

She put off reaching for the door handle another moment, turning to investigate the desert once more. No green rocks, no black machines, no evidence of other human life. So what made them appear? What kept them back?

Her mirrored self cocked its head to one side, a thread of an idea weaving itself through the puzzle. She connected it to each scene, each situation, and squinted as the thought weaved itself into a true possibility.

Her eyes popped open, and with sudden renewed vigor, she yanked open the car door. She fished around for her hobo bag of a purse, warmed by its untouched days in the sun. Her phone lit up when she hit the *on* button. Breathlessly, she watched the bars struggle to hold ground.

"Come on, come on." Several long seconds passed before two solid bars came and stayed. Heart hammering, she punched some keys and waited. Instinctively her teeth clenched when Charlie answered.

"Where the heck are you?" was his first question, followed by, "and who is Brie?"

"Never mind all that and listen up. Do you and Victoria still want to take the girls to Hawaii?"

A pause filled the line, then a cautious, "Yes."

"Then I have a deal to make with you."

§ § § § §

The men had heaped more wood than necessary on their on-going fire, drawing curiosity from Donavan as he trudged back to camp with an equally weary Brian.

"Hey!" Harley called out, his figure obscured in the growing shadows of night. "Come see this!"

Donavan and his companion rallied a bit of half-hearted energy and jogged over to the site where the rest of the crew scrambled to grab various tools and hurry out of sight again.

"Where you been?" Harley barked with a tone that implied more excitement than annoyance.

"Thought we found something," Brian spoke up for Donavan. "But it was nothing," he finished before Harley could ask.

Donavan swallowed his gratitude that Brian tried to make light of his disappointment. He had been so sure, Brian a willing wingman. And just like all the times before, a dead end. No monsters, no green rocks. This new camp commotion resurrected a glimmer of hope.

"What's going on?" Donavan asked.

"Got something." Harley picked up a shovel and jogged down a slope outside the neighborhood leading down the hill where the others had gone.

Donavan's feet hurried to catch up, attempting to squash his hope which rose so quickly with each false alarm. But when he circled left around the base that supported the houses to the south, the setting sun caught an anomaly in the rough, jagged terrain. An area of the hillside, flat and smooth, bared its face to the dying light where eager men dug away at the dirt that concealed its sides.

Brian grabbed onto Donavan's sleeve, his eyes widening while picking up his pace.

"Pete. Am I seeing things or does this mountain have an enormous *door* under it?"

§ § § § §

Smoke billowed from the car in a thick cloud that had lost itself in the dying sunlight. As the night sky fell, Laney prayed that the glow of the flames and heavy smoke were enough to attract attention. RJ's attention.

If not…she was screwed.

She had gambled on the fact that her warden would watch her from a distance, that he truly wouldn't leave until she had driven away. If his job was to make sure she didn't drive into camp, he couldn't be far.

Using fodder from the surrounding desert and a lighter—one of the many random items floating in her purse's depths—she started a blaze. The burning car would either be her savior or condemn her to a slow death.

With every beam of sunlight that weakened, fear grew stronger. A distant coyote's cry made her shudder, but she reasoned that most likely she would die from exposure in the next twenty-four hours and not from an animal attack. Well, if she were going down, she hoped it would be over quickly.

Movement in the darkness caught her ear, and her heart pounded despite her resignation to just die where they left her. It wasn't a motor hum or an animal shuffling. Standing with her purse to arm her, Laney reconsidered her death wish and decided she'd at least go out swinging.

A grating noise moved just beyond the car, but the light of the fire made it difficult to see outside its glow. She was too scared to call out and possibly draw unwanted attention to herself. Okay, well, the flaming car might make it a bit impossible for that.

RJ rounded the front of the car and stood staring at her in all of his perfectly chiseled form, looking slightly exasperated or teed off, she couldn't tell which. He held the handles of the wheelbarrow in a solid grip.

She shouldered her purse and marched over to shove his broad shoulders, which didn't budge him an inch.

"What took you so long? I was scared to death, you jerk!"

He picked her up by the waist and once again dumped her into the pushcart. She found her goggles and helmet there, along with a flashlight. "You best be taking me back to camp, mister!"

"Donavan's not gonna be happy."

"He can go pound sand. And *you*! Don't you ever turn on me again. I don't care who you think you *arrrrrr*—!"

Her words drowned out in flight, the wobbly cart rattling into the darkness headed north, a mere flashlight beam leading the way back to camp.

"There's something under the mountain." RJ picked Laney up out of the wheelbarrow and dumped her onto the ground, staring unaffectedly at her as she regained her balance on her weak ankle and shed her headgear.

"Ok, I'm going to ask *what* in a second, but first of all, let's talk some manners." RJ's scowl failed to intimidate her despite the huge, unanimated formation he had resumed. "You're human, okay? Not a rock, no matter what you may think. We are friends. You do not throw me around or drag me anywhere, got it? If you want me to move, you ask; and then if I need—"

"They found something."

Apparently not an etiquette book. "What exactly?"

"A door." He pointed in a vague direction along the edge of the neighborhood in the darkness, answering her next question.

"What's behind it?"

He shrugged. "Gonna open it tomorrow."

She paused. "Wait, how do you know that? Did you *leave* me alone out there?"

"I came back," was his only defense.

RJ moved toward the fire without another word and minutes later Donavan separated himself from the others, the set of his shoulders affirming the news of her arrival did not sit well with him.

"I've figured some things out," she said before he got too close. He stopped in front of her and planted hands on his hips.

"Me, too. Like that you are—are unbelievably tenacious and need a good smack upside the head!"

"Seriously, Donavan, I know what makes us *work*."

"We don't work!" He threw up his hands in a sign of exasperation. "That's why I sent you away! RJ told me—" teeth clenched. "Did you have to blow up the car?"

"Technically, I just set it on fire. Don't be so dramatic."

"Do you have any idea—?"

"Listen to me, Donavan!" She grabbed his sleeves and didn't care that it made him recoil. "Would you just listen to me for a second?"

He sucked in a sharp breath and grabbed her hands. "Do you still not feel that?" he asked.

For a split second, Laney was so overcome with sympathy that she thought about lying. "No. Nothing." No shock, no vibration. But thrill—how did she tell him that a simple pass of his hand on her skin enlivened her more than anything she had felt in a long time. Something deep inside, so long hurting and painful, burst into hope when he came near. She felt every bit as tortured as he did.

He dropped his hands and stared at her as if exhausted from an emotional shed. "Then how is it that we work, Laney?"

"Well, I don't know that for sure. What I am pretty sure about is what *doesn't* work."

"Meaning?"

"I give you more power sometimes and other times nothing, right?"

"Yes. My theory is that the closer this group came to us, the more it increased. The times we lacked connection, they were farther away." His shifting eyes in the glow of their flashlights told of a lingering irritation at her line of thought.

"More than that. What was the one factor that was always the same when you grew strong with me?"

Donavan squinted skeptically at any correlation. "Tell me."

"The kids weren't there."

A puzzled expression replaced doubt. "The kids…"

"Think about it. The day you brought down the glass door—Urie, Ella, and Parker were all at your mom's, away from us. The night you came alone to my apartment—my girls weren't there."

Donavan ran a hand through his hair and remained quiet for a while, lost in thought.

"Tell me," she continued, more confident she was right, "did you ever feel *super* when any of our kids were around?"

"No," he admitted. "No, never. But … it could be coincidence…" He didn't seem convinced.

"I think the kids are blockers or something."

"That's good then," Donavan nodded. "If that's true, then they're safe from these monsters, that is if they are sensing us. Maybe you would be safe with the kids. Right?"

Laney's jaw tightened. "That is, if I had a ticket to Hawaii. I sent them there with Charlie." She held up her hand to stop him from speaking. "I'm done with you bossing me around, hear me? I'm in this." He sighed and looked away. Her need to rant returned: "What were you thinking having RJ leave me alone in the desert like that?"

He sighed heavy and deep. "Do you realize my only goal was to keep you safe? I need you to be safe, Laney." He gripped her shoulders slowly, as if using the pain of it to punish himself.

"I know," she softened her response. "I get that."

His eyes searched hers, and when his face brushed closer to hers, closer than it had in forever, Laney forgave him everything. She slowly reached up to hold his face in her hands in experimentation. The evening at his party immediately came to her mind, and she remembered the comfort his touch had brought and wished she could do the same for him. That night, the girls had been in the next room, perhaps the buffer they needed to keep him from this electricity that she produced in him. He closed his eyes with a deep breath and moved his hands to cover hers on his cheeks. She let his forehead rest on hers and listened to him breathe, soaking in every second of his nearness.

Abruptly he let go and stepped away. "I always think it will get easier."

"I'm so sorry. I'm sorry that it's not easy to be near..." Something Tag had said in her dream came to mind, something that had bothered her. "Do you think you feel this way—this tingly, attraction to me— because I give you super, super powers? Or do you think I make you strong *because* you feel this way about me?"

He grimaced. "Are my powers because of my feelings for you or my feelings because of powers? I'm sorry, Laney... I honestly don't know."

"So if you fell for someone else... maybe it would be the same." She shook her head firmly, dismissing her own words. "No. No, I'm sure I'm supposed to be here. I'll find a way to prove it. We'll figure it out together."

"And let yourself get killed in the meantime?"

"Donavan, I twisted my ankle. It's almost completely better. Next time, I'll be more careful."

"We all can't be there to save you every minute."

"But we all have each other's back, right? I wasn't a total loser during our simulation."

He closed his eyes and nodded. "True."

"That's all I'm asking. I'll always be by you and you always have Brian as backup. And I know—I just know, Donavan—that I'll figure out something I can do that helps the rest."

He gave her a patronizing smile and gingerly pushed back one of her stray curls. "I think you may have already, honey. You are highly entertaining, and we've been so bored without you."

She swatted his hand away and looked across the moonlit desert where the others sat at the fire, bodies turned in their direction. Jacob, his unmistakable build silhouetted in the shadows, stood in an undeniable pose of leadership as the others sat. Laney swallowed and wondered what he thought about the car fire, the drastic measure becoming more embarrassing than she had expected.

"Tell me about the door," she said to Donavan and together they headed toward the campsite and her next tongue lashing.

The retaining wall served its purpose well from all appearances. One side of the mountain took an odd drastic drop that looked like folds in a fabric of earth. To utilize the space and keep erosion from overtaking, the southeast end of the community had actually been built up, leveled and held into place by a concrete wall covered with stucco to match the design of the houses. Several houses had their foundations built upon this plateau the wall created. They had the advantage of having their unfinished back patios overlook the desert from a cliff-like vantage.

At both ends of the wall, the desert took over and the folds were allowed to remain in their natural form. Almost completely covered up by one of these ripples of vertical dirt was a door, a massive metal construction with only jutting hinges to prove it true. The color and seamlessness of the entrance made it otherwise almost impossible to detect. The band had worked together all evening while Laney had been gone to uncover its fifteen foot width and seven foot height.

"See what you missed?" Brian asked.

Tag and Jacob moved to the door and renewed their attempts to find a way in. The huge slab, ancient and unembellished, had no handle or gap in space between it and the frame. It rooted itself, solid and formidable, into the hillside.

"It swings this way. The hinges face out, but even after we've hammered the pins off, the door won't budge." Tag continued to squint at the frame in bewilderment. "Ideas?"

"Blow the sucker up," mumbled Harley, inserting a fresh cigar into his mouth. "Laney, ain't that your department?"

"I. Set. It. On. Fire," she said, rolling her eyes. "What about a crowbar?"

Tag snickered, but Jacob's patronizing smile made him pretend to cough instead and study the structure again.

"There are no bad ideas," Jacob reminded his men. "The crowbar?"

"Won't fit in the crack," Harley said. "Can't even get a fraction of a hold. And obviously not big enough."

"What if we all got behind the trailer and tried to ram it down?" Brian asked.

They all turned his way.

"Okay, there are *some* bad ideas," Jacob corrected himself. "We can't destroy the trailer, Brian. Next?"

Donavan came to stand close to Laney. "Any way to get a hitch connected to it?"

"Again," sighed Tag as he walked away from the obstacle, "what are we going to attach it to? I had thought about—"

Laney let the men banter around her as her eyes took in the large barrier between them and who knew what. Some vague lettering etched into the metal just above the frame had distracted her. Maybe it was just scratches—no, she could make out an E first, or a slanted version. Then something that looked like an N but she couldn't be sure. Talk of using water pressure, RJ and Donavan's brute strength, and fire (Brian's half-jesting idea) filtered around her and Harley, now at her side.

"Harley, what's that say?"

Harley's eyes followed her pointed finger.

"Huh? Nothing. Looks like whatever was there has worn away too much to read now."

"Can you reach up there?"

Harley complied and used a bandana to scrub at the letters crudely scratched across the metal.

E, N, O, R.

The next letter had disappeared and the next was just a faded scratch. Maybe there was more before the E.

Laney backed up quickly, stumbling on her mending ankle and bumped right into Jacob's hands. He gave her a quizzical look.

"Laney? What is it?"

She grabbed at the purse she had thrown into the mix of supplies and started fumbling through it. "I... I know that. I've seen it before."

"What?" Jacob asked. "The door?"

"That name."

"What name?" Donavan asked.

"Señor Epus."

"I don't understand," Donavan said. "Who is Señor Epus?"

"I don't know," she said, digging her cell phone out of her purse. "But I know someone who does."

Chapter 27

A five-minute argument ensued whether they should destroy the cell phone on the spot or allow it. Every signal put them at risk of being found, Tag insisted. He pulled a begrudging Brian into the debate, and he suddenly became interested once he handled the device.

"Where'd you get this?"

"The phone?" Laney asked. "From my dad."

He held it up to Jacob for inspection. Jacob frowned. "It's a Napstar."

No one registered understanding as Brian and Jacob exchanged looks.

"A phone designed by the military a decade ago," Jacob explained. "Not many used it. It doesn't work through a regular satellite."

"How are you even getting service?" Brian asked. "Who's your carrier?"

"I honestly don't know. I inherited it from my dad when I got divorced... and broke. He's paying the bill till I get on my feet again. Now can I have it back?"

"She can't be making calls and jeopardizing our position," Harley rumbled.

"That's just it," Brian said, handing the phone to Laney. "It doesn't work with a regular network. It can't be traced. Or intercepted. Or anything. It's a foolproof phone that shouldn't even be in operation. You need to find out how your dad got ahold of that."

Laney eyed the old flip phone with the monochromatic Napstar imprint on the back. It had never occurred to her that the relic was unlike any she'd ever seen. But it didn't matter at the moment. She needed to make a call.

"Mark?" Laney spoke after selecting a never-used number in her contacts. "This is Laney. My fall break's going great, how's yours? You gave me your number, remember? You put it in my phone.... Ummm, no." She bowed her head to let her hair fall forward to block out onlookers. "Sorry, I'm busy tonight... that's not why I'm calling. I want to get ahold of the Radst—I mean, Wayne. Yeah, no, it's about our next play.... Sure, sure, that sounds great.... Could I just get your nephew's number for now?"

She repeated the digits out loud as he gave them to her. "Okay, great.... Yeah, you too! Huh....? No, I can't tomorrow. I—I'm busy... Friday? Umm..." she ventured a peek through her hair and saw Donavan and Brian staring with arched eyebrows. "Let me call you back.... No, I'll call you... I got to go, okay?"

"Mark, huh?" Brian asked.

"He's just a coworker. And he happens to be the uncle of the kid I need to reach."

She punched in the number and turned her back on the boys once again. Her heart was pounding as the phone rang, then stopped. No connection. Wasn't this supposed to be a foolproof gadget? She moved around trying to get two bars to come back and immediately hit redial when they did.

§ § § § §

Wayne Radison thought he heard his phone ring and gave his nightstand half a glance as he continued to slaughter zombies. The quick side-eye cost him his life. He threw down his controller, sinking back into his oversized chair that took up most of the corner in his darkened bedroom.

The phone didn't ring again.

He picked up his giant Styrofoam soda cup and sucked at the ice. Empty. Probably he should get out of the chair he'd slept in for the last couple nights and actually make some breakfast. Too lazy. He kicked at the stack of wrappers at his feet and found half a sleeve of Oreos. Good enough.

He had just popped the first two in his mouth when his cell phone went off again. He glared at it suspiciously and let it ring a second time. Not many people called him. His few gamer friends usually communicated over the X-box and his techy friends rarely left their introverted state to use any form of socialization other than DMing.

On the third ring, a mild curiosity helped him struggle out of his chair. He scowled at the number he didn't recognize but thought it might be fun to antagonize a wrong number or salesperson for a change of pace.

"Hahwo?" he managed around the remains of his cookies.

"Wayne? Hi, this is Mrs. Whyte. How are you?"

Wayne grimaced at the phone as if it had just spoken a foreign language. He sucked the chocolate off his teeth and swallowed again, subconsciously making himself respectable for his teacher.

"Uh, good.... How are you?"

"I know this is unusual, calling you, it being break and all... I hope I'm not disturbing you?"

Wayne glanced over at his rumbled chair and the mess it hopelessly tried to conceal in the dim light of the dropped blinds. "No, not really. What's up?"

There was a long pause, and Wayne checked his phone again. A shy Mrs. Whyte wasn't a person he knew. "Mrs. Whyte?"

"I have a really serious question to ask you."

"Okay," he said tentatively. He moved back to his chair and flopped down against the pillow that engulfed him. "Yeah?"

"Well, I know you're really hush-hush about all the doodles and such on your notebook, but I have something like that I really need help with."

The Radster provided the pause this time. "I'm not sure...."

"Well, I came across a name and it looks familiar. I think I saw it on the back of your notebook."

Wayne threw his pillow aside and sat up, listening. "What name?" he asked cautiously.

A quick inhale on the line and then, "Señor Epus."

A thick, loaded silence filled the line from both parties now. Wayne had made his private life especially private, and she had to know she was crossing the line into it.

"Where did you hear it?"

Mrs. Whyte told him of a ghost town in the desert and the mysterious door and its inscription.

"I'm not sure," Rad finally said. "It may not be the same thing... except...look, Mrs. Whyte, I like you—I mean, like *respect* you. You're a good teacher and you've helped me and stuff... it's just, well... there's just some stuff I can't talk about."

"Wayne, I know. Believe me, I know." Another break. "I'm in the middle of something. Something really weird. I'm trying to make sense of it all. And right now, all I know is that name—"

He looked around his room, his eyes falling onto his backpack. He debated.

"How weird?"

"Excuse me?"

"You said something really weird was going on. What did you mean?"

Silence told him that she was debating as well. He got a cold sensation in his veins.

"Rad, can I trust you?

"Mrs. Whyte, you're going to have to if you want me to tell you anything about that name."

"Touché." She briefly described how giant machines she called Oil Eaters had attacked them—her friend, Donavan, and herself—how they narrowly escaped to the desert. She talked about men with powers, supernatural things she couldn't explain. "They're all somehow connected, Wayne, and we don't know how. These guys, they're—well, they're like nothing the world's ever seen."

"But I have."

"You have what?" Mrs. Whyte asked.

"Seen it. I know what you mean. I can tell you what I know now. But you have to promise me you will never repeat it to anyone else. I swore I never would."

"Okay."

The phone gave way to static as Wayne readjusted uncomfortably in his seat and checked to make sure he had closed his bedroom door. "I'm not a hero. I never shot that guy in the convenience store. Neither did my dad. There was someone else the day of the robbery. Someone I can't explain."

"Wayne, are you talking about the time you were in the middle of the holdup? Back in junior high?"

He found it absurd how hard it became to speak with a lump in his throat. "Yeah." Slowly at first, he did his best to describe something too incredible to put into words—but then more rapidly, the words spilled out when it finally registered that he found the one person who could possibly believe him. Someone would finally understand. Finally, he could tell the story of the scared boy in the convenience store and the man with the *Señor Epus* tattoo.

§ § § § §

Laney shivered inexplicably while she listened to her student's account on the other end. It could only mean one thing. *There's more of us.* She made Wayne go over the description again, all the details about a man who had similar traits to her new friends in their size and build, skills, mystique... and a tattoo he said haunted his dreams.

"Do you think it's his name?"

"Sort of."

"An anagram?" she asked, thinking back to the doodles on his notebook. She rearranged the letters in her head but needed paper. She came up empty.

"No. A semordnilap."

It took Laney a minute to think of what that meant.

"A word that has meaning read both forward and backward...." She scrambled over to the door so she could visualize the letters. Señor Epus. Supe Rones? Super Ones.

"Wayne, what do you think... Wayne? Wayne! Dang it."

Laney scurried back over to the others.

"The call dropped. But if you look at the letters on the door—the first S is hard to see—but if you put an S there, you can read it backward. Super Ones."

An exchange of puzzled glances and shrugs.

"What significance does that have to your friend?" Jacob asked.

Laney reluctantly relayed Wayne's tale, emphasizing that they were the only people who knew of Wayne's encounter. He'd never told anyone else about the man with the tattoo who had moved with lightning dexterity, who stood over his father and revived him, then left them with a threat to ensure secrecy.

"Wayne seemed to think this guy had more than speed and a body of steel: healing properties. So does this mean there's another one of us?" she asked.

"Perhaps the real seventh member," mumbled Tag.

Laney gritted her teeth. "What makes you sure there's only seven of us? Does anyone know for certain how many? Rheinland can't even be sure."

Harley silenced Tag from further comment with a withering look. Jacob rubbed his chin, contemplating the new information.

"I don't know about our numbers. But if this guy is the only other one of us, he could have left this message on the door. If we are the Super Ones—"

"Of course we are!" beamed Brian.

"—then it could have been here for us."

"Or someone else knew about him and was trying to lure him here," Harley suggested. "Or lure us. Heck, we don't know any more now than we did a minute ago."

"If he was one of us, why hasn't he made himself known?" Donavan asked. "The rest of us are together because we've been called together. If he's the same thing we are, why hasn't he been called to us?"

"Well, I think it's a good sign, this Epus guy. That it's marked on the door," Brian interjected with Tag nodding in agreement. "We're 'Super Ones', right? It was meant for us to open. We need to—"

A loud clash of metal interrupted Brian, the sound breaking like thunder over the group. They flinched and spun to see RJ standing in front of a crumbled metal sheet that used to be the closed entrance. Dust rose from the large hole, dark and daunting, now in place of what RJ had demolished. RJ, unimpressed by his own feat, jerked his head toward the new opening.

"Less talk," he told them.

§§§§§

The impatient group of gun-happy men turned to cautious investigators before Donavan's eyes. The cave appeared deep. A thrown rock skittered along the floor after it dropped, no back wall evident. Laney's flashlight inspection gave Donavan the odd impression that she wanted nothing more than to rush into the hole and find out exactly what it hid in its depth. Not a single male moved so rashly.

"Don't look at me," Harley had instantly growled when curiosity piqued. "You know what happens to a black dude when they send him down first in a horror movie, right? I'll be the first zombie sandwich."

"You're so stupid," Brian said, slapping Harley's chest with the back of his hand. "Zombie's don't eat sandwiches."

Tag and Jacob brought some of the mobile gadgets from the trailer; a distometer, Brian explained, could use sonar to help map out the space beyond the darkness. He was no expert on using the device, but he managed to learn a few things from his initial surveillance with it.

Tag scrawled madly on some paper while he whispered with Brian and pointed over figures that came and went on the screen. Then they did some temperature and infrared readings and then some more sketching.

In the meantime, the others geared up, eyes wide open, praying they hadn't opened a trap. But mystery outweighed caution. Everyone wanted in.

An hour later, Tag brought them all around to view the crude map he'd created.

"The entrance remains eleven feet wide clear to here. Then it breaks off into three tunnels. The one on the left and right seem to be reinforced. There are hollow spots here and here, so possibly... side caves?"

Brian chimed in, eyes wide with anticipation. "There's heat coming from here, perhaps an energy source." He pointed to the path to the right.

"Good," Jacob said, looking every bit as eager to descend as the rest of the posse.

"What if those things are down there?" Laney spoke up. Donavan surveyed her for signs of anxiety, but his impression remained that intrigue dominated her apprehension.

"They're huge," Harley said, rolling the stub of his cigar in his fingers as if to determine if there was enough to start the expedition with. "Don't think the robots w'd fit. 'Sides, how'd they get down there? We just opened the gate."

"The center tunnel," Brian interrupted, "I don't have a reading on. That's the part we don't know about. Maybe it's deep... or maybe reinforced with a material I can't read through, I don't know."

"Can you detect movement?" Donavan asked. "Life? Metal? What about electricity or ventilation?"

Tag shook his head. "The only heat we detect is here." He pointed to the spot on his map Brian had. "No movement. That's about all I know."

"If this door was so well sealed," Laney spoke up, "then what's down there? Something that shouldn't come out?"

"Or there could be another entrance," Tag added. His tone implied a civility toward Laney that Donavan had never heard before. This was a good sign, especially if they were all spelunking into hell together.

"We've been all over this mountain a dozen times and we've never seen a thing," Harley said. He continued to eye the ghostly house frames. "This entire 'hood is just one huge cover-up."

"Who would go through all the trouble and why?" Donavan pondered.

"It's like gravy on a griddle," Harley squinted. "Makes no sense unless you plan on eating your underwear."

Brian and Tag shook their heads simultaneously while Donavan and Laney tried to suffocate their laughter. RJ dumped a pile of helmets and belts at their feet and turned to move up the mountain for more supplies. His size had reached its zenith during their conversation.

"This is it, folks," Brian said, grabbing a helmet. "Feels like we should do a 'one for all' thing or something before we go down."

"We need a name first. Like, you know, Super Ones," Harley suggested.

"We need it classier," Brian scowled as he buckled on a utility belt. "Like the writing Señor Epus, how it's backwards."

"But that sounds singular; we need plural," Laney suggested. She didn't flinch when Donavan helped her pull on an oversized vest that looked like it may have seen action before.

"How about just Super?" Jacob put in, surprising them all with a contribution into their trivial debate.

"Let's do the scrambled thing with the letters," Brian amended. "Something more mysterious, less obvious."

"Like Puser?" Donavan tried half-heartedly, but got head shakes in return. "Repus?"

"How about Uspre?" Brian said. He snapped on his chin strap and gave his helmet a test thunk. "Cuz it has the 'us' right in it, like we're a team."

No one knew what to say until Tag answered with, "Yeah, that's it." He hit Brian's helmet in confirmation of the newly named brotherhood. "We're Uspre."

"*Us-pree?*" Laney asked, cocking her head to the side. "Cuz there's only one *e*, so technically it can't be the *ee* sound—"

"Yes, *Us-pree,*" Tag said with a sincerity that bewildered Donavan. "We ready, Uspre?"

They let the name settle over them and acceptance followed.

"Good," Tag nodded, all seriousness. "It's go time, *Uspre*!"

"*Uspre*!" they answered back and headed toward their underground destiny.

§ § § § §

The gaping mouth of the cave taunted Laney like a clever giant luring his next meal into his belly. She donned her helmet and canteen with the others, moving forward as they prepared. Insanely eager herself, she grew acutely aware of the new danger they had manufactured by blowing open the only barrier between themselves and their enemy. Zombie sandwiches, indeed.

No sense reminding the others in all their bravado that this could be a trap. They'd been over that. Their answer was to leave RJ behind as the rear guard. His size made it near impossible for him to go further inside with them, but outside, he could serve as a formidable obstacle to anything that may come in after them.

The guys gave their big friend swats of camaraderie as they moved passed; Laney tried for a fist bump, but RJ just eyed her balled up hand like an insult. So Laney swatted his arm like the others and mouthed a long "ouuuchhh" at the hard contact. The tiniest of smiles surfaced on his lips before she disappeared into the eerie darkness ahead.

They stayed in formation while they advanced, Jacob and Harley first, which they confessed to be habit. When Harley's senses had worked correctly, this lead worked best. He could detect any threat immediately, and Jacob's bulletproof frame made the pair hard to get around. They placed Donavan and Laney just yards behind with Brian and Tag—another natural pair—bringing up the rear.

They selected the tunnel to the left first by way of a solemn game of rock-paper-scissors between Brian and Tag. Flashlights, looped around wrists by their attached straps, served as the only means of light. Laney knew she was to grab Donavan's jacket if any danger approached and that Brian behind her served as a fallback. They refused to give her her own weapon since she had little experience with their models, a fact that irritated Laney and simultaneously relieved her from the heavy responsibility.

The tunnel proved to be a floor of dirt and stone, carving its way under the mountain. The roof above them was reinforced, but when it narrowed to a little more than six feet high, it gave a slight claustrophobic feeling even for Laney, the shortest of the bunch. Her shoulder tension eased, knowing none of the Oil Eaters could make it in or out of this shaft. A long suspended pole appeared in their beams, revealing that a handrail of metal protruded from the wall. The metal, smooth in spots with periodic rough patches from age or lack of care, indicated more human intervention. The air seemed dense but not stale, a soft *husshh* echoing in the space ahead.

After several yards, the dirt floor ran into metal, corrugated sheets that resounded under their footfall. Tag and Brian's map proved to be as accurate as they could hope for. They discovered the open spaces they had mapped going off to the side were actually rooms with heavy metal doors jutting awkwardly from the rock.

With a nod from Jacob, Donavan put a shoulder to the first one, and it popped open with a resounding clang. Laney heard the safety come off every weapon, each person assuming either a defensive or offensive position they had rehearsed many times.

"Brian, check this out," Donavan said after glancing in.

Brian nodded from his post at the door and traded places with Donavan.

"Sweet."

Laney, her back to the wall opposite, got a glimpse of a machine, a high chair-less table, and glass cabinet doors.

"It's like a medical bay or lab of some kind," Brian said for the benefit of those without a good view.

The next door held similar supplies. The third, almost identical.

"It's a whole dang underground building," Harley mouthed around his cigar.

Laney ran her hand along the metal rail for security, the path flickering between dark and light in the beams of their flashlights.

The air moved again, a subtle whisper of a breeze still surrounding them.

"There's an opening around here somewhere," Jacob said, shining his light high to check out the ceiling.

"Found it." Laney swallowed past the lump in her throat when she no longer felt the wall. Her light showed her that the metal bar now stood independently, using only the floor and vertical supports. There was no wall left to hold a mount behind it.

They pushed past her and turned their beams to where the wall should be. Their expressions sent a chill through her. "What? What is it?"

"Nothing," Donavan said, moving closer.

"Donavan," she warned, not in the mood to be left out of play.

"No, I mean it. It's... nothing." All their light together couldn't penetrate the vast open abyss to the right of the tunnel where the wall had evaporated. Jacob tossed a rock into the unknown and listened for several seconds for its drop.

Brian whistled softly. "Could be forty, fifty feet down."

"Seriously," Harley mumbled, "what the monkeyshine is this place?"

Chapter 28

The metal flooring, a scaffolding of sorts, created a ring high above the open cavern. More rooms with metal doors pocked the rock wall along the way. Each space appeared hauntingly empty. Most doors held a small rectangular window that revealed the same languid equipment, dust covered with inactivity. Jacob stopped having Donavan force the locks open as they sidled their way counter clockwise toward the rooms on the right. Brian plowed forward to the mapped area of detected heat.

Like the other rooms, the door to the marked red spot held fast but opened quickly when Donavan's muscle coupled with Laney's touch broke it down. The accompanying crash resounded unanswered through the cavern behind them. They were in this grand hole all alone it seemed.

The contents inside turned out to be much different than the other rooms. Laney had never seen a missile before, but she was certain the long narrow capsule in front of the group had all the makings of one.

Wordlessly, they moved around the metal canister, its body lifted off the floor with huge brackets. A distinct green glow reflected off the wall on the far side of the object. Their inspection, led by Brian and a beeping wand of some sort, didn't send the geek squad into panic, which helped Laney to keep her cool too.

"There doesn't seem to be a detonation device attached," Jacob said.

"No," Tag agreed. "Whatever is inside is producing energy, but it doesn't look connected to anything."

"Seems nuts that someone would leave this here," Harley commented. "Has to have some kick to it to be up on blocks like this, locked in a strong room, don't ya think? This what them black bots protecting?"

"See any black bots?" Tag countered.

Brian crawled underneath to shine his light from bottom to top of the fitted metal while Tag ran his hand over every seam. Brian stood and pondered, peering into a small window, the only break in the casing, where the green light shone back at him. It distorted his features with a sinister radiance. He moved his flashlight beam up the wall, around the corners, until he hit on a metal box in the corner of the ceiling.

"There."

The container had the looks of an enlarged cable box or modem, closed up except where cords and buttons poked out, dusty and unlit.

"It's a conduit, I'm sure," Brian said. "If this thing is an energy source, and if it connects to the box up there, then it could be the power source for this place."

"If?" Donavan asked.

Tag nodded in agreement at the wall box. "I doubt it's up there to set this contraption off."

"You doubt?" Harley snarled. "Wanna get yourself a little more sure before you go clipping the red wire or something else stupid?"

"What is 'this contraption?" Laney directed her comment to Donavan, afraid to voice her ignorance too loud. "Is it a bomb?"

Donavan shook his head, but not convincingly. "I don't think so, but... maybe."

"So now what?" Tag asked.

"Let's see what's down there," Jacob said giving the 'fall out' signal for retreat.

"I have an idea," Brian said. "If I can get these two connected, I might be able to power this place up. There are overhead lights in all the rooms, a good sign that there's something around here to generate them. Maybe we can get some light before we explore more."

"And maybe we light this place up in grand finale instead," Harley said with a firm headshake. "This thing seems potentially lethal."

"Vote?" Tag asked.

This looked like standard protocol as the others' accepted the proposed question; Jacob gave a nod of consent and four hands shot up, hers not being one of them.

"Go for it," Jacob said. "You and Tag stay and see what you can do, but no more than fifteen minutes. The rest of us will head down below."

Laney and the remaining Uspre filed back out onto the whispering cavern scaffold. They made it back to where the paths first branched at the start of the circular balcony and prepared for their descent down the metal staircase anchored there.

Soft clicks joined the white noise of the cavern. The blink-blink shudder of bulbs and then the lights were on, a track of industrial-sized utility lights suspended on beams below them.

Laney breathed in quickly and tried to translate to her mind what her eyes took in. The ground bubbled with piles of up-heaved earth that rose up sporadically, like mounds of mold disfiguring the surface. Equipment in an array of sizes and shapes formed a scattered pattern around the dirt piles. Some looked like digging apparatus, some were types of small movers. Under the row of lamps sat a line of huge vats, tall but squat, like mammoth sumo wrestlers with swollen necks that connected to a series of pipes. The pipes reached up to the beams and networked their way around the room.

Brian and Tag joined them, Brian's spectacular display of fist-pumps advertising his success with the lights. The two descended the six landings of the spiral staircase until their feet met with the dirt floor.

Jacob graciously let Brian lead, his eagerness difficult to contain. Even though the lamps gave the room a decent luminance, the group used their flashlights to sweep the corners and materials hanging overhead. Jacob ran his hand along one of the vats, twice his height and impossible to see around.

"Brian?"

"This is crazy," Brian assessed. "It looks like a distillery, you know, processing something."

"Like?"

Brian threw his hands up, palms upturned.

More questions were voiced than answered while they made their way around the backside of the tanks. Tag hit one of the metal sides with the butt of his flashlight. It tinged hollow and echoed for several seconds.

"Oh, my—"

Harley never finished his sentence. His flashlight had come close enough to the wall behind a tank to send back a reflection. Stretching across the floor, the entire support under the scaffolding was made up of a rock wall, the likes of which Laney never dreamed existed. Layers of emerald and blue, purples and indigo, winked back at them in fabulous bands of rich color. The layers flowed in dips and crests in spectacular radiance, reminding Laney of the inside of an abalone shell before being polished. The effect left them breathless. No wonder Harley couldn't find words.

"Home of the green rocks," Jacob said. "One mystery solved."

They all approached the wall for closer inspection; for some reason Laney's first thought was *What a shame RJ couldn't see this*. If they came down together alone somehow, he could get a chance.

"Can I grab a sample?" Brian asked.

Jacob nodded, but no one could find a single broken rock to take. None of the loose gravel on the ground had any tone other than dull brown. The ones on the wall proved hard to extract. It took some doing before Brian had a chip worth hauling with him. He fumbled it in his hands for a moment.

"It's oily, like oil shale. But it's so solid. More like metamorphic." A quick nudge in to the ribs from Harley got him to tuck it into his vest so they could move on.

The circular cavern appeared to only have one entrance, the one they came through. But a survey in the back of the cave revealed a break under the scaffolding. The ceiling pipes dipped down and dove under the upper rooms bottlenecking into a passage. The group followed with cautious steps and sweeping beams of light to the unlit tunnel, nearing the soft roar that had filled the cave from the start.

Once through the corridor of rock, the pipes overhead led into a second cavern with tanks of a larger, taller size. Some were more like tubes than tanks, reaching to the ceiling in transparent plastic rather than silver canisters. A green-hued liquid swooshed upward then coursed back down in an undulating vertical column.

They stopped, soaking in the mesmerizing pattern of emerald highlighted with a ribbon of yellow and flashes of blue. A single beam of sunlight broke through some unseen cut in the rock ceiling, highlighting all the facets in a breath-taking uncanny display. No artificial lights other than the tubes lit the room.

"No green rocks," Jacob pointed out. The walls in this cavern stood solid brown and ugly.

The group stepped into the hollow of the large space to find the source of the roar tucked behind the pillars of churning, tubed water. A thick independent stream cascaded from a glowing hole in the ceiling, its appearance another anomaly in the dry desert. More incredibly, the waterfall hit the floor and disappeared into a neat pocket with not a drop missing its target.

"How in the world—" Laney began when clatter echoed into the chamber.

Every head turned toward the first cavern they had left behind.

Harley cursed and turned off his safety.

"They found us."

Laney didn't need Donavan's hand to push her down; she hit the dirt voluntarily, taking a rock in the gut when she landed. Urgent voices broke out around her:

"Over there—"

"I got him—"

"MOVE!"

A mad scramble—trained feet flew toward cover behind one of the few piles of rock in this part of the cave. Laney's desperate fingers reached for Donavan's jacket. Her heart pounded so loudly she had no idea how many bullets had been expelled when Donavan twisted his body to take aim beside her from behind their mass of rocks.

Coming on their right—a big metal monster with its slick, black, eyeless hood. Laney called out; Tag brought it down with two shots and continued firing off toward the tunnel. The heap of machinery collapsed in front of her and earnest sweat broke out on her forehead despite the chilly room.

"Don't let them block us in!" Jacob yelled, but the others were already working with hand signals and maneuvers that had them progressing over the fallen machines and directly toward the advancing ones.

They had almost reached the passageway when three more Oil Eaters whirred on their ungodly legs, lunging out with stiff arms as if they lived for nothing more than to tear this squad apart.

The bots reached Tag and Jacob first.

Tag fired a single deadly shot at the neck joint and sent his assailant down in pieces.

"Shoot them at their neck," Laney yelled to Donavan who had been squeezing off round after round at two remaining machines. "It only takes one shot if you get them where they connect." He nodded, almost unperceivable, jaw set in determination. His intensity rallied Laney's bravado, and she dug in her heels, ready to flee when told. Near them, Harley's shot took down one, then another, before Donavan could.

Then silence.

Jacob motioning them forward, the group scurried through the tunnel toward the tanks along the walls as a means of cover rather than the rock piles and equipment in the interior of this cavern.

The vats created deep shadows from the dim overhead lights. Uspre put more space between each of them now, one person sidling up a silver tank before the next person followed.

Brian moved ahead of Laney, Donavan behind. She crept toward the vat that concealed Brian and dropped her flashlight just as she rounded the curve of the tank. Cursing that she hadn't been using the wrist strap, she hastily scrambled after it before it could roll out from the cover of darkness.

Her hand reached and found the cool metal she couldn't grasp. Not the flashlight. A foot. A long, angular, metallic foot.

Laney's glance upward didn't make its way to the head of the giant body before her scream echoed through the cavern. An enormous black claw caught her at the throat and lifted her high off the ground in a split second. Behind her, crunching metal resounded as a second robot collapsed under Donavan's mighty strike.

Laney swung wildly in the air, grasping for breath in the clutches of the inhuman brute; more bullets and shouts deafened her before the roar of the time-train came. Everything froze. Something had a tight grip on her dangling foot.

Brian.

With labored heaves, he used his free hand to climb up the monster closer to Laney. His face dimmed under her blurring vision. She reached for him, but instantly returned her hands to the strangling claw, trying to get the weight of her body off her constricted throat.

"Not sure how this is will work," Brian spoke rapidly in the frozen chaos. "I'm going to take this guy down and when I do, he's gonna fall, and I don't know if I can hold you in the warp then. He falls; you jump!"

She gurgled a reply from blue lips and a shot rang close. Sight left her, but she felt the sensation of falling, her neck free, a huge breath filling her. In a weak attempt to obey Brian, she kicked out. Dust engulfed her when she hit the ground hard and in the next instant, Donavan tented over her, protecting her from the toppling shell of armor.

"Let's move," he commanded, tossing the debris aside like ripping free from tissue paper.

Laney latched onto her partner and ran with everything she could force from her aching body. The others followed and together they raced in blind confusion down the first available offshoot from the cavern.

Then another set of impossible doors appeared, lining the organic scenery with manmade openings.

Donavan put a shoulder to the most accessible door. The interior, a long angular space, glowed with dim lighting to the rear. Footsteps pounded behind as Jacob—who had overshot the door—doubled back, and Tag trailing Harley and Brian barely passed through the doorway when the soft whirl and metallic scrape reached them. Tag turned and hit an incoming menace with a loud zap that sent his own body flying backward with an agonizing cry.

Donavan picked up the discarded door and jammed it back into place while all available hands grabbed a large metal lab table and shoved it toward him. Donavan picked it up like a toy and rammed it up against the entrance. It held. The door rattled until, for good measure, Donavan found metal cabinets nearby and heaved them onto the stack.

The semi-dark room grew quiet, and Tag, who had been scrambling to regain his footing, collapsed into a grateful heap. Jacob came to his aid, but the author of jolts just waved him away.

"You okay?" Brian asked him.

"Well, it didn't feel good," Tag said feebly, rubbing his arms and swaying a bit.

They inspected the perimeter of the room, safe for the moment. They scoured the walls, the floor, the ceiling, and the surrounding objects for unfriendlies.

"All clear?" Jacob asked with wariness.

Affirmations all around.

"Now what?" Laney whispered.

"Don't worry," Harley mumbled over his ragged cigar. "They too big to be in here even if they get past the Pete blockade."

Brian took one of his gadgets out of Tag's pack. "The walls are the same thickness everywhere but here." Brian pointed his gizmo to the back wall. "There should be a vent or opening somewhere."

Jacob held his hand steady over a spot.

"Feel anything?" he asked, and Donavan held his hand up beside Jacob's. Apparently he did feel something; he jerked his chin to Laney who obediently joined him. She grasped his back without a word while he swung a mighty punch into the rock. While gaining a set of bloody knuckles, Donavan created a fist-sized hole that emitted sunlight. A small stack of smashed rock crumbled at their feet.

"We have our way out," Donavan said, shaking off the dust. He punched the opening wider. "Brian, crawl out, and I'll send Laney to you."

Brian struggled through with a grunt, the rock grapping at his gear.

"Needs to be wider!" he called into them after it had taken a full minute to escape.

A stirring caught their attention, and simultaneously all eyes turned toward the door.

"They're coming," Tag said incredulously. "I have a feeling that door is not enough against a team of them."

"Just try it, you sorry pieces of junk," Harley snarled.

"Let's move," Jacob countered, pointing to their newest exit route. Donavan turned to the wall and began punching, the hole growing by force. Laney glanced around the room and found thick rods used to support a utility shelf. She raced over and tugged.

"Donavan! Use this!" The words had no sooner left her mouth then the door, table, and cabinets flew in every direction and a claw snagged her t-shirt fabric in its clutches.

The smashed remnants of their barrier rained over her, but panic befriended her amid the chaos. In a mad wriggle and drop, she had her t-shirt over her head and emptied. She scrambled backward like a crab in her battered cami until she bumped into a muscled calf.

Harley reached down and picked her up by her arm with one hand while he continued to fire at a line of black-bots crawling over the debris. He tossed her toward Donavan before she could find her feet. In a swift movement, Donavan had her around the waist, smashing the rest of the wall with a single blow of his free hand.

The rumble that followed overwhelmed the senses, but through the confusion Laney found each man struggling to hold their own. Tag, caught up in hand to hand, found his weapon knocked loose from his grip and it skittled into the rocks.

"Leave it!" Harley growled, shoving the man toward their exit out the side of the mountain. Tag quickly followed before a new wave of robots appeared, and Harley, with a roar that would have intimidated a grizzly, charged them, while the remaining team retreated and held the ground behind him.

Harley had effectively cleared the field, and the mad scramble for the hole became a "you first" standoff before Jacob pulled rank and forced Harley out. From outside the men shouted their bravado, leaning in to grab hold of Laney next, now free from pursuit, when another beast, out of nowhere, cornered the three within the cave. Jacob, trying to use his body as a shield, ended up on his knees while Donavan, too close range to fire, began using fists. Brian shouted, his arm thrust through the opening at Laney, but beyond the attacker taking on the three of them, she could see shadows approaching the doorway rubble.

Ignoring Brian's call, Laney dropped to the floor to scoop up Tag's fallen pistol.

"Laney!" Donavan's voice echoed above the din, but Laney aimed and fired at the upcoming row.

Jacob overcame their closest assailant, and Donavan wrapped an arm around Laney's. As if under a will of its own, the aim turned deadly to the next robot and the next. Laney tucked into the hollow of Donavan, his arm outstretched along hers over the gun, together firing and taking out every single giant, every single shot.

Not wasting another second, the three, free from all menaces, scrambled out the escape route into the blinding mid-day sun. Without waiting for a consultation, Donavan used his fists—battered from his earlier demolition efforts—to smash into the rock wall from the outside. The resulting avalanche sealed the hole with a collection of large rocks that even RJ would struggle to get back through.

The crew held still, patiently waiting for the enemy's next move. But the dust settled around them in silence, and slowly, shoulders relaxed, deep breaths whistled in and out.

"Well, Shooter," Brian grinned at Laney through a long exhale, using both hands to sift dirt from his dirty blond scalp. "Looks like you finally earned yourself a real nickname."

Chapter 29

The gang assessed each other's injuries more for bragging rights than concern. Their wounds would soon disappear with the miracle aid that came from within their bodies. The daylight of the open desert revealed a clear view, void of black robots, melting away remaining jitters into the healing process.

Uspre had survived their first battle, the first with Donavan and Laney, at any rate. Donavan tried to join the others in the rehashing of their success and downfalls, but the woman by his side had sent his blood singing. *A lot.*

This wasn't the typical touch-me-not zing he normally encountered. No, that felt like a mere precursor of what was to come. Somehow touching her just now during heavy battle had become an intoxicating mix of electricity and thrill that took control of his body and wouldn't leave.

He shook himself, stamped his feet as if to drop the dirt, flexed his hands pretending to get the healing process going, but it was no use. His body was on fire and wired to *go.*

And there she stood, picking tiny rocks from her scraped elbow with a grimace. It couldn't be. It was just not possible that she felt *nothing* still.

She shot him a look and a bashful smile that sent his hopes soaring. He had to know.

He took her hand firmly in his, and her face lit up with surprise. He all but carried her away from the debris of the rockslide, finding a slight recess in the stone that blocked them from the others who continued their war stories only a few feet away.

Laney backed against the mountain as if startled and tripped on the way. His arm shot behind her waist causing her breath to rise sharply and her eyes widen. He didn't give her space and all but pinned her against the rock in an urgent attempt to capture her undivided attention.

"Do you feel it? Did you?" His voice came out raspy and needy, matching the tide of energy that surged more rapidly now in a strong, steady course.

Things were different. Everything was different. The shock that always set his teeth on edge had found its groove and raced through him in a charged, circulating pattern that had him on the brink of utter chaos. Yet it felt incredibly *right.* Maybe working together—acting together in the face an enemy—had forced his energy into a rhythm. It pumped through him now with exhilaration hard to contain.

Laney dug her fingers into his biceps and clung to him. She opened her mouth to speak then closed it.

"Well?"

She nodded, eyes bright.

The rush of elation threatened to break the dam keeping this new power in check. "Yes?"

"Yes," she barely answered before he kissed her. Every doubt he had disappeared like the softness of her lips crushed beneath his. He imagined clearly who he was, what he could do, and why he was here. Everything made perfect sense as he unabashedly absorbed her presence into his own.

Best of all, he was no longer alone in this consuming head-to-toe makeover.

She finally felt it too.

It took tremendous strength of will for Donavan to pull back, leaving his arm snug around her, his other hand bracing himself away from the rock. His forehead rested on hers, their ragged breath in unison filling up the space of the small alcove they had found.

When he could speak, Donavan gave her some room, enough to search her eyes and find them glistening. He slowly grinned.

"We found it, Laney. We found our groove."

"I... that was crazy."

His smile widened, and he leaned back. "But what a heck of a rush."

Turning back to rejoin the others, he grabbed her hand and found her shaking. He scowled in bemusement. There wasn't any part of him that felt unnerved. Never had he been so invigorated and empowered.

"You alright?" he asked.

"I might need to sit down."

Brian, Tag, and Harley began a slow clap behind them, returning Donavan to reality. Not as discreet as he had thought. He didn't want an audience right now, but he didn't drop Laney's hand. Nothing was more important than this moment. Her features held something, a look veiled in the depth of her eyes. Something he didn't feel, couldn't understand. Fear? No. More like... uncertainty.

"Lane? Is it gone? The feeling...."

"I—"

"Every. Time. Did you see that?" Brian said, joining them. "Not a single bullet missed its mark." Dirt streaks ran heavily down the right side of his face, smearing the blood that came from a cut in his head. The area surrounding his eye socket remained white and clean, creating a warrior-meets-Phantom-of-the-Opera mask atop his slanted grin.

"Lane?" Donavan probed, not wanting her attention diverted by Brian's comical appearance and jesting. Not until he had a clear answer.

"She missed a few," Tag growled, trying to ignore large scratches etched in the flesh of his forearm now turning a healing pink.

Donavan dropped his hand, and a slow blush spread over Laney's face. "You don't feel it, do you?" he frowned. Her eyes filled with apology and her mouth opened, but nothing came out. "You never did," he said, guessing more than accusing. No denial from her followed.

Jacob answered Tag. "No, she didn't miss a shot. Not when Donavan was with her."

"You just seemed so eager," she whispered. "I didn't… I don't want to let you down."

Donavan's shoulders collapsed in a defeat from a different type of assault, and he turned away. He couldn't bare the look of incomprehension in her expression, not after what he felt.

Tag checked the position of the sun. "If we head back that way, we should find home around the corner."

"Right," Donavan agreed absently. He heard Laney move behind him, but he forced himself to step away or he'd suffocate under the thought that he'd be alone forever within this transforming one-sided power.

Brian wriggled his eyebrows at Donavan as he passed; Harley held up a high-five that went unanswered. Jacob joined him in a steady march back around the mountain in wordless support of whatever cosmic pull he battled.

The others trailed close behind, but the sound of Laney's voice was impossible to block out as she let Brian engage her in rapid dialogue of what she'd seen and felt. Donavan tried not to listen, tried to work on being *normal* to the point he missed the obvious changes around them.

It was Jacob's sudden sprint toward the first house of their ghost town that pulled him back to himself. He turned to exchange glances of question with the other men when Tag cursed and broke into a run after Jacob.

Harley stopped in his tracks, and Donavan whipped around to scour the landscape for clues.

Around them, remains of fallen Oil Eaters scattered the desert floor like giant fallen crows, the angled arms poking up like broken wings. High, low, some in piles, some torn to shreds, dozens of metal bodies.

"RJ—" Donavan breathed simultaneously with Laney, and their feet were in motion.

They found him slumped by the cave entrance, his weapon a useless toy next to his over-sized rocky hand. The door had been shoved back into place and huge boulders sealed them in place. What looked like coagulating blood pooled on RJ's shoulder. His face, turned away from their view, didn't move at the sound of their voices.

The men blocked Laney from helping until she tersely reminded them that she could aid the most. True to her word, as soon as she knelt and took RJ's rough knuckles into her palm, the giant dissolved into a manageable size. Jacob and Brian did a quick evaluation while the others kept their distance.

"The blood is from his eye," Jacob said, which became obvious to them all when they turned his head and found an empty bloody socket. "Let's get him up."

§ § § § §

Laney welcomed the cool chill of the evening and might not have noticed the jacket Donavan draped across her shoulders if it weren't for RJ's groan. She had been sitting for hours now, holding RJ's hand in the twilight. The fire barrel glowed from the center of the structure, ghostly independent of the other houses as it floated up higher on the hill from its neighbors.

"How's our patient?" Donavan whispered to Laney.

"Lost an eye," RJ slurred. "Not ears."

"Cranky," Laney answered for the injured. Donavan crouched beside her seat on a short upturned barrel. She forced herself to meet his gaze and regret returned. The way his eyes had blazed today, the strength in his arms, his kiss—she could lose her breath even now just thinking about it.

But the look of disappointment that overcame him when she had admitted she lacked whatever it was he felt—that burned even hotter in her mind. She reveled in the fact they could fire a gun with deadly accuracy when together, true; but no electricity, no magic power prompted her. If anything, a heavy dose of fear laced with her drive, something she was quite certain Donavan did not feel.

If only she had continued to lie... if she just let him think it was a supernatural force for her as well.

Here in the semi-darkness, Donavan's face held no lingering signs of turmoil over her lack of emotion. His eyes—the gentle, warm ones that always captivated her under normal circumstances— reassured her. She couldn't be more thankful.

"I still don't understand," she spoke, keeping the conversation off of *that*. She leaned toward him and lowered her voice. "How could his eye be...? I mean, I watched you all do that instant healing stuff. Why wouldn't he? Won't the eye just..." she simply mouthed the last words, "*grow back*?"

Donavan shook his head. "Jacob keeps reminding me that we are all mortal. None of us are invincible; if it's damaged completely, there's nothing left to repair. He thinks since it was...." Instead of words, he used his hands in the coming starlight to illustrate an explosion to the face.

Laney recoiled at the painful thought of RJ's suffering in a battle he alone faced. Donavan tucked a strand of her hair back behind her ear and mumbled an apology. The simple gesture gave her some solace.

"Could everyone shut up now?" RJ groused.

"Thanks for the jacket," she smiled grimly, "but it's best if you don't come too near."

Donavan nodded in understanding as RJ's body shifted beneath his blanket. He kissed Laney on the top of her head and rose. Warmth flowed through her.

"Remember we've got your location secure. Nothing can get up here without our notice. We'll rotate guard duty throughout the night."

But they know we're here. Laney wanted to join the others at the campfire and talk it out. What was going on underground? The lab, the robots, the tanks, water, green rocks—it was all so baffling…But they had blocked both possible exits, one by Donavan and one by RJ.

And now RJ... poor RJ. He needed her right now, and that was all that mattered.

She told Donavan good night and resumed her hand-holding vigil. RJ's breathing returned to normal once Donavan had gone.

"Quite a few stars out tonight," she reported lamely and then realized that describing visuals could be cruel to someone who had just lost half their sight. He met her comment with silence, and she thought maybe RJ'd drifted off to sleep for a minute.

"Jacob... he thinks the eye's gone?" the question finally came.

"He doesn't know," she lied horribly. "We'll just have to wait and see."

He grew silent again, and she sensed he knew the truth. Her heart sank, heavy with guilt. "I'm sorry," she heard herself saying. "It'll get better," was all she could think of to say.

"Really?" he scoffed. "I feel like I've been made into a useless one-eyed dummy."

"Nonsense," she interjected, taken back at his rush of words. "You'll be our Cyclops and clobber masses of machines in a single swipe. Legendary. Just wait and see."

"Cyclops?"

He'd never heard of a Cyclops? Shocker.

"They're wicked one-eyed giants," she said, then quickly added, "like wicked cool."

RJ let that sink in. "Tell me the story," he said, and she was sure she'd misheard.

"You... want me to tell you a story? So you like when I rattle on? I thought —"

RJ interrupted with a huge sigh. "Story."

"Right." Laney decided to recount Odysseus' adventures with a bit of a tweak. She tried to make the Cyclops more glorified figures than the dirty, drooling group of characters that lived in her imagination. RJ's expression reacted under the bandage to different moments in the tale, encouraging Laney to further embellish the diabolical creature into the most fearful opponent Odysseus had ever encountered.

RJ's body relaxed even as faint coyote howls blended into the crackle of the fire. Laney rubbed the fingers of the hand he had kept in hers.

What else could she do? RJ, one of them, would never be the same, and all she could do was sit and tell him stories. A lump formed in her throat; her heart broke for her friend. Friend? Yes, surely RJ had the right to be called that.

Eventually, a yawn escaped her weary body and soul.

"What happens to him?" RJ asked just as she thought she might go lay down.

"Who? Odysseus?"

"That Cyclops."

"Oh. Well... he...." Lost his eye trying to imprison men for his lunch menu? Got outwitted by the hero? Not the ending a one-eyed warrior needed to hear. "Odysseus got away, but the Cyclops terrorized his corner of the world with his fierceness. He's epic."

Laney couldn't tell if she had sold it or not, so she quickly prepared her sleeping bag next to him and settled in for the night. She made sure the medication Jacob gave her was close by and that she stoked the fire well. Her injured ankle felt the strain of the day and needed equal rest now.

"Good night, RJ," she whispered softly.

"Good night," he answered. "Good story."

Laney couldn't say when, but at some point the sobbing began. Perhaps it was the pent-up emotion that hadn't had a chance yet to vent, an overflow of the "my-life-as-a-divorcee-sucks" buildup. Perhaps the incident with Donavan confused and frightened her as much as it intrigued him. But mostly she knew the reality of their danger had manifested itself with the loss of RJ's eye. His sacrifice overwhelmed her, and when she was certain he was asleep, she broke down. She didn't want to but somehow needed to. Some tear-shed would cleanse her and bring her back to proper functionality.

So she cried softly into her bedroll until the pain, unsubsiding, felt like it would rip her chest apart.

At some point, she slept and dreamt. It grew cold, so she stoked the fire and raised her head to view the unwavering stars—consistency among the chaos—when she heard the sound of her own crying. She stood by the small flames in her dream, watching her body shake with sobs next to the huge lump that was RJ sleeping beside her. Through the darkness, she fought for a glimpse of the men below. It was a lucid dream, so maybe she would just fly down to see them. Wouldn't that be cool if her power were to fly? What better time to try than in a dream?

She climbed to the highest point on the house's frame, amazed at the feel of the rough wood in her hands, and thrilled as a breeze caught her and ruffled the hair around her face. For a brief moment, she was free. Free from fear, free from pain, free from worry. She took a deep breath and was just debating if she should fall forward or actually jump into the air to achieve flight when sleep robbed her of ever finding out.

"Again?" The news that the party planned on a second tunnel expedition had been announced over breakfast. Another descent didn't really concern Laney. She expected the guys to poke the sleeping bear because, well, they were men, but it did surprise her that they plotted it do it so soon after their rocky battle.

"What exactly's the gain?" she asked.

Tag ironed out the crinkled map he and Brian had been working on. Brian turned his enthusiastic work toward Jacob.

"Here," Brian punched out. "And here and here. It's hard to detect. Well, I didn't know to look for it yesterday. But I've gone over this area," his hand swung in a wide arch to different spots on the mountain. The sweat V that lined the front and back of his shirt testified to the morning hike he'd taken. "And here, there are more tunnels. A network of them. Some of them seem so small they might not be anything more than air shafts. Some dive deep. Others disappear and pick back up, wind around. Aside from our mine beneath this mountain, passages web out everywhere. Like a giant prairie dog community." He paused to rub his chin and left a dirt streak in its wake. "Can't find a single opening to any of them. The tunnel we used, the one with rooms on the side, seems a natural passage they took advantage of to build on."

"Who 'they'?" Harley asked, working on his first cigar of the day.

An exchange of glances.

Tag eyed Jacob with deep grooves in his creased forehead. "Ideas?"

"Rheinland didn't know anything more than the Oil Eaters would be here."

"How did he know that?" Laney asked.

"Same as we do," came Jacob's answer. "The call, the feel of it."

"But he knew that we'd be sticking around," Donavan put in. "Why else have the trailer full of exploring devices and artillery? He must have known something about the place, the caverns."

"No. He just knew...." For the first time, the confident Jacob seemed at a loss for words.

"How reliable is this Rheinland?" Donavan persisted.

"He's tight," Jacob shot back too quickly.

Laney recalled the pictureshow Jacob had given Donavan. Calloway-the-good-looking and Ozegovich-the-plain flashed into her mind. They had been the object of Jacob's informative review, not Rheinland.

"He's never steered us wrong. Ever," Harley said, coming to Jacob's defense, but no one appeared reassured by this news.

"We need to call him," Tag frowned. "I'm going to say what Donavan's thinking. This feels more like a setup than a mission."

Harley turned on him. "What did you say? After all we've done with Rheinland—"

"Just sayin' it cuz Pete's too scared to."

Laney swallowed and glanced back at the house where RJ still slept. Maybe she should have slept in another hour, until all this testosterone had been worked off.

"No, it's fine," Jacob said, grabbing Harley's shoulder before he could move toward Tag. "We need to consider... all possibilities."

This admission sobered them all.

"What are you saying?" Brian finally spoke.

"I want to do this without phoning in Rheinland." Their leader let that acknowledgement settle over them along with the blanket of tension that followed.

"Why?" Harley persisted. His wide eyes told Laney this news would not rest easy with him. "Why would he hide info? We could be killed!"

"Harley, you know as well as we do," Jacob said patiently, "that this sucks. We came here expecting to find answers to the attacks, to the appearance of these things in the city. What we found are more questions. Don't you think it's odd Rheinland didn't know about the underground hideaway? It's not like him."

"So we ask him our questions! See what he has to say—"

"I'm not ruling that out," Jacob held up his hand to end Harley's tirade. It impressed Laney all over again how Jacob knew perfectly how to speak to each of them. "I'm just saying, for now, we do this alone." He jerked his chin in Tag's and Brian's direction. "So what do we know?"

"I've been thinking," Tag said slowly. "No robots until we turned the lights on. What if that power box—that green mama-bomba—activates the robots as well as the electricity?"

Heads glanced at Tag. Slow nods of agreement made their way around the circle.

"Robots found their way out before—during that earthquake or whatever," Harley countered. "Right? What about then?"

"Dunno. But what if we can get in there and turn that box off?" Tag continued. "Then we can keep looking around to see what's with the place."

"Is that the end game?" asked Laney. "To look around? What do we hope to find?"

Brian pulled the golf ball-sized rock from his packet, the facets of green instantly winking in the morning sun. Natural light made its iridescent qualities peak.

"I know this much about geology," Brian said, pinching his fingers together to illustrate a tiny space. "But I know what oil shale is. And this isn't it. Except it is."

Harley huffed. "And you give me crap about being obtuse."

"Oil shale is sedimentary rock," Brian continued. "Easy to break, kinda. This isn't. This is metamorphic. It's tough. And it's green."

"So what makes you think it's oil shale?" Donavan asked.

He reached out and rubbed the rock down Donavan's arm. It left a visible slick behind.

"To be sedimentary, there would have most likely been an ancient lake here. Not sure the likelihood of that. It's tight oil in those layers, tough to extract. That it's so hard makes it more like torbanite, but it's green. I don't know. If it's on the charts, I don't know where the heck it fits in."

"That equipment below," Jacob chimed in. "Has all the makings of a mine. A refinery."

"Wait," Laney said, thinking over what she knew about the topic. "Mining? For oil shale? So what, fracking?"

"Need lots of water for that," Harley scoffed.

"Well, we got water," Donavan said with a shrug toward the scum pond that suggested his uncertainty.

"You would need a lot more water and different equipment than they got," Brian said. "What do all those vats, pipes, and such remind you of?"

"A brewery, if we're being honest," Donavan replied.

"Right. It's as much a distillery down there as a refinery. I think we need to find out what's in those tanks."

"What if that's the job of those robots?" Laney asked. "What if all they do is help refine... whatever that is?"

"Seem awfully aggressive for worker bees," Harley commented. He still didn't seem settled ever since Rheinland had been put under suspicion.

"Could be," Brian nodded. "Lucky us, we got our first bots to autopsy! Tag and I might be able to find what makes them tick. Obviously they could use other power sources if they made it into the city, so we want to be as sure as we can about that before we venture down."

"Good idea," Jacob agreed. "Harley and I will try to figure a way to get back in."

"The plan being—" Laney decided not to finish her question as she examined the look of determination on the surrounding faces.

§§§§§

Donavan let the others prep for their assignments while he debated about telling Jacob what was on his mind. All the vague loose ends made him uneasy. He didn't want to descend back into their beautiful Hades until he knew more.

There was one way he could think of to do that.

Laney saddled up close, a troubled frown echoing his thoughts.

"So we're doing this?" she asked.

"Yeah. We are." He saw Jacob break away from Harley for a moment to refill his canteen.

"What about RJ? We can't leave him out of this."

"Why don't you stay with him?" he said without glancing her way. "Hang on, I gonna talk to Jacob a minute."

He missed any further worry that may have crossed her features as he moved quickly beside his leader.

"I want to call a buddy of mine," Donavan cut to the chase when he had Jacob alone. "He can get us information."

Jacob seemed taken back. "It's a really bad idea to include anyone from the outside."

"We're talking my partner of five years. He's not only trustworthy and loyal, he will have access to things others don't as a member of the police force."

"What kind of intel you looking for?" Jacob asked.

Donavan sucked his cheeks and wagged his jaw as if the words soured his mouth. "An update on Vincent Valentine."

Tag reluctantly held out the Napstar phone to Donavan when Jacob explained the situation to him. Jacob moved on with RJ, leaving Donavan to make his call. But Tag didn't relinquish his grip on the phone without a warning first.

"We don't include others... purposefully," Tag said between gritted teeth.

Donavan waited for more explanation that didn't follow. "I'm listening."

Tag released his hold and glanced around to see if anyone else was within earshot. The tension in Tag's shoulders told Donavan that he'd like to avoid this conversation, and Donavan's phone call had pried it out.

"There's a reason the rest of us aren't married, don't have girlfriends... no kids." Tag's eyes were intense and burning black in his brown skin. "They find what makes you weak and they use it against you."

Donavan's mind raced to his own family. "What are you saying? Who are 'they'?"

"'They' are whoever the hell shows up at our doorstep. Once they find we can't be messed with—not physically—they go straight for our—" Tag's voice broke, and he swallowed hard, rushing on in anger, "—for what we love. We never thought it could happen to us, but we've come up against some pretty ugly people."

Donavan pondered this, keeping still as he let the heat simmer off of his comrade. "You lost someone." It was a statement not a question.

"Yes," Tag answered, still heated.

"How?"

"They killed her," was his terse reply. "When we interrupted a little shipping operation in New Orleans... they found out I was engaged, and she was murdered."

Donavan cast a glance at Laney; Tag followed his vision as he continued. "I don't know what your deal with her is. I don't understand how any of this works any more than you do, but I know this. Neither of you are like us. You have kids, families. You come from a normal life that hasn't been disturbed." He took a step backward as if propelled by bitterness. "Make that call, but just know what you're getting into. You've been warned."

"Appreciate it," was all Donavan could say, but he was already talking to Tag's back. He sighed and gripped the phone tightly. Was he sure? The answer was no, but then again, he hadn't been sure about anything in a very long time.

Michael picked up the call on the third ring, his voice exploding into the phone when he heard Donavan's voice. "For the love of—Donavan, where have you been?"

"Michael, it's a very long story. I don't even know where to begin."

"Well, you've missed the train wreck here! The captain—you have no idea what I've been through because of your hiatus. So where *are* you? You falling off the grid doesn't look good for your defense, you know."

"I'm camping out in the desert."

"You're what?"

"I'm trying to find out who's behind this mess and all the... evidence... led me here." He gave Michael as much information about the coordinates of their location as he could manage from the information Tag had supplied him. "I need to know about this community that was being built here. It was abandoned, but it looks like it had been built overtop some other operation. I need your help."

"You? I could use some answers, too. Donavan, you have no idea—"

"Michael, I don't have a lot of time. Please. Listen. I need Valentine to talk—"

"Donavan, that's what I've been trying to tell you!" Even though Donavan's claim to fame was being the unruffled one of the two, Michael could be equally patient, so Donavan's stomach churned as his partner's next words came out in abnormal high pitch velocity. "Valentine's not here!"

"What? They released him?"

"No. No, they wouldn't." Michael's voice gained control again. "Donavan, some weird crap has been happening. I don't even know how it... you aren't going to believe me."

"Michael... " Donavan took a deep breath and shot a look over his shoulder at his odd group of friends. "I've met a man who is *bulletproof*. Literally. Cannot be killed with bullets. Another guy—he can stop time. I'm in the middle of weird. What you got?"

Silence. A curse. The phone rattled as if being moved to the other ear, and Michael's voice dropped low. "Are you high?"

"Michael! There's no time. I am deadly serious. Have you ever had reason to doubt me? Tell me what 'weird' you got."

A pause. "He disappeared. One moment Valentine was in his cell and the next—*poof!* – gone."

"Disappeared," Donavan repeated to himself.

"There's not even a clue on the surveillance cameras. In one frame he's there, taunting the camera with that smirky grin of his, and then he moved to the back of the cell and was gone. It's... not possible. The chief looks like he's going to have a stroke any second. Nobody's talking about it; we don't want to sound... crazy. But the bars were good, the door locked, the footage clear; he had no visitors—it's just... disturbing, Donavan."

"Watch your back, Michael," Donavan said grimly.

"I am. Every second. What about these guys you met?"

"They're the good guys, but I can't talk about it, Michael. Not now. But I promise I'll fill you in whenever I can."

Chapter 30

"I want you to do me a favor." Laney's announcement made Tag's eyebrows arch in surprise.

"Me?" He stood up and wiped the glisten off his brow. He had been bent over a broken robot for some time along with Brian, trying to unravel its mysteries.

"Shock me again," she said.

Brian set down his wire cutters and squinted up against the sunlight. "What d'you say?"

She took a deep breath in, bolstering her nerve. Even though she had promised herself she would quit getting ruffled by jabs about being powerlessness, Donavan's flippant directions that she should stay with RJ stung her. She was dealing with the exclusion as best she could when she had overheard his conversation with Tag about the phone call.

Like in her dream, Tag had voiced his concern about her lack of assets and the cost of Donavan's devotion to her. Just when she thought Tag no longer hated her. Just when she had earned the nickname Shooter. Just when she had committed herself to Uspre and left her life behind....

Tag stared at Laney as if she'd lost her mind. A stress vein rose on her neck, but she stuck her chin out and matched his glare.

"You want me to zap you again?" he asked with disdain. "What're you up to?"

A slow tremble started in her toes and quivered her whole body. "I need to know. I am meant to be here, and there has to be a reason. Shock me."

Tag squinted hard at her, then slowly rose, taking her in from top to bottom. He cracked his knuckles and shook out his hands.

"Knock it off," Brian shoved at Tag's shoulder. "What do you think you will prove?" Brian asked Laney. "He laid you out once."

"Hit me," Tag taunted, tossing his head back.

Laney took a deep breath, but Brian stepped in between them. "Are you *crazy*?"

"Brian, I know I'm more than just a sharp shooter, more than a... a sidekick. I feel like I'm changing. I'm just not sure how." Not a real lie. She did feel as if bravery could dominate her pain and panic now. "I want to try our test again."

Brian shook his head. "Not gonna happen. Let's take a more logical approach."

"That's no fun," Tag sneered.

Brian corralled Laney over to Tag's end of the trailer. He pulled out a chair, patted the seat, then dragged out a small white board and marker that he perched on top of some equipment.

"What all you got in there?"

Brian ignored the question and gave a thoughtful scowl, the marker tapping his lips several times.

"Okay, let's start at the beginning. Your childhood."

Laney dutifully sat as Tag leaned against the trailer and observed. "What about it?"

"Normal?"

"Yes… I guess."

"No serious accidents? Illnesses? Radioactive spiders?"

She shook her head.

"Okay, think. Adolescence. What about then?"

"Normal."

"No one has a normal adolescence," Tag commented.

"True." She shrugged. "I don't know. I couldn't jump off a building if that's what you mean."

"What could you do?" Brian pressed her. He wrote *building* on the white board and added a big X over it.

"Well, I was on the swim team for a little while." She pushed away images of Arie's powerful body surging ahead in the pool lane beside her. Brian wrote *fishy* under the crossed out building.

"Fishy?"

"Keep going."

"Gymnastics."

The marker squeaked: *flips*.

"Um—oh, rock climbing, hiking, riflery—"

"You gotta be kidding," from Tag.

Brian scribbled and waved her on.

"I played lots of sports that I was pretty good at. Softball, volleyball, soccer…."

Tag laughed under his breath as Laney read from the board *likes to play with balls*.

"Real mature. Ok, I rode motorcycles. I was never afraid of heights. I've cliff dived in Hawaii, para-sailed, bungee-jumped off bridges, and climbed water towers."

"Impressive."

"Snorkeling and scuba diving in underwater caves. Big game fishing with my dad."

"So any of that make you feel any different? Any unusual occurrences when you were doing those things?"

Flashes of parties rose on flames of distant campfire memories. A handful of rowdy teens being stupid just to have a good time. Arie's face across the campfire, laughing too loudly. Zane. Rachel. Corie. Hunter. Faces she'd forgotten the names of. But the feeling she didn't forget. The sound of the motorcycle's tires singing in the rain around treacherous curves, moments of thrilling climbs, hanging by only the fingers of one hand as she reached for another hold several stories above the ground, the panic driven on by adrenaline at seeing her air gauge low deep beneath the rock of a watery passage.

Had she felt anything? The first eighteen years of her life had been about feeling everything.

"No. Nothing extraordinary."

"Okay. So think out-of-the-ordinary."

"Like what?"

"Like things that aren't normal. What's weird about you? Just, whatever."

"I was born with a web toe."

An *ewwww* from Tag.

Frog feet went up on the board.

"Keep going."

"I could snap perfectly at age three. I can twist my tongue like this.... I have never cut my legs shaving. My nose twitches when I smell lavender. This fingernail grows pointy and all the others rounded."

"Okay, enough," Tag said. "You're freaking me out."

"Tag! Laney, go on—"

"I don't know!" She ran her fingers through her highly tangled mess of hair. "I used to be able to hold my breath for a long time.... I can knit a scarf.... I won a cooking contest with my apple cobbler." She dropped her head into her hands in frustration.

Brian finished writing and she heard the marker tapping against his mouth again. "I think I see a pattern here."

Tag snorted. "Yeah. A mean cook with mad needle skills. You know what we call that? A *mom,* not a superhero."

Laney moaned.

"Water." Brian tapped the board as he spoke. He had circled *swim, frog feet, diving, cave scuba,* and *holds breath. Fishing* had a question mark by it. "Your talent might have something to do with water."

"There's only one way to find out," Tag said with a slow draw. He grabbed Laney's chair and pulled her backwards on two legs. "Someone get me a hose."

"We're not water boarding today, Tag."

Laney threw her weight forward and got the chair to fall heavily back onto all four. She stood up and pointed to the rocky hill before them. "The pond. I'm going to check it out."

"For the record," Tag sighed, "this is a highly unscientific form of investigation—"

Laney marched forward, not waiting for Brian's comeback.

The pool of water that collected in a ravine off the slope to their north consisted of shallow, murky water covered for the most part by thin layer of green slime. Undaunted by the rough hike to get there, Laney climbed the untamed boulders—some deposited by nature, some with the help of artful arrangement by the designers of the community to make the small valley less wild. Random Saguaro cacti, arms tall and spiny, mocked her effort with their stolid prickly posture. Her ankle throbbed by the time she made it to the waterline, but she pushed aside the discomfort.

"This oughta be rich," Tag said from behind her. He and Brian had followed her up the hill.

Laney sat and took off her socks and boots. She glanced over the ridge to find her ascent hadn't gone unnoticed by the rest of the crew, either. Jacob, Donavan, and Harley looked on in curiosity but made no effort join them.

"What exactly is the plan here?" Tag's voice laced with his usual amused sarcasm.

"I don't know, okay? I'm just...." She waded in to her knees as her toes gripped the rocky bottom with each step she took, the stones cool and slick. "I just have to figure this out," she said in a whisper. "Please, just show me...."

Nothing happened. Laney inhaled deeply and closed her eyes. She took one more step so that her fingertips lingered on the surface. It's thinking time, RJ would say. It was a little difficult with Tag scoffing behind her, Donavan glowering from afar, and Brian practically bouncing on his heels in anticipation.

Nothing.

Gingerly she advanced, seizing onto images of Arie in the pool, the underwater cave, the cliff dive. Think water. Think water.

Maybe she needed to go under. A glance down at the green foam and slime floating in patches made her hesitate. To go under she would have to lie on her back or lie face first since the pool wasn't very deep. Stepping forward, a jeering remark came from Harley on the rim as he joined Brian. Her fist clenched. She took another step and the ground underfoot opened up. She found herself sucked into complete watery darkness. There was a moment of panic, arms flailing underwater, a moment of incredulous wonder, and finally a sense of calm. She wasn't dead, and that's all that mattered.

The water stung her eyes, but she forced them open and hung suspended in disbelief. Under the surface, the liquid glistened with a green hue that, unlike the eerie glow of the power source they found or the jeweled glow of the rock, wrapped around her in an incredulous mix of bright color and transparency. The view under her treading legs filled her with awe.

Laney took in as much as she could before her eyes felt hot and her lungs were bursting. She kicked herself upward and swam only a few short feet before her feet gripped the bottom again. The spot where she took the plunge had been an inexplicable hole in the center of an equally implausible mountain lake. Shouts reached her ears. The bank filled with bodies that occupied the far shore as she climbed out.

"I'm fine," Laney hissed, standing again in the shallows, dripping with slime. Tag's body shook with laughter even though the cupped hand over his mouth tried to conceal it. Donavan stood hands on hips, his expression one of calm concern. Harley and Jacob seemed more intrigued than amused.

"What happened?" Brian called from the far side.

"There's a hole," she seethed, arranging her disgusting hair away from her face. "Right in the middle."

"How deep?" Jacob asked.

"I didn't measure."

"Could you touch bottom?"

She scowled down at her drenched cami and its new shade of dirty hazel. "What do you think?"

"It's our way in," Laney said as she toweled off. "That cavern, the one with waterfall and big glass tube? It funnels up to this pond. Or the pond funnels down, I dunno which. But I could see through the floor. There's rock and silt over most of the pond's bottom, but there in the middle where all this water leads down to the cavern, it's pushed away. It's a glass floor—or ceiling, I guess."

"So you think we can break through?" Jacob asked.

"Don't see why not."

"After that, what? Can we repel down?" Harley's question turned to excitement.

"Could work," Jacob nodded. "Harley and I haven't found any safer way in."

"What were you doing in there?" Donavan asked Laney.

"It's not important," she said hurriedly, trying to block out Tag's grin. At least finding a way *in* saved her from the embarrassment of another failure. She couldn't breathe under water or walk on it or transform into something super. She felt the same as ever. "What have we found out about the robots?"

"We know that RJ can rip the heck out of one, for sure," Brian commented. "Other than that, Tag isn't able to find an independent power source. But they seem to have a reserve tank—or I think that's what I found on one of them. It was empty but was slick inside. Maybe the Oil Eaters need to eat oil when they stray from their main power."

"Lots of speculatin'," Harley grunted.

"It's as good as we got," Jacob said and the others nodded in agreement. "Time to make a plan."

Chapter 31

Laney had repelled several times in her life, but it had been awhile. She worked the gloves on by bending and stretching her fingers, balling her hands into tight fists and releasing. She pretended it all had to do with anticipation and not a thing to do with anxiety.

"Ready?" she asked her partner.

RJ nodded; no gloves fit over his granite hands. His face remained expressionless behind his eye patch, but he held her rope steady and nudged her forward.

"Easy," she laughed with a grimace. "We aren't all as resilient as you."

Cracking the bottom of the pond had been a relatively easy Step One of the plan, but now came the speed work. They had to get into the cave and to the power source without getting tracked by their nemesis. Harley and Jacob had gone first hoping that the few Oil Eaters that roamed free could be avoided or taken down before the rest of Uspre joined them. Bets were on the fact that they inhabited some of the "rooms" since they all came from directions other than the waterfall cave.

Tag and Brian descended next. With luck, they'd make it into the primary cavern, up the stairs to the top level, and to the mystery missile without interference. Their job was to disconnect the power as quickly as possible. Donavan roped down behind them to follow for their protection.

Last came Laney and RJ. Her persuasion, fortified by RJ, left the team no other option than to include them. If RJ stayed close to Laney, he could protect her and keep to minimal size through the passage that connected the rooms. Once in the large cavern, the space would be ample enough to allow him to move more freely as his gianted self.

The dark cool air sucked at Laney's feet as she slowly moved down the rope. Donavan waited at the bottom, but he served as more of a lookout than an assistant. She prayed for a soft landing and reached the muddied surface sooner than expected. It took a moment to adjust to the wonderland again: the soft hush of the waterfall, the green tube still in place despite the cracked lake, the smooth brown walls.

She came to her senses in time to move out of the way for RJ whose normally passive face transformed into awestruck at his surroundings. Donavan jogged ahead with a nod, playing his role as backup to the ones ahead.

All was quiet in the cavern of tanks. Jacob and Harley circled back in their direction after their sweep. No other Oil Eaters to be found. Soon lights flickered off overhead.

Brian and Tag had reached their goal and had successfully shut the place down. Step Two—check.

The cavern remained ghostly silent as the group converged to the center on the lower level. Once there, RJ hung back enough to let his growth spurt occur as gradually as possible.

It didn't take much for Donavan and RJ to crack a tank with Brian close by to extract a sample. The tank was almost free of product, but enough residue remained to satisfy their scientist. He scraped the goo into his container in the creepy hush of the distant waterfall and thick shadows of the tanks. Step Three, finding out what the tanks held, check.

Laney breathed easier now. All that remained was to find one of the labs upstairs with working equipment in order for Brian to analyze the slippery green liquid. Piece of cake.

§ § § § §

The men stood guard alongside of Donavan, canvassing the room while Brian worked quickly to apply a solution he had concocted of who-knows-what to slide along with a drop of green goo. Syringes, vials, liquids from bottles with long labels, all stood at the ready beside the variety of slides he had created. Every guess he'd made out about the labs turned out to be correct. The supplies all pointed to a refinery, the rooms for measuring and analyzing samples of mined earth.

The gang watched with ignorance as Brian settled behind the microscope a second time, then a third, with no humor in his features. He just shook his head after each attempted experiment. They let him contemplate what he viewed without interruption.

Donavan sidled up to Jacob. "They haven't found us."

Jacob nodded.

"Doesn't this seem –"

"Too easy?" Jacob finished.

A heaviness fell on Donavan, and he gripped his weapon tight in one hand, a flashlight focused in on Brian with the other. A battery pack carried by Tag served as the hookup they needed to run the microscope. As time ticked by, the shadowy room didn't help continue their earlier enthusiasm for success. This part of the plan, the most important, failed to bring the immediate enlightenment they'd hoped for.

Donavan's eyes fell on Laney and the shift of her body indicated she wanted them out of there as much as he did. She stayed near the doorway so that RJ, who remained outside on the scaffold, could manage his stature. Her glances in his direction revealed her compassion for the odd-man-out. Donavan softened. She was trying so hard. Talented or no, she deserved an *A* for effort.

Brian sat back with a sigh and clasped his hands behind his head with waning exuberance.

"Well?" Jacob asked.

"It's something organic. Something completely natural." He rubbed his face vigorously for a second as if to stir up new thoughts. "It's a simple substance. Not radioactive, not chemically induced, not anything. But what, I don't know." His words dripped with bewildered disappointment. "I miss the internet."

"That green stuff is a completely natural compound." The voice, not one of theirs, spoke from the corner of the room.

Weapons whipped into combat stance at a man in a white lab coat who appeared from nowhere. Donavan sidestepped to Laney, but Brian had already jumped off the stool to move in close to her. He may be a goofball, but he came in handy in battle, that one.

The man in the white coat raised his arms in surrender posture and walked toward them. Behind the stranger, Donavan could make out a dim light coming through a cracked doorway. In the dark recesses of the room, they hadn't noticed a passage to an adjacent room.

"Now gentleman—and lady—I didn't bring you here to have it end before you got the answers to all your questions. Shoot me and you will face our metal friends as cluelessly as you did yesterday."

Without questioning, Donavan and the others snapped the safety off their guns.

They had him surrounded. No one spoke for endless seconds as the trained soldiers analyzed their options, points of exit, any sound of approaching robots.

"Perhaps you could lower your weapons so we can chat?" the man asked. He didn't look particularly surprised at their presence or disconcerted to be at gunpoint. He appeared miniature at first until he stepped closer revealing he was of average height, only slightly shorter than Donavan. He wasn't old, perhaps late 40's, but telltale grey appeared at his temples and peppered his head. Thin lips set themselves over a wide chin, topped with small, unexpressive eyes.

"Who are you?" Jacob spoke up.

"An obvious first question," the lab coat replied. "The second would be, *What are you doing here?* followed by, *What are those horrid black machines?* But the real question on your mind, the one you really want to know is, *Why are we all here with those monsters?* Ah, I can answer them all, even that last one you are afraid to find the answer to."

No one replied or moved a muscle.

"Guns are rather extreme, don't you think? I am obviously unarmed," the new arrival continued.

"Forgive us for tucking our manners into our back pocket," Harley growled.

Jacob came forward, dropped his weapon, and patted the guy down while Harley moved in as backup.

"I assure you, I only want to talk," the man continued, unaffected by Jacob's hands running over his body. "Whether you kill me or not, even if you take me hostage, the outcome is the same. I cannot hurt you, only give you information you desperately want. The Oil Eaters are everywhere and could overtake you whenever we want. So, please, lower your weapons and talk with me."

Jacob nodded as Tag made his way to a strategic position between the new arrival and Brian.

"Ah, you would be Tag," the man said with a smile, unpleasant laugh lines creasing his face. "Your thinking is that if I try anything funny, you send voltage through me, correct? I assure you that won't be necessary. Let me start with introductions since I am at a distinct advantage. My name is Carl Thackray, Dr. Carl Thackray. And you are the elite. I have waited a very long time to meet you." A hint of sentimentality laced his words.

"How do you know us?" Jacob asked.

"We have a mutual acquaintance, you and I. Someone who knows all about you."

Donavan's jaw flexed, his old theories jumping to mind. Jacob displayed all the qualities of a trained interrogator and registered no emotion on his features. "Continue."

The odd grin broadened as the doctor folded his hands in front of him. "First, may I introduce you to a colleague of mine. Dr. Hassle?"

A second figure appeared from the slim door, even smaller in size than his predecessor. A man with a shock of slick, disheveled dark hair took his place next to Dr. Thackray, eyes heavily guarded by dark eyebrows. While Thackray's countenance made Donavan leary, Dr. Hassle fit the mad scientist mold to a tee. His eyes darted from one person to the next as if marking each one off a list in his head. He shoved his hands in his lab coat pockets that covered worn jeans with legs too long and scuffed at the hem, a harsh contrast to the neat trousers Dr. Thackray donned.

"Where shall I begin? Should we go somewhere more comfortable?"

"This ain't no pillow party," Harley groused. "Spit it out."

"Harley. You have been the biggest help to us, you know that?"

"What the—you outta your mind?"

"The five of you did a very good job of keeping your identity under wraps," Thackray continued. "Your existence might yet be a secret if it hadn't been for our machines...."

"That's not what they're programmed for," oily head spoke up.

"Yes," Dr. Thackray said, "I'm getting to that. You see, Manchester Industries has been on a quest for a long time—this is quite a story— are you sure we can't sit down? I, for one, would prefer it." He nodded to Hassle. His cohort disregarded every weapon and marched toward the stools along the lab table only to receive a thorough pat down from Tag. With an even deeper scowl of annoyance, Hassle dragged a seat back to Thackray. Hassle himself remained standing, hands shoved back into deep pockets.

"So you control those machines?" Donavan prompted. "You sent them after us to kill us?"

"Of course not," Thackray said at the same time Hassle nodded his head in affirmation. Hassle caught himself and let his crazy eyes dart to the floor. "We are getting ahead of ourselves," Thackray continued. "I think I should explain who I am, first, and why I'm here.

"Seven years ago, they discovered a very unique rock by accident while surveying this area. It took someone with adequate curiosity to get the unusual qualities tested."

"The green rock," Donavan said.

"Yes, the very same. There's nothing notably intriguing about it at first inspection. Just a pretty, oily rock. But that's exactly what it has going for it. Oil."

"I knew it!" Brian smacked his fist against his thigh. "What type of rock is it?"

"Much more dense than shale, but not as dense as coal. Incredibly extraordinary. Unlike coal which takes a massive amount of heat, time, and pressure to create oil, our new find can go through a relatively inexpensive, quick solution and—*tada*!" He did jazz hands for emphasis.

"It becomes oil," Brian repeated in disbelief, squinting at the two scientists.

"Well, oil is a loose term, but, yes! Not only that, it burns cleaner and hotter than anything else on this planet." His enthusiasm lifted him off his stool for a moment. "It doesn't have off gases or dangerous by-products. The easy extraction and refining properties make it the most valuable commodity we've ever—"

Hassle cleared his throat and Thackray paused. He sat back on his stool.

"Well, it's simply an amazing rock."

"What's the job of those big black beasts?" Harley interjected before the scientist could ramble more. "And what help did you get from me?"

"Long story short," Hassle cut off Thackray when he opened his mouth to speak. "Easy to extract and refine; not easy to find."

"But with enough money," Thackray broke in, "anything is possible."

"Right," Hassle sighed. "They gave us the cash to design our MOLe's—Mobile Oil Locaters—and they found this place. They are incredibly accurate in their search."

Donavan wanted to ask *whose* money but let Thackray continue.

"Collection was going well until you all showed up," Thackray said.

"Until we showed up?" Jacob asked. "Those machines found *us*. We followed them here."

"Not exactly," Thackray murmured, wagging a finger. "You moved in too close on that last mission of yours. The one where Tag rode his motorcycle to help you overtake some human-trafficking coyotes? Just ten miles east of here. Even before you touched a single rock, our MOLe's—your Oil Eaters—knew you posed a danger to their existence."

"How?" Brian scoffed. "They do what you program them to!"

"Well, yes, I was getting to that. We programmed them to collect and protect our investment. That they recognized you as Elite—" More laugh lines appeared that still failed to illuminate Thackray's eyes. "Remarkable. Even now I'm amazed at it. The technology works beyond our wildest expectations—"

"It's flawed," Hassle interrupted again, and shut Thackray down with a jagged glare. "It started tracking you when you came in close. They've been haywire ever since. A glitch in their security mode. Regardless, they are still excellent at their original programming. They can find these rocks—they are the *only* thing that can detect them buried underground."

"Rocks which you're converting to oil for a great deal of money, I'm supposing?" Jacob asked.

"We sent our first sample to Slession Oil and instantly found ourselves under investigation. Red flagged. Our product was the purest form of oil anyone had ever seen. Naturally, we attracted the most powerful buyer in the US. But they're not interested in just buying the product."

"The government?" Donavan guessed. "They want to take over your operation."

"Very good; yes," Dr. Thackray nodded. "So we are trying to keep our cave a secret, but our MOLe's keep seeking you out. We finally did the only thing we could think of. We planted a bit of rock in the city and let the robots come to you. Our hope was that they would take care of you far from here. Instead, you came. The question is why. How?"

"You have your secrets," Tag answered, "we have ours."

"Ah, now, we were just having a friendly chat with our cards on the table. Doesn't that help with our rapport?"

"I like the idea of us going somewhere more comfortable, as you say—getting on some common ground to have this conversation," Jacob said.

Donavan shifted a glance to Jacob. He still had questions he wanted Jacob to ask: how long had these guys been tucked in this hole in the ground with Uspre running around above? How long had they been watching? What about their entrance and exit to this place? Not that they would provide all the answers. Everything Thackray said made Donavan believe that they would go to considerable lengths to keep their secret hid.

In the near distance, the low hum of a motor caught his attention. No one moved as the hum multiplied. Donavan ventured a glance to the door, but RJ's figure was out of view, causing an uneasy feeling in his gut.

"I think we will stay here, thank you very much," said Thackray behind a humorless grin.

Jacob raised his pistol again, hesitated, then turned it around and tossed it at Thackray's feet. Thackray bulked at the weapon that did nothing to prove his bad-guy status. "I never hurt an unarmed man," Jacob explained.

Brian's hand moved over Laney's, and Donavan braced himself.

"I see. The idea is that I would pick up this gun to threaten you with, correct? You will have to do better than that. I know you can only use your abilities when—"

"Oh, for crying out loud," Hassle spat as he snatched the gun from the floor. "Just get it over with!"

Hassle whipped the gun in Tag's direction, and the group completed their hand-chain with Brian in a split second. The familiar collapse of normal caved in and slowed Thackray to nothing more than a Madame Tussauds' character. Donavan intended to step forward, only to find his feet frozen in place. He sent a questioning glare to Brian to discover that he was suffering the same fate.

In the center of the circle of the room, wearing a very unbecoming smirk, stood Dr. Hassle moving in real time with Uspre, gun poised in their direction. Voice leveled, he spoke as if to himself: "Perfect. Two down, four to go."

Chapter 32

Endless undulating pain coursed through Donavan until his body demanded an outlet. Pulling away from the source of his torture, he heard a terrifying scream that he first thought was his own, broadcasting the fire that tore through his every nerve, every cell. Only when he willed himself to submit to the unavoidable could he open his eyes and focus on the others.

Thackray and Hassle had brought them into this chamber, sealed by a solid steel door. All impressions of a mine or abandoned laboratory vanished within this room; in their place, an equally implausible round room made of silver and light. The center of the room boasted an innocent-looking dropped floor with circular seating—only the seats turned out to be anything but benign. With forearms overlapping as they sat facing each other, the band of soldiers with gritted teeth and bulging veins endured an unrelenting surge of pain as they sat helplessly strapped into place.

The men in control had placed Donavan to the left of Laney with her next to RJ, who appeared to be in the worst shape of all from what Donavan could make out through his water-filled eyes. Almost completely human next to Laney on one side, his body distorted and wretched out of shape with his forearm the size of a large ham as it remained fastened to Jacob's on the other side. The enraged misery in his cries crushed Donavan further, and he had a quick, passing thought that at least the giant had but one eye to witness the others' agony.

Harley separated Donavan from Brian and Tag to his right, partners caught in an inescapable trap. Tag's eyes, red and huge, bulged from his head while his whole body shook, drool running down his chin. A constant stream of words ripped from Harley's throat, none of them pleasant or comprehensible, as his head thrashed side to side.

"Quite a conundrum, isn't it?" Thackray's voice echoed in the chamber. "Sitting next to the one that should be able to save you and yet utterly helpless? My, my, isn't technology something."

Jacob tried to maintain eye contact with a stony glare, but he grimaced and snapped his eyes shut against the torment that coursed through the armrests.

"Please," Laney cried. "Please... stop...."

"Let her go," Jacob managed, but there was no power in his words coming from his chin on his chest.

"It's very uncomfortable, I'd imagine. My advice is to relax as best you can for a minute." A grunt could be heard from behind a control panel that curved a notch out of the rounded wall. Hassle's oily head peeked up. Donavan could barely make out his eye roll before he ducked down again and allowed Thackray to continue uninterrupted. "The duplicitous beauty of my own invention—I had Dr. Hassle's help, of course—," another grunt, "is that it captures you in the only way humanly possible: by using your strengths against you."

Brian moaned in unmasked pain, losing consciousness as he slumped forward.

"You see, the discomfort we inflict generates an automatic super-power response. But when one person fights to break free, the others suffer. As you use your strength, you deplete the others. Who knows? Forcing your way out may even kill someone. Quite fascinating to witness. A masterpiece created with Harley's help."

Harley delivered something resembling a heated denial.

"Oh, not directly, to be sure. As we used the MOLe's to find you, we found ways of gathering your DNA: toothbrushes, hairs, discarded bottles. All your DNA samples proved normal. No amount of testing could give us any clues to your gifts or why the MOLe's wanted you. It was Hassle's idea to try the impossible." He rocked on his heels as if waiting for someone to ask him to explain. After a dramatic pause, he continued. "We decided to get DNA samples *agendo* – while you were in action!"

A gurgly noise escaped Dr. Thackray's throat, something close to a giggle. He approached the chairs to examine his captives, down in their helpless circle. "We reasoned that if we could get a sample of your DNA *while* you were using your powers then—theoretically—we would be able to produce countermeasures to stop it. You may recall the dark, rainy night in the park when Tag's motorcycle led us straight to you. Oil Eaters—a clever name. You were almost right about that—the presence of oil gave them an advantage, an insight, you might say.

"Alas. You took out the bots so completely that night, the risk we took of bringing them out into the open proved to be almost in vain. We realized retrieving fight DNA would be very difficult, almost impossible, if it had not been for Harley."

Donavan could almost hear Thackray grinning from behind him.

"Harley was kind enough to simply leave a sample at the scene. His cigar butt."

A new stream of random words projected from the object of conversation.

"I had to work like a madman,"—a mumble from behind the half wall—"to find how his genetic composition operated and how to counter it. Countless hours—you wouldn't believe the consternation it caused me. In the end, it wasn't even something we needed to inject Harley with as we first thought. As soon as he neared the mine, it became obvious that arming our robots with the information gave them the power to render this mutated gene useless. Harley became completely harmless."

"I'll... show... you... harmless," Harley tried to growl, but it came out like an old man's garble.

"I didn't know if it had been a fluke or if Hassle and I could duplicate the results. Then Brian! So fortunate for us that you used your skills while bleeding. You cut yourself while saving Laney in your time freeze. The blood left on the MOLE worked quite well. How else would one extract DNA from someone who can freeze time and escape without a trace *while* they're doing it? What a lucky stroke for us!

"Obviously the same process that worked with Harley's worked with Brian. We were able to use it against him just now." The demented tormenter clapped his hands with childish glee as if he had been born to play the role of mad man. "Thrilling! I had no idea if it would work... well, quite disappointing that I didn't get to come along in the time travel but very thrilling for Hassle! He's quite sorry about having to use Laney at gunpoint to get you here, aren't you old pal?"

Donavan missed the humor in his joke and glanced at Laney who had tears in full flow down her face. She had bravely put up a fight, but in the end, having her at gun point enabled Hassle to force the rest of them into chairs. Their liability? No, it could have been anyone, he told himself.

Memories blurred and logic failed under the blanket of pain. Two down, Hassle had said—Harley and Brian... four to go. That meant the rest of them... minus one: Laney? Did they think of her as non-super?

"It will only take a few minutes to gather the rest of your DNA. But why not run a few more tests while we have you? I'm sure you're curious about your gifts as well. Hopefully it won't take long. All this conflict, while quite exciting, is also very exhausting."

"We have them where we want them," Hassle mumbled. "Why not just knock them off?"

Thackray glared at his colleague. "We discussed this, Dillon. Controlling them has far more benefits than destroying them. Just think of the possibilities!"

Hassle mumbled again something Donavan couldn't hear beyond the sear of pain circulating through his superhuman genes, fighting for survival.

"It's time to begin," Thackray said and before Donavan could wonder at the meaning, Hassle turned the dial on the slim control panel—and if the most intense pain ever imaginable could multiply itself by a thousand, it did.

Donavan's back arched involuntarily, and the noise he'd kept inside so long erupted like a volcano, releasing itself in a loud continuous scream drowned out by six other tortured voices.

§ § § § §

Laney slammed her head back into the seat as her spine arched and her cry joined the others, but ever so briefly. The pain was too much, had been before the turn of the dial, but now—now it separated her from herself and threw her into the abyss of unconsciousness.

Slowly she felt herself revived, fear of the returning pain tensing her muscles. She didn't want to wake. She didn't want to see if she had unwittingly killed someone by passing out or to find herself thrown back into the torture for another round. But her body came to life in a newness absent of agony. Dare she open her eyes?

Her curiosity overcame her need to hide from the truth, and she gradually let her eyes flicker open to watch Hassle move away from his panel and slip out the same door Thackray had. She stood in a recess of the steel wall where each panel divoted in and then back out again like the outline of a flower, the dents imitating the rounded petals. One niche contained the door that disappeared into a flattened petal top. Her gaze fell on the center of the room, the middle of this sinister flower, and there she found a quiet, heart-wrenching sight.

The men she had fought so clumsily alongside now slumped in a sunken circle of connected chairs. They had succumbed to the torture; every head bowed in submission, in weariness, in half-consciousness. The strongest individuals she had ever met, reduced a pile of motionless muscle, eerily void of life other than an occasional groan, a faint twitch of a muscle.

Laney threw a hand over her mouth to restrain a sob of anguish from escaping. Her Donavan. Her strong companion, her hero… the distress on his features twisted her gut and caused her body to shake.

Before she could move, her eyes locked in on what her view had been slow to perceive. Pressing herself into the depression of the wall panel, she threw her other hand over her mouth and held them both tightly, blocking both air and scream. There beside Donavan, lashed to the chair, forearms touching, was the head of the last person she ever expected to see there.

Herself.

But it couldn't be. She wildly scanned the room, trying not to make a sound beneath her covered mouth, trying to understand what she was seeing. Reluctantly, she brought her gaze back to the chairs and clamped her hands tighter. She stared directly at the top of her own head when she realized she needed to breathe.

Inhaling slowly, she dropped her arms to her sides and pinched both legs. It hurt.

Not a dream.

But if she were there....

She looked directly across the room over the low torture chairs and found her reflection staring back from the polished steel.

There was, without a doubt, two of her in the room.

Her heart hammered so wildly at first, she thought she'd pass out. This was different than stopping time or bullets or zapping someone. *She could somehow double herself.*

All fear scattered as instant jubilation filled her veins. She knew what she was! She was *one of them* in the most mind-blowing, crazy way she could imagine.

But how?

The faintest of memories teased at the edges of her mind, a familiar feeling, an awareness…but she couldn't work it out at the moment. The urge to *do* something *now* was far too great.

She forced herself to survey the room calmly and look beyond her bound comrades. Could their captors see her? Did they have a two-way mirror in one of these shiny panels? The controls. The door. Wall panel. Wall panel, wall panel, wall panel, all the way back around to her. Nothing else.

She gingerly took a step out, but before her foot touched ground, a very small whirr hummed directly above her and she pulled her foot back in. She pinpointed the source. A surveillance camera.

A huge swallow of relief; she had almost revealed herself. Following the line of vision of the lens, she tried to predict the width of its view. Could she possibly get to the control panel without being detected? Possibly, but the knobs, the only ones she had witnessed Hassle maneuver, lay on the far side in definite view of the camera. A small half wall built around it blocked the rest, like a sound booth in the back of a studio.

Think! Think! If only super genius were her power…

Nervously she inched toward the half wall, sliding her hands along the smooth metal, sucking in her breath and gut. *No more cheeseburgers. I promise. Just please keep me out of the shot.* She tried to move carefully, but the thought the doctors could return any minute kept her adrenaline high and her steps quick.

At the half wall, she counted to three and mounted it like a balance beam. She stood on top, her back still pressed to the wall away from the camera. The curve of the room made her jut out further now, and she panted for control of her motions. Having a brand new view of her old motionless self didn't help.

Reaching down to remove a boot took an agonizing minute. She tried to hold it in her right hand and keep her left hand along the wall for balance until it had wriggled off. She gripped it and took aim.

One, two – three!

The boot hit the video camera mount at an awkward angle, ricocheted, and hit her square in the mouth. Scrambling to keep her balance, she bit her stinging lip and pretended she was in a gymnastics competition. Stay on at all costs. Sweat ran down her brow, but she ignored it and took a deep breath.

The boot had landed in the booth after it assaulted her, next to the stool Hassle had used. It could have made it into the camera shot and alerted someone. She was running out of time.

Laney wiped her nervous palms on her cut-away capris and with small controlled movements, took off her second boot while balancing on the six inch width of the wall. This boot came off faster, a sense of urgency driving her on. This time she put the boot in her left hand and practiced the angle. She sucked as a lefty but throwing it across her body might give her the angle she needed.

The boot cracked into the mark and thudded loudly. Laney winced, but saw the camera had spun on its mount facing at an awkward angle toward the ceiling.

Perfect!

Jumping into the walled booth, Laney ducked low and searched the buttons hopelessly. None of them were labeled with anything that looked remotely like English. What she wouldn't give for a simple *OFF* switch.

She found the dial she thought Hassle had used and turned it backwards ever so slowly. The results weren't great. Brian crumpled his head almost into his lap; Tag took a huge gasp and started shaking again. She, that is the *other* Laney, stirred but didn't lift her head. This relieved and disappointed her all at once. She had no idea how that worked, meeting oneself, but felt like she needed better mental preparation to survive that scenario unscarred.

All things considered, best she turn the knob back where it was and leave the men sagging, heads drooped, all but motionless once more. The chairs remained locked.

Think! Laney poured over every detail. The control panel. Being strapped in. The lock. *The lock!* Dr. Thackray had used some sort of key, a large steel piece, like a thick blunt knife, that he had stuck into the wall and turned when they first entered. A key he kept strapped at his waist. It had illuminated the room, both the light above, the controls, and the lighting between each seat.

Avoiding another glance at the unfortunates, Laney made her way to the steel door and pushed. Unlocked! Of course, why would they be expecting anyone to exit, bound as they were?

Laney made her way out into the dimly lit hall where she recognized the green eerie glow that filled the air, carried on dust molecules that floated around her like small warnings.

No black troublemakers around.

She inched her way down the hallway until she could hear the voice of Thackray coming from the room next door, the lab. He wasn't talking exactly—the voice dipped and rose and contained various pitches as if he were... singing?

Laney came up to the door and pressed her ear close enough to hear that Thackray *was* singing. She was just in time for the chorus of "Man in the Mirror."

Chapter 33

Laney's heart beat so loudly she couldn't tell if the door squeaked when she nudged it a fraction of an inch. She hugged the wall outside again, trying to catch her breath. Never in all this craziness had she thought a moment would come when Uspre's fate depended on her. She could hyperventilate this very second thinking of the magnitude of it.

No, she scolded herself. *No, you won't.* She inhaled deeply to calm herself even though Thackray's horrendous Michael Jackson rendition broadcasted his chilling madness. But she could stop him. She *had* to.

Laney inspected her hands, shaking ever so slightly, and an image appeared of those same hands, a dozen years ago, so ready for adventure, for danger, for *anything* that made her feel this way. It had charged her, filled her with life and purpose. Today, that was the person she needed to be. The girl without fear; the girl that made things happen.

The door inched open under Laney's steadied hand, her breathing now under control. Thackray sang away, *"I'm starting with the man in the mirror!"* but didn't come into view. The lab table had been loaded with various white machines that lit up, vibrated, and gave a series of beeps and bings. The lights blazed overhead, leaving no shadows for cover.

The crack grew wide enough for her to poke her head in, and in a moment of wisdom, she got low so that she took a glance far below his eye level. Thackray stood, humming now, concentrating on some papers and holding up matching vials of something with latex gloved hands. He was alone.

Two other tables stood between Laney and the doctor. She waited, patiently channeled her nervous energy, and when his head turned just a little—she dashed on sock feet in her crouched position behind one of the tables without producing noise.

Nice, even breaths. Good. That's good.

The thick key hung from Thackray's waist at the front of his open coat.

She turned to survey the room as best as she could, glancing under and over the supplies beneath the tables. Her eyes fell on a pile of guns. *Their* guns. She took a moment to consider the stash, remembering that they were all loaded; no one had fired any rounds.

It grew quiet in the room; Laney squashed all tremors of panic and waited. Thackray's legs walked around to the end of the table, stopped, paused, walked back. Her eyes moved back to the arsenal. With her body crouched, she spider crawled sideways up and over the shelf under the table until she straddled it. Slowly, balanced on three limbs, she stretched one arm out. Could he see her? Hear her?

The cool metal touched her fingertips just as she heard scraping and clanging from the lab tables. *Don't panic!* she yelled at the rising tide within. The noise did not imply he had spied her, so she carried on inching her fingers around the handle of the pistol. It was killing her to have her back to him, to not know what was happening, but the gun was hers and all she had to do was stand up.

Crawling back out of her three-handed bridge while carrying a gun threw a snag in the plan. She rocked back to raise her left hand off the floor and prayed she didn't lose her balance; with a heave, Laney pushed into a squat between the tables again without a sound.

Big breath.

Laney rose, snapped off the safety, and pointed the firearm in Thackray's direction all in one smooth motion.

Thackray startled and dropped a glass tube.

"Hands up," Laney demanded, utterly pleased with herself.

"How did you…?"

"Oh, I'm sure you have lots of questions," she mocked, moving around the table toward the scientist. "Your first question is *how did you get here?* which would be followed by *where are the others?* and lastly *what are you going to do to me?*" She stopped several feet in front of him. "All your questions will be answered in good time. Key, please."

Thackray glanced down at the squared tool with a look of incomprehension. He scowled and then looked up at the video monitor that had a beautiful shot of a ceiling tile in all its glory. "The key? This? This isn't a key."

"You used it to activate the room next door. Cough it over."

He seemed to gain some courage then, his eyes narrowing. "Hassle?" he called. "We have some very surprising company."

Laney resisted the urge to slap him quiet; the younger doctor entered from the side door he had previously used. She backed up and waved Thackray out from behind the table. Understanding, the doctor kept his hands raised and joined Hassle at the furthest end of the room.

"Turn it off," she said, making her voice strong and confident.

The men exchanged looks, and she could tell their confusion kept them from reacting.

"How did you escape?" Hassle asked, glancing at the monitor that held no clues. "The extractor can't still be on if you are here—or are they are all dead?"

"You don't get to ask the questions," she snapped; the word *dead* made panic surge up again. "Turn. It. *Off.*"

More glances and Thackray slowly unhooked the wand-looking piece of metal from his waist and tossed it at her feet.

She should bind them somehow, make them lay face down on the floor, and then what? She couldn't leave them with a pile of guns and she couldn't take them with her or they would see...her. The other her.

What I wouldn't give for a roll of duct tape.

She glanced at the door and saw for the first time the same rectangular key hole compartment near the light switch as in the adjoining room.

"What's that do?"

Neither men said a word, and her anger mounted. Donavan and others remained trapped in eternal pain until these knuckleheads did something.

"Turn it off now!"

Thackray jumped out of his skin, but Hassle only narrowed his eyes.

"Or what?" Hassle asked, eyeing Laney doubtfully. "You going to shoot me?"

Laney aimed at Hassle's leg and pulled the trigger with only a second's hesitation. She hit his foot. Apparently her aim hadn't improved any without Donavan. Close enough.

Hassle cried out and doubled over; Thackray watched in shock as blood seeped out of the shoe onto the floor.

"It activates the generator on this level, the ones connected to the MOLe conductor—the, the missle-looking thing your group found. It, it supplies, uh, a source of power—oh please, don't shoot me," Thackray managed in a terrified rush.

Laney walked over to the doorway, gun still trained in the men's direction, and extended the key when a thought hit her. Jacob was right about letting emotion control your decisions. She had almost made a flawed one.

Across the room in the gun pile, she found one of their flashlights, clicked it on, and headed back to the key hole, inserted the rectangular rod and turned. For five seconds the sound of a dying jet engine filled the cavern outside their door; all lights dimmed to black out. Laney stood with her flashlight on her captives, Hassle's expression seething with as much anger as pain, biting his lip against crying out further.

She waited. But not long. The sound of a mountain moving with a tremendous roar told her that RJ had freed himself next door. Secretly, she hoped he'd execute a Kool-Aid Man crash through the wall. But the clang of the chamber door and more shuffles in the hallway told her they had escaped via the conventional method.

"In here!" she called and wondered nervously what herself—the other self—was thinking right now.

Jacob cautiously entered the room first and took in the situation. He nodded at her with a look of satisfaction. He didn't seem startled at all to see her. With a quick hand motion, he signaled the others in. Laney turned the key to crank on the lights again. The crew quickly grabbed their weapons from the pile while Laney held her breath and waited for the last member of the group to walk through the doorway, but *she* never came. Donavan squeezed her upper arm in a reassuring gesture and took over as point man on Hassle. "You will have to tell me how you managed that," he said.

"Is that all?" she asked softly so only he could hear. "Is…are there…is anyone else with you?"

"RJ? Don't worry," he grinned, no sign of the abuse he'd endured reflected in his features. "He's larger and more awesome than ever. He's right outside."

"Anyone…else?"

Donavan looked confused. "What do you mean? Who?"

She shook her head, feeling a little less in control of her nerves. "Nevermind," she murmured. Everyone seemed healed and ready to reap revenge on the two madmen that had almost taken them to the brink of insanity. "It's all good."

§ § § § §

In a matter of minutes, the sadistic scientists had gone from controlling the world's best torture chamber to becoming hostages in their own domain.

Tables turned, Donavan thought, cracking his neck with satisfaction, his body rapidly completing its rejuvenation. *How do you like us now?*

He had no earthly idea how Laney could have escaped first. The blinding pain had locked them into place so securely, every struggle making it worse on the others. His memory blanked after Hassle had turned the machine to maximum pain. He only recalled endless fire that not only burned through every cell in his body but kept him paralyzed.

He watched the others shoulder shrug and back stretch themselves to normal, weapons pointed in the general direction of the tormentors as a new spark of life flowed through their once impeded veins.

"You fools," Thackray scoffed, coming back to himself again. "Don't you think I can summon our army in a second flat? Look where you are!"

"I assume you would have done it by now if you weren't a skinned cat climbing his way up a chicken tree," Harley growled. Brian rolled his eyes with a slight shake of his head. Thackray raised an eyebrow in bewilderment, but couldn't produce a comeback.

"Your robots won't be much interested in us when we have you to lead us," Jacob said. "Let's go."

The two prisoners followed Jacob's pistol point to the door when Laney whitened. "No, wait."

She barely had the words out when Hassle reached into his pocket for a syringe with a wicked long needle. He threw his arm around Thackray's neck, standing on tiptoe to keep hold, poking the tip of his weapon into the folds of the scientist's neck.

Thackray vaguely struggled, the needle proving to be larger than his courage.

"Back up," Hassle hissed.

Harley scoffed, but Laney held up a hand. "Listen to him," she insisted. Donavan glanced at his partner with concern. Her cheeks were pale, eyes wide.

Hassle glared at her with daggers sharp enough to take her down.

The "hold up" signal came from Jacob, and he gave Laney his full attention.

"I shot him," Laney said, pointing to the floor. The telltale red stain proved her words. "Right before you came in. I shot him in the foot."

"He looks good enough to walk outta here," Tag said. "No piggyback rides if that's what you're suggesting."

Jacob's already sober features turned grave. "Take off your shoe," he ordered.

"I'm not taking requests at the moment," Hassle spat out, giving Thackray a tighter hold. "Now back up!"

Thackray squirmed to look downward at his companion's foot. "Dillon? Dr. Hassle, what's going on?"

With a grunt, Hassle kicked off his footwear to reveal an almost healthy foot. Red spots slowly mulled into new baby pink skin before the groups' eyes, sending goosebumps creeping over Donavan's flesh.

Harley breathed an oath while the others stared jaw-slacked.

"What the—how did you—," Donavan stumbled over his words. "How did you become one of us?"

Chapter 34

"What is he talking about?" Carl Thackray asked, staring at Hassle's foot incredulously. "What does he mean?"

Hassle released a huge, aggravated sigh and lowered the syringe to his side.

"Dillon? Is it true?" Thackray persisted, obviously troubled. "How can you— "

With no more regard than if he were swatting a fly, Hassle jammed the needle into Thackray's thigh and collapsed him mid-sentence. The scientist fell to the floor, seized up, and flopped around like a landed fish. Laney flinched, her brave facade forgotten in the face of brutal, unsuspected violence.

Jacob wasn't so easily daunted and moved forward to grab Hassle when a weird shadow fell over Hassle's features, almost as if something else in the room had just passed over them.

The occupants of the room moved in a weird rhythm, as if trying to swim upstream. The feeling gave the group a collective pause that kept them at bay for the moment, Donavan waiting for the swaying force to pass along with the rest.

"I have wanted to do that for *sooooooooooooo* long," Hassle said, rolling his head around his shoulders as if he had relieved himself of some huge stress. He looked drugged himself and within a moment, he groaned and staggered like a drunk man. The group could only watch, stupefied as his hands trembled, until they were no longer his hands. It was like he was Hassle everywhere else, but someone had affixed another person's appendages to the sleeves of his lab coat. The color in his face changed, not just paled or reddened, but swept through a spectrum of shades until he became a paler version of himself…for a moment. A slow moving moan grew from his throat and with eyes blazing, his features altered altogether until the noise escaped with a roar.

Simultaneously, the crumpled body at their feet shriveled, ghosting away before them. At what seemed to be the same second, an empty lab coat lay before them and Hassle, no longer Dillon Hassle but Carl Thackray, stood before them in his place.

In the series of crazy, unexplainable events of the day, this one rocked Donavan on his heels. Jacob, the closest to the metamorphosis, tried to reach for the new Thackray, when the din outside the room grew so loud the vibrations shook the floor and caused it to tilt. Hassle escaped Jacob's grasp as the wall exploded open. Hassle's transformation had blocked out the sound of the whirling motors that now deafened the room.

The next moments filled with dust and confusion as RJ's large arm followed a black machine that crashed into the room. With a quick yank, he pulled it backward. Harley was swinging, but more wall collapsed in what appeared to be RJ's best efforts to keep several more metallic giants from entering the space. Each of them battled for breath and space, while the cloned Thackray bolted for the door.

Tag stayed on his tail despite the slanted floor that almost sent him sliding out the door onto the high bridge, feet away from a long drop. The others followed clumsily, hearing the metallic wails before they could see their owners, Donavan holding fast to Laney. He wasn't sure if the entire underground structure was giving way or the destruction resulted from another attack, but the lab held no protection either way.

The bridge buckled under the weight of machine and man that tumbled toward the staircase, Thackray leading the way. He reached the landing and suddenly spun on Tag, close at his heels, just as Tag realized that the opposite side of the staircase, clouded with eerie green dust, contained more metal robots ready to block his way.

Everyone tried to find footing and back up the stampede, but, too late, they were blocked in on either side with the giant monsters, their eyes glowing lifeless slits. When the group froze, the machines paused, and as if following some unheard command, sat on the haunches of their hinged leg-like appendages like obedient pets.

"Now," the man said with a sweaty off-centered smile that held the same maddening twist as the real Thackray. "Where were we?"

§ § § § §

"How the hullabaloo did you do that?" Harley asked. Laney looked over the edge of the scaffolding and trembled a little at the height. No dialogue had been allowed when Hassle-Thackray, now one and the same, had lined up the group single file, shoulder to shoulder against the wall of the bridge, weapons useless next to the endless line of bots that encircled the crooked path to the left and right. She forgave Harley his question since it burned in the back of all their minds. But she mostly wondered how long the damaged metal flooring would hold them.

"What? Shape shift?" The man they knew as Thackray had become something else. Hassle within his body; Hassle with attitude and hostility in his clipped words. The man looked uncomfortable in his new flesh and suddenly stripped off his lab coat from where he stood on the main landing below them. "My power, dear boy. Not very convenient, but there it is."

"Who are you then?" Laney asked. Okay, she wanted to know more than how to get off this rickety platform too.

He laughed bitterly. "We're back to the *who*, aren't we? Who? That's a very good question. I wish I knew."

Squirming with agitation, he unbuttoned his shirt and shrugged it off next. His body, nude now from the waist up, revealed a series of scars, some patterned like surgical remnants, some more random, scattered along his torso and arms. He dug his hands into the pocket of his pants, but turned up nothing. He cursed and retrieved the dropped lab coat to seek out the pocket contents there.

"Your name," Jacob demanded, more on edge than Laney had ever seen him.

A small square of paper appeared from the pocket. Hassle-Thackray smirked and opened the square to full size. All signs of Thackray left his voice when he spoke, eyes on the document. "Who am I? I'm Russel Martinez. I'm Vincent Valentine. I'm Dillon Hassle. Take your pick."

"Did you say Vincent Valentine?" Donavan asked, his voice as edgy as his captain.

"Yeah, you would be familiar with him, wouldn't you? A petty thief turned industrial saboteur."

"He escaped the cell," Donavan said, reflecting his conversation with Michael. "How? He was in custody."

The new Dr. Thackray looked impatient. "I took the place of some homeless bum."

"You just take the shape of whoever you want, when you want?" Brian asked.

"Seriously? Would I be *here* if that's how it worked? Why wouldn't I go be President or a rock star or the richest man alive if that's what I could do?" He gestured at Harley. "Give me your T-shirt."

"You gotta be outta your pea-sized mind if you—"

"Harley," Jacob scolded.

"You kidding, right? Well, if that don't beat all."

Harley took off the piece of clothing, wadded it up, and threw it at the man who looked grim and determined.

"So enlighten us," Harley said, punctuating each word with his own impatience.

"I can only take over the body of a person who died." Hassle unwadded the shirt and shoved his head through the neck hole while the others simmered in shocked silence.

"So you're a zombie right now?" Brian asked.

"What do you think? I look like a zombie to you?"

"I'm gonna say you've looked better," Tag put in.

Thackray bristled. "You prissy boys march around, banding your powers into some kind of super team like you got it all figured out. You don't know squat. You blindly follow everything Rheinland tells you and stick to the cluelessness of what you really are."

Laney heard less and less of Thackray in his voice. The edge of Hassle's attitude had made it into the hiss of his words.

"I am *nobody*. I became nobody when I became you."

"Became?" Jacob asked.

"You all voluntarily came here," Thackray sneered, as if Jacob hadn't spoken. "I wish I had a choice. To suddenly bounce into being another person, randomly, without warning—what kind of power is that? What kind of life is that?"

"Here's one idea," Harley said. "How about don't kill no one."

He ignored Harley too. "Any of you tried *not* being super?" Thackray turned to sniff an armpit and recoiled. "Dear lord, when's the last time this was *washed?*"

Harley threw his arms up in exasperation, but Jacob eyed him into silence.

"The poor homeless dude that shared the cell with Valentine didn't have long to go," Thackray sighed, yanking the shirt back off. "I can possess anyone dead/dying. Here I am. I took the body of my dead cellmate and got released the next day while Valentine simply vanished." His arms swooped up as if illustrating the escaped spirit, the t-shirt dangling from one hand. He whipped it back at Harley.

"So," Laney paused as if processing it all. "Now you're stuck as Thackray until you kill—or someone else dies?"

A dismal smile froze on the doctor's face for a second and then the morphing began all over again, quicker this time than it had after Thackray's death. A swift shadow moved across his features, a lot less groaning and twisting around; and in less than a minute, a brand new man stood before them, a man with a greasy black ponytail and shifty eyes.

"Valentine," Donavan confirmed for the rest of them, the words falling from him like all the air was being sucked from his lungs. "So you can change back to as many of the dead souls you've possessed as you please?"

Donavan's heart pounded as a more pressing question pushed its way forward in his mind. *What do you know about Kelly?* He hadn't forgotten Valentine's innuendos the day they met.

"It's not like I get to pick and choose so easily!" Valentine was saying. "It's not like changing clothes."

He didn't elaborate, as weary lines etched his brown face. He picked up the paper again and read it one more time over before folding it slowly, almost in sorrow, into a neat square once more and tucking it into the pocket of his dirty jeans.

"So why are you here?" Jacob asked. "You want to take over the Oil Eaters—the MOLe's? Or control us?"

"Control you?" The notion seemed to amuse Valentine, and he grinned. He took a remote from his back pocket and punched at a few buttons. "Ha, no, that would be Leon Rheinland's job, wouldn't it? I don't need to dominate you; I know exactly where to find you. And the MOLe's—the most incredible advanced technology ever to complicate a mining operation. I can't wait to leave them in this godforsaken hole in the ground." He concluded his remote manipulation, and the robots rose to their full height, the legs extending to tower over them all.

"Okay, I'm missing the big picture here," Tag said. "Why are we here if you don't want us or to take over the dig? What exactly do you *want*?"

"You, Tag, of all people should understand," Valentine spoke from clenched teeth. "I. Want. *Out*."

Chapter 35

Laney hadn't watched many war movies growing up, only a few black and whites with her dad. She remembered a vague, detached feeling, not understanding the fear and drama surrounding each soldier, only grappling with the disgust of Hollywood blood that flowed from gaping wounds. She tried to relate with those scenes now, trying to channel the image of a tight-lipped sergeant with his weapon posed at the ready and simultaneously *not* connect with the wild-eyed private who had to sink his heels in to keep from running. Mulling over the handful of confrontations she had recently put herself through with these men, she never thought of this as "war"...until now.

Shoulder to shoulder, with RJ at one end and Jacob at the other, they stood rigid, suited up with protective gear supplied by the orchestrator of a mad game they had been commanded to play. At either end of the line stood a black monster, stoic and on guard, to ensure Uspre kept their places. However, these new centurions were a smaller, more mobile style of MOLe's. They fit on the upper tier as if they had been made for it, helping give the weakened structure less weight. Regardless of size, they held the same tough armor and deadly claws. Even worse, the metal warriors below them now wore gun mounts in place of one of their arms.

"When I woke up this morning, I pictured the day ending much differently," Brian said from his place in line.

"Yeah, really?" Harley gruffed. "Didn't picture yourself thrown into an arena of combat bots fighting to the death, did ya?"

"What's he want?" Tag said so low his words were almost lost. "If he wants to end it, why not kill himself and be done? What does he gain by our deaths?"

"He knows something we don't," Jacob said from Laney's far right. "Something Rheinland never said." The bitterness in his voice couldn't hide. "How's everyone feeling?"

"Do we have our powers back? Is that what you mean?" Brian asked. "The fact that I'm standing *here* and not *there,*" pointing to the back exit of the cave, "should answer that for you."

"I'm blank," Harley said. "And ticked that he took my last cigar."

"Did the extraction process affect anyone else?" Jacob continued.

"I noticed you didn't try to take a bullet for us to find out," Tag growled. "I couldn't get close enough to zap Thack-Hass while he was locked and loaded, so I got no idea. But RJ is large and in charge, so that's a good sign."

RJ grunted, and Tag gave him the standard chin jerk of solidarity.

If Laney was ever going to fill them in on what happened in the torture chamber, now seemed like the best time. Her heart hammered in her chest as she opened her mouth to tell them she had finally found her power, was finally an "asset." The trouble was, she still had no idea how she had done it. She didn't want them to rely on her doubling herself when she couldn't rely on it herself.

Donavan gave Laney's hand a squeeze, and she shut her mouth into a weak smile in return.

"You okay?" he asked.

She couldn't help but laugh a little. There was every possibility they were about to die, and he wanted to know if she was okay. He smiled too; count on Donavan to know she needed a little reassurance. His calming demeanor would forever be the rock that anchored her to him.

"Donavan, I have to tell you something."

A flicker of emotion she couldn't read crossed his eyes, and he shook his head. "Not now."

"But—"

A distant clanging interrupted them: loud and dissident, the sound of moving metal that had none of the hum and perfection of the MOLe's.

"Well, look at you!" a booming voice echoed through the cavern. "Ready to battle with the best of the best." From the direction of the tunnel, a figure appeared, walking stiffly with what looked like metal braces about his legs and down his arms, hands wrapped around grips at the end of the support.

"What in the—" Harley's words fell from lips that blubbered in the absence of a cigar.

"There's no reason we shouldn't all go down in a blaze of glory." It was Hassle now that spoke to them from the clunky suit before them. He made his way with great awkward steps to stand near the scaffolding where Laney could see his grim smile. "This gizmo gives me a fighting chance."

"Is that what you call those horrifying chairs?" Donavan shouted back. "A fighting chance?"

"Eh," Hassle answered with a shoulder shrug. "Hassle—me, I guess—designed those chairs for Thackray. He was really into the whole figuring-us-out thing. He's the bio genius wanting to get to the DNA. Well, he's me now too, right? It didn't work, so...." He held up his arms ensconced in metal sleeves, rigged with buttons and gadgets, to complete his answer.

"If the MOLe's were after Uspre, why didn't they detect you?" Jacob called down. "Why weren't they trying to take you out?"

"And why couldn't Thackray extract my DNA and *un*-super myself?" Hassle said. "Trust me—I've asked all the questions and found some pretty unusual properties about my own genetic makeup. Don't think I'll take the time to fill you in.

"Besides. The extraction only works temporarily. Eventually, powers return. A bug Thackray was trying to work out."

Brian and Harley exchanged hopeful glances.

"So then the world continues spinning as always, taking our unnatural bodies, our pathetic, untamed, unpredictable," Hassle's fists clenched, and his voice rose again as his list grew, "pathetic, meaningless, *uncontrollable* lives, and carries on as if we are nothing!" His chest heaved, having worked himself into a frenzy. "Aren't you *tired*? Aren't you done being something you have no control over?"

"Listen, Hassle—" Jacob spoke firmly, "—what's your real name?"

"Some days I can't even remember," Hassle bellowed.

"Well, you're one of us. I know you believe the rest of us have had it easy compared to you, and maybe that's true, but we've suffered a lot too. We know what it's like to be the outcast, to have to try to figure this all out. No one's blaming you for how you got here. The only blame you will bear is for what you do here today, to your own."

A silence drenched in tension filled the battle floor. Then a buzz began, and Hassle's plated suit began to unfold. The plates attached to his legs and arms elongated into a complete armor, wrapped around every part of his body, and morphed him into a menacing robotic giant. He towered over the MOLe's behind him; his eyes became those of a hooded emotionless beast. He had become an enormous version of one of their dreaded Oil Eaters.

"You aren't the only one who knows about this place!" Jacob yelled. "You don't think others know about it? Any minute now...."

"Any minute now, what?" Hassle's voice had transformed into a synthesized slur through his mask. "Someone will burst in and rescue *Uspre*? Believe me—the only person who knows I'm here knows exactly what I'm doing. And they aren't coming to save the day."

Harley whipped Jacob a quizzical look. Laney wanted to ask Harley's question for him—did Hassle mean Rheinland? Or the others in Jacob's pictures, Ozegovich, the businessman, or that playboy type, Calloway? Jacob only focused ahead when the sinister sound of a gun loading sprang from Hassle's suit and mega gun barrels erupted from the back of his forearms.

"Awww, snap," Brian muttered.

"You're nuts!" Tag yelled. The desperation in his voice echoed the same thoughts growing in Laney. "Look around you! This discovery has to be worth millions of dollars, and you just gonna throw that away? You, you could be rich! You could be a, a hero!"

From the metal sleeve on his arm, Hassle pushed a button and the pipes from each of the tanks changed from silver to a soft green, slowly at first, until the soft glow became fluorescent bubbles that churned and pushed their way in a steady course. The flowing liquid illuminated the room, making the layers of colored rock glisten on the walls tucked far back in the recesses. If not for the sinister way the green substance activated the Mobile Oil Locaters, the room would have made a spectacular backdrop to the most surreal moment of Laney's life.

"There's nothing left," the robotic voice boomed. "The rocks paneling this cave are all that remains. After today, there will be no more colored stone to exploit.

"So let's get the showdown started," Hassle continued. "Here are the rules. You have one minute to take cover and create a strategy before my MOLe's come after you. That's as much help as I can offer."

"If we're going to do this," Jacob yelled frantically, "let's take it outside! Give us a fighting chance! We are outnumbered and over powered! Brian and Har—"

"I can't do anything about your power raping," he said. "Who knows? It may kick in when you need it... or not."

"Of all the cockamamie, crazy crap—" Harley began his own tirade that Laney tuned out as she turned to the man beside her.

"Donavan," Laney whispered. Sweat beaded on her forehead, and she could feel her hands quivering on her weapon. "Donavan, there's something you really should know. Not that it matters, but, I need to tell you—"

His firm hand grasped hers again without hesitation. He brought his face closer to hers. "You don't have to say it."

An alarm began to blare, producing panicked curses from Laney's support group.

"Don't have to say—?" Laney asked in confusion. "No, you don't understand—"

His hand left hers to caress her cheek; her face warmed with a glow she couldn't control. "You can tell me when this is all over," Donavan said, still wearing a reassuring smile she knew was far from what he felt.

"Oh... no," she said, rattled by the tender moment amid the chaos. He must believe her to be on the edge of an emotional confession and in her frazzled state couldn't think of how to dissuade him. "I mean, okay, yes, to that... but I really need to tell you—"

"It'll be like hide and seek," Hassle's robot broadcasted over the alarm. "They have their eyes closed." He gave a little laugh that translated to downright creepy when boomed through the synthesized speaker. "You hide, we'll seek. Sorry, you won't get a chance to be 'it'. . . Aaaaand we're counting. *Sixty. . . fifty-nine....*" Each number became more monotone than the last, until the words fell flat, void of emotion, emptying the metal giant of any sign of humanity. "*Fifty-eight... fifty-seven....*"

The Oil Eater beside Jacob began to whirl. Before Hassle hit fifty-six, Jacob flew to the stairs, the rest of his band close behind. They hit the floor automatically in a team huddle, eyes wide and breaths audible.

"Okay," Jacob said, "we know that the tanks make a good cover—"

"We need a position higher than that," from Brian.

"To be more visible?" Tag challenged. "Let's take cover."

"Someone's got to get a bird's eye," Harley agreed with Brian.

"There's no room on the balcony; we could get blocked in—" Donavan added quickly.

"There are two entrances we know of," Tag was saying, "both blocked—"

"Obviously there's more," Laney tried to contribute. "They got in some other way than the broken ceiling."

"If we split up—" Harley swung his head in every direction, checking out the options.

"We leave ourselves open," Tag interrupted.

"You climb up the stairs, I can take them out," RJ rumbled.

From the robot standing yards away the count continued. "*Forty-three....*"

Panic had them all talking at once, their voices tripping over each other.

"—never make it that far—"

"—how do we—"

"—the only way this will work—"

"No," Jacob whispered coarsely. The group turned toward their leader, deep stress grooves carved into his brow. "We don't split up."

Everyone paused for a second. Laney wasn't sure what they were thinking, but her heart surged with compassion. It was easy to see how the weight of Jacob's responsibility for Uspre's well-being plagued him.

"I know this is hard." Donavan spoke calmly to their leader, "but we all know how this will probably go down. We understand there's a good chance we won't make it out of here. You have to accept it's almost certain that we won't survive if we stay in a group.... If they corner us...."

"Time," Laney whispered nervously, the countdown now at thirty-five.

Jacob's shoulders sagged as if he would physically break into pieces under the strain.

"Give me RJ," Brian jumped in. "I need cover, he needs size."

Jacob vaguely nodded, and Tag spoke up, too. "I'll go with Harley." He looked at Harley for conformation and found it. "We'll try to get a high position. Like that dirt mound over there. It gives us a good all-around view and some protection from the digger machine."

Brian frowned at Tag. The open stance had been Brian's idea, but his friend had just offered to take the dangerous post in his stead. Tag only nodded his confidence, and Brian looked away.

"Laney has me," Donavan said. "Stick with us, Jacob."

"Okay," he said slowly, "Okay." Then lifting his chin with what was probably false assurance, he repeated more firmly, "Okay."

Harley clapped him on the back, and Laney felt their unity like a stifling hug. No one wanted to see Jacob shaken; no one could function if he fell apart now. And no one would dare acknowledge his weakness, not just for his sake, but for the way it hurt the morale of them all.

"Time to move!" Brian said with forced cheerfulness.

"Into the rabbit hole," Harley nodded, wiping at his cigar-bereft mouth.

"Let's take the right." Brian cuffed RJ's arm. To the right, piles and piles of rocks and scraps of metal stood solid amid an odd array of equipment.

"*Twenty-eight...twenty-seven...twenty-five. . .*"

"He skipped twenty-six!" Laney said incredulously.

"The Mad Hatter," Harley nodded and un-shouldered his weapon.

"Alright, another team takes position at the far end," Jacob said sounding in charge once more.

"On it," from Tag.

"Laney, Donvan, and I will cover this corner. If it becomes necessary, we each head for a passageway if we can. One of them has to have another exit; it's our best hope for finding a way out."

"*Twenty-one....*"

No one moved, and in the next seconds that followed, Laney thought she might collapse with emotion while the band of brothers eyed each other and stepped forward as if for the last time, clasped the shoulder next to them, across from them, nodding, wordlessly conveying their fear, their strength, their commitment.

Then Tag and Harley took off to their given position. Brian and RJ paired up, but RJ paused a moment before Laney. She caught his big hand into hers and stared as it warmed and changed under her touch into something personal and human.

"Be careful," was all she could say.

"Got it, Alice," his voice ground out, that incredible sound of sandpaper smoothing out a grit of words.

"Alice? Hey!" She would have laughed outright if the final seconds of the countdown weren't ringing in her ears. He got it—Harley's *Alice in Wonderland* references. There would always be more to this guy than she knew, than she would ever likely get the chance to know. "Okay, Richard." Lips tightened on the stony face. "Ronald? Ralph? Oh, please don't tell me it's Rocky? It's not *Rocky*, is it?"

Donavan was pulling on her now; Jacob had already started jogging to his position.

"It's... R...J!" The animated rock squinted down at her with a gleam in his one good eye.

Welling tears threatened to damage what little cheer her small smile could offer before she sprinted away with Donavan into the shadows.

Chapter 36

Laney wasn't ready for *one*. How could she be? Hiding in dark corners like rats with the loosest of plans and a thread of hope? But the countdown ended, and the room exploded with more action than any war movie could have prepared Laney for.

A vat in front smashed like a burst thundercloud before Donavan, arms wrapped around Laney, could even get off a single shot. They splayed onto the flats of their back, the impact separating the couple. A sleek black arm aimed itself at their prone figures as Laney pulled off a round with a yell, but it went wide right without both Donavan's hands guiding. A split second later a shot would have taken out Laney had Donavan not used his strength to shove her hard in the opposite direction. She had no time to look back at Donavan as instinct took over and she dove behind the next silver canister.

Jacob, using the same cover, hauled her to her feet with his free hand. With the other, he shot down the same black bot closing in, but as it staggered to its death, a second one followed it, very much alive. This MOLe came between the separated group; Jacob hesitated before his shot, Donavan within his crossfire.

"*Get down*!" Donavan's command was barely audible over the continuing blare of the alarm, but without hesitation, Laney and Jacob hit the deck as bullets dinged the metal like an off-key xylophone. The floor cracked like an explosion when the bots and debris fell around them. Laney cupped her head in an attempt to stop the assault of sound, her eyes squinting in the process.

Use the fear.

She pried her eyes open despite the commotion to see, through a swirling cloud of dust, a vaguely familiar sight—Donavan had pulled a pipe from its connection on the tank, causing the apparatus above and below it to break. Connecting pipes overhead swayed and bent, sending loose ends crashing to the floor, and Donavan, with a pipe of the perfect handheld diameter, swung like a bat around him with speed and force impossible for any mortal. Good to know the extraction hadn't damaged his prowess.

The pole made contact with the sleek black bodies in the semi-shadows, eyes dying under the impact. Jacob shot in continuous rounds to Donavan's right at the tier above, dropping one or two bots from the height but always, several more took their spot. Laney watched their left and behind.

When no bots crowded them, Donavan dropped his weapon, running to scoop Laney up while Jacob covered them. Wordlessly Donavan braced her shooting arm, whipped her around the next vat, avoiding steam that cascaded from the broken pipe above, and began a volley of shots in the center of the room where the piles of debris crawled with the misty outline of a dozen more predators. Like mad ants driven from their hill, the endless stream poured out before them. Jacob took their side to the left and shot at the necks of a couple rounding the corner, so close that when they fell they created an instant barrier for the next wave coming. Jacob advanced, and Donavan pulled Laney with him to join. Within minutes, they had cleared a small area by constructing a makeshift fort of black metal arms and track wheels. From this viewpoint, out from under the canopy of the scaffolding, their shots could take wider angles to the tier across the room, but should any robots approach them at ground level, the three of them could be sitting ducks.

Silently Laney prayed for Tag and Harley's success in clearing the MOLe's that rolled above them.

Two figures appeared on the horizon and then dropped again behind the rubble. From Laney, Donavan, and Jacob's hideout, rolling hills of dirt and debris stood between them and the open floor space. They waited; Tag and Harley appeared again over a mound, and Donavan turned his partner's gun in their direction to clear out the bots that chased from behind. Harley bled profusely from his bicep, but ran like an angry man on fire, his mouth a gaping hole without a cigar to keep it clamped shut.

Donavan stopped shooting to examine the piece of trashed metal that protected them from above. Grabbing hold of the side, he ripped steel like it was paper and pulled Laney up so they were standing in the gap, looking out the homemade sunroof of a totaled vehicle. From a standing position, they covered the two charging men without endangering them…much.

Tag and Harley sped by as if pushed by an invisible wave and dove under the scaffolding's protection where a section of the cave carved out a dark alcove. A huge shadow flashed over the hideout, and Laney reeled around only to find herself scooped up along with Donavan by two large rocky hands. RJ. He took them with him to the wall's recess with Brian running ahead.

Jacob charged out of their inferior screen and, after taking out the last bot on the horizon, raced with his crew; within a moment, the band of seven—dirty, injured, and at a loss for breath—converged into the recess, the last barrier before the battleground.

"Above us," Tag tried to speak between pants, "we brought down enough to create a roadblock up there. I don't know if they'll try to climb over each other or what, but there's a stretch of bot-free bridge up there, for what it's worth."

Harley moaned and Laney gasped to see his gut oozed blood from under the damaged forearm that he hugged around his waist.

"Brian—" Jacob didn't even finish the question before Brian shook his head hard.

"No, I'm not back in the freeze business yet. Gonna have to live this out in real time."

Jacob nodded in acknowledgement, but Laney sensed their commander didn't have a back-up plan.

"I need to leave," RJ boomed. "I'm visible; they'll find you."

"Easy, big guy," Brian said, clapping his friend's side that nearly reached head level. "They already know where we are."

As if to prove it, Jacob fired shots toward the new set of MOLe's breaking the perimeter they had just cleared.

Harley cursed, and Tag walked over to a bot fallen at an angle among the shadowed rumble. "Donavan, help me." In a few seconds they had the insides gutted and propped the shell up as a huge backboard. They forced Harley into his new resting chamber.

"What the h—don't you dare—!" But the large man wasn't in any shape to fight them off.

"You need to heal," Tag said matter-of-factly. "Stay in there till you're strong enough to break out." Tag slammed the front cover over Harley and snapped it shut.

"If he doesn't have his power back yet," Laney asked weakly, "can he still...will he heal?"

Brian and Donavan exchanged a glance, but didn't answer her.

The Harley-turned-mummy produced muffled curses and violent rocking while Tag helped hold the line with Jacob.

"We need a way out," Donavan said.

The plan had been to split up, but here they were, all together and getting ready to go down as one. A lump in Laney's throat kept her from voicing her fear. She wished now she could tell them about her power—wished even harder that she could use it. But what good would it do right now? There would just be two of her trapped with the others.

"Seems like time to split into the tunnels and see what we got," Brian said.

"Just feels like we'd be mice running a maze," Donavan huffed. Tag and Jacob shouted for help and then the inevitable battle began all over as another wave of robots moved in at rapid speed.

"How do we get them to not sense us?" Laney yelled over the din. "We can't ever hide if—"

"They're protecting the green stuff, right?" Jacob answered. "We need to get rid of that."

"Or distract them with it ..." Donavan's voice trailed off as he looked upward. Brian, prone beside him, followed his gaze and rolled over. They discussed something Laney couldn't hear over the gunfire, breaking metal, and the siren that sounded above them like an erratic nightmare.

Together Donavan and Brian shot at pipes and holding tanks; nothing happened for several long seconds, no evidence even that the bullets hit their mark. Then a sudden green spout erupted from a pipe.

"Better hurry!" RJ rumbled. More bots took the hill in front of them. RJ picked up something resembling a large ladder, ripped it in half, and hurled the pieces toward several robots, knocking two machines off their tracks.

Laney latched onto Donavan, and with their combined aim, spouts soon poured open all over the room. One pipe sagged from its mount, burst, and sent liquid flowing like a green curtain over the equipment below it. Pops and sputters joined the din until, without warning, an explosion broke a tank wide open. Suddenly the room came alive with a blue-green flame that covered every surface the oily substance touched.

Black bots stopped in their tracks; several swiveled their heads. Then, as if by some telepathic communication, a row of MOLe's headed toward the fire while another row headed straight for Uspre.

"Well, that potentially made things worse," Brian commented and turned back to taking them down.

"The fire..." Laney didn't finish her statement, knowing the rest must be well aware of the trap they'd set for themselves. The endless enemy blocked the path to the stairs, the route to the tunnels growing with flames. She looked up at RJ who scowled with concern at their new dilemma.

"Get out of here," Jacob barked. Bullets flew so rapidly near them, it sounded like hail on a tin roof. Donavan took one in the arm before Jacob issued his command a second time. "Head for one of the passages! Now! *Go!*"

Too many of the MOLe's had advanced, and the group dug down deep from their position to take out what they could as a wave of heat moved over them like a sauna turned on full force.

Laney lay prone beside Donavan until he moved his body over hers, pushing her into the metal and dirt beneath them. She held out her arms to help aim, but the heat and pressure made it seem hopeless that she would ever hit a mark.

A figure rose beside her, and she knew before she looked it was Tag.

"Get down!" Brian yelled, but the other man wasn't listening. He took in the scene before him with a determination that startled Laney.

"Everyone get grounded," Tag said.

"*No!*" Brian screamed as a bullet ripped into his thigh. "Tag, don't do it—"

In the next instance, Laney whipped backward, pulled with Donavan back onto the dirt by RJ's large hands. He didn't hesitate to grab Jacob and Brian next, a bullet zinging off Jacob's chest without a dent.

"Jacob!" Donavan yelled in surprise, clutching his own injury tightly against him. But Jacob's relief was evident. He had his powers intact; then so might Tag.

Tag didn't look back to see if anyone had listened to his order. He grabbed hold of a broken metal pipe and charged into the fray, holding the weapon in front of him like a horizontal javelin; he buckled from a shot that hit its mark just as a hissing sizzle filled the ground before them. A row of bots made contact with the pole, and, in a split second, all the way down the line, metal touching metal, machines dropped like electrified dominos. At the initial contact, Tag flew off his feet, away from the fried bots, straight up to the scaffolding. RJ jumped with incredible agility for someone his size, caught Tag by the leg, and yanked him to earth.

Brian angled himself to let Tag fall onto him, becoming a human mattress under the limp body. A gaping wound in Tag's shoulder spilled blood, and the hair on his head smoked around his charcoaled face. Laney fell beside him, wiped the smudges, and patted his cheeks with urgent taps, trying not to cry out.

"Field's clear," Donavan reported just as a thunderous crash broke from behind them.

"Lock me up in danged coffin, will ya?" Harley shouted, tearing open his temporary holding tank; the blood at his torso had left dark stains on this shirt, but ceased to flow. "I'll rip Tag a new—*what the*—who let him fry himself before I got to him? *Tag!*"

"We have to move," Jacob said quietly.

"I'm not leaving him," Brian whispered from Tag's side, but already smoke thickened the air above them. The soft blue shine of the quiet flames in the distance replaced the strange green glow that had once colored the wall.

A crazed laugh echoed around them, the sound loud and synthesized. Hassle.

"Well, who do we have left?" His large stiff frame appeared on the far side of the centerline, his armor still intact. "Roll call!"

"You coward!" Donavan yelled. "Where have you been?"

"This isn't as easy as it looks," the robot laughed. "My first time in this thing; well, *this me* that is." The mirth in his tone left a clammy sweat on Laney's skin. "But I'm ready to go; so, who's next?"

"More bots coming," RJ commented, ignoring their mad tormentor who continued his rant. "Jacob?"

RJ was right. The cavern seemed depopulated, but from the depths of the tunnels, the all-to-familiar sound of whirls and clicks began. Donavan egged the menace on, trying to buy them time.

"What do you need a suit for?" Donavan badgered. "This fire will take us all down!"

"Beautiful, isn't it?" echoed the maniacal voice. "When it's pure, there is none of this smoke, just that crazy clear blue flame that comes from an absurd green rock—"

Harley hissed down at Tag all the while Hassle spoke. "Wake up, you stupid, selfish idiot!" He raised his fist and dropped it onto the motionless chest with a dull thud.

Tag's eyes flickered for a second before rolling back into his head. His chest heaved.

Laney felt a nudge at her shoulder and turned to see RJ pointing.

"That tank is water, not green stuff; it runs together and down there," his index finger indicated a spot Laney couldn't make out from her lower vantage point. "Looks like it's headed to a drain."

Laney slowly nodded. For the first time, she noticed that the tanks varied in shape and size, water and green glow each housed separately. "The falls in the other cave. It fell into a hole, too. The water's way out."

"Our way out," Brian cut in.

"Could be," Laney said tentatively. How big could the drain be? She wiped her palms on her dirty jeans and tried to focus amid the chaos. They needed a plan—*now*.

Brian jerked his chin toward Harley's chamber and eyed Tag. Harley gave an, *"Oh, heck, yeah,"* and helped lift Tag's sagging body into the metallic carcass.

"It has to be now," Brian said, clutching Donavan's arm to pull his attention away from Hassle. "We'll follow the water flow out of here, hopefully, make it to the drainage tunnel or at least a safe place to hide Tag until he heals. But we leave now before another round of uglies gets here or that fire takes over everything."

Harley had already twisted the metal armpits of the disassembled robot over his shoulders to hang on to like broken backpack straps. He dragged Tag's cocoon behind, and Brian jogged next to him, not looking back for verification.

Jacob turned to Laney and Donavan. "Go before the fire gets the best of you," Jacob nodded in agreement. "I have business here."

"You'll have to beat me to it," Donavan said, reloading and taking a stance by his side.

"Wait, who—Hassle?" Laney asked.

Already Hassle had seen the two men with their metal stretcher making a break for it. He turned his large gunned arm in their direction, but not before Jacob and Donavan sent rounds into the giant's body, enough to rock him on his heels. Hassle turned and fired back. Jacob pushed Donavan down, stood his ground and shot, confident in his proven bulletproof abilities again.

"Let's keep him on this side of the cavern; it'll give them a chance," Jacob said. "RJ, hang back with Laney a minute, and you should be able to make it through the escape route."

A crash and roar down the passage alerted them to the arrival of their next series of attackers. The air filled with a thick blanket of grey as the smoke sucked at their caged air around them.

Donavan turned through the haze, his eyes telling of the difficult decision he faced.

"Laney—"

"Go!" Laney coughed as she inhaled. This was no time to argue or try to prove a point about her usefulness. "Stop him; you don't need me to take him down. And he's *gotta* go."

The flames grew, and the room became a wonderland of aquamarine and blues, licking their way across the tanks and equipment. The MOLe's headed for the source and unfastened their claws into usable tools that disconnected tanks before they exploded. The machines did what the designers had programmed them to: protect this product. Most of the structures were too far gone; the robots only accomplished getting themselves caught in the fire. They collapsed like dying insects, squirming and then motionless in the flames, their precious resource unsecured.

RJ, who took in the scene with more gravity than Laney thought possible, grabbed her hand and gave Donavan a nod. "Got her." Donavan returned the nod and moved behind Jacob. He gave Laney one more glance and startled her with a wordless message on his features she hadn't prepared for.

He doesn't think he will make it out of here.

"Hey," he called, "tell Parker I got to battle a Transformer."

She choked on her reply, her face unexpectedly wet. "Tell him yourself."

He nodded and disappeared over the ridge behind Jacob.

Chapter 37

The two remaining Uspre stood frozen, rendered speechless by the view of the rabbit hole they'd been left alone in. Robots poured into the cavern; small fires and creaking pipe gave the room a ghastly appearance of flames and smoke. Above them sparks sputtered like mini shooting stars against a sky of eerie grey-green. Laney gripped RJ's hand tighter and closed her eyes, while his fingers melded into human-size within her grip. When she opened her eyes again to look up at him, he seemed to read her fear.

"We'll make it," he said.

Above his head she took in the scaffold, out of reach, yet free of flame and robot. If only…

Laney cocked her head to the side, an idea forming.

"RJ? What if—"

"Turn that tin thing off?"

"Right," she agreed slowly. In the distance, gunfire reminded her that Donavan still fought for their life. "It could turn everything off, right? Shut down the robots again maybe. How do we—"

"I boost you."

"What about you?"

He leaned down and cupped his hands. "I'll get you up. That rail?"

"RJ!" She grabbed his shoulders instead of stepping into his makeshift riser. "I'm not leaving you behind."

A slight grin. "I'll be right behind you. Don't need a lift with you not here."

She mentally calculated his size without her and the distance between them and the overhang. He would reach it.

With a solid launch from RJ, Laney reached for the pipe and caught it while her heart remained lodged in her throat. She ignored the fact that her feet swung too far from the floor for her to fail. Robots moaned into view giving her the motivation she needed to grit her teeth and swing her body onto the scaffold in an agile if ungraceful move. RJ teetered on the small size so she quickly moved away, running down the bridge in the direction of the missile room.

It only took a second to realize her presence had attracted the smaller robots of the top tier. She whipped around to find that they came from the backside of the bridge too. Within a minute, she would be surrounded if she stayed on this perch.

RJ landed onto the frame with a heavy slam that seemed to echo throughout the cavern already flooded with noise. She ran back to him and held out a hand, sizing him down as they raced toward the door. They would beat the MOLe's coming toward them only by a breath. Laney threw herself into the doorway; RJ followed and smashed it shut with a heavy clash of metal shaking the frame after them. If his stress level had heightened, he didn't show it. His face wore the eye patch with the same grim look as always.

"Do it," he told Laney, jerking his chin toward the interior of the room.

She opened her mouth to protest—then snapped it shut.

The canister was gone.

"RJ? We have a problem...."

The door rattled beneath RJ's hold. He gave a quick glance back at her, then did a double take.

"Wait. Look up there." Laney pointed to a box high on the ceiling with conduit pipes protecting the wires. It still connected the panels of thin cabinets along the wall even if the mini-sub had been removed. "Brian said the energy that thing produced would be stored or realigned somehow. There?"

Not sure of how Brian reached it, Laney scrambled for her own solution. The metal table in the corner, heavy and awkward, took all her strength to move into place.

"Hey," from RJ. Another chin jerk told her that he wanted one, too. She wrestled a second table and barely scooted within RJ's grasp before he scooped it up and mangled it into the shape needed to hold fast the door.

Laney didn't stop to watch him complete his task. She vaulted herself up onto the table and opened the cable box as quickly as possible. A mess of wires stared her in the face. Exactly what she had feared. Red wire? Green? She moved them all to the left, then right, and found a message scribbled in sharpie beneath one: Brian's scrawl! It read *THE RED ONE.*

Without hesitation she pulled the wire and yelled in satisfaction as she heard a rearrangement of the commotion outside, the far off hum below dying down. But the banging outside the door persisted, loud and determined. She scowled down at RJ.

"They aren't stopping," she said. "But, how?"

RJ listened, his set features showing no surprise or relief. After a moment of what appeared to be deep thought, the man of stone climbed onto the table with her and used his large fist to smash a hole near the cable box, high enough to be out of reach of the smaller robots outside. RJ gripped the newly created window and hoisted his body up. After a moment he lowered himself, and without asking, grabbed Laney by the waist and held her up for her own inspection of the cave.

"It worked! Well, down there it did. The big ones have all stopped! And the lights—they're out! So why aren't these—?"

"The key," RJ said knowingly, letting her drop to her feet. "They used a key to power the upstairs."

Laney pictured the key she stole from Thackray, the turn switch that had created power and then outed it.

"Two different systems?" she asked weakly.

He nodded.

"So these smaller robots…they run on, what, batteries? Remote?" Laney slid down and sat with a *thunk* onto the table. RJ jumped down and surveyed the room and its useless contents before he joined her.

"Shoot our way out?" she asked hopefully, but one glance up at his far-off stare told her the truth she already knew. There were too many.

"Well…at least we gave the guys a fighting chance, right?"

RJ nodded again, but still did not make eye contact.

She reached out and grabbed his hand.

"So we wait till they come up here."

He was silent; not even a nod. Laney swallowed the lump forming in her throat.

The banging outside the door persisted. Above them, a gentle smoke rolled in, taking its time in filling the room with its poison and suspense. RJ's hand, her only anchor, became warm and softened under her touch. She clutched it desperately again and hoped that he couldn't make her out for the coward that she was.

"Tell me one of your stories."

An instant *phfffttt* passed through her lips. She arched her neck to look up at her companion. "Stop it. I'm pretty sure my story-telling actually annoys you."

"Maybe. But," he shrugged, "it helps you."

Images flashed in Laney's mind of her story times, nervously rattling on while he listened patiently…all her tales came so quickly when *she* needed to calm herself. Another perceptive insight from this mysterious Uspre.

"Sorry," she managed, adding another lump to the collection her throat had been gathering all day. "Not very chatty at the moment."

The door shook so violently that Laney jumped. RJ squeezed *her* hand; she glanced up again.

"What really happened to him?" RJ asked, an attempt to distract her from their impending doom, she was sure. But the curiosity in his voice tugged at her heart all the same. "The Cyclops?"

She examined his profile—the rough angular skin of flexible stone that had made her flinch at their first meeting, now the only true comfort she had in the middle of this twisted madman's game. How could she have ever been frightened of his appearance? He was like a statue, a work of art, that became more awe inspiring, more breathtaking the more she stared.

She turned her head away in shame. "You don't want to know."

He didn't answer, and she hated herself for telling him that lousy lie of story in the first place.

"I was wrong before," he said.

A steady *bang, bang, bang* echoed through the thickening air of the room.

"When I said I wanted to be alone?" he sighed. "I *did* need you. I did need…family." He gazed at her with a steady warmth he'd never given her before.

Their conversation under the stars the night she twisted her ankle came back to her. Laney had tried to convince him they were all in this together.

She felt her chest tighten as she struggled to breathe the harsh air; he had said "did need" not "do." Her instant haughty comeback caught in her throat, unwanted tears streaming down her cheeks that would have burned if the temperature in the room wasn't already dramatically rising. The fire, the smoke, or the robots—one of them would soon bring them to their end.

Then she remembered....

"RJ...I think—" The words were wrapped in a sob. She inhaled hard to try to speak but ended up in a sputtering cough.

"I need to tell you—" more coughing—"how I escaped the chairs."

RJ was lost in contemplation, defeat at their door.

Suddenly sharing her news *now* was the only thing that mattered.

"No, listen! I...I was in the chairs, and then I wasn't."

He scowled down at her, and she fought another cough to plow on. "I mean, I got out of the chairs because *this me* wasn't there in the chairs. There's two of me, RJ. Or there was."

The frown turned to an arched eyebrow that indicated his doubt.

"Seriously!" She jumped up to stand over him on their table perch. "RJ, I found out my power. I can recreate myself. I duplicate!"

His eyes widened, but she held up a hand to stop any interruptions. "I don't know how, but I passed out in the chair, and then *THIS me* woke up or was created, or whatever. I saved the rest of you.... I just don't know what happened to the other me. Or maybe this *is* the other me, both me's put back together. But for sure, I can become two persons. If I could do that now..."

RJ jumped up so quickly, Laney would have fallen off the table if he hadn't caught her. He turned to the wall and began punching their spy hole wider and wider around the surrounding black box.

"RJ—"

"We're getting you out."

"What? How?"

He punched several more times, his punches in time with the robots' against the door. The hole in the wall grew into an 18" clearing.

"Grab this." RJ tapped the metal pipe that ran the wires within their room to the outside in the spot he had worked his construction. With his humanlike hands, he lifted her up again. She dutifully held on and he let her hang by her own weight. The slender pipe strained in its bracket, but held.

He nodded in satisfaction.

"You'll fit through there." He gave his standard chin jerk. "You're far enough above them; they might not be able to reach you."

"Maybe, but—" a coughing fit took her again. How could his stony lungs take in the thick air?

The door boomed off its hinges and would have flown across the room if RJ's jam hadn't bounced it back into its frame. The constant banging continued, the door moving a fraction of an inch each time.

"Go. Use the pipe to cross over to the beams. I'll distract them."

"*Now*?" Sweat trickled into her eyes, but she forced her voice to work. "The beams are on fire, RJ!"

"Try. Move fast! I'll buy you time."

When she attempted to let go of the pipe, he grabbed her by the waist and heaved her up again.

"No, it's stupidity! *RJ! Stop!*" Laney tried to twist around and cling to him. He all but shoved her out the crawl space, giving her no choice but to grab the pipe or fall out headlong. "It's suicide! *Stop*!"

"You're our only chance, Laney."

She couldn't remember a single other moment he had used her name, and the sound of it in his sandy tone brought on more burning tears.

"I won't go without a fight," he said calmly. RJ jumped off the table and scooted it out of her reach to go stand before the bulging blockade he'd made. The smallest of changes began. She realized too late what he already knew; without her, he had half a chance of surviving. Staying with her had prevented him from growing into an obstacle for the menaces that waited on the other side.

"RJ," she whimpered. She dangled from the pipe, unable to wipe at the cascade streaming down her face. He stood firmly in place, not looking her way.

"Reginald," he corrected her. "It's Reginald Justice."

A sob ripped from deep inside Laney's chest. Her sweaty hands stung from the heat and pain that matched all she felt inside.

RJ grabbed the crumpled debris away from the doorway, and the first incoming black beast met with his fist and flew backward into the others.

"Go *now*!"

She didn't wait to see the second robot hit him before she scurried out her escape hatch.

Hand over hand, knees and feet clinging to the pipe secured to the ceiling, Laney pulled herself out of the hole RJ had created, trying to block out the sound of the fierce fight behind her. Moving far from him—it could save him, she told herself over and over as her back scraped a swatch of skin from beneath her shirt, but she stifled the cry and pulled hard, finding the pipe outside the room hotter by far than inside.

A MOLe must have seen her; the loud scraping below told her it neared. Something plucked at her shirt and missed. Fear propelled her forward, clutching to the conduit as long as the grip of her toes could manage, in a mad scramble to be free from the overhang. Once out of reach of the machines on the upper deck, her legs gave out, and she swung by her hands high above the cavern. Nothing could grab her from the wall now, but the temperature of the pipe made her grip even more insecure.

A robot flew off the edge. RJ smashed down onto the metal bridge right after, a MOLe pinning him against the grid flooring. She couldn't watch; fear would paralyze her if she didn't move now. Her focus needed to be getting her feet onto the beam that ran the length across the cavern.

She went quickly, scooting her hands as fast as she dared to keep a grip. A *snap* barely registered before the pipe dipped several inches, and she produced the scream she'd been trying so hard to contain. The thin conduit had finally tired from bearing its extra weight, the final incentive to drive her to the beam before all hope went up in flames. If there were ever a time she wanted her clone to appear…

But there was just her. Just one of her. And just enough time to swing masterfully from the sagging rail to another one attached to a beam. It groaned under her grasp, but she gritted her teeth and hurled herself onto the beam. The solid eight-inch width did little to settle her panic. The heat had intensified, and the view from this height dizzied her.

The small fires of five minutes ago now blazed out of control, the sickly smoke pocketing the room in off-colored pools. She had found a gap of breathable air for the moment, although the surrounding clouds moved around her with swirling, probing fingers, as if seeking a set of lungs to invade.

In the moment of clarity, she considered options. The beams crisscrossed the ceiling, but some were too tight to the top to walk or crawl on. Some were dead ends; flames licked others. Below, bots squatted in frozen contortions now that she and RJ had disconnected their power source.

A blast rocked the room. Laney swayed on her beam as a second smaller explosion shook her again. Decision made for her, she scurried to a vertical girder for support, only to find its heat so intense, it scorched her back the moment she leaned into it. Stupidly, she reached for it and burned her left palm.

Desperately she spun around, searching for a way out when her gaze fell on two figures at the front of the cave, miniature replicas of two men she knew well: Donavan and Jacob. Their fight for life was against the sealed passageway.

Behind them, no sign of the huge Hassle. Had they beaten him after all? It didn't matter much if the fire that licked at their heels closed any further in. In a few minutes, they would lose the one space free of flames. Above them, the water tube from the other cavern connected in its clear tubing.

Her mind instantly made the connection, and she took the cross beam that traveled beneath the water tube, her burned back riddling her with pain. A break in the pipe ahead revealed her accurate assessment; water leaked down the side and dripped down below, putting out the flames in a small spot, adding to the smoke billowing toward her.

Running as if her life depended on it, she launched herself onto the tubing, landed and clung to it in a bear hug. It gave a loud crack and spilled its contents toward the two men below, but already their forms grew lost in a cloudy inferno.

Her body screamed louder than her voice when the heat became too much. She fell before she could jump onto the beam beneath and landed with a heaviness that took her breath away. Unable to communicate to her battered hands fast enough, she slid off the side and scrambled to hold on to the lip at the bottom of the girder.

That's when she saw him.

Under the metal scaffolding, surrounded by frozen MOLe's that he had helped disable, lay the body of RJ. No longer a statue of a human, not stoney or gianted, but in the mortal proportions of a man who had never seen the heroic end of his sacrifice. Now just a lifeless form sprawled amid the burning rubble.

The cry that ripped from Laney's throat was the last thing she remembered before her body gave way to free fall.

Part III

Chapter 38

The bedroom door vibrated as Wayne shoved one more time against it. He couldn't turn the handle far enough, precariously loaded as he was with packages of nacho chips, cheese doodles, PollyAnna's Deluxe Snack Cakes, and a large green apple Slushy. Not willing to set any of them down, he arched up on his toes and came down on the handle with his hip, successfully gaining entry. It was his own fault for weighting his door and equipping it with a heavy duty entry lock. He saw it as a security must-have for his privacy just as his junk food stockpile served as a necessity for brain power.

In the semi-darkness of his bedroom, the teen dropped his snacks and set down his cup by his gaming chair. He retrieved the large chip bag from the pile, and after it resisted standard methods of access, he slapped it open with a pop. The reward of his impatience spilled directly into his seat.

With a mumbled curse, Wayne ate some fallen goods while he scooped other handfuls onto the small table covered with candy wrappers. His mom would have a cow if she laid eyes on this new level of mess, but he pushed the thought of the impending tongue-lashing aside. Plopping directly onto the remaining crumbs, Wayne directed his attention to his laptop, its glow pervading his solitude.

Aside from his computer, four more screens he had begged, borrowed, and swiped sat to his left and right. Their faces arched down at an angle easily seen from his low seat, each one dark and blank without a mission to engage them. Yet.

Putting in his earpiece and tapping a few keys, Mrs. Whyte's student waited, eating chips and sipping the icy liquid, knowing he had signed in early. The Uspres wouldn't be online for another few minutes. He wasn't anxious—far from it. Eagerness smoldered from every nerve, but he held it in check by his determination to not screw this up. And…to know.

That was the thing. Knowing. Why him, why his dad, what role he played in this supernatural kismet. Had someone used him that day at the convenient store to cover up a death? To aid a super hero? Was he the kind of person who could face a gunman and do something? Or a cowardly kid that would live in the shadows all his life?

Minutes of life had ticked by in a countdown to a day he would either know or find a way to forget. Today, the countdown took a decisive path. Today could be the end of the wondering.

The chips were half gone by the time the blank screen came to life, the image of the interior of a van glowing in greens and grays in front of him. He licked the salt from his fingers and wiggled into his chair for maximum comfort, ignoring the crunch that came from his bottom.

"Uspres to Radster. You got us, over?" a faintly recognizable voice asked.

A small grin slipped onto the normally unanimated face of the youth. He pushed up his thick glasses and adjusted his earpiece in nervous anticipation.

"I got you, Uspre. Go ahead, over."

§ § § § §

The men inside the surveillance vehicle would have seen a fresh morning transform the beach below them had they glanced out the front windshield with Donavan. They had parked their nondescript white van tucked into a side lot, down a dead end street so that they faced the ocean below the cliff. He hadn't been to California since Parker was little. A small reminder of better days, a reason to press on. Now, behind him, there were four men in close quarters making a plan that held onto the thinnest shred of logic. Far from a Cali vacation.

"Tag? Harley? Ready?" Jacob's voice called from behind, shaking Donavan from his seat. He moved to the back, letting a curtain close behind him blocking out the ocean view.

Tag nodded somberly, but Harley grumbled his assent.

Jacob eyed Harley, but said nothing.

"Something's been bugging you," Donavan said, donning a small earphone. "Let's hear it, Harley."

"This is just stupid," the man growled.

Brian and Tag continued with the equipment check as if they hadn't noticed Harley's tone, but Jacob stopped and gave full attention.

"We've been over this," their leader said calmly. "We have limited options."

"Limited? That's what you call it?" Harley snorted and made a show of fishing a cigar out of his pocket. "*Options*. You act like the only thing we can do is the one thing that will get us killed."

"Harley—" But Jacob got cut off mid-sentence.

"No, you asked, now you listen." Brian and Tag tensed and shot Donavan a glance for support. No one spoke to Jacob that way; but no one seemed brave enough to silence Harley. "We did what we were supposed to. We went into that god-forsaken desert and faced a bunch of over-protective robots, and blew the lid off the little secret mining operation—literally. We're done. We're healed and free from that sadistic murderer. He's dead; everyone thinks we're dead. We've never had a chance like this in our lives to disappear without a trace. We should just be moving on."

"And what about the canister?" Jacob countered.

"For all we know, the fire destroyed it."

"Then what is this?" Jacob jabbed his finger at an oval-shaped blip on the screen in front of Brian.

"You going to keep falling for the same trick over and over?" Harley spat. "What exactly did this last mission accomplish, huh? We lost a good man and a decent woman, all for the sake of what? We don't know nothin' about that blip, but we just keep moving in the direction Rheinland points us no matter what the cost."

The silence hung heavy in the van as a slim line of sunlight finally made its way through the curtain up front.

"He doesn't know." Jacob spoke the words evenly.

"Who?" Harley barked. "Who doesn't know what?"

"Rheinland. He still doesn't know we're here."

"For the love of—then what is it we doin'?"

"It's my idea," Donavan inserted. "I brought us here."

The dark eyes clouded and deep lines rounded the cigared lips. "Figures."

Donavan's muscles tightened, but he didn't reply until he checked his emotions. It hadn't been an easy decision to make. After they had made it out of their earthly hell, burning chaos that could have been their permanent demise, they had struggled to regroup and heal in time to make a getaway before authorities showed up. Donavan refused to go far, camping in the desert scape, awaiting evidence that Laney and RJ—Hassle too—had made it. After all, they were Uspre. He didn't know all that meant, but he wanted it to mean they were invincible, more than human.

He had watched Laney fall, a nightmare that replayed itself over and over again in his head, after she had broken open the life-saving water pipe. Still, he couldn't believe, couldn't *feel* that she had gone. He hoped beyond hope...One unidentified body had been pulled from the wreckage...RJ. Just a mystery man to the authorities. But no Laney.

Donavan's brain, refusing to rest, mulled over the pieces of the mystery still unsolved and focused on one name. Someone who should have helped them far more than he actually had.

Donavan raised his chin. "You're right. We don't know *nothing*, but the one thing we weren't supposed to know about was about that missile-looking capsule. Rheinland didn't tell us anything about the underground bunker and never mentioned any possible energy source. But Thackray...you heard him. He knows more about Rheinland's involvement than we do." This was the thought he let consume him, the one that kept him from spiraling into a dark hole of loss for the woman who'd slipped away so soon after he'd let her into his life.

"It could have been Hassle feeding him info," Harley replied.

"Maybe, but if Rheinland had any intel at all, if he knew enough not to send us in there with any type of oil-powered machines, then he knew more than he was letting on."

"I've been here before," Jacob spoke up and jerked his head to the house on the screen. "Twice. After I met with Rheinland once, I followed him. He told me about a contact of his that was helping gather information that he didn't want me to meet. For my safety, he said. I tracked him here. Now," he poked the blimp on the screen again, "that thing is here."

"You understand you talking about turning your back on the one person on the outside that's helped us sort through all these years of trying to make sense of all this—of this crazy crapshoot life—" Harley pinched his lips shut and began rechecking his weapon, shaking his head as he did.

"Brian found a van company in the area that made a delivery here the day we were caught in the cave. While we strapped in for battling Hassle, they could have removed it, must have. And now a week later, the same van company has been hired to make another move for tomorrow." Jacob looked at Brian for confirmation, and he nodded in affirmation. "Tonight's our chance."

"There's a party tonight at the house," Brian chimed in. "The capsule is in a basement or under the side of the house. That's what you need to find out. How do we get in without going in the front door?"

"So the plan is to find the capsule and disarm it so we can, what, save the world? Shheez." Harley puffed up to boiling point.

Tag nudged his friend to get his full attention for a moment. "What else you got to do?" Harley just stared for a long minute before exhaling. "Come on, man," Tag continued. "I ain't going in there without you. All for one and all that BS." Donavan looked away from them, knowing the enthusiasm Tag gave wasn't genuine. Tag had been stoic and aloof ever since that cave.

"Uspre to the Radster," Brian said into his mic. "You got us, over?"

Silence, then static, then the voice of a teenage boy. "I got you, Uspre. Go ahead, over."

"I think I got you patched in. Give it a try."

"We've done our research on Ozegovich," Jacob spoke to Tag and Harley. Donavan brought himself back to the conversation with visions of the photos Jacob had shown him coming alive in his mind. Ozegovich: rich, 40's, business type. "You know that. Not just details about his funding of Rheinland's projects but his connection to this house, to Calloway." Max Calloway: good-looking playboy type. "Brian's tapped into their camera system, we have the entire layout, and every detail of tonight's event noted."

Brian nodded. "Believe it or not, this place is condemned. Yesterday, officially. It and every other house on the street." Donavan wouldn't have believed it just by looking at the huge elaborate homes that topped the cliff. But the vacant streets spoke the truth. "The beach erosion has the integrity of the cliff in question so they evacuated the neighborhood. This party—a last, illegal hoorah of the rich and reckless."

"Think the police just might notice?" Harley asked.

"I think for a few bucks they are going to look the other way. Yesterday—today. I don't think they figure it will get anyone killed letting them gather for one more shindig."

Harley seemed to consider this. "Might be fun to see a houseful of snobby folk end up in the ocean."

Brian ignored that and continued. "Once we get a lay of the land, we'll cut the power source. We'll aim for the lower level first where we see the missle-lette—there seems to be three floors. The party on the main floor by the looks of the delivery drop offs." He nodded to another screen.

Harley exploded into a low roar. "That don't mean we're going sneaking around dark passages we've never been in before, right? Have we learned nothing about *our lack of prowess underground*?" Silence stifled the room. He whipped his gaze over to Tag. "You? You got nothing to say about this?"

Tag shifted his weight and shrugged. "Prowess is a good word," was his answer. "And I think you actually used it correctly."

Brian snorted and exchanged glances with Tag. Harley shook his head, but a nudge in the shoulder got him a friendly grunt back. They were back in it, all of them together.

A tap on the back of the van's door repeated itself in a quick coded pattern. Tag opened the door, and Michael jumped in, swinging the door shut behind him. He brushed off his dress slacks then eyed the others in their dark t-shirts and cargo pants.

"How'd I look?" he asked, arms wide, palms up. His grin held a hint of *how'd I get myself into this* mixed with *you all owe me big time.*

Donavan walked over and adjusted Michael's collar even though it was perfectly in place. "You sure about this?"

Michael shook his head. "Of course not. But I'm the only one of you knuckleheads good-looking enough to get through the front door."

Donavan grinned back. They *did* need Michael's face, not for his looks and charms— although it would be a huge selling point to get into a West Coast party uninvited—but because he had never been seen with the gang. He wasn't Uspre. They hoped whoever moved the canister didn't keep tabs on Donavan's police partner, Michael.

"Anyone follow you?" Donavan asked.

A quick head shake. "Not a soul in sight till I got here." Michael brushed down his sleeves as he spoke. "Know how you asked me to check up on the builders of your little ghost town? Ozegovich's name was all over that."

Donavan exchanged looks with the others, another connection falling into place.

"Um, Mr.—" a young voice spoke over the intercom.

They had all forgotten the youth for a minute. Wayne Radison, Laney's student, had been the best outside source they could find to give them the tech support they needed. Brian hailed him as his younger, geeky doppelganger.

"Brian. Just call me Brian."

"Um, Brian, do you have a view of screen 5B?"

"I can't see all the screens at once. I gotta flip through. Why, what's up?"

A pregnant pause filled the van.

"There's something you're gonna want to see."

Brian fumbled through the channels until he found the right image. Curiosity brought the others over too. Seconds ticked by as they tried to make out the grainy image. A woman. Almost out of view in the front corner of a room. Strapped to a chair. Motionless.

"What in the world—"

Donavan grabbed the screen, and immediately threw it back as if it had bitten him. No discernible features, but an unmistakable mop of curls couldn't be concealed.

"Jacob." His voice trembled with emotion. "I'm going in."

"Don't be stupid," Tag said, his voice calm despite the antsy hand that ran through his hair. "You can't be seen. Everyone thinks we're dead."

"Well, hello, Mr. All For One," Harley rumbled, "of all times for us to do *something*– "

Jacob nodded in agreement. "Brian, I'm going to need you to get some things.... I have a plan."

Chapter 39

"Laney?

Her name.

"Laney? Can you hear me?"

Beyond the fog in her head and the unbearable throb that coursed through her body, it was good to hear a voice. An oddly familiar voice, like a distant memory coming to life. It comforted Laney to know that at least she wasn't alone any more.

The voice continued; it was saying something. She should listen, she knew she should, but the pain returned and the voice grew into an irritation. It might completely wake her from this doped slumber and make her start feeling.

Feeling didn't seem like a good idea.

She clung tighter to her medicated unconsciousness.

"Laney!"

She wriggled her body in protest to this insistent interruption only to find that the restraints caused her further agony.

The chair. In her impaired state she had forgotten. The horrible confining chair they strapped her in when they had wanted her out of bed. They wanted something from her. Expected something. She didn't know what and tried to care but couldn't. All she could do was drool and let her head bob helplessly. She was stuck in a body working diligently to repair the nasty burn down her back, the main reason she embraced her captors' forced drugs.

Her shoulders rocked. The annoying voice was shaking her. This was the newest form of torment since she had arrived here.

Here.

Where was *here*?

The agitator roughly captured her face in a warm pair of hands and shook some more until she was compelled to open heavy eyes and see that the voice did connect with a familiar face, oddly out of place, as if in a dream. Yes, she must be dreaming.

Except a dream never carried this much pain.

"Michael?" It came out more as a groan than a question.

"There you are. Stay with me, Laney. I got you."

"Michael? Why…why are you here?"

"I found her," he told someone she couldn't see. "She's alive."

"Oh, no, Michael," she heard her voice say. "You better go. These people…they aren't nice."

"Hey, I'm here to get you out," Michael jostled her more and peered closely to make eye contact.

"Michael."

"That's it, Laney. I need you to wake up a bit."

"You have great eyes."

He chuckled softly. "So I've heard."

Her head drooped. "Why do you have so many shoes?"

"Laney, I need you to snap out of it. Jacob told me to give you this." He placed something in her mouth and followed it with a squirt of water. She obediently choked it down. "We have to move quickly."

"You have four feet. It kinda freaks me out …"

Her body shook again, this time with a vigor that sent pain coursing through her seared back. It brought her sitting up sharply with a gasp.

"Laney, I need to get you out here, honey, but it's gonna have to be on your own two feet."

She tried to remember something. Something important.

"Michael. I died."

"No, you didn't. I got you. It'll be okay, but you need to help me here."

"There's two of me."

"Let's get you moving, and it will help clear your head."

Laney strained to focus, concentrating on her friend's four shoes until they became two.

She pulled her head up and zeroed her gaze in on Michael as he rose from his crouched position.

"That's my girl."

"You look nice."

"There's a party going on downstairs, Laney. I snuck in as a guest. Now I need to sneak you out as one."

Laney looked down at the clinical gown that men in surgical masks had given her after they transported her here in some van, already drugged by a merciful shot to the behind. There hadn't been a moment of rational thought in the hours—days?—that followed. Only exams and IV's. And wonderful, welcome injections.

"I'm going to a party?" She tried to make sense of it but couldn't get the pieces in place. They shouldn't be celebrating. There was a sadness lining this dream that drove her toward the pleasure of unconsciousness as a means of escape. It nagged her now, and she frowned, trying to pull it to her. To remember more.

Her hands suddenly became free as Michael released her bindings, and she would have pitched forward in the chair if he hadn't braced her. She wobbled and clung to him, unable to use her hands as gripping tools just yet, when the memory slashed its way to the present and ripped her apart all over again.

"Michael." Her voice came out hoarse and constricted with emotion. "They're gone. All of them, gone."

"Who?"

"Donavan. Everyone. Gone." She collapsed into his arms as the last word came out as nothing more than a croak.

"No, honey. No, they're not." He shoved something in her ear, something tiny, only a thin strand that came down around to the back of her neck and carried the miraculous sound of his voice to her.

"Laney? Oh, thank God."

"Donavan? Donavan, where are you? Are you dead?"

A small laugh from the earpiece. "No, Laney. I'm here." There was a pause before he spoke again with a voice saturated in emotion. "We're gonna get you out. Just listen to Michael. Do what he tells you."

"Okay," she answered.

"Donavan," Michael interrupted.

"Yeah, I know," her earpiece answered. "Laney, I need to switch channels now. You'll be tuned into Wayne. He's helping us from the outside."

"Bruce Wayne? Batman's here?"

"Hey, Mrs. Whyte," the youth's voice came through after a crackle. "Um... how are you?"

At present, Michael was unceremoniously undressing her. She kept a hand on him for balance, tottering as he unwrapped the gown from around her, stripping her to her underwear.

"Wayne? Radster? Um. I'm okay. Just, maybe, a little confused." Her voice rose in uncertainty as she squinted. "So what's the plan?"

Michael shed his suit jacket to reveal a small pack splayed out across his back like a thin parachute. He removed it and produced a short white brocade dress, the pattern concealing any wrinkles that may have been present.

"Ooo, pretty. For me?"

"Brian found this rather quickly which actually concerns me about his knowledge of the female wardrobe; but he assures me it will fit you. Can you manage?" He was holding it up toward her for her to step into, the zipper open facing her. The sooner she could not be in her underwear in front of him, the better, so she climbed in and turned with another wobble that nearly toppled her. He grasped her shoulders from the back, steadied her, and went to work slowly, slowly working the zipper up over her bandaged back. The thickness of the material camouflaged it well.

A noise outside the door froze them in the act.

"Wayne?" Michael whispered. "We have company?"

"No, you're good," the voice in her ear said. "Someone passing, just a lost guest, I think. Everyone's on the main floor partying like it's 1999. This guy is headed toward the party, too."

Michael hastened the final zip with a sudden tug that produced a groan from Laney.

"Tell Brian a size larger wouldn't have hurt," she mumbled.

"No, I won't tell her that," Michael said into the invisible line that hung down by his lobe.

"Tell me what?"

Michael's lips tugged in amusement. "He said that you wouldn't have looked hot then."

Her heavy head bobbed in a weak smile and her eyelids drooped with weariness. "Can we go now?"

"It's not quite that easy."

A pair of palest pink pumps fell from Michael's bag, shoes of flexible gel-like material, and Laney slipped them on, admiring their style and fit. Friday night shoes.

"We're upstairs and they have stationed guards at all the stairs and doors," her savior informed her.

"Guards?"

"Bad guys with guns under their jackets."

"Oh."

"Down the end of this hallway are two bathrooms. One's a powder room. You're gonna need to, um, powder up." That thought brought an involuntary hand up to Laney's impossible curls, the movement almost knocking her over. Michael caught her by the wrist and gained her attention again. "Then let's try to blend you in with the party downstairs and out the door."

"They'll see me."

He held up a pair of hipster style glasses not unlike the reading pair she owned. "This might help. We're going to take the stairs behind the kitchen—that's how I got up here. We'll take the front door out. They're busy checking everyone who comes in, but no one that leaves."

"What's the party for?"

"'I believe the theme is The End of the World As We Know It," Michael opened the door a crack and scoped out the hallway.

"By R.E.M.?"

"I think, my dear, this might just be the real deal. This house may be next to slide off the cliff into the sea."

"What? So why am I here?"

"We were hoping you could tell us. Someone thinks you're the last living Uspre, we're guessing."

Laney let that sink in.

"Ozegovich, Rheinland's funding buddy, owns this house, but so far we haven't seen a trace of him." Michael coaxed her body closer to the door, but Laney grabbed Michael's forearm in a tight grip that stopped him in the doorway.

"So the others—they all made it out? RJ?"

His face flashed sympathy that was Laney's instant answer. She took a step back into the room, and Michael closed the door once more to hold her by her shoulders. "Laney, I know. This is hard."

"You don't understand. It's because of me. We lost him because he was saving me—"

"Laney—"

"Tag was right. That's why none of them are in here saving me. Just leave me. I don't belong—"

"Listen," he shook her, helping the heavy lids lift farther off her eyes. "I've only just met them, and I can tell this group is unlike anything this world has ever seen. They're tough, strong, beyond comprehension. And they're loyal. They are not leaving without you. They need you."

"Where are they?"

"They sent me in because I'm the only one that won't be recognized. Laney, we can get into all the details later, but right now, I got at least five men shouting into this stupid earpiece that they will show you their eternal devotion as soon as you get out of here."

"Mrs. Whyte?" a timid voice spoke from her own ear. "He's right. The party's in full swing; everyone's distracted. This would be a great time to get moving."

Nausea clawed at her detoxing body, but she let Michael guide her out into the wide carpeted hallway, quiet and unpeopled. The mild thump of bass woofers and cheers rose from the opening at the corridor's end where a balcony curled into the head of a staircase.

"Here, this is the door to the powder room. Do what you can." He handed her a small case along with his backpack. "Use this and then throw all of it away. I'm going to scout again and make sure the back stairs are still an option."

Laney, numb and aching, entered the powder room with its sleek tile floor and marble countertop. A bright mirror laughed at her, throwing her disastrous image back. Bruising and thin scratches flecked her skin, cheeks surrounded by an unruly massive tangle of curls.

"Wayne? Can you…see me?"

"Uh, no. I just tapped into their security cameras. There aren't any in the bathrooms."

"This might take a while."

"You have about two-and-a-half minutes."

"Seriously? Being *super* is not the same thing as a miracle worker."

"I don't think they can go undetected for much longer. Harley and Jake are closing in on the device—the weapon or whatever it is—on the lower floor. Once they breech the security there, it's only a matter of time before they're on to us. We got to get you out first."

The fact that Wayne was using "we" did not escape Laney's soggy thought process. He was in this too. She picked up a brush and went to work. "Then you've got two-and-a-half minutes to explain some things to me."

After three minutes and twenty seconds, Laney emerged from the cool room into the warmth of the hallway. There was something comforting about the dark patterned carpeting, low ceiling, and crown molding that laced the edges. The powder room with its brightness reminded her too much of "the room," the realness of it all sinking in as the drugs wore off. She had no memory of leaving the cave, only of pain and medication as her back was treated.

Hassle? Rescue workers? She had nothing to go on other than she had seen herself fall, seen herself sprawled over the debris of the cave floor. She didn't recall any details of the place, the time, the hands at work around her. Pain was all she knew, that she wasn't free...and that the others were gone, which was worse than captivity.

Pain.

The impression of reoccurring pain found its way to the foreground of her thoughts. Had there been a time, out of the select few moments her selves split, that pain *hadn't* propelled her there? She ran through the scenarios in mind—her twisted ankle, the torture chamber, her burning back. It must be the catalyst! In desperation, her body had found a way to survive.

A slow excitement built and for a minute took precedence over any escape plan. She knew something important, something meaningful.

So why wasn't she making a second Laney now? Her scorched back screamed in frustration as the answer eluded her.

But Wayne was right: the time to wrestle with it all wasn't now. He had kindly reminded her of this in his adolescent fashion after his quick recap of their journey to this location, a entire state away from their cave battle. He didn't tell her how he'd exactly hacked into several surveillance networks to accomplish his job, but she probably wouldn't have understood that part anyway.

The hallway was dimly lit by glowing sconces spaced down the long wall leading to a draft of noise. Michael was nowhere to be seen.

She should stay put and wait for his return, but her weary body groaned under the strain of her exertion. A divan, nearly at the end of the hallway, beckoned her with its soft velvety cushion. She swayed toward it, cautiously, in the opposite direction she assumed Michael had gone. Sitting was a slow process, but she settled gently, steeling against the torment the dress caused as it pressed into her burn.

A great banister kept the protruding balcony safe from the immense drop into a great room below, where music pulsed and laughter rose in waves. Her curiosity almost had her on her feet to sneak a peek when a figure appeared from the top of the staircase and came to lean over the rail.

Laney stayed rooted, the man oblivious to her in the shadows. Her options were limited. Should she try to make it back to the powder room for cover? Or keep still?

The man wore a tuxedo and slouched on his hands in such a way that his shoulders hunched about his ears. Despite his relaxed pose, his jacket protested this undignified position. A minute passed, and he fished a cigarette out of his pocket then flicked open a lighter.

Laney sent glances back the long hall, but still Michael did not appear. The stranger half finished his smoke before he turned around to exhale in her direction, leaning on his elbows. His slacked recline created another awkward pull of his buttoned jacket. Moments passed before his eyes adjusted to the poorly lit corridor.

He erected himself, restoring honor to his tux. Laney swallowed, knowing she was made. He shot her a sheepish grin.

"I'm probably not allowed to smoke this up here."

She smiled back and tried not to bite at her lower lip.

"Okay, Michael? She's got company," Wayne said in her ear. "You headed that way?" Undoubtedly he'd put Michael on the same channel.

"It's such a pain to go outside, you know? Just thought I'd sneak upstairs."

She knew she should probably answer him. Or run. Or something. But he didn't appear to know who she was so just maybe it was safer to stay put.

"Michael?" Wayne hissed. No answer.

"What brings you up here?" the figure asked her.

Laney opened her mouth to respond just as Wayne piped up. "Oh, crap. That's *Max*. Maxwell Calloway?"

The pictures, the ones Jacob had spread over the rocks. This guy—the playboy. Calloway, the rich friend of Rheinland's buddy, Nick Ozegovich. The information scrambled through Laney's mind like files dumping out of a drawer.

"Talk to him," Wayne was saying as she stammered a collection of *uhhh's* and *umm's*, "and let me see if I can track down Michael on his original channel." A crackle and then silence.

"The noise down there…just a bit much," she finally managed.

At the sound of her voice, Max gave a curious tilt of his head. It was as if he were reading more into her words than what she actually said. She eyed him back, wondering if he knew her.

"That I can understand," he said and entered the dark passage. Laney held her breath as he leaned down to put out his cigarette in the potted plant beside her. "Have you ever been here before?" His bent figure brought his face closer to hers where he examined her in detail.

"No. My first time."

"So how'd you know Nick?"

The conversation could start down a dangerous path here. Laney willed Wayne or Donavan or someone to speak into the micro thingy dangling under her wispy curls and tell her what to do.

"I don't," she continued without any other option, donning the role of actress as best she could. "My date does."

"Ah," he was smiling in an odd way that neither concerned her nor charmed her. A row of small perfect teeth gleamed at her. "Dragged here, then? You have an excuse. I can't see how anyone would want to subject themselves to ostentatious mayhem voluntarily—oh, I'm sorry." He gave a little laugh. "Perhaps you *are* having fun. Don't mean to be a killjoy."

"No, no, it's okay. Not a fan of the 'ostentatious mayhem' myself."

"Well, you ain't seen nothin' till you've seen the big oaf down there—he's a *five*, tops—trying to steal this girl, who's a positive *nine*, from her boyfriend. I'm pretty sure the battle's about to begin. Thought I'd have a better view up here. A smoke and a show." He held out his hand. "Come on. Take a look."

Uh oh. From the railing she might be seen. "I'm a tad afraid of heights."

"Don't blame you," he smiled, but didn't take his hand away. "You fall from this height and hit that marble and *splat!* It's over."

She gave a little nervous laugh and examined his face for any guile in this graphic description. An odd familiarity weaved its way through her disconnected memories—his shock of bleached blond hair cropped tightly around his squarish face with the most piercing blue eyes imaginable. Ice reflecting sky. She couldn't have ever met him before and had seen photos only for a few minutes. Surely, she would never forget those eyes if she had met him in person before. Still...something....

Unwittingly, she offered her hand and let him pull her to her feet while her mind raced. He brought her to the balcony where he leaned on an elbow. He didn't look at the scene below but instead used the full lighting to take in every inch of her. She would have blushed at his scrutiny had she not scolded herself: *Play the role. Don't let on you're a stranger here.* "True," she continued his line of jesting. "It's not the height I actually mind. It's the splat part I'd like to avoid."

He smiled. "So no parasailing?"

"Never."

"Hot air balloons?"

"Not happening."

"So what *do* you do for fun?"

"You mean besides celebrating the end of the world? Well, if I survive this, I'll let you know. The way they're carrying on, they might just send this house into the ocean before the night's over."

"Ah, so it's not just the noise you hate. It's the idea of falling into the ocean from like a mile up, is that it?"

She tried to create a natural laugh. "Could be."

"How about your date?" he asked with a slight arch of an eyebrow that created a heart-stopping effect when coupled with those eyes. He could have been a magazine cover with that look. A misshapen tuxedo never looked so good. "You avoiding him as well?"

"Oh, that," she said offhandedly. Be playful? Disinterested? "Let's say I can enjoy his company just fine from here."

He laughed a little and stuck out a hand. "Maxwell Calloway."

"Hello," she stalled as she shook it. "Alexandria." Amid the stack of nicknames she may be called, no one ever called her by her full name. It felt safer than using an alias she'd forget.

A sparkle in his eyes lit up his face for a moment, and Laney's body tingled with caution. *Did he know her?*

"Well, it's nice to meet someone else who's brave enough to take a break from *that* for a little while."

She nodded and stared down into the crowd, venturing closer to the edge. The bottom of the staircase ended in the direction of the front door, hugging the wall as it curved away from the balcony. But there appeared to be a million swaying, noisy people between the stairs' end and the door. Woman wore tight cocktail dresses or billowy beach covers, men in tuxedoes or board shorts, a weird concoction of the fancy and frolicy, just the type of attire one would expect from an "end of the world" party. Whether there were "bad guys with guns" or not, she couldn't tell in the tangled horde.

What if she went for it? Were her legs steady enough to get her to the door by herself? Then what? She didn't even know where to run to. Why wasn't Wayne talking at her?

"Are you okay?"

Dang. She would have to work harder to conceal her expressions. "A little queasy, I think. Too much to drink, not enough to eat."

"Well, there's a cure for that downstairs."

"Oh, no, I'm fine. I couldn't eat anything."

"Worth a shot. Come on. We can't hide out forever."

"You sure about that?"

He gave a boyish grin, one that said he'd win this argument. He moved in closer and offered his elbow.

She placed her hand in the crook of his sleeve, and he mercifully let her have the banister on her other side when they descended. "Sad to *sea* you go!" read one of the huge signs across the entry way. There was the band, excited ribbons and balloons dancing along the walls, a huge dessert table, waiters with trays of drinks—perhaps enough of a distraction to let her get lost in.

Her legs wobbled at the end of the stairs, and she tried to grip the handrail as long as possible before Max swept her away into the crowd, chasing down a server. Within a minute, they both had tall flutes filled with a bubbly spirit.

"The best champagne," he practically had to yell over the din. "You have to at least try it."

The thought of alcohol without food started to churn her stomach before the liquid even touched her lips. She pretended to drink, turning her head to check out the scene, until someone bumped into her injured back. She winced and spilled some of the liquid, but Max didn't seem to notice or care. He stayed close, his icy eyes taking the commotion in with amusement.

The band changed its tune, discarded the celebratory overture, and replaced it with a less jarring rhythm. Max plopped their drinks, his empty, onto another passing tray and spun her onto the makeshift dance floor.

"Your date won't mind, will he?"

"Well, he tends to be the jealous type," she ventured. His hand was nothing but a shadow across her back, and, still, it sent needles of agony through her. Other couples crowded around her, unfamiliar faces, laughing, crazy with the intoxication of being in a building that may plummet them into the ocean without warning.

"Perhaps we shouldn't make a scene of it," she said as calmly as she could manage, trying to keep the front door within her sights. He was gliding her now, expertly, as someone who actually knew how to wear a tux would do, without breaking his gaze for a moment. Their bodies moved along the outer corners of the room.

If she had been bold, if she had been steadier, if all the movement and pain hadn't made her feel like vomiting just then, she would have bolted. They were passing a hallway; that could work. She just needed to gather her strength.

"It's uncanny really," he was saying. "So unreal."

"What's that?" They spun nearer the entrance, the queasiness waning, strength growing in the need for escape.

"The resemblance. It's... wow, I can't believe you're here." Something like a boyish relief filled his face then, only to be darkened by a distant grief. "It takes me longer and longer to remember...."

He knew something she didn't... or something she *should*. She flipped through the photos from the desert through her mind. The dapper man with women on each arm in most shots, the long coat, bowler hat, and the Aston Martin.

"I don't follow you," she answered when her mind could not produce any concrete connections.

"I've never met two people more perfectly the same—really, there's not a shred of difference. I get that you're twins, but..." His voice trailed off and his blue eyes pierced her with an intensity that froze her.

"Twins," she echoed lamely.

"You could be Arie," he laughed. "Your voice, your manners—your hair, for crying out loud. Not a skosh of difference."

Laney grew pale and felt her knees buckling.

"You... you know my sister?"

He threw back his head and laughed, the noise unnoticed by the chattering throng. It rang with slick charm and a hint of malice. "Know her? Alexandria, she had my *children*."

Confusion and fear tangled up her ability to pull away. Max's hand pressed into the center of her damaged flesh as if he knew all about the hidden injury. An involuntary cry broke from her lips that he shielded from nearby ears by pressing her into his shoulder. Her weakened knees would have buckled beneath her had his forceful hold not held him to her.

"Arie," she croaked. "Where is she?"

"I wouldn't have chased you across two states if I knew that. Haven't seen her in years."

I want to live in the land of adventure, no regrets... fast cars and men in bowler hats... she had said that rainy night years ago. Laney squeezed her eyes tight and tried to conjure any other image than Arie at that high school party.

"She's alive?" she whispered, unable to meet his icy gaze.

"No clue. It's something we're going to figure out together." She tried to tear away, but he firmly held her until she thought the pain in her back would rip her in two.

"I need *them*," his voice, now dark and heavy, whispered into her ear.

She didn't have any fight left, the tumultuous thing happening within that she had never been conscious to experience before. It was happening. *Now.*

"They're gone," she breathed. Did he know Uspre lived? She had to at least try to protect them.

"Who? The Uspres?" he laughed softly into her ear. "No. They're not. They're all in the basement as we speak. I don't need *them.* I have *them.*" Anger had edged its way into his tone, his face becoming an echo of a tortured soul. Those eyes....

"Zane?" The truth slammed into her fear, multiplying it with unchecked speed. In answer, he dug his fingers into her back until she cried softly, tears of pain and shock streaming down her makeup-ed face. *No! It can't be!*

"You said *them.* You said you needed—"

"I meant the children, of course. My kids."

A violent constriction grabbed at Laney's chest, and all her mind could allow her voice to do was repeat the words he had just uttered.

He captured her chin as if to savor every second of the agonizing realization as it broke through. "Urie and Ellie are more mine than yours. I'm their father, Alexandria. And I need them."

Craccckkkkk.... Rippppp.... Split.

Chapter 40

"Laney?"

Awakening again. *Again?*

"Laney, umm... Mrs. Whyte?"

No pain, no heavily medicated fog, no scattered thoughts of confusion. This awakening felt like the first awakening of man at the dawn of time. So clean, so perfect, so... *unreal.*

Laney took in a smooth, clear breath and exhaled slowly as she opened her eyes. She stood in her soft, flexible pink heels, leaning against the wall in the hallway upstairs. A tingle coursed through her body, and every nerve vibrated with it.

"Mrs. Whyte?" The voice spoke directly into her ear. "Don't panic. Oh, crap. Okay, don't worry. Um, okay, I'm looking for the others…"

"Wayne?"

The merriment of the party, still going strong, floated up from below and brought a sense of safety in numbers with it. She had no idea how this worked, how she got here. But she knew one thing.

Beyond a doubt, she had split again.

The deep pain, both of body and soul, had done its work and provided an outlet by duplicating her body out of danger. Two Alexandria Whyte's lived at once.

"Mrs…Whyte?" A confused teen spoke into her ear.

"Wayne? What's happening?"

Silence.

"Wayne?"

"I don't know... Mrs. Whyte... where's your mic? I can still hear Max speaking to you. Can he hear you speaking?"

"Wayne, check the cameras. Upstairs."

A distinct crackle followed by soft curses, and a series of rustlings followed.

"Holy sh—, oh sorry, Mrs. Whyte, but…oh, shoot, wow. Mrs. Whyte, there's two of you!"

"Yeah," she said breathlessly, her energy and clarity slowly turning into need. A need to move. A need to do something. *Now.* She had an odd sense of the other "her" and the emotional disaster that affronted that her. This Laney wouldn't go there. This Laney, palms sweating and fists clenched, set her jaw and refused to give into the terror and confusion that built like a rising tide against the vitality of her "newness," free of back pain and brain fog.

"Tell me what's going on."

"Okay, you're going to have to give me a minute, Mrs. Whyte. I can hear *both* of you... this is so trippy! I don't even know which one of you to listen to!"

"*How about the one that's freaking out?* Wayne, tell *me* what's going on!"

"Okay, okay, so Jacob and Harley moved down to the lower level to extract the bomb."

"Bomb?"

"Well, no one's giving it a name. That big canister thing? Looks like a bomb to me."

A chill flicked across Laney's skin. She started moving down the hall, rattling locked doors as she went. "Go on."

"They beat the security system down there—well, actually it was mostly me, but they're the super heroes, so whatever—and they got inside. I lost Donavan, Brian, and Tag in *underground tunnels*, can you believe it? There's this cool network of tunnels here—which is probably what is causing the integrity of the cliff to weaken, hence the evacuation protocol. *Anywhoo*...I lost communication with Harley and Jacob, too. Think they're too deep down."

She paused, processing this new intel. "Michael?" she asked.

"I can't find him. He's been off grid since he left you."

"Find him."

"I've tried—"

"Wayne. Find Michael. That's what you focus on." A sound down the corridor halted her in her tracks. Most of the doors along the passage had carved in archways barely big enough for Laney to hide in. If she flattened herself, maybe....

"Wayne," she whispered. "Everyone's distracted. How do I... what do I...?" She swallowed and exhaled. A quick peek out from the worst hiding place ever revealed she was still alone. She slunk across the hallway to the place it all broke off to a tee giving her ample room to conceal herself around the corner. It took a minute to examine this body number two.

"Wayne, this—this split happens because the real me, or the other me, is in pain. That's what I think. And then, maybe then... when she's *not* in pain any more... she becomes one again. But I think that, probably, she can also... die. I mean if there's enough pain...."

A silence told her that Wayne was doing some processing of his own.

"So... you think that's what's happening now?" he asked.

"Yeah, I'm assuming. Because I split, it means the other *Laney* could be in danger. And if... well, if the pain is too much... that would be bad for her." She nodded her head while staring at a fixed point, mentally reassuring herself that her thinking was clear. "But there is *this* me. I'm here, so that's good. So while I'm here, let's make me useful, okay?"

"There's—there's an office," Wayne spoke, his voice no more sure than hers.

"What?"

"The only room with a security camera up here is an office. Like a den? That means there should be something important there, right? Maybe...like paperwork and stuff?"

"Good, good. Yes." The fact that her super self had decided to land *this* Laney here in the hallway must be significant... right? "Which one?"

"Third one down on the right on the main hall. Next to last door. But Mrs. Whyte, someone's coming up those back stairs."

Laney wasted no more time and Scooby-dooed her way zigzag down the hall, from frame to frame on tip tops, until she reached the next to last door on the right. Locked.

"Can you get me in?"

"Do I look like Houdini? What do you expect? I can't just—oh, right, yeah, it's an electric lock."

Laney heard a satisfying click, and the knob turned under her pressure.

"I'm going in, so see if you can find Michael while I investigate. And, Wayne? Keep an eye on me. You know, the *other* me."

A pause. Then, "This is so crazy weird."

§ § § § §

Just beyond the perimeter of the yard, three men crawled below ground for a dozen yards, elbows digging into the damp soil to make their way through a narrow passage to a spot where they could stand up. They brushed the dirt off as best they could and readjusted their headlamps.

"Makes you really appreciate the green caves," Brian said with a huff.

Donavan gave a half smirk. Brian wasn't wrong; the solid dirt caverns in Arizona, old and dry, made navigation much easier than the loose soil here by the sea. Humid and sandy, it easily crumpled under the touch, not giving much in the way of confidence to the three volunteers taking this route closer to Wayne's "bomb."

Tag readjusted his ear piece. "Still no Michael?"

They took turns shaking their heads, and Brian jerked his chin toward the separated tunnel ahead. Donavan lagged behind, navigating around roots and rocks, using his light to expel a darkness thicker than the Arizonan tunnels. Underground tunnels... but no green rocks. None of it was making sense, but he went along with the best plan they had. Let Michael retrieve Laney; they would disarm the bomb or remove it.

Sound swished like a passing train before Donavan even saw men approach them. Brian's time warp had quickly captured the two gunmen, and with equal fluidity, Tag had released his zap, sending them flying backward before their guns went off. Donavan witnessed it all as a woosh and a flash. The impending attack had been too quick for Brian to pull him in the lock with him.

Brian and Tag high-fived without even making eye contact. They continued ahead, winding in a labyrinth that moved toward the house. Two more gunman suffered the same fate as the previous ones, just as a single attacker appeared from a cutout in the cave wall. Donavan had a shadow to conceal him, charged the man, wrestled the gun upward before it could go off, cracking the man squarely in jaw with the same impact of speeding bus. He fell into a heap and didn't move again.

Donavan picked up the fallen gun, emptied the magazine for good measure, and moved on. A glance and nod from his friends felt right. Truly they were Super, *Uspre,* when all of them had their powers working in unison. How could anyone get a jump on them and circumvent their defense?

That was his last thought before the floor opened up and swallowed the three men without warning.

§ § § § §

The glass in Laney's hand shook when she brought it to her lips, so she set it quickly back down on the bar. Either Max—*Zane*—did not notice or did not care. He unstopped the bottle he'd just recapped and immediately topped her off. He grabbed his own full glass and leaned over the polished marble between them to give his most cocky smile yet, set below the icy blue eyes she remembered from all those years ago.

"Cheers," he said. Flashes of the last party with her sister swirled into a potent mix of memory and emotion: shoulder to shoulder in the hunting cabin crowd, rain pounding the roof, Zane's controlling smirk...

Laney didn't reply or raise her drink, thankful that, while he stood, she had a barstool beneath her to keep her stable. The wet bar and pool table took up the whole of the small game room adjacent to the large party-filled entryway. The crowd continued dancing, drinking, and otherwise ignoring the man that had dragged her in the side room to "chat." But she was vaguely aware that the *thing* had happened. Somewhere out there a *new* her was walking around...she assumed.

"Zane," she finally breathed. "When did...I don't understand. How...?"

He only smiled, leaning so close she could smell the whiskey on his breath. "It's so uncanny...you'll just have to give me a minute."

"How are you now in Max's body?" She forced herself to ask the questions she needed to know, even though the thought of the answer scared the crap out of her. "Are you...one of us?"

He took his time memorizing her face before stepping back for another sip. Then he splayed his hands out on the bar much to his tuxedo jacket's chagrin as it hunched awkwardly around his shoulders. "It's been a long time, Laney," he said, ignoring her question. "Do you remember the last time we were together?"

She squinted hard at Max; it *was* Zane…wasn't it?

"Prove it to me," she challenged. "If you're Zane, why didn't you recognize me sooner?"

At this, his smile faltered. He looked away, downing the rest of his glass. He held the empty tumbler to examine the drops left, then set it on the bar too hard. "Crazy, right? I *am* Zane; so why can't I have the memory of Zane all the time?"

"I don't understand."

His shoulders jerked up in question. "Me either. That's the problem." He took a paper from his pocket and set it on the bar in front of her. The well-creased square, several inches wide, appeared to be the same square Hassle had had. She opened it and read a maze of scrawled description, times and dates, odd scribbles, all undecipherable except the top rows.

Zane Allen Talbott

Mason High School, Cortez, Colorado

Arie Whyte, Wife

The date after that had been scratched out and then rewritten and then scratched out again. More names and dates followed.

"What is this?"

"My cheat sheet."

"For what?"

He gave a wry smile. "So I can remember."

Instead of asking, she waited patiently for Max to pour his liquor, take a large swallow, and follow it with a tight pull of his lips before he continued on.

"Yes, I'm one of you." His voice dripped with sarcasm and weariness. "Accidentally. In fact, I'll venture to say, I'm the only accidental Uspre there is."

"Explain it to me."

"Okay, let's start with Arie. She knew looooong before you that she had the Uspre gene."

Laney sat up straight as if pulled by the arch in her eyebrows. She fought back the instant throb this caused her back. "Arie? How? What's her power?"

Max smiled and just shook his head. "She's Ariel. Being Arie is her superpower."

"You're not making sense."

"She didn't understand, either, when we ran away together. To get out. It was because of her power she felt so caged. She hadn't figured out yet that because of her power she *couldn't* get away." He leaned in to add conspiritively, "It never lets you. It traps you."

"Tell me what you're talking about! Where is my sister?"

He took a deep breath and exhaled as if the story already exhausted him. "She didn't know. The two of us were just out of here. Fleeing life, or running toward it, or whatever. And then there was the accident." He emptied his glass a second time with less of a grimace. "We crashed my bike. I don't remember how, just speeding along and then—phhhttt, light's out. Ended up in the ER." His voice had grown dark and his eyes veiled. "We took out a family in a van who veered off the road to avoid us. Such a...mess.

"I just remember seeing nurses running around me, a blur of scrubs, me not having a clue what happened, not knowing where Arie was, and seeing Chen lying there."

Emotion overwhelmed him as he stared off into a memory. "I was dying...I mean the other me..." He huffed and tried again. "We were both dying, me and Chen, the little boy on the gurney. All of us half in the hallway of some little hospital, no beds or rooms available, just spilling into the halls, all the tubes, calling codes...he was so small, and he was dying. I needed a transfusion...which was ironic since there was *so* much blood everywhere. I told them to leave me, help him. He was just a little kid... And I had done that to him."

He upturned his glass, but the tumbler clung to the moisture left, so he sighed and continued without repouring.

"I was dying. Felt the life sucking from me, but I kept telling them to save the boy, save the boy." A humorless internal laugh jerked him slightly. "Sounds heroic, doesn't it? I watched them coding him, and that's the last thing I remember...and then I woke up. I woke up Chen."

"You...woke him up?"

"I woke up as Chen."

"I don't—"

"I didn't understand either!" Max sent his glass sailing down the bar where it smashed onto the floor, causing Laney to jump in her seat. "One minute I'm Zane, the next I'm Chen! I'm watching Arie cry all over me across the hallway, like having an out-of-body experience. My parents—Chen's parents—were in bad shape from the wreck, so I was all alone, trying to figure out how to..."

Max paused before starting a new train of thought. "Then Arie let them put Zane in the body bag. I watched them wheel him away, and I was screaming, 'Hey, stop! Don't take me away!' But it came out gibberish. Took me a whole day to realize that I was speaking Mandarin."

"So...that's when you found out you were Uspre?"

He waved the idea away with a swipe of his hand as if erasing a whiteboard. "Not that easy. My parents recovered, took me home, and I lived through the hell of a grown man in a Chinese kid's body for a year...couldn't stop crying, couldn't get the hang of it all. PTSD is what they told everyone.

"The worst part about it is that I grew more and more Chen and less and less Zane. I held onto who I was with both hands as much as I could. Wrote it down." He nodded at the slip of paper in front of them. "Kept notes. Until one day I realized that Chen had something really great working for him. Intelligence. That kid was some kind of whiz. They put me into some fancy- smancy school where I was top of the class. Me. If only Arie could have seen her boyfriend as smart. But dang if they don't work you to death in those crappy, smarty schools. Started craving a way out again. Wanted away from it all, an out, but I was like ten. Where was I gonna go? Back home, to Zane's life in my new little Chinese boy body?

"So I used his brains to my advantage. Researched this transformation, this body swap from every angle—something beyond the fact that it had happened at the precise moment of both our deaths. There had to be another factor.

"I learned to hack computers and got a hold of the hospital records from that night. By that time—" He stopped abruptly, his mind again going somewhere else reflected in the distance of his gaze. "I had forgotten so much. When I opened our charts and saw a picture of Arie...I couldn't even remember her name."

His voice had softened to this confession, and it took him a minute longer to speak again. "I couldn't remember the touch of hand, the sound of her voice…literally. The longer I stayed in Chen's body, the more I became him.

"Nothing in their medical records gave me hope. So what'd I do?…I went into a spiral…smart kid like Chen knows how to get things…can't even remember what I started on that time. Speed? Adderall? Doesn't matter. Six months later and I was a drug dependent mess…again. That part of Zane sure knew how to stick around."

"So you were Zane trapped in Chen's body? How did you get out?"

"First, I needed to figure out how I got in."

"Did you?"

"Took a while, but after years of exploring my suspicions, yes, I believe I did. The transfusion."

"The one Zane got in the hospital?"

He nodded in slow affirmation as if Laney would suddenly catch on, but the connection eluded her.

"I found out who gave me the blood for the transfusion," he continued. "Arie. I had Arie's blood in my veins."

Max picked up the knife beside an uncut lime and absently began stabbing the cutting board. The action did nothing to calm Laney's frazzled nerves. Her burned back that had felt supported by the bar stool now tightened and pulsed in rhythm to her heightened blood pressure. She had a feeling this story would end badly.

"And you believe that Arie is, or was, Uspre?" Maybe if she kept him talking long enough, the men would come find her. Could Wayne still hear her?

"*IS*!" Max shouted with a deep stab of the knife to punctuate his voice. "Don't you get it? Once you're Uspre, you can't just *stop*! There's no way out." He let go of the blade stuck in the board with a wide jerk of his arms that sent his tuxedo jacket scrambling for dignity, and Laney for balance on her seat. "I am now, forever and always, one of you and can't do a dang thing about it!"

"So your power," Laney said, unable to control the tremble in her voice, "is to change? You're a shapeshifter, too? Like Hassle?"

"Too? Oh, come on, Laney. You're smarter than that. Haven't you figured it out by now? I *am* the shapeshifter."

A violent trail of goose bumps ran up her spine and spread the length of her limbs.

"I am Zane, I am Chen, I am Valentine and Hassle and Thackray and Max. I am the Uspre who is *everyone*, and the Uspre that's *no one*." A slightly off-key laugh escaped him, one even he must have known sounded crazy. He quickly wiped at his mouth to suppress it and reached for the capped bottle. "I lost myself long ago, and now I'm just this mashed up compilation of people I don't even like…but I'm stuck with." He poured his glass full and tried to add more to her already filled one. It spilled over her rim, onto the bartop, unnoticed, while he sealed the bottle back up.

"You…you have to…kill someone to take them over, though. Right?"

He shook his head then drank. "They have to die; matters not if I kill them or they die in front of me another way."

"But then you can convert back to those other people? You—you did that in the cave. You went back to being Hassle after Thackray."

"Yup. Nifty, huh?" he mocked her question.

"So why don't you just change back to Zane? You don't *have* to be anyone else."

He gulped the rest of the contents and eyed his new glass as if considering whether to send it smashing into the other one.

"Ever hear the saying, 'Timing is everything?' I died. Me. Zane, the body, not Zane the soul. And I died within moments of Chen. If I had died before the transfusion, I would have been *phhhtttt*. Had Chen not died, who knows? Maybe some other poor stiff in that crowded ER hallway would have gotten to be Zane. But I died after the transfusion, then Chen died, and lucky me, I got to be him."

The icy blues eyes clouded over, and Zane's stare turned directly into the heart of Laney. She leaned away when his words grated out, "The curse of Arie. Her blood saved me…then damned me."

"Arie. She shapeshifts?"

"Come on, Laney, she's your twin, for crying out loud! *Think.* What's the one thing Arie was *really* good at?" Laney's mouth flapped open and shut, fumbling for an answer that would appease him.

Zane smirked at her wordless groping. "Uspre she is; shapeshifter she ain't."

"Okay, okay," Laney finally managed. She'd push the Arie puzzle aside for now. "So you're Zane, and you are Uspre. You can take over people's dying body, and it makes you less and less yourself, which has got to be horrible, I'll admit. But I don't understand your involvement here, with this guy—Ozocho-what's his name? And Thackray? What are you aiming for? Why trap us or *eliminate* us? Just—just *join* us! We are all figuring out this super—super curse together!"

He huffed softly, a *you-don't-get-it* twist of the lips forming. For a moment, his agitation simmered, and he slowly removed tumblers from the shelf beneath the bar to set on top, upsidedown.

"Put the *Us* in *Uspre,* as it were." He counted the glasses and spread the group so they didn't touch one another. "What a very Laney thing to say."

His index finger danced from one glass to the next. "Your friends had a bond for quite some time, but this call—this time it was different. Brought them together without them knowing why. It even roped Donavan in for his first Uspre experience." He splayed his hand over the bottoms till his fingertips brought in the collection. Each glass became a representation of the men. "Any guesses?"

She couldn't think. The pain in her back seemed to double, and the panic in her chest wouldn't let her breathe properly.

A weak shake of her head.

"I'll give you a hint. It's green."

"The rock," her small voice answered.

He picked up the lime and placed it in the center of the glasses with a nod.

"Yes," Zane spoke in a patronizing tone, "the rock." With a clink, he pushed the glasses to gather around the citrus. He pulled out another tumbler. "You." Another. "Me." A third. "Arie." He set all three on the outskirts, like three points of a triangle around the circle. "Not called."

Laney scowled. She pushed away pain and fear to focus.

"Why?" she breathed in unison with Zane. Their gaze locked, and she found for the first time something other than bitterness. There were questions he wanted answers to, just like them.

"I came because Donavan felt me," her words fell before them. "He...he knew I belonged before I did. How did you?"

"We can't sense the rock," he explained visually by removing the lime momentarily and indicating the three glasses on the outskirts, "but it seems we have a connection to the gang itself." He shuffled their symbols closer to the group.

Laney nodded despite herself. Her bonds tied her to the men, not the green stone. "Arie?"

"I honestly don't know what she knows, but I have to assume she's more like us than them."

Laney rubbed her neck, a thought forming that Zane gave words to in a lowered tone.

"We aren't like them." He toyed with the glass that represented Arie, his head bowed over his display. "You, me, your sister. We share the same blood. And for whatever reason, it's not like them."

The explanation made her nod subconsciously. They stared at the containers in silence for several long moments, more questions moving forward from the recesses of her mind than answers.

"So," he exhaled loudly, dropping his shoulders, "what I do know is that the bond for us three is not breakable. Blood or no blood, we are all kismically *connected* even if we aren't *called.* He cupped his tumbler and moved it back and forth. "Why can't I leave?" Then he grasped the Arie glass. "And why isn't she here?"

"What do you mean you can't leave?"

"I mean I'm trapped, Laney!" His left hand slammed his glass down, and her pulse ran rampant. "This *thing*– " he ground out the words, "–inside of me! It won't let go! I can't fight it, I can't leave it, I can't *be me!*

"And what's worse is that all the nasty, dependent habits Zane have followed me, no matter who I try to become!"

Each word had led to a new crescendo, his face growing red.

"*And so,*" he clapped his hands together loudly, causing her to jerk away. Control came back gradually, and he picked up the lime again. "And so we disarm them all." A thin bar rag served as a wrap for the fruit which he dropped again, covered, into its place. Palms up, he paused for her inspection.

"The canister."

"Precisely." He tipped each cup over onto its side and let them roll haphazardly around the hidden lime. "Works as a de-powering tool for most. Not all."

Three glasses remained upright.

"Not for us."

A slow nod of agreement. "Try'd killing them all off—no luck."

"It *was* luck they survived! We—we fought our way out of those chairs—they just barely made it out of the cave."

His head began to shake. "No. Not luck. A thread." He picked up a glass from its side and held it up. "RJ." He released the tumbler and let it smash onto the floor behind the bar. "I watched him drop. I *felt* him go."

Tears pooled instantly in the corners of Laney's eyes.

Zane found her abandoned glass of liquor and sipped loudly. "I felt him go, and I can't believe no one else did. In here," he pounded his chest, his tuxedo contorting at the movement. "I watched you. I saw you on those beams and thought by the way you cried out that you had felt it too."

The moment RJ had died—she desperately wished the drugs they had given her would wipe the memory away—but there it was in a vivid frame by frame slowmotion in her mind. *Had* she felt it? Was there a thread like Zane said? All her body could recall was the heat and the pain, physical and emotional.

A huge grin now from him despite her renewed grief.

"But then something even more incredulous happened. I watched you *not* die."

Laney swallowed and wiped at her dampening cheeks.

"I know now what you are," he whispered and then drank. "You are indestructible."

If he only knew the whole of it. For now, it gave her more resolve to fight knowing that he had misunderstood her actual abilities. The other Laney would be safe for the moment.

"Indestructible? Tell that to my back," she said, finding her voice. "I can't heal myself like the others. Whatever you did to save me—"

"Quiet," he snapped. "Don't play me for a fool." The rest of the drink disappeared down his throat. "You are the only one who cannot be killed." He tapped the bundled lime. "Take the power away," then began pushing each glass off the edge with a sickening crash, "and one by one they *can* be destroyed. Then their thread gets thinner and thinner. Oddly, my body gets stronger and stronger. I believe yours does too. Their power goes—ours increases."

Laney balked a his statement.

"There is a catch." He picked up the tumbler that represented him and held it in the light. "The chair, the robots, the battle—I have a suspicion that it's not within my capability to take any of them out. That 'luck' of theirs? It defies any attempt by these hands to conquer them. You, however…"

"What are you trying to say?"

"It has to be you." He set his glass down and slid it toward hers. "You have to be the one. You kill them off, the thread breaks, I am enpowered, then we find a way, my blood sibling, to make me permanently stable.

"But I need time to figure out how you're going to lend me your power. With your guardians out of the way, it's going to make experimenting much less difficult."

A vice of horror gripped her, her hands clutching at the lip of the bar. "That doesn't make any sense. You just said a minute ago… we are alike. I *can't* kill them any more than you can!"

"Not so," he said, his hand splaying over both their tumblers. "My theory is you're the *only* one who can. And once I have my daughters back—"

A phone behind the bar rang in a couple of sharp patterned tones.

Laney's mind was reeling at the implications of his words. What did the girls hae to do with any of this?

Max picked the receiver and listened for only a few seconds and hung up without saying a word.

"It's time, darling Arie-look-alike," Calloway-Zane drawled before swiping the remaining tumblers from the bar onto the floor with the shrill splintering of glass. "Let's test this theory of mine, shall we?"

Chapter 41

How could anyone get the jump on them? had been Donavan's last thought before the ground collapsed under him. His arms and legs flailed in empty space, but only for a second before hitting a hard surface. A shower of soil and rocks followed, covering his body. After a moment of shock, he righted himself, coughing through a screen of dirt. He caught a glance of Tag and Brian in the same situation, slowly removing their soil-clad bodies from a shallow grave.

Aside from his backside, which presently was killing him, Donavan could find no other injuries. He'd wait the posterior pain out, knowing it would soon dissipate. In the meantime, he examined his surroundings between hard blinks, starting with the ceiling that had just disappointed him. Broad holes, perfectly square in design, showed that the tunnel above had come with a very clever trap door. Hinged metal doors now swung freely above his head, the perfect way to capture an Uspre.

Through the surprise, danger finally registered, and Donavan jumped up despite his hind quarter's reluctance. Several armed men trained their sights onto the three new arrivals. Before any of them could react, a henchman sent a dart sailing at Brian that hit with a *thwawt* directly into his thigh.

Brian couldn't even complete a glance down at the projectile in his leg before collapsing under the influence of whatever drug it delivered.

Tag roared, but when he took a step forward, the sound of another safety went off from their captors. Donavan weighed their options. There were three of them, only two Uspre, now disarmed.

The man behind Jacob walked to one of the six support beams that braced the room. A phone box attached itself to the wood there. The man took it off the hook and spoke a message, short and to the point.

"Sir? We got them."

No sooner had he placed the call when the door off to their right burst open with Jacob leading the charge. Bullets were exchanged, Jacob taking many that flicked off like raindrops, and when Harley flew in behind, taking out a fourth man hiding in the wings who appeared out of nowhere, the count became five Uspre to zero gunmen.

"Good news," Harley said around the cigar in his mouth. "Got my *prowess* back."

§ § § § §

Laney stumbled and cruel hands raised her back onto her feet again as pain continued its relentless course through her body.

"Where are we going?" she asked behind clenched teeth.

It was a needless question, just something to say for Wayne's sake. She should have screamed—she knew that now—should have kicked and hollered to draw attention to the madman when he'd dragged her out of the game room toward a large wooden door that could be an exit. Except it wasn't. Behind it, a series of long, dark stairs wound its way downward like some medieval dungeon entrance.

Her frantic thoughts pulled together some truths; Calloway was taking her to the lower level where Wayne had last seen the others. The plan must have been to draw them all here from the get go. She hadn't been drugged to save her from pain, but to keep her stationary. The green rock had enticed the other Uspre, and now they all had once again converged into the same location. This was a grand trap, even more reason she should bolt.

But hope wasn't lost, she told herself as she banged and tripped her way down the stairs at Calloway's rapid pace. Michael was still out there. And that was something.

And *she* was out there. Laney #2.

That last hopeful thought gave her a small amount of confidence to press on. To join Donavan below, to help him subdue Calloway—Zane—and wipe that infuriating grin from his face.

The staircase had narrowed, dark as night, save for a torch-styled lantern mounted on the wall to mimic Middle Aged lighting. Whoever had built the home had gone to great lengths to incorporate the secret paths beneath the structure. It might have been crazy cool if they weren't so outright creepy.

"It's time to put you to work," Calloway breathed, the cold glint in his eyes caught in the dim light. She spooked at the tone of his words, and when he felt for a door handle, she squirmed out of his grasp. She fled back to the stairs, only to be recaptured against his body, a gun barrel poking her in the ribs with a fresh outbreak of back pain following.

"Laney," Zane's look of insanity, etched in her memory from all those years ago, mirrored itself in Max's drunken stare. "It's in your best interest to do what I say."

Terror awakened anew. "Don't you touch my girls!"

"Oh, I won't hurt *my* girls, Alexandria. I'm not *that* crazy." He thrust the gun handle in her direction with such confidence that she flinched. "No, I have a better pawn to maneuver to win this game; let me explain how you're going to kill Uspre for me."

§ § § § §

The den, small but well decorated, remained silent in stark contrast to the party in the great hall below. The music bellowed at full volume, and in response, a hundred bodies tested the ability of the house to cling to the cliff one more night, their feet pounding out a rhythm to the music.

The Laney of the upper floor softly closed the door and waited a moment to see if anyone had heard and followed. No one appeared. She glanced over to the large desk that consumed a good portion of the space. Behind it, the entire wall contained built-in paneled wooden cabinets and filing drawers. A small lip separated the top compartments from the bottom, providing a thin shelf for a few picture frames and office supplies. Carved out in the center of the glossy wood work sat a small bar in the nook—a couple of opened bottles, several clean overturned glasses—set against the soft shine of a beveled mirror. She stood behind the desk, taking it all in, and wished she could ask Wayne for help. But she wanted him to find Michael more; she could find something here on her own, surely.

"Okay, Nick," she whispered. "Show us why we're here."

She gingerly sat in the huge leathered swivel chair and surveyed the contents of the desk. Nick Ozegov-it-whichever-his-name-was functioned as Rheinland's money source. That much she remembered from Jacob's briefing in the desert. An investor in bio matters; so probably would be interested in the green rock. So had Rheinland pulled him into the mining operation?

Laney nodded to herself in affirmation that this made the most sense. The missile-looking thing was here because Nick wanted it. The possibility also meant that Rheinland, Jacob's contact and Uspre supporter, knew more than he'd told them. And if Nick did fund the mining operation, it meant he must have hired Hassle and Thackray, too, or at least known about them.

So where was Nick? It was his house, his party, but no Nick. Not that she had seen.

While connections and questions crisscrossed through her mind, Laney opened the desk drawers and shuffled through papers. Not a single thing that told her anything; but then again she really didn't know what to look for.

The last drawer on the bottom left was locked. Ah ha. She found a letter opener and began digging around the lock like she'd seen in movies and got the lock to open in under two minutes. Feeling accomplished, she rifled through folders, convinced they would contain the intimate secrets of some grand malicious scheme. Instead, she found boring reports and employee records that meant nothing to her.

"Wayne?" she asked reluctantly. "What do you think I should be looking for?"

It took a few seconds and some static before she got a response. "Zup."

"Nothing looks important; help me out here."

"Try the laptop."

Laney stared at the device in front of her on the desk. Duh. But it came with a predictable locked screen. "Password protected."

"Okay, stand by… here we go. Try the password that unlocked the security grid: 10177101."

"Yes! I'm in—Wayne, you have got to be some kind of genius—wait. Wayne?" A slight chill made her shudder. "It's another one of those backward codes. Those numbers are my birthday. That's my birthday forward then backwards! Why does this guy have my birthday as his code?"

"Dunno. Gotta go; still listening for Michael. And Mrs. Whyte?"

"Yeah?"

"Max is taking you—the other you—downstairs, and there's no reception. Sorry, but I've lost Laney number one."

Chapter 42

"Well, I can't tell if we just got tricked or we pulled one over on them," Tag said, examining every inch of the room they were in.

"I don't like it," grumbled Jacob. "Their main goal was to disarm Brian. That's not good."

"We'll be fine," Tag scowled. "He nodded toward the canister in the corner. "Let's deal with that thing. Quickly."

Donavan and Harley pulled on the hatch that contained the green glow, but it wouldn't budge.

"Find something to pry it," Donavan suggested.

"Arm yourselves first," Jacob commanded.

There was a shuffle around the room, men securing weapons and hunting among the spare materials in the underground bunker.

A large door at the end of the room opened, and all the men took aim until they saw the arrival.

Laney walked in alone, hesitantly, as if propelled by an unseen force. Pale faced, her mask of horror could be seen in the shadows far before she moved into the light. Her hand held a pistol that she slowly raised in their direction.

"What the—"

"Laney, stop where you—"

"Whoa, whoa, whoa—"

Uspre's voices toppled over each other, Donavan taking a step forward, his weapon raised in one hand, the other out toward her as if it would block a bullet sent his way.

"I'm sorry," Laney said in a small voice. Her hand shook as she raised the weapon higher. "Please, nobody move."

"How many doors *are* there to this room?" Tag snapped, throwing his hands up in frustration.

"Two," Harley mumbled. "Count—one, two. Ain't hard."

"But the trapdoor up there—"

"Don't count. Okay, maybe that's three."

There inconsequential banter, something they were all used to, hid their actions as they separated themselves out of Laney's range, maneuvering toward her peripheral line of sight.

"No, stop!" she struggled to speak. "I have to do this. You don't understand."

"Have to do what, honey?" Donavan asked patiently. "Tell us what's going on."

She moved backward, to her right, making her way to the canister they had abandoned. She fumbled for only a few seconds before the green light shone bright, replacing its soft glow for a powerful green spotlight that arched across the room.

"Laney," Tag hissed. "Turn it off."

Jacob shot Tag a look. "Your power—"

Tag shook his head briskly.

"I have to do this," she continued. "He's making me…please…I don't know what to do…"

Max appeared from the darkness behind her, his satisfaction a stark contrast to Laney's fear.

"Good girl." Max's voice held a quality of softness that gave Donavan a wariness throughout his limbs. He gripped his weapon tighter when Max continued, "What do you think of our girl here? Huh? Is she Uspre or not? What do you think?"

"She's one of us," Jacob spoke up. "You wouldn't be interested in her if she weren't."

Max nodded. "True. But none of you figured it out in all this time. You still don't recognize what she can do, do you?"

The men were silent, eyes pinned on Laney.

"You're looking at the one indestructible Uspre. The only unkillable one of us that exists. Did you know that?"

"My gosh," Harley breathed. "You really are a madman, aren't ya?"

"The last green rock," Max continued like Harley hadn't spoken, right here in this capsule. "Calling you. And you arrived right on time."

He placed a hand on Laney's shoulder, a gesture that brought new emotion to his features. "Time's up, Laney."

"He thinks only I can kill you," Laney managed, finishing an explanation Max hadn't.

"Do it," Max said, noticeably squeezing her shoulder tighter.

Laney nodded slowly. "I'm so sorry, guys. It's just…Michael doesn't deserve any of this."

"Oh, yes," Max said with a sardonic smile, "I almost forgot." He held up his hand and through the doorway behind him two men entered, dragging a body with them, a man whose face had been bruised almost beyond recognition. They dropped him and brought him up on his knees before them, hands bound behind his back.

Michael—head bowed, shirt ripped and bloody, slumped back on his heels.

"Laney, take care of Donavan first; get the most difficult out of the way."

"Laney, don't," Donavan pleaded.

Max took a step back into the shadows. "He goes or Michael goes."

§ § § § §

Upstairs, Laney's head reeled as she opened file after file, moving from shocked to numb with each bit of intimate detail she read. She didn't know what she expected to find within the laptop. But the folders with each of the Uspre's names laughed back at her as if she had finally uncovered the cruel inside joke of it all.

The first files she uncovered had given Laney the connection they had been looking for. Documents verified that Ozegovich had funded the mine, gathered information about its contents, and lined up buyers—a group called REDLINE that may have been a government agency. She wasn't sure about that, but as she clicked through documents, the initials LR caught her eye several times. Leon Rheinland? A sick twist of her stomach hit, but she moved on as rapidly as she could.

That's when she'd discovered the Uspre files.

Each file contained detailed docs of their past. Not just high school and grade school easily-researched information, but specific classes they had taken, essays they'd written, names of hangouts they'd frequented with friends, parents' backgrounds, pet names, military records, even faces of neighbors and friends long ago forgotten. Medical records, separate candid photos of all of them at random locations, personal preferences, and allergies...the data went on and on. She found charts and spreadsheets that went into mathematical equations. Though never mathematically inclined, it seemed to her the charts sought variables, common points. Whoever had gathered this information had been reaching for a tie between them all.

Laney lingered over Tag's file for a little longer than the rest. It contained the tragic story he had kept so tightly to himself.

Tag had been in a relationship. Laney swallowed as she read into the pain. Love—he had been the only one of them who had been attached to someone else, it seemed, within the last five years, save Donavan who had only just discovered his powers. Tag had been engaged to a beautiful, brown-haired girl for five months. Preus Bisset. And then her life had ended in a boating accident. Another boat had been spotted leaving the scene, the police report read, but never found.

You of all people should understand, Thackray had told Tag in the cave. Having someone close to you when you sought a secret life became a liability. It had been what Tag had been trying to tell her that night by the fire.

Without meaning to, Laney's mind drifted to that night, to the conversation. She was sure now that it had been the first moment she had doubled. The other her in pain, lying on the hard floor of a half-built house under the medication of only aspirin, had split allowing her that moment with Tag. And again when she had been in emotional pain with RJ she had doubled to contemplate flying off the wall of the house. Pain was the trigger, to be sure. In each instance, it seemed like the other *her* could stay in its place or vanish or merge.

Sweat beaded on her brow as she tried to solve out the question of what became of the other her. Now, with both Laney in dire straits, it seemed like a good time to know.

Voices in the hall jarred her back to reality. She froze and waited till they passed, then squinted at some numbers typed at the bottom of the fact sheet next to the word "ring."

Giggles in the hallway from a bunch of women who likely felt naughty to explore the section of the house closed off from the party. She had to think, and fast, before someone discovered her in here.

Some numbers were sectioned off by hyphens, three sets of double digits. A combination?

Laney glanced back at the desk, the drawers, and a filing cabinet. All had standard locks.

Maybe the numbers were nothing. But all of this gathered information was creepy and invasive. There had to be more than just data that Nick or Max wanted.

She swiveled in her chair to look at the bar and woodwork behind her. She opened each drawer along the middle, each unlocked and filled with junk, mostly. Some were empty. No rings. No combo locks.

Next she opened every cabinet under the drawers. More files and files, and *hello*...a safe. Laney cracked her knuckles and entered the combo. The safe made a satisfying click, and the door swung open.

She inhaled sharply and began to sweat all over.

"Mrs. Whyte?"

"Wayne, please. Don't you think we are past the formality now? Call me Laney."

"Yeah, well, Laney, we got some goons coming up the stairs."

"I just cracked open a safe."

A pause. "*Cool.* So? What's in there? Gold? Jewels? Plans to rule the world?"

Laney slowly opened the door trying to quelch an irrational fear creeping up on her. "Some more files. And a cloth bag of some sort."

"Diamonds!"

"No, some miscellaneous stuff...a watch, a medal...a ring..." Laney's voice trailed off as a lump dominated her vocal cords. "Wayne...this is stuff that belonged to us."

"Ummm...weird. Like this guy's been stalking you? Oh, shoot, Mrs.—er, Laney—time to go. They're checking all the doors."

Laney set the bag in her lap and almost closed the safe when the lettering atop a file caught her attention.

ARIEL.

Heart hammering, Laney grabbed the file and glanced at the fact sheet on top. There was a picture of Arie that Laney had never seen, a face that had aged like hers, no longer a teenager, proof that she lived, that she was out there.

"Wayne—" she breathed.

"Laney, get out now! Dang, I think it's too late. They turned down your wing."

"My sister—wait, it's her birthday date. Wayne, the security code."

"What?"

"The code. It's my birthday, but it's also *hers*."

"Okayyyy…"

"This guy knows her. He knows my sister! We need to find this Nick guy!"

"You won't be finding anything if you don't get out of there. You need an exit plan, *now*."

Laney grabbed all the papers out of the file, folded them into a thick sandwich, and shoved them down the top of the tight dress without much success. They wrinkled and jammed, sticking out the top like a broken origami crane. She ignored them and turned toward one of the junk drawers where she'd seen a flashdrive, found it, and shoved it into the laptop. All the folders were in a larger folder of their own, so she hit copy and waited for them to load while she looked around the room for options. A door and two windows. Some small vents. Not much.

The door handle rattled, and Laney bit back an exclamation. The file, still loading. She ran around the desk and grabbed one of the chairs facing her. She jammed it up under the door handle snuggly just as she watched it give.

Running back to the desk, Laney checked the download. Done. She snatched the thumb drive and dumped it into the cloth bag with the rest of the small contents. The sack came with a delicate drawstring cord that she tightened and looped around her wrist.

The door shook.

"Laney—" the voice in her ear warned.

"I'm working on it," she hissed back.

Laney pulled open the window's long drapes. Outside a considerable drop. Of course.

Laney looked left and right. Nothing. Then up. A ledge. Not really a ledge. More like a lip. But within reach. It could work.

"We need a distraction," Wayne suggested.

"Good idea. Oh—I got it!"

Laney ran around to the bar and grabbed a bottle of liquor. She apologized ahead of time for the expensive accelerator it would become and began making a trail from the curtains to the door to the vents while she told Wayne her plan.

"Uh, Mrs. Whyte? That's not the kind of—"

"Got a better idea?"

"I think you're overestimating the strength of that chair."

"It'll hold."

Laney scrambled back inside and tossed every loose paper she could gather from the room and doused it with more alcohol, resisting the urge to throw one back for good measure. The door burst open, finally betrayed by her only friend, the chair, allowing two large men to charge forward. From a humidor on the bar, Laney grabbed a set of matches.

She made it across the room to the window as she simultaneously struck a match and let it drop.

The room set ablaze, Laney pushed back to her new best friend, the open window behind her. Both men stopped in their tracks and called out to others. The fire fought for a hold after the initial liquid burned off, but the curtains on the furthest window, wispy sheers alongside denser fabric, burst brightly up the wall, setting the alarm off in a loud get-out wail throughout the entire house.

Chapter 43

"Pull the trigger, Laney."

Laney stood frozen, for what, three, four seconds? It felt like a lifetime, looking from face to face, trying to plead forgiveness with her eyes. Donavan tried to answer back with his.

"You have until the count of three to put a bullet in Donavan, or I have my man take out Michael."

The darkly clothed man that had dragged in Michael clicked the safety off his gun and aimed it at Donavan's best friend, just a regular good guy who had unwittingly stepped into this crazy man's drama.

Laney tried to steady the gun. "I am so sorry," she repeated as the men yelled again.

She pulled the trigger.

Her aim went right, past Donavan, into Jacob.

Jacob took the shot in his shoulder and collapsed. Laney cried out, letting the gun fall with her to the floor.

Max moved in behind her and roughly pushed her down toward the weapon.

"Pick it up." Max's nod toward the gunman could have been nothing more than a flick, but without a word his gunman accepted the sign and shot Michael in the back.

Donavan's partner fell like a dead weight to the ground, the blood pooling quickly around him.

The men all shouted at once—Harley collecting Jacob off the floor, Tag keeping Donavan from charging Laney. She was on her feet again, gun in hand, Max's hand firmly entangled in the back of her hair, keeping her erect. He had pulled her several feet, away from the mess he had created, into the shadows. The tears that flooded from her eyes illuminated her cheeks, her mouth gaping in a noiseless cry.

"Well, we discovered two things, didn't we," hissed Max from his cover behind Laney. "That you *don't* have your powers at the moment—the canister *works*.

"And secondly, we learned *I'm not bluffing*." The voice of Max rose to an ugly pitch. "Laney, take them out or Michael isn't the last casualty. And I will go after Parker and Nellie, so help me! And don't get cute. Anything happens to me and Donavan's family is toast."

Donavan froze and searched Laney's eyes for answers in the dim lighting. She stared helplessly back, silent tears still streaking her face. His gaze fell on his fallen comrade, lifeless in front of him.

"Alright, alright," Donavan said, shrugging off Tag. "Okay, Max, you win. *You win*. Let her go, stop hurting her."

Max stayed put, but he didn't argue back.

"Guys, hands up. Let's do this," Donavan pleaded with his band of comrades. The other men warily complied. "Now let her go, Max. We won't resist. We give up."

§ § § § §

Laney stumbled forward when Max released her with a shove. Zane/Max himself remained back in the shadows.

"There is no surrender, Donavan. There is just elimination. Laney, I'm losing patience. Donavan first."

"Jacob," Laney said weakly, her heart constricting as if it had taken the bullet itself, "You understand—"

Jacob nodded and held up a hand from his uninjured arm. "Yes, I know. It's okay, Laney. It was a good way to test our powers."

Laney swallowed in relief that the straw she grasped at had been understood. If Max was wrong about any of this, then Jacob would have been able to withstand a bullet. She noticed he wasn't healing now either.

They were powerless. All of them.

Except her.

"I want you all to know…how very sorry I am—"

"Five…four…" The voice from the shadows began the countdown.

"Look, we all know you're not bluffing," she spit back at Max. She had angled herself now so that she could turn her head left to see him in the darkness while the men were more to her right. "Everyone is cooperating. But you are going to let me say goodbye, for God's sake. You at least owe me that, *Zane*!"

A tense silence followed.

Laney held the gun out in a steady, two-handed motion, directly at Donavan. He had separated himself slightly from the others, and she used this to her advantage.

"I loved you," she said simply. Her body rocked as she shifted her weight from side to side in what she hoped looked like anxiety. "And you trusted me. You all did. You believed in me. And I'm asking you to believe in me just a little more." Her swaying was leading her further back and to her left and as if by some unsaid suggestion, the men shifted their bodies slightly left to, the complete circle now rotated a fraction around the fallen figure of Michael. Every inch would bring her closer to the canister.

Laney nodded, tears still plentiful as she spoke. "He's right. What Max said is true. I can't die."

Donavan's eyes narrowed at her. "What are you saying?"

"I'm saying I'm indestructible." She turned the pistol then and pointed it into her stomach.

An outcry from the men filled the stone-walled basement, the sound echoing within the chamber.

"Laney," Max warned.

She wasn't going down without a fight. Her mind had been wrapping itself around every scenario she could think of to get them out of this mess, and it came down to this.

Donavan moved toward her, but Max barked from the shadows, "Not another step, Peterson!" that stopped him in his tracks.

"Don't bring him closer," Laney warned, still moving to her left in her rocking motion as she spoke. "Not close to Michael. He's staying away because he doesn't want to possess yet another victim, isn't that right, *Zane*?"

"You're going to regret—"

"What?" shouted Laney. "Isn't this what you wanted? You want to see if there's a way you can possess a permanent, imperishable body, right?"

"I know what you are," he countered in a dark quiet voice from the depths of the back of the room. "But you need to off them *now*."

She lifted her elbow high, chin jutted defiantly, sidling more and more to her right as Max called out the order to his men.

A sudden blaring alarm drowned out Max's voice, with a shrill so loud it seemed to shake the house on its foundations. The men flinched, but Laney didn't lose the opportunity to dive straight at the kill switch on the canister before one of the henchman fired in her direction.

§ § § § §

The flames upstairs ringed the small den, aiming for the curtains and furniture fabric with their greedy fingers. Men charging into the room gave pause, but Laney didn't wait to see how brave they would be.

She climbed out onto the windowsill, slim and unwelcoming. She arched her body outward while clinging to the open window in an underhanded grip. The wriggling action did nothing to keep her tight dress in place or make her back feel any comfort. Before she realized what had happened, the papers trapped in her bodice worked themselves free and spread their wings like an uncaged bird.

Laney cried out as some documents landed back into the room, and others scattered into the wind. One hand desperately grabbed at the fluttering chaos and managed to hold on to several which almost cost her her second life. She clung to the window again, the cloth bag dangling from one arm, the other hand trapping a wad of two or three papers as it gripped the sill.

The men had found their courage and moved toward the window with a shout.

There was no more time to think.

Cramming the remaining papers into her mouth, she bit hard and let go with both hands giving herself enough room to launch off the sill upward. Fingers dug into the ledge above and from that moment on it was a mental exercise as much as physical. From the travel of voices, the grassy slope below must be filling up with evacuating guests now. A cooling mist hit her legs, indicating the sprinkler system had been activated inside the house.

She ignored all else but reaching the roof. Set in competition mode, she focused on nothing more than not falling—a determination to win propelled her just as much as fear.

Swinging by just the grips of her hands, she landed a foot up on the ledge, and Laney swung the rest of herself with more ease than she imagined. Unlike the windowsill, this ledge provided room and stability to allow a moment of examination of the eaves above. Gutters and drain pipes provided possible hand grips.

"There she is!" she heard a man call above the growing din. Taking only a moment to remove the papers from her mouth and shove them deep into her bodice again, Laney hiked up her skirt as far as it would go and used every hand and foot hold available to start climbing up the wall toward the roofing. It gave her a small reassurance to know that if she fell, she wouldn't *die.* But the fact that two of her already existed and the second her was probably in peril at the moment, she wasn't sure *this her* should use death as a security net.

So she climbed and didn't look back.

The rooftop offered a moment to regain her breath. Another shout behind her and she was off, running up the small peak of this portion of the house, bare feet clinging to tile with agility that denied the fact she clambered some thirty feet off the ground.

The small peak merged with a larger portion of the house, another climb that would test her rusty skills and restrictive clothing. She almost turned to evaluate the position of the pursuant voices when the first shot rang out and zinged off the tile to her right.

Laney charged the new peak with all the speed the distance would allow her to gain; with a surge of adrenaline, she made the rooftop and began running the ridge like a clumsy balance beam when the second and third shots flew by, the third shot pinging off a tile just ahead of her feet.

She didn't stop.

Scared but focused, she charged ahead, not knowing if the fire she set had provided a distraction or destruction for Uspre, or what the fate of her other self had come to. Would she somehow know if the other Laney perished? She had no time to contemplate the paradoxical implications of her powers.

More shouts told her they were closing in on the roof now, more shouts below. Trails of smoke began to wisp their way around her legs and then disappear into the growing twilight.

Ahead, a glorious seascape peeked over the treetops, the sun starting its descent as it dared her to follow.

Laney never broke stride. She sprinted straight off the roof toward the shadowy trapeze of branches in a great tree that could hold her if she could make it—when the fourth and final bullet left its chamber and found a solid mark.

Chapter 44

The large silver capsule died with a whine, taking its powerful radiance with it. In its place, the placid soft green glowed once again.

The alarm blared in an urgent chorus, adding chaos to the moments that followed.

The gunmen, off guard, faced men who had their supernatural skill back, and were caught up in a whirlwind of Harley's fast fists in a frenzied dance around the motionless body of Michael. One last man fired a bullet from yards away, only to find it intercepted by Jacob's body. Jacob took the impact and kept coming despite his bloody shoulder. He disarmed this last gunman and cracked him across the skull. The man fell, and Jacob dropped the gun with decisive rage.

Tag had eyes for only Max, however, crossing the distance that separated them, throwing himself at the lunatic with a growl.

Max saw him coming and bolted. With the slam of some unseen lever, a trapdoor that mirrored the one in the ceiling opened wide on the floor, and Max fell out of sight. Gone.

Without hesitation, Tag dove headlong after him, just making it through a second before the door snapped shut with a loud clang.

"Four doors?" Harley yelled. "Whoever heard of a room with so many dang exits—"

Brian groaned, distracting Harley; Jacob raced to find the lever and activate the door again. Nothing happened. "It must be locked from the other side."

Donavan dropped beside Laney, a rag doll lying next to the power switch of the capsule. The blood that surrounded her confirmed that, despite his prayers, she'd been hit. Her eyes glazed over and Donavan panicked, scooping her head into his hands. Indestructible? Is that what she had really believed?

Brian, revived and somewhat stable, joined Jacob at the trapdoor. Harley located a rusty screwdriver to help try to find a way to pry it open.

A new alarm, coming from the capsule, entered into the confusion. The loud beep came and went, followed close behind by another. Then another.

Brian's head snapped back to glare at the canister. Stumbling over to lean on the long metal tube, he pried with the tool into the face of the glowing compartment.

"Well, guess we weren't wrong about the bomb part," Brian slurred. "Looks like we got ourselves a full minute before this thing blows." Jacob leaned in to examine what Brian pointed out.

Laney moaned, and Donavan pulled her toward him, clearing the messy tangles that escaped her updo from the whitening frame of her face. "Max told me…if I didn't…what he'd do…"

"Shh," he reassured her, his own heart electrified at her touch in that bittersweet shockwave only she could render in him. He held her tight and let the power surge through him, ignoring the terror of her condition that loomed over him. "Don't worry. We'll get you out of here."

"No," she smiled weakly. "You won't…but it's okay. You trust me?"

"Yes, of course." His voice shook and he swallowed hard to keep himself steady.

"Then let me go," she said, and squeezed his hand. "It's okay…I can't die."

He gritted his teeth, trying not to scream over the nonsense Max had convinced her of, holding his disbelief in silence.

As if by some cosmic cue, smoke began to seep from under the large wooden doors at both ends of the room, adding urgency to the pinging canister timer and blaring alarm.

"We got about fifty seconds, folks," Jacob said, his voice confident in command again. "Let's get going. Brian, Harley—" He jerked his head toward Michael with tight lips.

Harley nodded and made his way to Michael's motionless body. Brian hesitated a moment, seemingly torn between loyalty to Tag, his need to disarm the mass weapon, and duty to the fallen.

"Go," Laney said, and her voice faded into a wispy breath. "I'm okay…you'll see."

"Laney!" Donavan shouted, but the light had left her eyes and energy drained from his body as if someone had pulled his plug. "No!" he shouted, but Jacob pulled him roughly to his feet.

"Pete—Donavan, we have to go."

"He's alive!" Harley called out. Through the thickening smoke, Donavan watched Harley hull the body of Michael to an upright position. Jacob hurried to his side and pointed to a door barely visible now. He motioned to Brian to join him.

"I'm not leaving without Tag," Brian said, choking slightly in the contaminated air. "I got this, just go."

"Brian—" Jacob said with a warning in his voice.

"I'll handle it! If things get too hot in here, I got time on my side." His broad grin reflected he'd returned to his normal self, and he continued working with nimble fingers.

Harley shoved against the closed wooden door. "Uh, Donavan. Little help here." Harley's survey of Laney's slack body turned to a look of pity that added no comfort to Donavan's breaking heart.

Reluctantly, he took Harley's place at the door and began to ram it with his shoulder. Despite Jacob's returning powers, the gunshot wound had its effect, and he motioned for Harley to help him get up. Donavan's heart stirred to hear the groans of life coming from the noodle-like frame of his oldest friend.

"Hang in there, buddy," he called out. The door gave way and the three men pressed Donavan up the staircase into clean air.

They stumbled into the game room annex, getting their bearings, before Donavan turned back.

"Wait, Pete—"

"I'm going back, Jacob," Donavan said. "I can't leave her there—"

"There's no time." Donavan tried to push past, but his leader blocked him. "She's with Brian, Donavan. If anyone could save her, it's him. But if we don't go now..." Jacob's voice trailed off. His hand dropped off Donavan's shoulder, allowing the decision to hang between them. Face grim, Jacob took the other side of Michael, and Harley led them through the abandoned party room, already filling with ghostly fingers of smoke.

Donavan headed back down the stairwell until he reached the billowing cloud around the chamber's door. He called out to Brian but got no answer. He coughed and pulled the neck of his shirt to cover his face, but it was no use. Somehow the smoke had traveled by vent or tunnels to grow thicker here than upstairs.

His heart cried out as his feet retreated backward, one more glance within the room. Was it just the smoke, or was Laney's body no longer there?

Chapter 45

Amid white oleander bushes, bark chips, and a brisk chill, sparkling laughter filled the air unlike any that the woman in a deep pink jacket could remember. Perhaps the sound of it had always been the same and the newness of the day just purified it. The autumn morning warmed slowly to the rising sun, giving added dimension to the reassuring sounds of the children at play.

Or, then again, it could just be new ears heard it.

Laney took another bite of her pear, letting the juice drip from its skin to her lips. She wiped at the moisture with the back of the same hand, keeping her other hand cozy warm inside the pocket of the fuzzy fleece.

A second hand pushed its way into her pocket and intertwined its fingers with hers. It withdrew the captured hand and together, they hung by her side. She couldn't stop her heart from racing with Donavan so close, shoulder to shoulder, snuggly gripping her hand. Her cheeks colored to complement her jacket.

She couldn't help the smile as she chewed, but she kept her eyes directed ahead, watching the older woman on the far side of the jungle-gym brush dirt off a whiney, curly-haired girl and send her on her way. Nellie tipped her head Laney's way with the slightest nod and faintest smile. She crossed her arms again and continued to play sentinel to three children mixing into a throng of other careless, laughing kids.

"Any word?" Laney turned to Donavan in query. Her presence no longer bothered him, he said, the children once more acting as a buffer to the energy flow Laney supplied him. Whether Laney's powers were dampered or not with the kids around was still a mystery, one they weren't willing to put to the test any time soon.

"Brian and Tag?" she asked.

The pleasure in Donavan's eyes slipped to the hidden depths he so closely guarded. "No. Not yet. Calloway hasn't surfaced either." She looked away, but he caressed her fingers. "Maybe that's a good sign. It would be really hard to get one up on Brian and Tag when they are together."

"And we're sure—"

"No bodies were found," Donavan said with a confident edge in his voice. "Every indication is that Brian found his way into the trapdoor—it had been pried open. They'll be hot on Max's trail, and they won't let go until they find something."

She nodded and prayed he was right.

"And Michael?"

"Recovering. Was awake most of the day yesterday. He asked about you today."

"Really?" She had visited his bedside several times, but he'd always been under heavy sedation.

"Actually he asked if the new Laney was every bit as in love with him as the old one."

With that, she laughed, echoing the carefree sound in the children's noise around them, and Donavan's eyes returned to warm contentment. It was good to have her power now out in the open, a provable fact the others had seen. The Laney of the basement had faded from existence.

He said, "I reassured him that there was definitely a new love in your life, and it wasn't him."

Laney glowed in the intimacy of the remark, but tried to redirect the conversation to all the unanswered questions. The days after Ozegovich's party whirlwinded with activity while the police investigated the fire-scorched house. Jacob and Harley did their own investigation in the aftermath of the fire department's nightlong vigil to discover what they could about the disappearance of their friends. Not long following, the entire house collapsed from the eroded coast and water-soaked ground. The media concentrated on the sensational facts of a clandestine party that ended with an ironically epic end-of-the-world-like destruction. Beyond that, speculation of the owner's whereabouts or the origin of the fire carried little interest. The mention of the large missile-shaped canister never surfaced.

Laney, however, managed to get her first TV debut as a camera caught an unidentified woman sprinting across the rooftop, features too difficult to make out in the twilight. The video couldn't capture the bullet that ripped past her in her last leap of hope, lodging itself harmlessly in the tree branch she managed to snag and use to swing to safety.

"Harley?"

"Still with Jacob. They're working on locating the others." She knew without a doubt that that is where Donavan longed to be—

out there, searching for the lost men. But he had taken Jacob's advice and stayed with his family…and Laney.

"Have you talked to Wayne?"

A chuckle. "Turns out he wants to take credit for disabling the bomb before Brian did. He apparently had been working on it remotely same time as Brian."

She was sorry for the boy's sake that they had not unveiled the mysterious Señor Epus's identity…yet.

As if reading her thoughts, Donavan continued. "He's giving those files you copied onto the drive a good, thorough look-over. He hopes his answer is buried there with our data."

"Do you think...is it possible that Zane knows Rheinland? Because maybe Rheinland knows about Señor Epus, and about where Arie is."

Her voice trailed away at Donavan's sympathetic frown; she immediately regretted bringing up the subject. But Zane had said Arie was Uspre! She needed to know how Arie had known before her and what power Arie possessed. *Being Arie* is her power, Zane had said. What did that mean?

"We need to find Rheinland and ask him," she answered her own question, repeating the response Donavan had given her when they had discussed at length that her teenage acquaintance, Zane, had become the original shapeshifter. She had told him about the bag of trinkets she had found in the safe and the few papers she had salvaged, but for now they remained under her bed, awaiting the time the group could all examine the items together and make any sense out of them. It didn't stop her from bringing the papers out nightly and examining every word, every letter, wishing that the vague phrasings would provide a clue to her twin sister's whereabouts.

"Jacob will work on that, too, but Brian and Tag come first."

"Yes, of course." Laney took another deep bite into her pear, mid-nod. So much of what they didn't know centered around the man she had never met, the elusive Leon Rheinland who had brought the others together. Their genetic similarity, shared impulses, and their bizarre connection to the green rock—all created more questions now than when their adventure had begun. Nick and Max, two key players in the founding of the mines were both at large with Max now a muddle of personalities to deal with. Rheinland seemed to be their best shot at getting any answers since he was their direct link to Nick Ozegovich.

"With the green rock gone, it may be a little easier to find some unmanipulated answers to who we are," she continued as she wiped her mouth again, leaving a sweet trail of juice behind. Whoever understood the mechanism to build another canister, like Zane infused with Thackray and Hassle, only needed another green rock to once again "call" the men together and depower them. Without that exploitation, their fate seemed to be more firmly in their own grasp.

Who we are. Besides her urgency in finding her sister, unraveling the mystery of their powers was a priority that she hoped they all shared. Right now the others focused on what Rheinland had intended by sending them on a "death mission," and she couldn't blame them. Though they now knew her to be Uspre, she hadn't shared the differences in her genetic makeup that Zane revealed. It seemed more devisive than helpful right now.

She took another bite and grew silent in contemplation.

§ § § § §

Donavan removed his hand from Laney's and pulled his eyes away from the tantalizing gloss of her fruit-tainted lips. The wind carried a slight chill that gave him reason to thrust his hand back into his own jacket for warmth.

His pocketed hand came into contact with a secret object nestled there. His fingers passed over its smooth cool surface, turning it over and over till it warmed to his touch.

He had meant to reveal it to her today; did it have to be today? He couldn't remember anymore why he hesitated. They had barely let each other out of sight in the week that had passed, not allowing themselves to be alone without the children, the electricity coming on so strong for him then. But had he made the effort, he could have talked to her in private before now.

Perhaps at the playground was a bad idea. Or maybe it was the perfect time. He doubted himself a dozen times over and wished he hadn't brought it with him at all. He truly had no idea how she would react so soon after all this mess.

"There's nothing left for us to worry about," Laney finally spoke again. "The mines are buried, the canister destroyed...we are rock free. So no overprotective robots to attack us." She took a deep breath and released it slowly through her peared lips. "Ground zero. At least something to work with, right?"

She gave him a hopeful smile, and Donavan's pocket turned to lead. If they kept looking into the thread of their DNA and the Landon Biometrics connection, they might find answers to their origin; that seemed to be what Laney banked on. But he couldn't help wonder at the "mystery" part of their makeup, the one that led them to the door with an inscription that matched a tatoo, the one that called them together without words. To him, the mines were the starting point of how their abilities converged with their mysteries.

But no matter what, he needed Laney beside him, on the same page. He took a deep breath of his own and decided to put an end to his torture.

"Laney?"

"Hmm?"

"I've been thinking..."

She took another bite of the enviable pear. "Bout waa?" she asked with her mouth full. "Wan' some?" She held the fruit up to share, and at that moment, he was sure Eve couldn't have been more enticing.

"I—" He changed his course of thought, picking up the thread she had dropped. "Don't you wonder what the rock was? Is? Think of the amount of time and effort it took to extract it, to create giant mechanical creatures to mine it and protect it. And then to end up targeting Uspre instead? Don't you wish we could have a chance to go back—"

His words faded away when a familiar car rolled into one of the parking lots. Laney stiffened, but her plastic smile tried to hide it. Donavan emptied his hand and pulled it from his jacket to casually drape an arm across her shoulders. Her smile turned real, and he felt her relax. She didn't have to face Charlie and Victoria alone this time, and if he had his way, ever again.

"Are you sure this is what you want?" he asked.

"Yes." She even managed to sound pretty confident. "Yes. It's only for a few days."

Despite only having the girls for less than a week since the ordeal, Charlie had agreed to take the girls again for a few days out of the normal rotation. Laney wanted a chance to attend RJ's memorial service and additional time with the men in mourning without involving the children.

Charlie had also consented to let her take the girls to their grandparents for a week or two, as long as she could squeeze in a leave of absence from school. Laney convinced Donavan there were questions she needed to ask of her father, starting with how he'd come to own the non-commercial phone he had issued her. Twice she had tried to call her parents about this and about Arie, but told Donavan she'd lost her nerve each time. It had been Donavan's idea that she make the trip, to give herself time away, and to encourage her parents to talk about what they knew in person. Laney admitted that she wasn't eager to stay in the apartment anyway, not since the random doors opening and missing gun in the weeks leading up to their desert escapade—more unsolved riddles.

But how could he let her travel out of his sight so soon? Would it be as difficult for her to leave him?

Today might answer that for him. His mind traveled to the unguarded object in his pocket as Charlie approached.

Laney's ex had come alone, passing a cool Nellie on the way across the playground. That woman was a force to be reckoned with, and Charlie knew it. He withdrew his sunglasses with the overcast sky rendering them useless. The girls waved hi but made no attempt to run to him as they continued their game of tag with Parker and other neighborhood kids.

"Hi, there," Charlie spoke first. "Nice playground. What made you decide to switch up our meeting spot?"

"Things change," Laney said lightly, broadening Donavan's grin. She ditched her pear core into the nearest can. "Where's Victoria?"

"Tori's still feeling a little morning sickness." From the girls' report, their step-mom had spent a large amount of time in bed on their glorious Hawaiian vacation.

"Well, tell her I said hello and to hang in there. I hear the second trimester is much easier. Not that I would know." She glanced at her adopted daughters at play without the least bit of guile in her remark. "And thanks for doing this."

"No problem." He gave a tight pull of the lips and nodded at Donavan for the first time. He stuck out his hand, and Donavan removed his arm from Laney to shake it firmly. Word of their relationship had filtered its way to Charlie before today.

"Things do change," Charlie echoed.

"Let's make it for the best." Laney used a light, breezy tone. "We can renegotiate drop-offs and pick-ups if you like, and I'll be more flexible about time. I think having the girls in Hawaii was great for them."

Donavan stifled a laugh. *Great for them: translation – saved them from a demented mad man, kept you busy on your honeymoon, gave Laney leverage for her own vacation with the girls.*

"Sure," Charlie rubbed his chin and nodded, trying to hide a building fidget. "Just want to make sure…I mean I haven't heard much about you in the news lately," he directed at Donavan. "What's the situation with your job?"

Donavan let his trademark calm keep his expression in check. "The investigation is closed; I should be re-instated soon." How could he explain that his nemesis, Valentine, had simply vanished from his cell? The station struggled to do the same and hoped to bury the whole ordeal.

A vigorous nod. "Good, good. We all knew—" he started lamely with an erratic hand gesture. "Just wanted to make sure—for the kids' sake—"

Laney saved him from further blundering by calling to the girls to gather their backpacks and give hugs and kisses goodbye before going with Daddy. She held each girl's face in her hands for long seconds as if memorizing each detail before she said, "Remember, I love you *very* much," and released them to run toward Charlie's car.

Charlie seemed reluctant to join them, finally working up the courage to ask, "So what's your plan?"

"My plan?" Laney asked. Donavan returned his protective arm to her shoulders. "Oh, *our* plan." She smiled up at him, so close by her side, a fresh youthful blush making her skin glow. "Take each day as it comes, I guess."

Donavan could feel the weight of his pocket sagging against him in answer, but he said nothing.

The Whyte girls piled into the car with their father and waved as they drove off.

"You were great." Donavan pulled Laney to face him, his arm sliding to her waist. "Well done."

"It's hard to resent him anymore," she said softly, allowing an escaped curl to catch in the breeze and brush against her tempting mouth. "He kept my girls safe. They were far from this horrible train wreck we got ourselves into. If they hadn't…if Urie or Ella or Parker had gotten hurt…or Nellie! I can't imagine what I'd've done—"

He held her tighter, silencing her with his forehead coming to rest on hers. "A ton of *what ifs*. None of them transpired. We're here. All of us." Her face fell ever so slightly. "All but RJ, I know."

"He died protecting me."

"Any one of us would have done that to protect another."

"You would die for me?" she whispered, her eyes closed. It was all the encouragement he needed to lower his head and kiss all the pear sweetness from her lips.

When he spoke, he hadn't moved more than a few inches from her de-glossed mouth. "I plan on doing a lot of living with you right now, but yes, I would die for you over and over and over again, if I had your power to do so, you little enchantress."

She nuzzled into his chest and stayed there until the wind nipped with icy bites and drove a cold and lonely boy to them.

Laney broke away and smiled fondly down at Parker.

"I should go," she said, the air teasing more curls from their pinning.

Donavan came back to his senses and reached into his jacket.

"But you're going to pick me up for the service tomorrow, right?" she added. "And Harley and Jacob will be there, won't they?"

He answered, "Yes, of course. We'll all be together."

Nellie walked toward them, holding up Parker's abandoned sweatshirt.

"Okay, tomorrow then," Laney said, and blew him a kiss before turning to go.

His hand sunk deep into his pocket and remained.

"Come here, partner," Nellie's gravelly voice barked at her grandson. Then to Donavan, "Let me drive him home, son." The boy in question lit up at the prospect.

"Please, Dad? She plays the good music."

The offer surprised Donavan, but one look at Nellie told him she understood the emotions Laney created within him. Astute woman, his mother. Maybe he'd have enough time to catch Laney before she left.

"Yes, okay, thanks, Mom." He planted a light peck on her cheek, rubbed his son's bouncing head, and watched them hurry off the playground to a parking lot opposite to the one Laney headed toward.

He took a couple steps in the direction of the woman who had stolen his heart and built him into a new man in the wake of Kelly's desertion. But his feet betrayed the rest of him, and he froze in the middle of the grass, the laughter of the other children taunting him from the jungle gym behind.

"Chicken," he scolded himself and drew his hand from its cocoon to stare at the rock warmed to a soft glow in his touch. The layers of marbled green glistened and captivated in the same way they had when he held the first one in the rock yard all those weeks ago. This one, about half the size of his palm, was smooth on one side, as if it had been sliced or polished, while the opposite side remained in its jagged, natural state.

This was the last of them, as far as he knew. The only salvageable green rock left. It held the key to their existence, he was sure. Unlike Laney, he didn't believe it complicated things with some manipulation of Uspre's personalities; he believed it would direct them to the source of their power, to knowledge of why Uspre existed, even without the canister.

He just needed to convince Laney of the same thing. *And* not frighten her away in the process.

Not today, he decided. The cold air filled his lungs, invigorated him, gave him assurance he wasn't wrong. With his collar pulled up to protect him from the dropping temperatures, he turned and walked to his car, shoving the potent rock back into hiding.

Acknowledgments

This work did not come into being without the help and support of many others:

To the other four members of the Fab Five who spurred me on with enthusiasm: a huge thanks to Connie for volunteering as a Beta reader and to Cynthia who vehemently insisted on being in charge of the launch party long before the book ever saw its final edits. Your endearing, invaluable friendship cannot be described adequately with words, even by the best of writers.

To my amazing writers' group: your ability to kindly and cheerfully critique this work will not be forgotten. A special shout out to Darren for early edits, and Stephanie (also an early reader), Jenna, and Parris for their help with the last chapters during COVID quarantine. Robin, your ridiculously selfless aid to my cry for help with formatting astonishes me still. Thank you for such a kindness with that tedious task.

To my incredibly supportive family who will be shocked to find this mysterious book finally in print. Dennis, Dani, Jake, and Tyler—you are my own personal Señor Epus, forever and ever. And, yep, you're gonna have to read the book to know what that means.

To my sister, Debbie, whose unparalleled encouragement made me feel like this book was possible every step of the way. And now, *it exists!*

To the many other unnamed family members and friends who have cheered me on and vowed to read this. I acknowledge I have much work to do to turn this hobby into a profession. Your gracious acceptance of this first novel is humbly appreciated.

And, finally, but mostly importantly, to the Father of Love from whom all good things flow, I give all thanks and praise. Indeed, I am nothing more than a girl wrestling with words without Him.

Author's Note

Like so many authors before me, I will say I am a writer out of need. Not for money, not for fame, not out of boredom. It seems I was born with wild ideas rolling around in my head, writing my first book at age six, asking my mother every other minute, "How do you spell—?" Writing becomes a necessity for those of us looking for an outlet for the brain rambles. It allows us to be much more than creative—it gives our head space to breathe.

The idea for Uspre was not a singular concept. Several plot points or "scenes" hatched separately within my noggin and after co-mingling there for quite a while, they collided one day, and I realized that all the elements could work together. Laney and Donavan suddenly had superpowers to interrupt their romance, with a team of renegades rallying them into schemes that pushed them out of their ordinary lives.

Crafting those scenes gained inspiration from an unusual group of readers who piqued my attention: adults who read young adult fiction. Curious, I investigated deeper into what drew them into teenage action, adventure, and romance. The conclusion came as a small surprise. The age of the characters had little to do with intrigue. It more had to do with two key components: moderate language and appropriate intimate relationships amid nail-biting scenarios.

Therefore, while this tale contains all the fantastical qualities of a supernatural tale—weapons and life or death situations—I opted to give the rudiments of life a gentler, wider appeal so that both older and younger audiences might enjoy the journey.

A book, especially a series, lives by its reviews. If you enjoyed the beginning of this *extra*-ordinary adventure, please leave your review on Amazon or Goodreads.

Thank you for reading.

Ready for more? Visit www.dorenemclaughlin.com for your FREE copy of the Prologue for Book 2 in the Uspre Series.

The Heroes of Uspre

Un-Usual Suspects

Sometimes the battle comes from within…

Coming Fall 2023

www.dorenemclaughlin.com

Fiction2Reality